C000129310

Silver

Becca Bruton

Copyright © 2023 Becca Bruton

All rights reserved. No portion of this book may be reproduced, copied, distributed or adapted in any way, with the exception of certain activities permitted by applicable copyright laws, such as brief quotations in the context of a review or academic work. For permission to publish, distribute or otherwise reproduce this work, please contact the author at beccabruton@hotmail.com

Paperback ISBN: 9798859637966

For my family,

for all the love you bless me with, thank you.

And for all those who have ever, or have yet to find, someone who makes

them wish that time stood still... hold on with all your heart.

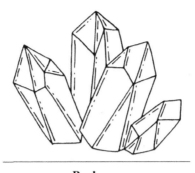

Prologue

"Well, don't be rude, Matthew. Let my Angel in." Slayton's silken voice snagged on the barbs hidden beneath.

Gin hated his pet-name for her. It cut through the ghost of the patient's screaming that still echoed in her ears as she stood frozen in the doorway to Slayton's office. She gaped at the fragile new life she held carefully in her arms. Only it didn't feel like her arms. No... she was gliding dizzily from somewhere above. Blinking away tears only showed her the ends of her chestnut brown hair, dripping crimson blood onto the already drenched swaddle.

"Who knew there'd be *so much blood* in childbirth?" Slayton mused as he studied her nauseating appearance.

Gin scrambled through her thoughts. Numbness coursed through her, but she forced herself to look up. Her silver eyes were even brighter tonight, puffy and waterlogged, glowing in the low light.

Slayton perched on the edge of his mahogany desk and clicked open his lighter. The sound made her flinch, sending a shiver tiptoeing down her spine as he lit the cigarette lodged in his thin lips. The embers burned bright red, illuminating his sharklike glare before letting the smoke encircle his head.

"So. Why have you bought it to me?" His tone was one of boredom.

Gin tried to speak, to convey the past few hours that she knew he'd heard, along with all the patients at the hospice. But the words clung to her pounding chest.

"She didn't make it... the mother... I-I tried. The bleeding just... wouldn't stop." Her voice felt raw and sharp as it left her, trying to make sense of the night's harrowing events.

The grand desk creaked as Slayton rose. Heart in her mouth, she dropped her glittering gaze as the stale smoke filled her lungs. Shiny tan shoes came into view as he stopped before her, crouching to the newborn's level. He took another drag, studying the slumbering baby, letting the smoke envelop them both before looking up at Gin. Her nose wrinkled softly.

"It's funny. I can't tell which are your freckles and which are splatters of blood upon your face." he mused, in awe.

Gin's stomach roiled as she shifted her arms, the drying blood sticking to her baggy t-shirt. His poisonous words seeped through her thick skin that she'd had to grow in order to survive here. But she stilled her tongue.

"So you killed her." he said, all traces of amusement vanishing. Gin's eyes widened and her cheeks prickled with heat.

"No." she whispered. "No, I tried to help. I did everything I could! If you had just called for a doctor like I asked-"

"YOU KILLED HER." His nostrils flared. Gin's words dried up as her body trembled. "You and your reckless need to help people. Your inability to keep from interfering has ended in the death of an innocent woman, leaving this baby all alone in the world. You just can't stop yourself from sneaking around my hospice, can you? Trying to be the saviour. But you're just an orphan, Angel. Nothing more." Gin's eyes stung as she stared at his shoes, shame pricking her cheeks. She shook her head slowly in shock as the implications of her actions twisted her gut. She'd only meant to help, but Slayton's words sank to the bottom of her stomach. Maybe it was her fault.

"Well, guess what?" His brows rose, wrinkling his over tanned skin. "An entire lifetime of meddling now lies at your fingertips. You have a whole tiny human to care for." he stroked a yellow stained finger across the baby's forehead, causing it to wriggle gently.

Gin had forgotten how to breathe as his words sunk in.

"I can't... I'm only fourteen! She needs a proper mother."

"Yes. But unfortunately, you snatched that from her. A shame that will be a burden for the rest of your life." He stood, straightening the buckle of his belt. His mouth twitched up as her brows furrowed with the rise of her shoulders. A swath of needles erupted over her back, tracing every scar. Every ghost of his belt...

"The price of your ego, my Angel." He flicked the lighter lid open and shut, lazily.

Gin crushed the sound from her mind and focused on the bundle in her bloodstained arms. How was she supposed to be a mother? How was she to raise a baby in this hell, to keep her safe from the monster before her? She was drowning in the numbing fear... until the strangest thing happened. A feeling, before anything, of being pulled from within. Her gaze lifted to the half-moon window next to the sputtering fireplace. She cocked her head, luminous eyes narrowing. Slayton's contented sneer slipped as he followed her gaze.

A lilac haze seeped through the gap in the heavy velvet curtain. It started at the top of the high ceiling, swamping the dark wood walls all the way to the polished oak floor, until it bathed the entire room in an ethereal light.

The hairs stood to attention along Gin's arms, breaking free of the dry blood. Slayton marched to the window and threw open the curtain. His sharp figure cut an eerie silhouette against the dancing lilac hue that now engulfed them all.

"My god... he bloody did it." he breathed, shoulders slumping.

Gin could barely think straight, walking through a fog of thoughts as Slayton ordered Matthew to take her back to her room. But as he shoved through her door, Slayton's voice pierced the silence.

"Be sure to call our friends at the police station, Matthew. Tell them I have a body that needs to disappear."

The door slammed shut behind her. Gin was back in the safety of her room. Only now she wasn't alone. She realised that she'd never be alone again. She knew very little about caring for a baby, but something deep inside her switched on at that moment. A reason and purpose beyond all others. She felt it in her chest, expanding.

"I'm so sorry. It's all my fault." she whispered, swallowing hard as images of the baby's lifeless birth mother erupted before her. "I promise I won't let you down again. I'll do whatever it takes to keep you safe." Her brows knitted and a small tear fell onto the blanket, but the baby slumbered on, blissfully unaware of the world she'd been born into. A world that Gin knew had to change. No more helping her fellow patients. No more hiding in the shadows of night to help those who so often went without the care they needed. She gladly took Slayton's belt for her actions... but she would not risk him taking his anger out on this baby.

Gin held her closer and sniffed the chill night air. She glanced at the window, remembering the lilac glow back in Slayton's office. But whatever had caused it was long gone. Had she imagined it? It seemed ridiculous now, but... that tugging sensation... it still lingered, urging her to the window.

She padded over to the full-length window, her heart hammering. She pulled the baby close, shielding her from the draft that seeped in through the window. Paint crumbled beneath her fingers as she placed a hand on the frame. As she peered out over the train tracks that ran parallel to the Hospice and the small town of Chestlewick nestled in the valley, everything looked normal. The street lights illuminated the warren of roads that hugged the park on the other side of the valley where the ruins of Lowndes castle-

Gin's roaming eyes stopped here. A gasp she hadn't realised she'd let out fogged the glass before her. She swiped it with the back of her hand and blinked hard several times. Where the tumbledown ruins of Lowndes castle had stood, with memories of playing as a child on her mother's good days, there was now a fully-fledged castle. It stood proudly on the edge of the park, unapologetically, as if it had always been there. The robust stone walls drunk up the light of the moon, as if made of moonlight itself.

Gin's breath caught in her chest, unable to drag her tired eyes away from the magnificent fortress. It made absolutely no sense and yet, there it was. Whatever that lilac haze had been, she was sure she was looking at the source.

What she would give to be free to run out of this hell, across the valley to explore. Maybe one day. She would live in hope until then...

"Hope…" she mused quietly, looking down at the fragile life she held. She tilted her head, her wavy locks and mother's red ribbon that never left her hair, spilled over her shoulder as she studied the baby's delicate features. The name was perfect. "Yes, Hope."

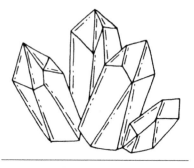

Chapter One

Four years later. 2018.

The warmth of the sun caressed Gin's olive cheeks that morning as she sat with Hope in their favourite spot of the garden at Slayton's Hospice. Tucked behind a flowering lilac bush, the cloying scent filled the air. She had a partial view of Lowndes castle on the other side of the Valley, just over the stone wall. She could sit here, listening to the beat of drums or call of trumpets if the wind blew in the right direction. It filled her with wonder.

Of course, they were never permitted to visit it, but it didn't stop her reading news articles from newspapers in the dayroom on the odd occasion they found their way there. Only when Slayton had made headlines about his latest charitable achievement, usually outdated by several weeks, but nobody minded. It was a glimpse of life outside this nightmare.

The castle, it seemed, had appeared that night, in all its former 15th century glory. But what's more, it had transported the people that inhabited it through time, and they were now a living historical attraction. All the ins and outs of how it all happened were never in the articles she read, the enigmatic owner never spilling the secret. The focus was always on upcoming events or the four famous knights that had apparently charmed the hearts of the world, showing off their skills and bravery in daily performances. The mystery around its arrival was still just that, a mystery.

Theories were forever cropping up. Some thought it an elaborate hoax, that Hollywood had hoodwinked them all. A well-known scientist was convinced that a localised tear in the fabric of time was the cause. And when those within the castle failed to speak and explanations fell short, the fingers even pointed to aliens. Whatever it had been, Gin knew in her heart no bigshot movie director had orchestrated it. That exquisite lilac glow had ignited something undeniably profound within her that night.

"Oh! Mummy, I did it!" squealed Hope, startling Gin as she strained to hear the distant music. Hope's head darted up, sending wild brown curls bouncing around her head. Her big blue eyes ignited with the fire of triumph as she held two linked daisies up to Gin, the beam on her face framed between two prominent dimples.

Gin's face softened as she beheld the little flowers, barely hanging onto each other. It was an enormous step up from the little pile of squished daisies beside her.

"You are just too clever." she said, taking the flowers carefully as they dangled by a thread. Holding them up to the sun, Gin's mother's many silver rings glinted on her fingers. Any thread to her was precious.

She picked up Hope's little pink hamster soft toy that lay next to the reject pile.

"You know, I think Penny would *love* a daisy chain necklace, isn't that right, Penny?" she said, turning the threadbare toy towards her, as if expecting an answer. Hope giggled as she pulled Penny in for a snuggle.

"Sorry, Penny. This one is for mummy's birthday tomorrow! *But don't tell her!*" she added in hushed tones, tucking her safely into the crux of her arm. Gin picked an imaginary piece of fluff off her short-sleeved yellow shirt, pretending not to have heard a word of their private conversation.

Though outwardly she played along happily, her insides squirmed at the reminder, half excited, half terrified. Tomorrow she turned eighteen. She would be an adult, legally allowed to leave the so-called *care* of Slayton's and move on with her life. But she had yet to bring it up with Slayton... or the fact that she was taking Hope with her.

The muffled sound of hurried footsteps on the grass behind them pulled her away from her thoughts. She squinted through the sun to see Kate trotting towards them. Sitting up taller, she placed Hope in her shadow.

Kate slowed, catching her breath, offering a small smile. Gin did her best to return it, but wasn't sure it made the cut.

"Hi. Listen, I hate to ask, but Sam could really use your help. Nurse Maggie is nowhere to be found and the other nurses are not in yet. His mum is having a bad episode."

"You know I can't help." said Gin, turning back to Hope, who was peeking at Kate with interest. Kate hovered, wringing her hands.

"Please, Gin. I wouldn't ask if it wasn't important. No one else knows how to."

"I said no, Kate. And you shouldn't be helping either. If *he* catches you... well you're just lucky he hasn't yet." snapped Gin, looking past her to the red brick walls of the Hospice. Being four years older than Kate, she had always protected her, made sure she always took the blame for her meddling in the past.

Kate let out a humourless laugh.

"I was there too, you know." she said, bluntly, with a darting glance at Hope. "I was by your side that night. I saw the same horror as you, but I still try to help around here. Where did you go? You used to be the one we all came to. You might as well have died that night too." she hissed, turning on her heel and marching off up the grassy verge.

Gin watched her stalk away, nausea churning her stomach. She was right. She might as well have died alongside Hope's mother. A wave of guilt washed over her for being able to hold the beautiful little girl every day while her real mother rotted away... God knows where. She never dared to ask what Slayton's men within the police force had done with the body.

It broke Gin's heart to stand idle while the patients here suffered neglect. But her meddling days *had* died that night, at least.

She heaved a sigh, turning her attention back to Hope, who was trying to make a hole in the next stem, furtively glancing up at her from beneath her thick, dark lashes. But her dimples had vanished, along with her smile.

"Sorry, sweetheart." she said, her eyebrows pulling together. "You know we have to keep our heads down. If we don't keep to ourselves, we risk getting into trouble."

"With Mr. Slayton?" she asked, quietly.

Gin pulled her knees into a hug and pursed her heart-shaped lips. Protecting her from Slayton was a full-time job. She never spoke much about him, only that he was the man in charge and she was to stay away from him. But as Hope was nearing her fifth birthday, she found her curiosity peeking about the mysterious man who mummy warns her to stay away from. And that scared her. The sooner they could leave, the better.

"Yes. But you and I will not be here forever. You remember my promise?" she asked, raising her brows, the morning sun making her silver eyes sparkle like diamonds.

Hope smiled then, going back to her task of poking her fingernail through the slightly limp stem.

"Yes, we'll have our own little home one day. With no one except us... and Penny!" she added, her eyes wide, darting up to meet hers. Gin smiled, her nose wrinkling.

"*Of course,* and Penny!" she said, tucking a loose brown curl behind Hope's ear.

It had clouded over by lunchtime as they headed back up the grassy bank towards the hospice. They stepped through the patio doors, and Gin's eyes took a moment to adjust from the sunshine. The temperature dropped as they made their way through the dayroom, avoiding those who occupied the baroque armchairs. Gin had her hands firmly on Hope's shoulders, guiding her along the path with as few people as possible, avoiding the cautious looks they received. It was rare that anybody tried to make conversation with her these days, and that was precisely how she preferred it. She kept herself and Hope tucked up in their room for the most part. It was a stark contrast to life before that dreadful night and she knew she was unliked by most of the patients and their families now. But if doing right by Hope meant alienating everyone else, so be it.

They passed the kitchens, avoiding the lunch hall, where soft chatter drifted in, and picked up a tray of food for lunch. Today consisted of what looked like leftover ham sandwiches from the day before, the outside of the bread somewhat crispy. Two oranges also sat slumped on the tray. Not a good sign. It was a good day when they rolled around precariously as she walked. The fruit inside was sure to be plump and juicy. That was a rare occasion, though. The norm was a sadder, more shrivelled affair, like today. But she never complained. It kept them alive, as was its purpose.

Gin's eyes darted around the barren whitewash kitchen. The chef was currently talking at the little serving hatch, a small queue of people forming behind. She nudged Hope gently. Hope smiled and nodded, walking over to the back of the room near the pantry. Tucked just behind the chrome bin was a hessian bag that she picked up before scurrying back to Gin, looking very pleased with herself. Gin gave her a small wink, and they marched out, keeping their steps light.

Climbing the dim staircase to their rooms, she caught sight of Maggie closing the door to Slayton's quarters. Their eyes met briefly before turning right towards their end of the corridor.

"Gin. One moment." said Maggie, catching up with them. Gin closed her eyes and sighed as she slowed.

"Mr Slayton would like a word…" she said, trailing off with a kind smile to Hope, who stood behind Gin, hugging her leg. Gin's heart sank.

"I can take lunch to your room with Hope and sit with her, if you like?" she suggested, smoothing her white pinafore. "And the bag of recyclables, I'm glad to see you found." a wry smile flickered across her face.

Gin frowned, looking down at Hope, who was inspecting the daisy chain she held carefully in her small hands, then back to Maggie. She was the only nurse who she had ever let help with Hope. Albeit at a distance, she had guided her when she was a newborn and honestly, she wasn't sure she could have gotten through it without her. Though she'd never admit it. Maggie also sustained her need for scraps of paper, pretty packaging or glass bottles, anything that she and Hope could use for crafting. Maggie often referred to their room as a cave of treasures. Everywhere you looked, there'd be some sort of carefully crafted piece of art.

Taking a deep breath and letting it out slowly, Gin reluctantly handed over the tray and ruffled her hand gently through Hope's mass of curls.

"I'll be as quick as I can." she said, avoiding eye contact as she made her way around Maggie. "Make sure she gets the bigger sandwich, please." she called over her shoulder, giving a reassuring smile to Hope as she watched them disappear into her room. It always left her with a pit in her stomach whenever she had to leave her, even though she trusted Maggie.

Biting the inside of her cheek, she turned to Slayton's door, preparing herself for whatever he wanted. It was never good.

She rapped her knuckles against the door.

"Come!"

The familiar overpowering smell of tobacco greeted her, making her insides churn. Slayton was sitting at his large wooden desk, tapping away at the keys of his computer, a cigarette perched in his lips.

"Ah, Gin. What… a… pleasure." he said, finishing what he was typing after glancing up at her, cigarette moving with his mouth. "Take a seat."

She hated how he always had the audacity to be pleasant to her, as if his politeness would make her blind to his punishments. But she did as he asked and sat at the farthest end of the sofa from him, watching the particles of dust dance in the rays of sun through the halfmoon window.

Slayton sauntered over to the fireplace, fiddling with the cuff of his crisp white shirt. She felt her heartbeat increasing with every second, racking her brain for any recollection of doing something that may have displeased him.

"Time. The currency of all brilliant achievements." he said, peering out of the window Gin had been focusing on, sending the slow dancing dust into a frenzied waltz as he swept in front. "You've been here, what… eleven years now? The longest out of all of my patients, in fact. Ironic that your mother, may she rest in peace, was here for the least amount of time." he said, laughing to himself at the sick realisation.

Gin's hands bunched up in her lap at the sting, her long nails digging into her palms. Hearing him talk about her mother, who he left to die, made her blood boil. She had been too young, too helpless back then to do anything but watch the neglect that led to her death. That's when she vowed never to leave anyone else to the same fate.

"And just like that, you will turn eighteen in a matter of hours." he said, still staring out of the window, one hand now playing with the lid of his lighter, the other tucked into the top of his belt. Her back tingled as she watched his finger caress the leather.

So it was here. The moment she would have to tell him of her plans to leave with Hope. She knew it would come, but it hadn't stopped her from hoping she'd be able to slip them both out the front door at first light. *Foolish*, she thought.

"I warn you, the world beyond these walls is not as you might think. There are people out there who would turn your stomach, Gin." he said, turning to look at her, his thin lips turned down in disgust. "If you thought I was, well... maybe *hard* on you, you will certainly be in for a shock out there."

Gin said nothing, lowering her eyes to her bunched up hands. She tried not to let his words seep in, tried not to imagine her and Hope out there amongst the dangers of the world. Truth be told, it scared her. But if it meant fleeing Slayton, she was prepared to face anything.

"But you don't have to worry. Because I have taken care of everything, to ensure your safety." he said.

Gin's gaze shot up, her eyes wide. Her heart plummeted at the look on his face. The way only one side of his mouth rose into a smile was more like a snarl to Gin, who knew him only too well.

"You didn't think I would let you walk out of here alone and directionless? Come now, you can't think so little of me?" He took a long and satisfied drag on his cigarette. He knew very well what she thought of him, but he also knew that she would never admit to it.

"I have, in fact, arranged for you to be taken in by a very reputable man who already has a, let's say, *large* family. I know him well and he has been waiting for a suitable person to take under his wing, to learn the tricks of his trade. And seeing as you have no experience of anything really, this will be the perfect pairing. A blank slate for him to work with, so to speak."

Gin's brow furrowed.

"Hope. What about Hope?" she breathed, afraid to hear the answer she knew was coming.

Slayton chuckled, poking his tongue into his cheek.

"Ah, Angel. She will stay here, of course! She is young and still needs the care and stability that she is used to." he said, his smile widening with each second as Gin's world was crumbling beneath her. Her mouth fell open as her eyes welled up with hot, angry tears.

"You know I can't leave her. I'm her mother, you gave me the responsibility of looking after her-"

"And look after her you have, but your time with that responsibility has come to an end." he said flatly, cutting her off, his head cocked to one side as he closed the space between them. He knelt to her level as she sat stock still on the edge of the hard leather sofa. She wasn't sure the air she was breathing was doing its job anymore, her lungs failing to support her need for oxygen. Slayton gave her a clenched half smile as he ran his fingers through a wavy lock of golden brown hair that fell over her shoulder. She froze, as she always did, not daring to move a muscle or to give him an excuse to use his belt...

"Let us not forget the reason Hope was in your care in the first place, hmm? We wouldn't want that getting out. You wouldn't last a day behind bars. Not to mention having to live with the look on Hope's face when she finds out you're not her real mother... that you *killed* her actual mother. Can you imagine the betrayal she'd feel?" His voice was sickly sweet and ran over her like honey, sticking to her, rendering her immobile. She had never thought about Hope finding out the truth. How could she ever risk the hurt that would cause her? She blinked rapidly, searching his small brown eyes, her tears now falling on to her clenched fists.

"Hope is better off without you. Far away from the damage you've done, and let's face it, are likely to do in the future." he said gently, tipping his head to the other side and pulling her into an embrace. Her body trembled as he ran his hands over her disfigured back, exploring the welts he had given her. She squeezed her eyes tight shut as though if she tried hard enough she could pop this whole moment out of existence.

"Please…" she whispered, panic flooding her veins, "Don't take Hope away from me. I'll even stay here, for however long you want, just *please* don't do this. "

Slayton released her and pulled back, all traces of the smile now replaced with his usual shark-like stare. He took the cigarette out of his mouth, stubbing it out slowly on the arm of the sofa, inches from her arm. When he spoke, his voice constricted, tempering his unhinged anger that constantly bubbled beneath the surface.

"You are lucky you are leaving, or you'd have a fresh wound to deal with for daring to question my authority." he said, nostrils flaring.

Gin stared at the charred spot next to her wrist, scolding herself for being so outspoken, the exact opposite of what she had taught Hope to do in such a situation. She clenched her jaw, still focused on the charred circle of leather, the smell of burning invading her nose. Slayton rose, making his way to the window again. She heard the flick of his lighter, open then close, open then close…

"You see? Timing is key." he said, staring out of the window. He flipped his phone out of his pocket and dialled. Gin held her breath, unable to speak or do anything.

"She's ready." was all he said, before ending the call, throwing his phone onto the mantlepiece.

"No…" she whispered to herself. It was happening right now, no goodbyes to Hope. Before she could legally walk out of here. Perfect timing, indeed. She gasped for air as panic consumed her. "Please! Don't do this! I'm begging you!"

"I already have, Gin." he grinned, turning to face her as she stood, her hands clenched at her sides. "I hope you do at least have the sense to keep your memoirs of your time here to yourself. We wouldn't want anything to tarnish what I've accomplished. Especially with Hope, so small and impressionable." he said, inhaling through his teeth.

14

She snarled like an animal as heat seared through her body. Slayton gave her a look of disdain. There was a knock at the door and Matthew appeared at her side. He shoved her brown leather satchel into her arms, apparently already packed with her few belongings.

"Goodbye, Angel." said Slayton as thick hands grabbed her arms, dragging her out of his office.

It was all a blur from there. The walls of the hallway passed her by as she screamed. At least, she thought she did. She couldn't hear herself. The world had gone silent. She tried to scream for Hope as her door disappeared from view and she was forced down the stairs. Nausea took hold as he shoved her along the long corridor towards the entrance.

Matthew was buzzed through the glass doors, and daylight seized her sore eyes. She had dreamt of this moment for so very long, but she'd always been hand in hand with Hope.

A smartly dressed man was leaning against an emerald green car, the passenger door open. He'd been pushing the gravel around with his feet until he noticed her, like a deer in headlights, as Matthew released her.

The man pulled himself a little straighter and offered a smile, his grey hair neatly swept to the side. Gin eyed the car with trepidation.

"Gin…" he rasped. Quick footsteps on the gravel told her he was coming her way. "Gin." he said again, stopping before her and reaching out to grasp her arms. She flinched, glancing up at his face, eyes wide. His face fell apologetically, his mouth laced with wonder under a handlebar moustache that curved up around the apples of his cheeks. She couldn't determine his age, for the smoothness of his skin contradicted his greying hair, seemingly both young and old. There was something familiar about him she couldn't place.

"Forgive me. I shouldn't have been so forthcoming. I'm Joseph Oldman. And I…" he let out a stifled gasp, searching for words. "I've been waiting for this day for a very long time." he smiled. "This must be so difficult for you. Leaving the place you've called home all these years and Mr. Slayton." He bit his lip for a moment. "I don't know how much you've been told about me or the home that I live in but, it certainly isn't your average family. And I know it will take some time for you to feel it, but my home is your home. I am certainly looking forward to having you with us. Very much so."

Gin swallowed through the pain of holding back tears and risked looking up at him.

"Are you ready?" he asked hesitantly, pushing up his sleeves to reveal a pocket watch tattoo on his arm. She was silent for a moment, wondering what he'd do if she said no, if she turned back to the Hospice doors. What punishment would await her... or worse, Hope. It sent her heart plummeting off a ledge. She was powerless to stop this.

"If I said yes, would you believe me?" she asked, looking away.

Joseph opened his mouth to reply, then shut it again. She sighed heavily as she walked around him and slid into the passenger seat. The scent of leather, citrus and polish hit her like a wall.

Gin couldn't bring herself to look in the wing mirror as they rolled out of the gated gravel driveway. The horror of her heart being ripped from her soul was too much to witness. She didn't see Hope burst through the open door, only to be grabbed by Matthew as he watched them go. Didn't see the tears roll down Hope's little cheeks or the daisy chain necklace, tied with a red ribbon, swinging from her hands. She didn't see the look of utter sorrow as she was dragged back into the hospice; the door slamming shut as Gin was driven off to an uncertain future... the gates closing firmly behind her.

In fact, she barely noticed Joseph talking at all as they drove through the town, so lost in her own heartache. She only took stock of where they were when she was being jostled about, the smooth road replaced by cobbled stone. They were heading up a lane flanked with beautiful old cottages on either side, the type that seemed to come straight out of a fairytale. Ivy crept up the walls to well maintained thatched roofs that overlooked whimsical front gardens, boasting vibrant flowers.

As the road rounded a corner, the towering outer wall of Lowndes castle filled the windscreen. She looked at Joseph for the first time since they set off, her brow furrowed.

He, however, was smiling as he continued up the lane towards the lowered portcullis.

"I told you it wasn't your typical home."

Chapter Two

Gin gazed from Joseph to the looming castle repeatedly, irritation rising in her chest as he chortled to himself at her confusion.

"This is a joke." she said, slumping lower in her seat to look up at the imposing grey stone walls on the other side of the moat. She folded her arms over her chest, heart pounding at being so close to the place that had consumed her imagination for so long.

"I assure you, it's no joke. I know it's a little crazy, overwhelming even. My family is not your average one. They've had a lot of adjusting to do, much like you will. But they're good people who have come to love the way of life that I provide for them."

Gin's eyes widened as she listened, suddenly placing Joseph's face.

"You're him. You brought them here from the past." she said, recalling him from the newspapers. Joseph flashed her a smile, cheeks flushed, and held a hand up.

"Guilty. The point is, I don't want you to be put off by appearances. I've worked hard to get to where I am now, where we all are. I made a lot of sacrifices along the way." he added with a sharp sniff as he brought his attention back to her. She looked away, the pressure already feeling heavy.

"Just give it time. Get to know us." he said, with a hopeful grin, his handlebar moustache curling up.

Gin scowled. She didn't want to give him or anyone else time. She could never be happy anywhere where Hope was not. But she couldn't tell him that, for fear of what Slayton might do if she spoke of her daughter.

"In fact, I believe we are just in time to watch the opening of the gates." He smiled in her direction, but she refused to meet his gaze. Instead, she watched out of the window, in quiet awe. As they continued up the long lane, a line of people appeared with backpacks and sun hats, as far as she could see. She pushed herself a little straighter in her seat, the queue winding on and on under a tunnel of trees.

"Are they all waiting to go in?" she asked, amazed at the sheer number of visitors.

"Certainly are." he said, grinning as he waved to a few people that had clocked on to who was in the car.

Gin's heart pounded in her chest. She felt sick to her stomach, this reality before her not connecting to the world she was so used to.

"What the…" Joseph trailed off as they rounded a corner to where the line zig zagged into roped lanes before an immense portcullis. "What is he playing at?"

Gin followed his gaze to where a tall, dark-haired knight stood atop a stone wall, leaning casually against the gate. He wore a metal breast plate but no armour on his legs, hands wedged in his pockets.

Joseph pulled to the side and cut the engine. She lost sight of the knight and took stock of Joseph's ruffled feathers.

"I apologise. It's just that I had arranged for someone else to raise the gate. Not Sir Col." She didn't miss the note of frustration in his voice as he unbuckled. "Not to worry! I'm sure there's a good reason. Shall we?" he asked, swinging open his door with more force than necessary.

Gin rubbed the ache in her chest, willing herself to keep it together. This was all a complete mess. But she'd find a way back to Hope, somehow. This was just temporary. With all the strength she could gather, she swallowed the painful lump lodged in her throat and followed Joseph.

She clocked Col, who had noticed their arrival as Joseph slammed the car door. The knight pushed himself off the wall and bowed low, his black hair flopping over his forehead. A sharp cut grin slid to one side as he rose, eyes trained in their direction.

Something dipped in Gin's stomach as he held her gaze across the sea of guests. She cleared her throat as she met Joseph's sidelong look.

"My Lords, Ladies and children of all ages!" Col exclaimed, drawing a sword from its sheath at his side and pointing it at them. "I want to hear a resounding cheer when I say *welcome to Lowndes castle!*" The crowd cheered and whistled a little, rippling over the bobbing of heads. A moment hung in the air before he lifted his eyes, surveying them.

"Well, damn." he said, leaning upon the hilt of his lowered sword. A chuckle rippled through the crowd. "That was awful." he said, shaking his head slowly. "You there!" he exclaimed, brandishing his sword at a teenage boy with shaggy blond hair in the front. "What's your name, Sir?"

"Uh... Eliot." answered the boy. His shoulders curled forwards as he clutched one arm nervously. A lady who looked to be his mother nudged him forward.

"Ok, we'll get this right. Don't worry, it's you and me and Eliot! Lords and Ladies, Eliot here will die horrifically if you don't get this right, ok? No pressure." he said, shrugging. "Eliot, stand here!" he ordered as he pointed to the space next to him. Eliot smirked as his mother ushered him forwards, her eyes set firmly on Col.

"Right! His life is in *your* hands!" said Col as laughter rippled across the sea of heads as he brought the sword to the base of Eliot's neck.

Gin's mouth parted and she shot Joseph a wide-eyed look. He frowned, shaking his head a little, resigned.

"See what you've done? I've sunk to threatening innocent children. Sorry, a young man, I apologise, Eliot. My Lords and Ladies! I said, *welcome, to Lowndes castle!*" he cried as his enthralled audience gave an almighty cheer.

"There it is! Eliot... you are free to go, for now." he said, releasing the boy back into the crowd. "Now! Before I can let you raucous lot into the castle, I need to know..." he stared dramatically around at their captivated faces, "that you are on *our* side. That you will sacrifice your children to the knight School, where they will train in combat to fight against our foes." There was another ripple of laughter.

"You will watch our brave knights in the Tournament and cheer, although, not like the first attempt or I'll have to threaten Eliot again," he pointed his sword at Eliot as a few cheers rose. "You're not meant to cheer for that!" he said, brows knitted, looking towards the culprits. "Really, I'm so sorry Eliot, that was uncalled for." The boy fidgeted on the spot, laughing. "You will cheer like Eliot's life depends on it, for your chosen knight in the arena!" The crowd cheered again as he slowly licked his lips. He was quiet for a moment, frozen to the spot, seemingly lost in thought.

Joseph sighed next to Gin, shifting his weight. She could feel the tension radiate from him, but she couldn't drag her attention from Col, pulled in, just like his rapt audience.

"The year was 1461. For many, famine, poverty and illness were rife. You'll meet some of those who suffered first hand. Then there are those of us who had come home from battle mere weeks before our sudden shift in time. You may have heard of it… The Battle of Towton, March 29th. It was one of the largest and bloodiest battles ever to take place on English soil." he said darkly, still rooted to the spot. His transfixed audience seemed to lean in a little more as a hush fell upon them. No more laughter. No more jokes.

"We were victorious. It drove out the House of Lancaster, Henry VI, an unstable king, along with his supporters, allowing Edward IV to take the throne. But at the cost of many lives." Gin blinked heavily. How was this possible? How was she looking at someone who lived in a completely different time? The things he must have witnessed sat heavily in the air.

He lifted his chin and pointed his sword at the gate.

"By stepping over this threshold, you will not only see history come alive, but through the eyes of those who *lived and breathed* it." He stood tall, drinking in the silence as he surveyed them. Until his eyes fell upon Gin, sending a wave of electricity through her body. Her feet had carried her closer to him during his speech. She now stood to one side behind the crowd, leaning against the jagged stone wall. She swallowed, being close enough now to notice the summer smoulder of his blue eyes under dark, angled brows.

Col continued, holding her gaze, but his own had taken on a narrowed intensity. She blinked, his scrutiny a surefire sign that he had seen the abnormal shade of her silver eyes. Her ears burned in embarrassment. Always the freak.

"We have already taken our journey of a lifetime… it's time for you to take yours." As he finished, he released her gaze and stepped aside.

Gin clutched her arms as goosebumps flecked her skin, despite the warm breeze that caressed the rustling leaves overhead. He had left her with the most unfamiliar feeling that still lingered somewhere in her chest.

The portcullis began to rise. A boy pulled at the ropes that wielded it, and a steady beat of drums played over the speakers throughout the grounds. She wasn't sure what was beating heavier, the drums or her heart.

Excitement swept through the crowd like a bubbling brook. She shrank back as they surged forwards, coming to a halt against something solid. She whirled to find Joseph's flinty gaze upon Col, who was sauntering towards them through the awestruck crowd.

"Well Gin, I was hoping to introduce you to Sir Louis at the gate, but… we'll start with this one."

She opened her mouth to tell him she didn't want to meet anyone right now, that she wanted to be alone, just as a voice purred over her shoulder.

"Well, well."

Gin spun round with a sharp intake of breath, finding herself facing those potent blue eyes again. Her stomach flipped. Thick black lashes fringed his piercing gaze, which widened slightly before immediately narrowing, paired with a one-sided smile that cut into his angular jaw.

"Oldman, you've finally got your new pet." he paused, "And it all becomes clear."

She watched his smile disappear, along with the double lines that hugged it, as he looked over her shoulder. Joseph cleared his throat.

"Gin, meet Sir Col. One of our knights." said Joseph, huffing as he crossed his arms.

Gin lowered her eyes as she nodded rather feebly, unnerved by the sensation his presence had provoked.

"The pleasure's all mine. Although, best not tell Sir Louis." That lopsided smile flashed again as she shot him a puzzled look.

"Speaking of which, where is he? I was expecting him to open the proceedings this morning." said Joseph, rather shortly.

"Ah, yes. He fell behind and had to prepare for the joust before your arrival. He has been rather flustered this morning, Oldman. I'm sure you understand why." he finished with a wide grin, as his gaze slid back to her.

Gin glanced around, the crowds of people excitedly whispering as they caught sight of Col. Her hand went to her hair, sweeping it back as a wave of nausea rolled over her. She just wanted to be out of here, away from the throng of people and Col's intensity, with some time to think. To process everything that had happened and how she was going to get Hope. Col's brows flicked together fleetingly, as if reading her flustered mind.

"Well, let's not waste time here, Gin." Joseph said, casting a scowl towards Col. "Maybe we can catch Sir Louis before the Joust begins. Introduce you properly." he placed his hands on her shoulders. A move that sent a flash of ice through Gin's body and prickled down her scarred back. She ducked out of his touch, squeezing her eyes shut against the fear of hands upon her scars. As if he'd sense their presence beneath her clothes.

"Mmm, Oldman has that effect on me too." said Col, noting her reaction as he sheathed his sword. "I should prepare myself for the tournament. It's about time Sir Louis faced me again. I'm sure he's dying to win his title back."

"Col, don't even think about doing anything stupid." Joseph's warning was a low grumble.

Col shrugged his shoulders.

"And ruin his big moment? As if I would, Oldman." He held a hand to his heart in mock horror. "It was nice to meet you at last, Sparkles." he said before bowing, backing up towards the open gate, hands buried in his pockets and disappearing into the crowd.

She frowned. *Sparkles*. As if she needed anymore attention drawn to her abnormal eyes.

"At last?" she said, more to herself, but Joseph shifted next to her.

"Well, ah… I've been preparing for your arrival for a while now. Everyone here is very eager to meet you." he said, ushering her forwards, without contact this time as he smoothed down his maroon waistcoat with one hand.

She looked over his shoulder. Through the gate was a large courtyard where visitors were milling around white tents, shrouded in wisps of smoke from fire pits. The same drums that she and Hope had listened carefully for across the valley thrummed through her ears. She felt a painful pang in her chest at the memory.

"This is insane. I mean, none of this makes sense! How is this real? How did this castle form from its own ruins?" she gasped. The reality of being thrown into the centre of the place that had burned a fire of curiosity within her for years, and knowing nothing of how it was even feasible, gnawed away at her.

Joseph scratched his cheek and glanced sheepishly around the mass of people.

"In time, Gin. All in good time. Come." said Joseph, an apologetic smile curling his moustache around his rosy cheeks. "For now… come home."

Her teeth clenched at the word. A word she knew this place would never be. That no place without Hope would ever be. Time was not something she planned on giving to him. But if she could get through this day, pretend to play the role of Joseph's 'new pet', then she'd plan her way back to Hope, no matter the cost. The secrets of this castle would have to remain that way for now.

She took a deep breath and followed him into the heart of the castle. The place that had consumed her dreams every night for four years.

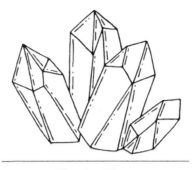

Chapter Three

Gin found herself being jostled through the grounds of the castle, stopping every so often to be introduced to one of the time travellers. Each one was as painful as the last, being gawked at as soon as they met her eyes. Having spent so much of her life cooped up in Slayton's, she was not used to meeting new people. And if this experience was anything to go by, she didn't care for it either. She couldn't fathom ever feeling the way she did right now, how she actually wished to be back in her room in the Hospice, hidden away with Hope. But she wished it down to her bones.

They followed the swarm of guests out of the large oval courtyard, away from the smoky fire pits and tents and over a stone bridge. The moat was dry, blooming with rhododendron bushes, the spicy sweet scent filling the air.

They rounded a corner and came to the top of a hill that ran down to a flowing river. Her mouth slackened as she took in the sight of an immense arena on the other side, different coloured banners flapping gently in the warm breeze. The sea of people they were following were all heading for it, converging over a bridge.

"Ready for your first Medieval Joust?" asked Joseph. She hoisted her bag on her shoulder and followed Joseph, who was eagerly making his way down, not waiting for her reply. She scowled, knowing he knew her answer would not be the one he wanted.

As they descended to the bridge, she noticed a small walled off overgrown garden and the thatched roof of a little cottage poking out from the rambling yard. It looked abandoned if she was honest, no care put into the garden like there was in the grounds. She tilted her head, surveying it quietly. It was so out of place from the grand surroundings.

"Oh, there you are!" came the singsong voice of an older lady trotting towards them, her hourglass figure swaying as she weaved against the flow of the crowd. Her brown dress cinched in at the waist with a white apron, and her heavy bosom spilled over the top, yet she was rather petite. Her white bobbed hair was not tied up like those she had seen in the market, but framed her aged tan skin that wrinkled into a warm smile.

"Ah, heavens, Joseph! You could have taken the poor dear's bag!" she said, shooting him a scowl, wasting no time in taking Gin's bag from her shoulder.

"Men, Gin! Honestly, whatever happened to chivalry!" she exclaimed, rolling her eyes at Joseph, who held his hands up in guilt. "Where are the other bags, dearie? I'll send for them to be taken to your room." she asked, all smiles again as she focused on her. But she didn't flinch at her eyes.

"Uh... just that one, actually." she said, looking at the bag she clutched to her bust.

"Oh... ok. Well, that's just fine." Gin clocked the surprise she failed to keep from her reaction. "You know, we've *plenty* of dresses for you here, so not to worry, dearie! Oh, how rude of me! I'm Daphne. I run the kitchens mainly, but see to our Lady Flora too and seamstress, *anything* really. You're a little later than expected, so you'll have to make your way straight to the podium. The knights are already waiting. Shall we?" taking a much needed breath, her eyebrows raised over sparkling green eyes. Joseph nodded at her with a wry smile.

"As always, Daphne, you are one step ahead of me." he answered.

Gin snapped her mouth closed, realising she'd be gaping at her as she'd tried to take in everything she'd said. Joseph led the way and Daphne waited for Gin to follow before muttering under her breath.

"More like five steps ahead."

They left the queue waiting to take their seat in the arena and entered a small doorway to the rear. It opened to a narrow wooden staircase, each step groaning below her feet. It led to a gloomy room with three opulent chairs facing a wall.

"What is this place?" she asked, stalling just beyond the threshold as Daphne poured three cups of water from a jug in the corner of the room.

"The best seats in the house, of course." said Joseph.

Gin looked towards what she thought was a wall that all three chairs faced, only to notice the slight movement as it swayed, a ray of light creeping in at the sides.

"It's a curtain." she said, more to herself than to them. Joseph opened his mouth to reply when a honeyed voice beat him to it.

"Oh, how very astute of you!"

Gin's attention swivelled to the stairs to see a lady staring down a delicate nose, her expression pinched around bright red lips. A sway of red curls cascaded over one bare shoulder onto an extravagant golden dress that billowed from her corseted waist.

Gin had never seen so much beauty possessed in one person. She dipped her chin, allowing a lock of hair to curtain her eyes that she loathed so much, feeling even more inferior in the presence of this newcomer.

"Lady Flora. Just in time to meet-"

"Gin, I presume." said Lady Flora, cutting Joseph off as she glided forwards, stopping only because the skirt of her dress brushed Gin's shoes. Gin shifted her weight as she bore her scrutiny.

Lady Flora's mouth parted slightly, gaze flicking knowingly to Joseph and then back.

Gin's shoulders heaved as she released a deep breath. She'd had enough of these suggestive looks she was completely out of the loop of. She bit the inside of her cheek, turning to Joseph, who was quick to display a smile.

"Showtime!" he said dramatically, falling into the middle chair and pulling his phone out. Daphne rolled her eyes as she walked towards Gin, handing her a cup of water.

"Here you go dearie. Take a seat. We have a brief wait until *showtime,*" she said, smirking. Gin pressed her lips into a fine line and took her seat, thanking Daphne, and waited in awkward silence. Joseph tapped away on his phone, illuminating his face in a grotesque manner, while Daphne saw that not a single hair was out of place upon Lady Flora's head.

As the beating of the drums intensified, so did the pulse of Gin's blood around her body. She still couldn't see beyond the curtain, but the ever-increasing volume of the audience told her that the arena must be near full.

She glanced at Joseph, who had at last put his phone down and was being handed a microphone.

"A few more minutes, Sir and we'll be good to go." said a young boy who popped his head around the corner of the stairs.

"Right you are, Podraig." said Joseph, straightening his shirt as Podraig gave Gin a nervous smile. He was about to leave when Lady Flora called him back.

"Oh Podraig, I know he's not your Master, but please let Sir Col know that I'll be on the right side of the podium today... seeing as my usual side is otherwise occupied." she said, looking at the top of the swaying curtain with a bored expression. Podraig nodded after a moment and took his leave.

"You are welcome to sit here if you want to." said Gin, looking straight ahead too. Lady Flora laughed lightly.

"I cannot simply sit in your chair. It's completely different. Mine is mine because of its decoration and status." Her brows knitted tightly. "Mind you, perhaps that's what you and your new *father* wish." she said, with a sour turn to her lips.

Joseph sighed, walking to the middle of the podium, gripping his temples.

"Please, Lady Flora. We spoke about this. It is not my inten-" the sound of trumpets cut him off and he spun on the spot immediately to face the curtain. "*Intention.*" he whispered with a little more gusto.

Gin tapped her foot, inhaling deeply. Whatever status Lady Flora had here did not interest her. But she wouldn't waste her breath. She wasn't hanging around long enough for it to be a problem. The thought of getting out of here as soon as possible and back to Hope was all that was keeping her from breaking into tears at the moment.

Pre-recorded sounds of battle echoed through the arena. Thrashing of metal upon metal, cries of men as they poured every bit of strength into the fight, and the thudding of hooves as their steeds carried them through the onslaught.

She quelled a small buzz of anticipation as the music that she used to strain to hear now engulfed her. The noise from the crowd died down as they waited with bated breath.

Finally, the podium curtains rose with the crescendo. She squinted against the sunlight that flooded in, the music returning to a soft thrum as she looked out to a packed arena. She shrank into her chair. The enormity of the crowd was now amplified by the burn of their eyes upon her and her onstage companions, the cheering and clapping almost deafening.

"Welcome! Welcome all on this momentous day for all here, at Lowndes castle!" boomed Joseph's through the microphone. "I'd like to take a minute to step out of the usual show that I know you are all extremely eager to see. Don't worry! Your knights are coming. But first, I need to make a very special introduction." He carried on, as Gin sank further into her chair.

"Life has been quite amazing since arriving, some four years ago now. I feel blessed beyond words." He looked at Lady Flora, who was wearing a plastered smile, so sickly sweet it could only be for show.

"My life has been a series of wondrous moments. But there has always been one thing missing." he said, hesitating before glancing at Gin. She shifted in her chair, angling away from him as ice carved through her body.

"Until now." he continued, curling the twirls of his moustache. Gin inhaled slowly, praying he would stop, that he wasn't about to say it. "It is with immense pleasure that I welcome not just a new member to Lowndes castle, but more importantly, a daughter. Something I thought I'd missed the boat for." Gin winced. He'd gone there. And he had not finished.

"Adopted into the legacy of this magical castle." he paused, tongue poking out slightly as the audience held on to his every word. Words that shocked Gin to her core.

"A castle… that I will one day leave to her."

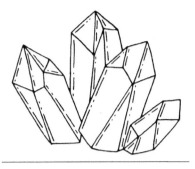

Chapter Four

The rest of Joseph's speech was lost on her. Gin's mind was reeling.

The castle would be hers?

It was inconceivable. She had nothing to her name except for the few things she packed in her backpack. And now she was to be left an entire castle?

She stared into nothing but was fully aware of Lady Flora's eyes burning into her, the cold welcome now becoming clear. She was the Lady of the castle in her previous age. Now it fell into Joseph's hands… and eventually hers.

She clenched her teeth. Her instinct to run was subdued as the bones of a stable future became a possibility. For Hope to have a future that was secure. Safe. Maybe she just had to figure out how to get her here instead of running back to the Hospice. And somehow, accept the reality of Joseph being her adoptive father. She closed her eyes; the word sitting ill in her stomach. She would cross that bridge another time. It meant nothing to her now.

"I shall not make you wait any longer!" she zoned in on Joseph's voice again. "Behind those gates, await none other than Lowndes castle's finest knights! No theatrics or actors grace this arena. These men have witnessed battle first hand, fought bravely, risking their lives for their country. Made history itself." he said. Gin swallowed. These mediaeval knights shouldn't be here. It was crazy. Yet here they were, breathing the very same air hundreds of years later; it took her own away.

"Today, they will endeavour to prove themselves to our beautiful Lady Flora, Stewardess of Lowndes castle!"

Lady Flora rose from her chair and waved delicately to the audience, the other hand placed softly over her cinched stomach. She held her head high, relishing the attention before taking her seat again. She produced a golden silk fan from within a pocket of her dress and elegantly waved it in front of her swan-like neck.

"Be prepared for them to transport you to a time they know only too well. Where *danger* followed them like their own shadows." Joseph wore an almost wicked grin as the gates at the far end opened.

A surge of intrigue roused Gin from her pit. She sat up straighter, as white smoke bellowed out from within, the beat of the drums rising once more.

Abruptly, a beautifully clad horse thundered out of the smoke, a pale blue and white cloak billowing over its back, revealing a flash of metal armour beneath. Metal plates glinted in the sun over its forehead down to its muzzle, and a small metal spike protruded from between its eyes, making it look like some sort of deadly unicorn.

The knight on its back was in full body armour with a matching blue and white cloak that streaked behind him as they flew down the right side of the arena.

"Sir Tarrick!" roared Joseph over the cheering crowd as Tarrick slowed to take the u-turn and was handed a white and blue flag from his squire. He raised the flag in front of the podium and bowed to Lady Flora as much as his armour would allow, to which she inclined her head slightly in acknowledgement.

Gin swallowed the dryness in her throat. All her years cooped up in the Hospice and now this. It was like being inside one of her dreams.

Tarrick gave a mighty war cry and charged down the other side of the arena, holding the flag high as it rippled through the air. The screams from the audience were now at another level.

A second later, another knight bolted out of the smoke upon his armoured horse. The cloaks that adorned both horse and rider were red and white.

"Sir Alistair!" called Joseph as horse and rider streaked through the stadium, taking his flag, bowing to Lady Flora and disappearing in a cloud of dust.

Joseph glanced at Gin with a loaded grin before announcing the next knight.

"I give you, Sir Louis!" cheered Joseph.

She was rigid in her seat. Something about this *Louis* made her insides twist uncomfortably, and she hadn't even met him yet. All the nods at her meeting him. Her nose wrinkled, the unsettling feeling mounting as his bright colours of yellow and grey streaked through the arena.

After bowing to Lady Flora, he trotted a few paces, coming to a halt before Gin and bowed to her too. She looked away, catching Lady Flora's attention, who looked as if she was sucking a very bitter lemon. Gin finally glanced at Louis, inclined her head shakily before sliding down in her chair again. Any further and she'd fall off completely.

Louis lingered for a minute before thundering away. The unease did not leave her after his greeting. In fact, it only magnified, camped out heavily in her stomach.

"Ladies and Gentlemen, our fourth and final knight... Sir Col!" said Joseph. Gin narrowed her eyes at the annoyance that he failed to keep from his tone.

Maybe it was her imagination, but the music seemed to intensify and the wait for Col to make his entrance seemed to take longer. Her eyes strained to see through the fog that clouded the gate.

Finally, a black and white clad horse and rider sent the smoke swirling as they hurtled out, hooves pounding the dusty earth as it rose behind them in a flurry. Col reined his horse in, approaching the podium as the cloak of black and white danced leisurely at its knees.

Gin licked her dry lips. It was perhaps the most beautiful, yet more domineering than all of them, snorting through the intricate armour on its head. Its front legs struck the ground as Col took up his flag. He wasted no time in taking off into full gallop back towards the gate, leaving Gin with a swathe of goosebumps, despite the warm sun.

Lady Flora let out a small huff as she watched him disappear, having received no bow from him. Gin flattened her lips, suppressing the smirk that rose in her affront.

"Now that you have met our four knights, the tournament can begin! Our first joust will see Sir Louis and Sir Tarrick battle it out for 5 passes along the wooden tilt barrier that runs the length of the arena. The aim being to hit their opponent on the breast shield with their lance while receiving a similar blow and, of course, *staying* on their horse." Gin listened as Joseph walked the edge of the podium with slow and methodical pacing as he soaked up their eager faces. "Scoring is as follows. A touch on the breast shield wins 3 points. A broken lance awards 6 points to the knight whose lance is still intact. Unhorsing wins 12 points to the seated knight. The opponent with the highest score after 5 passes will advance to challenge our current champion, Sir Col!" he said. He braced the wooden railing, looking out with a raised chin at the ramped up audience.

Gin hadn't realised, but she had scooted forwards in her seat, now perched on the edge, hands braced between her knees.

Louis was the first to reappear from the veiled gate as he raised the visor on his helmet to greet the cheering fans. The ladies, who had positioned themselves at the front of the barriers, waved what looked like hankies or silk scarves as Louis took his time nodding and grinning down at them. But Gin's brow furrowed as he made his way to her, stopping his horse and fixing his eyes upon her.

He blinked several times. Light brown stubble gave way to his smile and Gin gripped her sweaty hands tightly in her lap, shuttering her eyes. Her stupid eyes. She swallowed, but her throat was so dry it grated.

"Gin." said Louis, drawing her gaze to his, heart racing at being called upon. "You wave no favour. But if you'll allow it, it would be a privilege to ride in your honour today."

Gin did a double take, completely lost. But he was waiting. And not just him. The whole arena was cheering, eyes on her.

Joseph beamed at her as he stood tall. She genuinely wanted the ground to swallow her whole, a cold sensation erupting in her chest.

"Uh…" she floundered. "Um… ok?" she said, not having a clue what else to say, just wanting this moment to be over.

Thankfully, it was enough for Louis, who nodded, covering his grin as he lowered his visor and rode out to take his place.

"What was that?" she asked Joseph as he took his seat next to her.

"Showing your allegiance to your chosen knight. Traditionally, knights choose a lady to ride for and take their hankie." he said casually, crossing one leg over the other and gripping his hands over his knee. Gin turned her head to him slowly.

"What for?" she asked, perplexed.

"It's good luck for the knight. And exciting for the ladies." he winked. "You can purchase hankies at the ticket kiosk on your way in." he added, casually.

Gin whipped back to Louis, who she was certain was still watching her from the other end of the arena. She hugged her arms as the next knight rode out.

Tarrick followed suit, choosing his hankie from a quiet blonde lady whose husband stood stoically at her side, attempting to look half as manly as the impressive knight.

Once the knights were in their starting positions at either end, their squires marched in, making quick work of handing them their lances, each painted to match the knight's colour. Louis slid the lance out of Podraig's hands in one fluid motion.

Both squires waited for a nod from their knight to signal they were ready before raising their arms to Joseph. He stood and made his way to the edge of the podium, the music intensifying into an almighty crescendo of drums.

"May each knight fight with honour and valour!" with that, a trumpet sounded, making Gin jump, as they spurred their horse into action.

They raced along the tilt, leaving a trail of rising dust, each knight bringing their lance into position to strike their opponent.

Gin winced, bracing the arms of her chair as she prepared for impact, as if it were her own. Finally, *clang!* Both knights had struck the other's breast shield, and each squire held up a scorecard of '3'.

She blew out her cheeks letting out a breath she didn't realise she'd been holding as Louis reined his horse to a halt before the podium, letting out a guttural cry as a cloud of dust swirled around them. She heard a laugh from her right to see Lady Flora stifling a grin as she gave her a sideways glance.

"You modern folk, so perturbed at the smallest of strikes. You'd fail to last a day in our time." she mumbled, eyes ahead.

Gin gritted her teeth as she flexed the taut skin on her shoulder blades. She'd like to see how long Lady Flora would last under the wrath of Slayton's belt. To scar that beautiful creamy skin that she was certain had never felt an ounce of agony. She held her tongue, willing herself not to give her the satisfaction of knowing how her words had stung. She was at least grateful to have the ability to hold herself in check after years of having to keep her tongue in place or face the consequence.

The squires awaited their knight's signal and again flew down the beaten track to the roaring crowd. Gin heard a loud crack and witnessed Tarrick's lance shatter into splinters. Louis's supporters gave an almighty cheer and the scoreboard tracker saw Louis's points rise to '9'.

The next pass saw '3' points awarded to each as they slammed their lances into each other's shields, and no points to either on the fourth pass. Both knights let out primal roars of disappointment as they careened to a halt.

Gin leaned forward, elbows planted on her knees as the knights prepared to make their fifth and final pass. Even the crowd seemed to hold their breath as they waited. She pressed her normally full lips into a thin line.

The knights took their places, both horses puffing and snorting as they tired. The signal went up and Louis gave an almighty war cry as he spurred his horse along with all he had left. Tarrick worked just as hard, the beat of the hooves matching the beating drums.

Each rider's aim seemed to waver slightly as the weight of their lances, coupled with their fatigue, took effect. Gin craned her neck to get a better view of the imminent final blow. Her mouth fell open as it was Louis's strike that had Tarrick grappling with his reins as the blow knocked him backwards. His horse seemed unaware of his rider's plight to stay saddled as he cantered on to the end. She watched wide eyed, Tarrick was now almost sideways as he reached the other end.

Finally, a trumpet sounded, marking the end of the rounds, and Tarrick held steadfast.

There were cheers all round as the final scores went up, Sir Tarrick - 6, Sir Louis - 15.

Gin slumped back in her chair, watching Louis take off his helmet. He pumped his fist into the air and bowed deeply to Lady Flora, who nodded her approval with a dainty smile and Joseph rallied the cheering.

"Ladies and Gentlemen! Our first champion of the day, Sir Louis!" he said, puffing his chest out.

Gin's jaw ached from clenching her teeth throughout the joust. She rapped her index finger on the arm of her chair as Louis tilted his head, panting as he fixed her with a triumphant grin. The hair stood up on her arms.

"Don't keep us waiting, Sir Col!" shouted Louis, to the arena at large. "Ride out and face your champion!"

Gin watched as Joseph dragged a hand over his beard, taking a couple of steps backwards. She glanced sideways and Lady Flora's tightly bound chest was rising and falling with quickening breaths. They were nervous. She could feel it rippling off their bodies and it was creeping into her own.

Louis paced in front of the podium, eyes fixed on the billowing smoke that continued to emanate from the large gate.

"Come now, Sir Col! My people grow restless! They wish to see another victory!" said Louis, growing impatient.

There was a cheer from the crowd, though some groans erupted from those who evidently were not there to see Louis win against Col.

"I know you said no theatrics but there's no *real* danger in this… is there?" asked Gin as she looked sidelong at him, trying to gauge his emotions.

He took a moment before replying.

"There is always an element of danger, Gin. Even between two knights who play respectfully. Their lances are blunt, but that doesn't protect against wooden splinters the size of a knife if shattered, or a particularly hard strike that dismounts the rider." He wasn't looking at her while he spoke, playing with the tuft of his pointed beard. "In their day, it was solely to demonstrate their prowess. But when you have two knights who have a particular dislike for each other, skill and logic can sometimes be put on the back burner. Although we try to quell it, feuds sometimes make their way onto the field. There have been a few close calls when Louis and Col are matched." he said, releasing a breath through his nose.

Gin couldn't stop the involuntary gulp of air. Her gaze wandered slowly back to Louis, who had now mounted his horse that Podraig held steady for him as he still waited for Col to come out.

A ripple of chatter expanded over the audience, their curiosity of his whereabouts mounting with every passing second. Even Louis took a cursory glance towards Joseph, who shifted in his seat, made a move to get up and speak when a dark shadow of horse and rider emerged from the haze.

Col rode out, casual and controlled, his horse swaying the pair as it stalked into the arena. It was strangely more impressive than the almighty speed at which the others had entered on, the steady pace allowing the tremendous muscles of the imposing horse to be showcased.

The audience cheered as the tension lifted among them and Joseph deflated into his chair with a sigh. Gin couldn't decide whether relief or trepidation lay behind it.

Col made his way down the opposite side to Louis, who was drawing himself up tall on his horse as he slammed his visor shut. Col paid him no attention, his gaze fixed upon the podium, helmet tucked under one arm as a gust of wind ruffled his swept back waves of black hair.

Lady Flora licked her lips and rose from her seat, gliding over to the edge of the platform with a playful smile upon her delicate features. She pulled out a white silk hankie with black lace trim and ran it through her long fingers as Col approached.

Gin almost rolled her eyes, until she realised that Col's attention was not upon Lady Flora. Even as he took the hankie from her, his sky-blue eyes were, instead, fixed upon her.

That flutter in her belly reared again, along with the need to brush it off as quickly as it surfaced.

Joseph strode over to the front of the podium just as Lady Flora took her seat. She could feel her searing gaze without having to look.

"Sir Louis. Sir Col... may your match be fought in honour, valour and most of all, *respect*." he said, raising his hand to almighty whooping and clapping as the knights nodded their understanding. Although it may have seemed for the benefit of the show, Gin was sure it heeded as more of a warning to the pair and their imminent combat.

The trumpet sounded, and they were off. This time, Col wasted no time in gathering speed as they tore down the tilt towards each other, lances aimed for impact.

Gin's knuckles were white as she leaned on her fist, watching wide eyed and waiting for the strike. Both knights jolted back as the blow struck each shield. She winced, squeezing her fists tighter until her nails dug painfully into her palms. But she hardly noticed as Louis came to a halt in front of the podium, the silver blunt end of his lance glinting in the sun. Again, he let out a guttural cry as he swung his horse round. She felt sure he bared his teeth under that helmet.

Col waited patiently at the other end as Louis tried to gain control of his horse, who had gone too far to the side.

It was in stark contrast to the calming stroke Col gave to his composed steed.

Pass two came, and the pair charged once more. This time, Col gained what seemed like more speed than she'd witnessed so far, his horse's legs seemingly invisible as they beat the dusty track.

The unsteady start from Louis saw him miss his strike. But Col hit hard and true, dead on target.

Gin pushed herself up. Louis was sent twisting sideways as his horse carried on to the end.

A united gasp rose through the arena, followed by cheering for Col as he put all his might into slowing his powerful horse.

Gin blew out a shaky breath, sliding her sweaty hands down her thighs. She'd not expected to feel so much tension.

Louis staggered up while Podraig attempted to aid him, but ended up being waved off, his pride clearly taking the brunt of the blow. It didn't help that several groups of people had started to chant Col's name and many more followed suit.

The knights focused on each other, once again charging, giving every ounce of effort, readying to give and receive the next thrash.

She could hardly bear to watch and yet could not tear her eyes away as the strikes came. The pair struck the other's shield. However, there was a loud *crack* and with it, a shower of splinters came raining down.

It took a moment for Gin to decipher whose lance had broken, but the rage of Louis's cry gave her the answer before her eyes worked it out. He threw the remaining part of it to the ground as Podraig dutifully picked up the pieces.

Gin held her breath. Col was still silent, even in his growing victory and the cheering he didn't acknowledge it, solely focused on his joust.

The scoreboard was altered. 'Sir Louis - 3, Sir Col - 24'. Gin felt a rush of adrenaline as she saw Col's score soar higher, leaving Louis way behind. Despite giving her allegiance to Louis, a little fire in her belly ignited for Col to beat him. His game was expertly more dignified.

Louis let out a final gruff cry, and Podraig scurried over with a new lance. She watched him snatch it up, inspecting it while the crowd was busy cheering their support for Col.

Meanwhile, Col received a new lance too from what appeared to be the same squire that had been with Alistair. Come to think of it, she hadn't seen a squire with him until now.

As the two knights made their signal and picked up pace, she noticed something fall to the ground from Col's lance. A prickle tiptoed down her back and arms. Something wasn't right. Something was very wrong. The feeling flooded her veins with fire. And as Col thundered forwards it became clear. Instead of a blunt metal head, she could see the sun glinting off a pointed spear shaped head.

Her stomach dropped, her blood running cold as she watched him aim the sharp end directly towards Louis.

She whipped her head around to Joseph and Lady Flora, both oblivious. Rising out of her chair, everything passed in slow motion, and yet she was powerless to stop it.

She had to think fast.

Time was slipping away.

Eyes wide with panic, she looked around her. She ignored Joseph's questions and puzzled look but spotted the microphone that he held. She grabbed it and lunged towards the railing of the podium. Her heart in her mouth, unsure a word would escape the tightness in her throat, she shouted with everything she had.

"COL, STOP!"

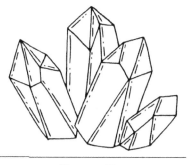

Chapter Five

Time slowed agonisingly as the world faded. Her voice echoed ominously around the arena.

Col's pace didn't falter, but Louis pulled back on the reins, trying to bring his horse to swerve away from the impending blow he'd now clocked. But it was not quick enough.

Gin's fingers gripped harder on the railing, as if it would somehow slow him down if she did it hard enough. But all she could do was watch in horror as Col's lance penetrated the underside of his arm through a gap in his armour. Louis's cry of pain cut viciously through the air. An ice cold shock unfurled in her chest.

She sagged, gripping the railing still as Joseph appeared at her side, staring in horror.

Louis had crumpled forward, clutching at his horse's powerful neck as it slowed to an agitated trot, fully aware that something was not right with its rider.

She met Col's gaze when he lazily lifted his visor, raising a dark brow. She was sure a feline grin ghosted his lips before he rode into the billowing smoke of the gate.

The shocked audience were now craning their necks to get a better look at what had happened. Gin sheepishly handed the microphone back to Joseph. She caught the flurry of Lady Flora's skirts and followed her as she disappeared down the stairs to the arena. Joseph's frantic apology reverberated around the silent arena as he suspended the show, asking the audience to exit calmly.

Louis sat on the ground, leaning against the wall of the podium, helmet and top half of his armour strewn on the floor as medics attended to the wound. She threw her hands to her mouth as the two men cut the wooden lance a hand's length from the entry point, earning a grunt of pain from Louis.

Lady Flora stood in shock, hands over her stomach as she watched, Daphne by her side, reassuring her quietly.

Louis met Gin's wide-eyed stare and his panting transitioned into deep breaths, chest rising and falling slowly. She didn't know where to look as she fought the urge to help him, and there was something else. A deep anger bubbled from within. Her wandering gaze didn't settle until it came upon the fogged up gates. Her ragged breathing stung her throat... and something snapped inside... her breath stilled. Anger and frustration pulsated through her veins, and it was all directed towards the one person she'd seen walk through that gate. Col. He had done this on purpose. Wounded Louis. Another monster who walked amongst men. Just like Slayton. Only now, she had nothing that kept her tethered back. No one to protect.

She confidently made her way to the cloud of smoke, veiling wherever Col had stalked off to.

"Gin..." came Louis's strained voice. But she couldn't turn. The magnetic force that compelled her to go after Col was just too strong.

"GIN!" he called, this time louder, putting every ounce of effort behind it.

It was as though every moment of injustice she'd tolerated, every beating, every punishment for just being herself, wanting to help people, had come to a head. It mixed with her frustration of being ripped away from Hope, to create something even more powerful. She couldn't explain it, but she didn't need to. She felt it and that feeling drove her.

The wind sang in her ears, drowning out Louis's calls, until finally the thick smoke enveloped her. She squinted against it, swathed by silence until it cleared and she found herself in a small courtyard, flanked by several stables on either side. At first, it appeared empty, everyone having run out to see the commotion in the arena. She scanned the empty stables nearest her when a clang of metal reached her ears. She paused, eyes darting to the source in the furthest stable.

She made quick work of crossing the dusty courtyard and came face to face with Col as he threw his breastplate to the floor. A dark brow raised over one piercing eye, taking her breath away momentarily.

"So nice of you to drop by. Come to help?" he asked, the corners of his mouth twitching. Gin's heart thrummed in her ears, fury flooding her body. She wanted to throw every insult under the sun at him, but words just didn't seem enough. Blind anger won control of her trembling body, tightening her fists and contorting her face. Suddenly she was inches from his face as he peered down his nose at her, and she threw a bone crunching punch to his chiselled face. It sent a shock of pain bolting up her arm to her shoulder as the adrenaline rushed to her head. His face snapped away from her before whipping around. He cupped his jaw, working it, brows knitted.

"Damn it, Sparkles! You could at least have taken your rings off." he winced, rubbing his smooth cheek. She gritted her teeth against the pain, flexing her fingers with a slow, satisfied smile. Everything told her she'd just crossed a line and that she needed to get out of here. And yet a swell of justice flourished in her chest.

But it was fleeting, gone as an arm wrapped around her and dragged her backward.

"Argh! Get off me!" she screamed, panting as the skin on her back protested, lightning coursing through her scars at the pressure of being held.

"What... on earth... are you thinking?" said Louis between pained breaths, letting go of her. She whirled to see him clutching his injured arm, and a wave of guilt washed over her. The end of the broken lance still penetrated his flesh.

"Oh God. You need to get back to the medics." She breathed, reining in her tremors as she crossed to inspect his wound. He winced, fixing his eyes upon hers. His face softened, as if his pain had vanished momentarily.

"You thought I was going to stay there while you marched off after *him*?" he asked, breathing in through his teeth as he glared over her shoulder.

"Oh, I don't think you needed to worry. Little miss punchy pants here was doing quite well without your heroics." said Col, padding up to her side, still rubbing his cheek.

Louis eyed his reddening jaw, narrowing his gaze. Gin clenched her aching hand, catching Louis's eye travelling to her fist. She huffed, cheeks burning, hardly believing what she'd done herself.

Their attention was diverted as the sound of hurried footsteps approached. Joseph marched into view, face blotchy with anger. She hid her hands behind her back, and glanced sideways at Col. He'd seen the move and his eyes travelled back to hers, his lips pursed. She swallowed involuntarily, sure she was about to be thrown out, just as bad as the man who had provoked such anger from her.

"For crying out loud, you two!" he panted, resting a hand on the doorway before spotting her. "Gin... what are you doing back here?" he asked, brow furrowed. She opened her mouth, not sure what excuse would come out. Fortunately, Col intervened before she had the chance to find out.

"I was just saying she should join us in a spot of healing. About time she knew what she was really getting herself into, don't you think?" asked Col, sidling up to Louis and hoisting him under his good shoulder. A muscle worked in Louis's bristled jaw. She frowned, looking at the three men. "What better way than to show her the power first hand?" Col cocked his head, looking into Louis's exhausted eyes. "Come. Heal yourself, brother." he smiled, but there was a darkness behind it.

"Brother?" asked Gin, gawping as she turned the word over in her head. The brothers both met her gaze, their silence her confirmation, only cut short by Louis's gasp of pain.

Joseph let out a sigh of frustration as he glanced around the empty courtyard, stamping a foot.

"Right. Get him to yours, *now,* while I clear up your mess. I don't want another *foot* out of line for the rest of the season after this stunt, Col. Do you understand?" said Joseph.

"*Crystal* clear, Oldman." said Col. Joseph paused, jaw jutted. "Don't you want to be there for the *big reveal?*"

Joseph shook his head dangerously slowly, looked to Louis, who was blinking heavily, not dragging his gaze from Gin.

"I don't want any part of what you're about to do in there. Just fix him. This is his moment, not mine." He slid a sheepish look to Gin, who was more confused than ever. "I'll see you at the celebration dinner tonight. Seven o'clock. We'll get back on track, Gin, I promise." he said, before skulking away, head hung. Her stomach dropped at the mention of a celebration dinner, but he was gone before she could object.

"Come on, Sparkles." said Col, patting Louis's hand that he held over his shoulder, "You heard him. Let's go heal my dear brother."

*

Col's place had actually turned out to be the small cottage she saw on her way down. She followed them through the first gloomy room, the windows still shuttered so that no daylight entered. Almost blindly, they made their way to a smaller room at the back. The shutter here had been opened, and she could make out a small round table and four chairs. Col helped Louis into one of them, groaning as he settled.

"Sorry about the mess. If I'd had more time, I might have cleaned up a bit." he paused, glancing around. "Maybe."

Gin ignored him, glancing at the mass of liqueur bottles and copious notebooks strewn over the table, even across the floor, and made her way to sit by Louis. His breathing was becoming more laboured, and from what she could make out, he had become noticeably paler. His face was still inexplicably soft as he watched her, as if transfixed. She shifted in her seat, a scowl forming on her brow.

"You're real... I always believed it, but... you're really here." he rasped, his copper brown hair warm in the soft window light.

Gin shook her head softly.

"I don't... I don't know what you mean." her eyebrows squished together. He laughed carefully, so as not to move the lance that Gin couldn't keep her eyes from for long. "We need the medics back, Col. You need to get them here." She turned to find him leant up against the door frame, hands in his pockets.

"Nope. As soon as my dear brother tells you the truth, he can do a much better and quicker job of healing himself." said Col, smiling at Louis with narrowed eyes. Louis's breathing intensified, his nostrils flaring slightly.

"You know I'm not going down that path, so why don't you just get the medics here, like Gin asked," he said through gritted teeth. Col's smile disappeared.

"Either way, you owe her the truth first. So I'd be quick about it."

Gin shot him a look of disgust. Her nose wrinkled.

"You're really going to make him tell me before you help?"

"Yep." he shot back, resting his head on the doorframe. She gritted her teeth and turned her back, eager to find a way of helping Louis.

"It's alright, Gin. Let my brother have his fun. I've played his games many times, I'm almost as good as him." he sneered, glancing over her shoulder.

"Hm, almost." agreed Col, suddenly appearing beside them as he threw a leather notebook onto the table. It slapped the wood and made one of the empty bottles roll slightly. Louis gazed at it, then at Gin, before dragging it towards him with his good arm.

Col slumped into the chair opposite them, placed three cups down, and unscrewed a new liquor bottle. She watched him pour amber liquid into the three cups, sliding them one each.

"She's not eighteen yet, Col."

"Oh please," he sneered, "and when the clock strikes midnight, she'll suddenly be able to hold her drink?"

Gin eyed the drink before her, then Col, the playful glint in his eyes daring her to drink. She'd never tried alcohol, but she'd smelt it enough on Slayton's breath.

"No thanks. Just tell me whatever you have to say so that you can get help and I can leave." she said, pushing the drink away and fixing Louis with a hard look. After a moment of silence, he nodded slowly and flipped open the notebook. Time had taken its toll on the creamy yellow pages, wrinkled and torn around the edges.

"It was our mother's," he said darkly. "One of the many she kept on the Crystals and the device that sent us all here." he said, biting his lower lip. Gin's mouth parted, her eyes widening. The truth about how they got here had always lingered in her mind. And here she was, surrounded by the knowledge that she craved.

"There's one part in particular you need to know. I'd uh… I'd read it to you, but… given the circumstances… I think you should read it yourself." He closed his eyes, clutching his side as he slid the book her way.

Gin inhaled sharply, looking at Col expectantly. Surely he wouldn't leave him like this.

"Better read fast." he said, swirling his drink slowly before taking a sip.

Gin felt a roiling heat in her belly as she snatched the book up, mouth pinched. He smirked and drank again.

She scrutinised the page. The writing was beautiful, feline and feminine as it swirled across the pages. She glanced at Louis once more, his weak gaze upon her as his shoulders rose and fell with each strained breath. Then she read aloud.

"My dear Louis, I feel compelled to share my recent vision that the Galaxy Crystal has bestowed on me, for it concerns your future. And I fear that your life may take you on a path where you may overlook this opportunity. Through no fault of your own, but that of what life has given you.

My dear son, you must dig deep to find the strength within yourself to let this be. There will come a time when the stars will send you the soul of another and, once found, the bond shall be unbreakable. Even if you try, with all your might, to forget, to pretend it was but a figment of your imagination, it will always pull on your heart. At your very core.

This soul will come in the form of silver…" Gin trailed off. It couldn't possibly be…

"It may not be apparent at first, but you may feel it before your eyes see it. I cannot put words to this feeling, for it will be so deeply profound that even the stars themselves cannot convey the words to me. It is a gift. It will find you, whether it be through friendship, partnership or a love that would put the heavens to shame.

But here is where you must be strong again. For this silver soul will be close to breaking." Gin's throat ached from the strain of reading what was becoming more

47

and more close to home… she glanced up at Louis, who gave her a sad smile. Her heart hammered against her ribs.

"I uh... I… I don't know if I can." she stammered, unable to talk as her throat constricted on her. She stared down at the notebook, cheeks heating as she tried to process the letter.

Col strolled over and crouched to her level. His eyes danced on hers as he slipped it from her hands and continued.

"And my son, I fear yours will not be far off, either. But much can heal, beyond the power of the Crystals, when two souls that were meant to be, come together. So don't lose hope. Don't walk away in ignorance. Individually, you will flourish for it and together you will ignite a fire that will be unstoppable. Together, your soul's love is more powerful than any Crystal.

My love and light, always, my dearest one."

He lingered on the page for a moment before puckering his mouth and closing it softly.

Gin stared sideways at him, mouth open as a shuddering breath left her lungs. Their gaze snagged, unable to pull away until Louis reached out a hand and slowly placed it on hers. The shock rippled through her body and she recoiled it to her chest; the force making the pain from her punch flare angrily.

"Gin, I…" he began, watching her wide eyes survey him.

"Too fast, brother." said Col, but his eyes were on Gin. Her mind was reeling. It couldn't be true. She couldn't be who they thought she was. It was ridiculous. And yet… she felt broken.

She knew that much.

She felt what little was left of her soul break the moment she was forced away from Hope. But *this?* This made no sense.

She rose on shaky legs, the chair scraping the flagstone floor. She couldn't be dragged into whatever fantasy they were weaving her into. Hope was who she needed to focus on. She'd let herself get swept up enough already with the whirlwind of events.

"I have to go." she started, but froze, hands flying to her mouth as Louis slumped forwards onto the table, sending his drink flying to the ground.

"Finally." Col breathed as he stood. "Thought he'd never keel over... shame about the whiskey, though."

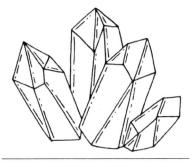

Chapter Six

Gin stared in horror as Louis lay unconscious, guilt burning in her chest at having let Col have his way.

"Why? Why did you make him tell me first? You had your *fun* in the arena. Why drag it out here?" she said, hands sliding through her hair.

"Because I needed to get your attention, without my brother drooling all over you." said Col, crossing to a large wooden chest nestled in the shadows of the kitchen. She let out a humourless laugh.

"Well congratulations, stabbing your brother certainly did that!" she spat, nausea churning in her stomach. "What are you even doing? You need to get him medical help *now.*" She slumped into the chair again and heaved Louis upright with all her strength. "The lance is still in place, which means it's still stemming the bleeding. But there's no telling what damage it's caused inside."

Col crouched beside her once more and placed three raw Crystals on the table, along with a drawstring hessian bag. She threw him a bewildered look, her patience running low. She may not have liked Louis assuming his absurd claim on her soul, but she couldn't walk away from a wounded person. Not anymore.

"Have you even listened to a word I've said?" she breathed. He gave her a lopsided grin that disappeared as quickly as it appeared.

"*Intently.*"

She narrowed her gaze, his sarcasm grating on her every nerve.

"Now it's your turn to listen, Sparkles."

She straightened. She had no idea who this man was, and so far he had given every impression that he was dangerous beneath that mockery.

"My brother wouldn't dream of breaking his vow to never touch the healing Crystals again. Not after our mother, Josephine, left them to *me* and the havoc they have wreaked ever since. Call it morals or sensibility. I call it plain old jealousy." he said, lip curling as he picked up the bag and one purple Crystal. Gin tilted her head, eyeing the Crystal, lips pursed. Her muscles tensed as he turned it in his long fingers, the light catching on its white points and illuminating the deep purple at the bottom. Her mind raced. She had heard of Crystals having healing properties… but surely he wasn't relying on them to fix Louis's wound.

"So, the healing today was always going to fall to me. Which allows me a window of time to talk to you freely." His magnetic eyes lifted to hers. Her head pounded, having spoken and listened to more people today already than she would normally in at least a week. She rubbed her temple.

"Trust me, you're going to want to hear what I have to say." he said, sensing her resistance.

"Why should I trust you at all? You stabbed your own brother just to talk to me!" she said, throwing her hands up, wincing as her injured hand throbbed in protest. Col's eyes danced to her curled hand and back.

"You may not like my method, but you might as well hate me from the get go. If you didn't, the rest of the castle would have made sure of it, anyway. Saves them the trouble." He smiled, but it didn't reach his eyes. "This is in your own interest. I promise." his gaze tiptoed around her face. She inhaled deeply, letting out a long sigh. A glance at Louis kicked her heart into gear. He was getting paler by the second.

"Alright. I'll listen. Just *help* him first." she pleaded. Col's smirk slid to the side again, eyes widening for a second.

"I can multitask, Sparkles." He opened his palm to reveal the purple Crystal. Gin scowled but held her tongue. "Amethyst. Relieves pain." He popped it into the hessian bag and picked up a greenish blue Crystal, flecked with specks of red.

"Bloodstone. Does what it says. Cleanses and purifies the blood." She watched him place it in the bag too, her body tensing with anticipation.

"And lastly, Opal. Healer of the skin." After placing them all in the bag, he tied it closed, pulling his head up and pressing his lips flat as he surveyed her.

"If you know the lance is stemming the blood, you also know what's going to happen when I remove it." His brows lowered.

Gin blinked several times. She couldn't speak though as she tried to shift the vision of the night she delivered Hope. How she watched her mother bleed out on the bed, the metallic tang that filled the room that still haunted her to this day. How she had scrubbed her skin raw for hours. How she'd had to cut her hair to get the image of dry blood sticking the strands together from her mind every time she looked in a mirror. It filled her core with ice at the memory.

Col bit his cheek gently.

"You… might want to look away," he said, gently. Her breath hitched in her throat as she pulled herself out of her thoughts, reminding herself that she had the freedom to help here. She watched, transfixed, as Col reached for the lance, speaking as he did so.

"My brother has been planning this day since our mother passed, twelve years before we even arrived here. You're the reason he stays away from every hot-blooded female that throws themself at him." He was about to grip the splintered lance when Gin reached out a trembling hand, taking it herself. Col narrowed his eyes on her.

"I'm no stranger to blood." she explained, fixing her silver eyes on his, which pulsed, never seeming to decide on which emotion to convey.

She'd dealt with wounds at the Hospice for a long time before that night. Patients regularly harmed themselves, but her urge to help always pushed past the horror of it. She just needed to find that person within who she had buried.

Col cast her a sceptical eye. She was sure he was going to stop her. After all, he had no reason to trust her. Only he didn't. Brows lowered, he nodded firmly.

His trust was almost enough to make her forget what she was doing. Her mouth dried as she calmed her breathing, still tangled in his gaze. She needed to still her shaking hands and find balance.

"Alright. You'll have to pull, hard and fast. There won't be a lot of time between removing the head and me having to apply a lot of pressure with these Crystals."

She nodded vigorously, trying to ignore the image of Hope's mother laying in a pool of her own blood. Because of her. She blinked hard, shoving the guilt down.

"But the bleeding... we'll need bandages. And what about infection? We'll need to clean it." she said, looking around helplessly at the lack of anything clean or sanitary.

"We won't need any of that. Your turn to trust me." he said, shifting on his crouched legs. She swallowed. She didn't trust anyone. This made no sense to her and yet, she knew she was about to follow blindly. With a slow nod of her head, he helped to brace Louis's shoulder. Her hand screamed in protest as she pressed it into the underside of his wound.

"Remember, hard and fast. And pull straight." he said.

She leaned in, Col's head just inches from hers, his scent infusing her senses. Leathery yet sweet, like blackberries, laced with whiskey. Being this close to someone other than Hope sent her heart attacking her ribs wildly, and the urge to back away was almost overwhelming.

Pushing through the blur and confusion in her mind, she took a deep breath, hoping to whatever higher power there may be that she didn't mess this up. Tightening her fingers around the end of the lance carefully, she *pulled.* Hard and fast. A grim, squelching sound emitted as the blade left his flesh. It sent her stomach roiling.

The blood the blade had kept at bay now spilled out over her legs. She watched, mouth agape. Col instantly applied pressure, the Crystal bag pressed firmly over the gash. His face contorted, back rising and falling as he strained to keep the pressure.

"Our mother's prophecy said that the soul connection may present itself through friendship, partnership or love." he said. She looked up from her shaking blood-soaked trousers and tried to focus on his words, trying to ignore the hessian bag. It was now scarlet between his fingers, the sticky blood oozing over them like some kind of garish Halloween fountain.

"So, before my brother gets his claws into you and fills your head with the fantasy he's already planned, just remember." he lowered his head to turn to face her, his cheeks flushed. "You are your own person, before anyone else's."

Gin wrestled with her ability to comprehend what he'd said as he removed the bag of Crystals to reveal completely smooth skin. Not a single drop of blood marred him. Her hands shook as she tried to speak, unable to tear her stinging eyes away from the miracle before her.

She felt something shift in her hand and found Col removing the lance head from her trembling fingers.

"You ok?" he asked, warily. She felt the drying blood on her hands crack as she flexed her fingers, and a familiar cold sweat accompanied a wave of nausea.

She was going to throw up.

She threw herself towards the backdoor in the kitchen just in time and aimed for a bush. She wavered for a moment, breathing the fresh air deep into her lungs. A damp linen cloth appeared by her shoulder, and she watched it sway gently in the breeze.

"Never liked that bush anyway." said Col, casually. Gin's chest caved as she blindly took the cloth and wiped her mouth, heat creeping onto her cheeks.

"Sorry."

"Don't be." he said, earnestly.

She straightened, turning finally, arching an eyebrow.

"What, no sarcastic remark?" she wiped her forehead with the back of her hand, embarrassment flooding her cheeks. Col puckered his lips, studying her for a moment.

"You forget, I've marched through battlefields strewn with the bodies of the injured, and worse. I've seen it turn the stomachs of even the most fearsome knights." Their eyes snagged for a moment before he winced slightly as he took in her blood-stained clothes. "I, uh… I can find you something to change into.

Daphne will get those cleaned up for you. She's a wonder with bloodstains." he said, disappearing into the kitchen again. Her eyes widened, not wanting to imagine what Daphne has had to clean up. She approached Louis with care. His shoulders rising and falling calmly as he slumped over the table.

"He'll be fine." said Col, gripping the door frame as he looked over his shoulder. "He'll sleep it off for a bit and be back to courting you in no time." He flashed her a feline grin as he left the room.

Gin scowled down at Louis and crossed her arms. The healing Crystals were incredible. She had no doubt in her mind of their power after witnessing it. But she had no intention of being courted by anyone, least of all someone who had already decided upon her future. Whether or not this whole soul connection existed, she would not be bound to it or anyone.

Col returned with a small bundle of clothes.

"This should do until you can get to your room and change. Before you do though… " he closed the space between them and her body tensed. He peered down at her hand she'd tucked carefully in the crook of her arm. "Let's heal that weapon." He arched a dark brow.

"Don't worry, I'll be fine." She said, flushing as she stepped back a little, their proximity stifling. He tipped his head and sighed.

"Oh, come on, how are you ever going to punch me again with a gammy hand?" A shadow of a smirk ghosted his lips. She shifted her weight, sucking her cheeks in.

"Well, you deserved it." she said, eyes lowering to his neck.

"Yep. And I probably will again, so… shall we?" He pulled back a chair for her. She pursed her lips, sceptical to let him help. But he'd healed Louis. And she really wanted the throbbing pain to stop. Reluctantly, she slid into the chair as he crossed back to the chest, rummaging for a moment.

"Apatite." He pulled a chair towards hers and held a bluish green Crystal in his palm. "This will help the bones and relieve the pain." He paused, his eyes doing that pulsating dance again, all in a blink of hers, trying to read her. She hugged her hand closer under it. The last thing she needed was someone to read her like some sort of horror book.

"You do it." he said. She blanched.

"I don't know… "

"It's easy. You wouldn't have been in my mother's vision if you didn't have some connection to these too." he said, dark lashes lowering to rest on the Crystal. She couldn't deny the pull she felt towards it. A flash of adrenaline flooded her veins, a glimmer of wanting to believe him. She stretched a tentative hand to pick it up, a small intake of breath hitching in her chest. It was warm to the touch, but more amazingly, it was vibrating gently. Her eyes widened as she looked up. He leaned forward, elbows on his knees and hands clasped before his mouth.

"You feel it." He squinted up at her. Her heart pounded as she nodded.

"Hold it in your injured hand."

She did so, the sound of it clinking against her rings as she closed her fingers gently. The warm vibration spread out through her palm, soothing and relieving all the pain and tension. The redness that had mottled her skin shifted back to her natural olive tone. She huffed a laugh. All she could think about was the impact that these Crystals would have if she could only get them to all the patients stuck at Slayton's. What if they could heal the mind as well as the physical body?

"They're incredible." She unfurled her healed fingers. Col took the Crystal, eyeing her.

"They certainly like you." He rapped his knuckles on the table. "It should have taken twice that long to heal. You're fast."

"It wasn't me." She sat back in her chair, shaking her head, staring in awe at her hand.

"Hmm." he said. Her gaze shifted to him, his mind obviously ticking over. She cleared her throat, keen to change the subject and curious about something.

"Why did you warn me?" she asked, pausing. He frowned, silent. "I mean, obviously you and your brother don't exactly get along, but… all this. Just to get one up on him?" she asked, nose wrinkled.

He tilted his head back, a gleam dancing in his eyes.

"Added bonus." he smirked, smile lines cupping his mouth. She folded her arms, sighing pointedly.

"Look." His broad shoulders slumped. "If this was important enough to transfer the energy of a vision to our mother, and you are who we think you are… then your soul really is broken." he said, gently. Gin stiffened, digging her elbows into her sides. She knew that already and didn't need a vision to tell her that. Living under Slayton's roof was sure to accomplish a broken soul. But to hear someone say it… she felt exposed. Her chin dipped, shame prickling at her chest.

"Hey, love could blossom and if so, congratulations, I look forward to *not* being on the wedding guest list." he shrugged, palms up. "But I figured it's only fair to know what rules my dear brother is playing by. As far as he's concerned, you were the love of his life the moment he found the prophecy. And he's *very* good at getting what he wants." He reached for his drink and paused midway to his mouth. "A heads up to a broken soul was the least I could do." He downed the rest of the whiskey, teeth bared, as he let out a soft sigh.

She blinked heavily; the day getting crazier by the second. Her own drink still sat untouched. She suddenly felt the reckless urge to drink it. She grabbed it, causing Col's brows to raise.

"I don't do love." she said, jaw clenched as she looked at the sleeping man, foolish enough to think she'd love him. She downed the liquor in one, embracing the burning trail it left in her throat, taking her breath away.

Col swallowed a laugh, clinking his empty cup to hers before saying,

"Cheers to that."

Chapter Seven

Gin sat crying in an alcove by the window in what she had been told was now her room in the castle. The limestone walls stretched high to a domed ceiling. It was too big and empty, void of the vibrant life her room with Hope had had. A large dark wood four-poster bed sat against one wall, deep red curtains hung from a canopy. Near to that stood a wooden wardrobe, but she had kept her bag packed, ready to leave as soon as possible. A screen veiled a wooden bathtub in the corner and an enormous fireplace heated the cavernous room. The alcove in the window had seating along the walls and a small wooden table that ran through the middle.

Daphne had shown her up, as Joseph was otherwise occupied with running the castle. She had mumbled something about thinking he should at least take the day off to be around for her first day, but Gin didn't mind his absence. In fact, she preferred it.

Daphne had failed to keep the shock from her face when she'd seen her in Col's clothes. A long black shirt that sat just above her knees, cinched in the middle with a plaited leather belt. He had no trousers that would have fit her, but it was a warm day and his shirt acted like a dress of sorts. It had covered her back, so it was good enough.

Now, alone in her room, she watched the busy courtyard below, knees hugged to her chest, letting the tears roll freely. The tents were busy with customers, buying trinkets and souvenirs, children role playing as knights as they battled with plastic swords on the grass, while a jester in red and green tried to muscle in on the play-fight.

The sound of the musicians rang out as they played a light and merry song, the background to what seemed like so much happiness. But all she could think about was how this was the background music to being locked up at Slayton's and that Hope was still there. The fire of anger in her belly was doused with a storm of sadness, each vying for power.

She nestled her chin into the crook of her arm upon her knee. That leathery sweet scent filled her nose again, and she realised she was still wearing Col's shirt. She recoiled, not wanting to be reminded of the events that morning. Using the sleeve of his shirt, she wiped her cheeks free from tears. She felt emotionally exhausted, but she needed to focus, to train all her thoughts on how she was going to get Hope. This place could be good for them. It was a safe future. But she still felt a reluctance to accept it. She didn't want any other family; she didn't *need* a father and she most certainly didn't need a husband, no matter how strongly Louis believed in the soul connection. If indeed it was even true. Her silver eyes and broken soul were a strange coincidence, but she was just Gin. There was nothing exceptional about her. No deeper meaning to her future, other than making the best life for her and her daughter. That was exceptional enough for her.

She wasn't lost in thought for too long before spotting two familiar figures sauntering through the stone arch by the bridge. Louis had regained consciousness and had changed into black breaches and a fresh, deep blue shirt. He greeted people with no ounce of pain or discomfort, making a show of his strength by wielding his sword to the crowd. He was followed by Col, who had also changed into a white shirt, the sleeves rolled up under a long black waistcoat with silver studs. His black breaches were tucked into long boots. He came up behind Louis, hands in his pockets, who stopped the show and braced his shoulder.

Gin's brow raised. Any animosity between the pair had simply disappeared as they posed for photographs of many eager guests.

Just then, Joseph appeared from the same stone archway, striding with arms held wide towards the two crowded knights. A mirthless laugh escaped her throat, the source of their sudden bond now clear as the sky above.

Joseph rounded on Louis and bowed his head to speak. A moment later, Louis's gaze rose to her window. Her stomach dropped, unsure if he could see her. He clapped Joseph on the shoulder, beaming as he continued to speak with his adoring public.

It was then, when she thought she was free of prying eyes, that she noticed Col squinting up at her window while he handed an autograph book back to a very pleased young lady, bobbing up and down as she inspected it.

Gin drew back, the cold stone wall nipping at her back. She didn't want to get any more involved with them. It was an unwelcome distraction. Apart from the Crystals…

She frowned, peeking out once more. But Col had vanished, leaving his brother and Joseph enthralling the crowd.

She wondered if the Crystal's healing power was common knowledge and if so, would he ever be willing to help those at the Hospice?

*

Gin spent the rest of the day hiding in her room. She found sleep eventually, exhaustion finally catching up with her from overstimulation. The four-poster bed had been a luxury she never thought she'd experience and wrapped her in guilt at feeling its comfort while Hope had none. The feather pillows made it difficult to raise her head when she finally woke to a rapping on the door.

"Come in." she said, bleary-eyed as she glanced towards the window. The sun had lowered in the sky, casting a golden hue on the light stone walls.

"Evening, dearie." Daphne trotted into the room with a bundle of towels in a wicker basket. She busied herself behind the folding screen.

"I've just sent for the hot water to be brought up and between you and me, I raided Lady Flora's bath essence supply. Best keep that to ourselves though," she added, hesitantly. "You've got a big evening ahead of you and you deserve to feel as wonderful as you'll look!"

Gin grimaced as she remembered the dinner party that Joseph was hosting for her. All she wanted to do was to stay snuggled up in her bed and sleep until she could figure out how she was going to get Hope back and Slayton out of their lives forever.

"Ah, Daphne... I don't think I'm going to go to the party." Daphne's head popped out from behind the screen.

"But... it's in *your* honour. Everyone is so excited to welcome you. One person in particular." She trailed off with a knowing smile. Gin screwed her eyes shut.

"Don't tell me you believe this whole *prophecy* thing is me, too?" She slunk back into her pillow, gazing up at the domed ceiling.

"Well, you have to admit, you fit the profile perfectly! Those eyes of yours, I've seen no others like them, and you haven't had it easy, growing up without..." She cut herself off and Gin twisted her head towards her, expression flat.

"Go on, you can say it." she prompted, not phased. "Without parents. I must be broken right? Trust me though. That's not what breaks your soul." she said, turning her head to stare at the ceiling.

Daphne wrung her hands and approached the bed slowly.

"I'm sorry, dearie. What you must think of me! I meant no offence." she said, perching on the end of the bed.

"It's fine." Gin said, eyes fixed above, "But I won't be forced into marrying someone because of a prophecy. Let alone one that says it doesn't *have* to be linked to love. So Louis can forget the plans he has for me." She was silent, waiting for Daphne to leave. But no such luck.

"Hmm, I see Col has already had words."

Gin pushed herself onto her elbows. Daphne pursed her lips.

"He just wanted to make me aware of my free will in all this." she said, brows raised. She felt an odd sense of protectiveness after he had tried to help her. Albeit, not in the good grace she'd have liked.

Daphne smiled kindly, her small blue eyes twinkling.

"Of course you do, absolutely. But all I'll say is, the pairing of souls like this is extremely rare. I've known of only one other true soul connection, and their love was enough to make you weep." she smoothed her apron, looking fondly into some distant memory.

Gin frowned, her chest tightening uncomfortably. Daphne caught her eye.

"And anyway, you still need dinner. So, get washed up, dressed up and cheered up. You can meet Louis properly with your head full of free will and see what your heart decides." she said, making her way back behind the screen. Gin rolled her eyes, but the mention of dinner was appealing, having had nothing all day. And she didn't need to worry about her heart. It was already taken by Hope.

"I've also got a lovely selection of dresses for you to choose from."

Gin's stomach hardened. She sat up and hugged her arms around her knees. Her back tingled, as if in protest. She'd not risk anything that would show below the base of her neck.

"Uh, that's ok… I, um, I'm not really a dress person." she said, baring her teeth and wincing as she waited for Daphne's head to pop out from the screen again. She was not kept waiting.

*

The music from the Great Hall drifted up the stairs to where Daphne was walking Gin to her dinner party. Gin tried to ignore the fleeting looks of disappointment Daphne kept giving her regarding her outfit choice. A thin knit pale yellow jumper, tucked into straight legged light blue jeans, rolled up at the ankle. Her mother's red ribbon tumbled over one shoulder from her half up half down hair do, her hair falling over her shoulders. She felt a little guilty for not wearing one of the many beautiful dresses that she'd suggested, but they would all have shown her scars. That was something she couldn't let anyone see, or she'd risk Slayton's wrath with the only thing she loved.

Gin's stomach danced uncomfortably as they neared the top of the stairs to the Great Hall, the laughter and chatter already in full swing. She swallowed, wishing she could just turn around and flop back into her bed. But she was hungry, and she had yet to figure out what she was going to do. So for now, she would play along and she would eat.

"Now remember dearie, they're all here for you." she said, smile lines erupting around her eyes, as if that should bring her comfort. It had in fact intensified the beat of a thousand butterflies in her stomach. But she offered her a smile she hoped would please her.

"I'll walk you to the end of the hallway." Gin spun to face her, terror flooding her body.

"No, please. Don't leave me to go down by myself. I can't." she said, shaking her head vigorously.

"You won't be alone." said Daphne, chin dipped. Gin's shoulders dropped along with her insides.

"Oh no, Daphne, please… tell me he isn't waiting out there." she grimaced, voice hushed, glancing nervously towards the end of the hallway.

Daphne took a deep breath and spoke carefully.

"Free will, remember?" she trailed off, staring into Gin's frozen face. "He just wants to escort you to your seat, that's all."

Gin looked to the ceiling, releasing the breath she'd been holding.

"Yes, but *he* thinks he's escorting his one true love to dinner." She raised her brows as the words rolled out of her at lightning speed.

"And he will *always* think that until you prove him wrong. Or… right." she said, calmly. Gin paused, dry mouth parted, letting the words sink in. She had a point about one thing. Louis needed to know that falling in love and living happily ever after was not on the cards. She gave a slow nod.

They continued down the hallway, the music and merriment growing ever louder. When she reached the archway, she turned to speak, but Daphne had stopped several feet away. She gave her a firm nod, smiling kindly.

Gin was on her own. Her heart beat sluggishly as she took a shaky breath and a few steps, turning left towards the top of the stairs. That's when the lead dropped into her stomach.

Louis stood waiting for her, one arm behind his back. As he met her gaze, a slow smile swept across his face and his chest swelled. Little did he know she was about to burst his bubble and dreams along with it.

She forced her feet to move forwards, running her hand along the bannister as she looked out at the crowd of people, talking in groups and laughing with friends. Thankfully, they hadn't noticed her yet. Her eyes travelled back to Louis as she finally reached him at the top of the stairs. He beamed before his throat worked. "You look wonderful." he said. She fiddled with her rings, avoiding his fixed gaze. His little attempt to compliment her did not go unnoticed. She'd put minimal effort in and it hardly compared to the sweeping dresses she could see below.

"Dresses aren't really my thing." she said, still scanning the large hall. The long table had been decked out with a feast she had only ever dreamt of. The amount of food was more than she had seen in a month at Slayton's, and her stomach growled loudly. Louis laughed softly. She pressed her lips together against the heat rising in her face.

"I'm guessing you haven't eaten today, what with all the drama my brother caused." He sucked the air between his teeth, his brows pinching. She eyed him sideways, wondering if Col had told him of their conversation.

"Thank you, by the way. I'm told that you helped." he said, tentatively. Her brow furrowed.

"It was nothing." she lied, trying not to let her mind wander back to the blood that had spilled from his wound. "I, uh, hope you're feeling well now." she said, shortly. He paused, his smile growing wider.

"I am now." He held his arm out for her to hold. She stared at it. Now was the perfect time to let him see how uninterested she was.

"Ah, yes, I can see!" she said, inspecting his arm. "You have fully recovered, with full... mobility..." she said, trailing off and beginning her descent, leaving Louis frozen in her wake.

Her eyes fell upon a huge roaring fireplace. Mounted above the mantle was a line of alternating sized daggers under a fan of spears. She let her gaze wander down to the archways on either side of the fireplace to where two statues of horses stood proudly, a knight upon each, both knight and steed adorned in shining armour.

Louis's quick footsteps soon caught up with her, as did the eyes of many in the room. Conversations turned to her arrival, and she froze at the bottom step. She lowered her head, angling towards Louis, whose gaze left her face, flitting around the quieted room.

"Alright everyone, mind your manners and your ogling." he commanded, his voice taking on an authoritative tone. She risked a scan of the hall to find that everyone had indeed listened and they were now deep in conversation once more. Her wide eyes met his, and he gave her a small smile. She nodded her thanks. He motioned towards the food-laden table and they started walking.

"They don't mean to be rude. They were curious about you to begin with and then you tried to save my life." He stopped, bracing the back of a high-backed chair. His eyes filled with a soft glow, and she felt the hair lift on the back of her neck, realising how her actions must have looked. She'd inadvertently tried to save the man who she was 'destined' to be with in everyone else's eyes.

"Oh, uh... curse of wanting to help people. I never could keep my nose out of it." she said through her teeth, crossing her arms as she digested this inconvenience. A deep rumble of laughter left him as he pulled the seat out for her. But before she could take it, a familiar voice greeted them.

"Ah, hate to take her away from you the minute you find her, but!" said Joseph, rounding the head of the table where two chairs sat. He pulled one out and beamed at her. "Gin, you sit with me tonight."

Gin watched as Louis yielded with grace.

"Of course. Your place is indeed by your father." he said, stepping back for her to pass. She couldn't keep the coldness from her face as she fixed Joseph with a steady look. A look that said more than her words ever could. That she would never accept Joseph or anyone as a father figure. Joseph's rather sheepish laugh broke the silence that hung between them.

"Ah, let's forget formalities for now, hm?" his grip tightened on the chair, "come, let's begin this dinner, in honour of your company." he said. Gin wanted nothing more than to get this ridiculous evening over with and to go back to hiding, so she took his offered seat.

Their tension seemed to lull, and she stared at the table as Louis came to take the seat to her left. It was then that she saw Lady Flora, sitting alone at the other end of the table, apart from a blonde haired girl who couldn't have been much different in age to Gin. She poured her a drink, which Lady Flora took without a sideways glance at the girl and drank, peering over the rim at Gin. She wondered if this was normally her seat from the daggers she shot at her. But she supposed that was probably the look she was always going to earn from her.

"Good evening, my dear friends. I am so glad to see everyone here!" said Joseph, his voice carrying the attention of the room as the musicians played quietly in the background.

Gin scanned the table and couldn't help but notice that not *everyone* was here. Col was nowhere to be seen. As this thought crossed her mind, the doors to the castle groaned open and in walked the man himself, casually leaning against the heavy door he'd just swung open. He held a hand to his heart in mock pain.

"Started without me? I'm hurt, Oldman, deeply hurt." As he said this, a wry smile played on his lips.

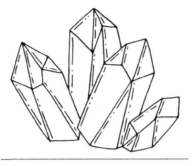

Chapter Eight

Gin caught the wind being taken from Joseph's sails as the pair stared it out.

"You can hardly expect me to wait when your attendance to anything other than duty is so rare."

"Well, I heard there'd be wine." The playful smile danced in his eyes as he caught Gin's gaze. She looked away, noticing the sudden fluster upon Lady Flora's face as she sat up straighter. Her eyelids batted wildly compared to the hard stare she received before.

Col didn't seem to pay her any mind, even though he was heading in her direction. His eyes flicked alertly to Louis, then to Gin. She twirled one of the many silver rings she wore around her finger, the chill of the vast hall loosening them.

As Col took the seat left open by Lady Flora, she fussed with his goblet, topping it up with more wine. Daphne and Louis exchanged anxious looks.

"As I was saying…" Joseph continued, raising his voice as spots of colour dappled his cheeks. "It is with great pleasure that I have gathered you all here tonight. An occasion I have been preparing for, for many years."

Gin ground her teeth. If only she'd been given time enough to prepare… to escape with Hope before her world was turned upside down.

"It's been a long time coming, and I feel extremely privileged to finally have someone on board who I can take under my wing. Someone who will one day take the reins of this magical place and all you magnificent people." he said, his broad smile curling his moustache almost to his eyes as he beamed down at Gin.

She shrank into her chair, cursing the back that held her in place. She jumped slightly as the bottle Lady Flora had been holding came down to the table with a thud. And there they were, Lady Flora's daggers were on her again.

"I hate to cast a shadow on this joyous evening, but I'd like to know why your full intention was not put before me, Joseph?" She was breathing through flared nostrils, keeping her expression quite flat. Col raised a lazy brow.

Gin leaned her forehead on one hand, gazing sideways at Joseph, her heart pounding. He let out a hearty laugh and threw his arms wide, his half rolled-up sleeves wriggling up further.

"Lady Flora, it makes perfect sense for me to have an heir. Unlike you and your travelling companions, unfortunately I *do* age in this timeline and I won't be around forever. I need someone who can carry on, to see that what we've built here is kept alive." he looked down at Gin, a solemn smile upon his face.

"Why me?" Gin whispered, unable to keep the question she'd been asking herself all day from rolling off her tongue.

Joseph's brow furrowed for a split second, one hand twisting a perfect curl of his moustache. She could hear her blood pumping through her ears as she waited.

"I have known Mr. Slayton for many years. When you were very young, I saw you at the Hospice and those eyes of yours, Gin... I couldn't shake them." He tilted his head to see them better. "Then, when I came to know of the prophecy, well... I knew it had to be you. I came to him to ask if I may adopt you when you turned eighteen and when I had established the castle, so that I might take you under my wing. But to also fulfil what was prophesied. This was your destiny all along." he said, glancing over her shoulder to Louis. Gin let out a breath of laughter, resting her lips on a clenched fist. She'd had enough of people telling her what her destiny was.

"All this time... he knew *all this time?* And he never said a word." She was talking more to herself now, a fiery rage building up inside her chest.

"There's one thing we can agree on," said Lady Flora cooly.

Joseph shot her a warning look and took his seat, bringing himself to Gin's level. She couldn't face him though, couldn't look at anyone. She scratched at a knot on the wooden table absently.

"Listen, I apologise for the way it was handled. Clearly it has brought you a great deal of upset." he began, lowering his voice to talk only to her. He attempted to take Gin's hand, but she tucked her hands into her lap. Joseph clasped his own and leant on his thighs.

"Please, let's talk about this tomorrow, hey? Tonight is for enjoying ourselves. To celebrate the future. And what's not to celebrate?" he said, raising his voice, looking around the table with a plastered smile.

Gin looked up, catching Col's eye. He was leaning back in his chair, one ankle crossed lazily over his knee, nursing a goblet that rested on his thigh. She couldn't stand the way he seemed to look within her. No thought seemed safe from him. He was however, oblivious to the efforts Lady Flora was making to fuss over him, while never unstitching his gaze from her. Whatever thoughts were going on in his head, she was only glad he kept them to himself.

Joseph dropping the subject was the easy way out, and she had no intention of making things any easier for him. Not on what had been one of the worst days of her life.

She drank deeply, letting the fumes fill her nostrils and burn her throat, the taste sweet, not unpleasant. She breathed out through her teeth as she let it settle. Then drank again.

"Everyone, let us feast, let us drink and dance and laugh, for tonight we forget our worries. Tonight, we celebrate." He raised his goblet to the table, "To family, new, old and– "

"How?" she asked Joseph, rather abruptly and louder than her normal voice. All eyes darted to her, their ears piqued.

Joseph turned his head slowly, as she squinted through the fog in her head.

"*How* is any of this possible? And don't give me the same 'in time' answer. How is this castle here? These people? What did you do?" she asked through narrowed, unfocused eyes. Joseph appeared to choke on the very air he breathed as he cleared his throat, his eyes darting around the table.

"Oh, I like her." said Col, grinning ear to ear from the other end of the table, hands crossed over his stomach.

"Col." said Louis, eyes narrowing slightly.

"Louis." he countered, a smile scorching his lips. "Do regale us, Oldman. I, for one, *love* this story."

"*Col.*"

"*Louis.*" he countered again, eyes flashing.

Gin took another long gulp of wine, watching the two brothers carefully over the rim of her goblet.

"It's ok, Louis. She has every right to know." said Joseph. Louis raked his gaze over Joseph before offering Gin a tight smile, his head inclined. He obviously held Joseph in higher regard. Even if it meant sticking up for him over telling his so-called *soulmate* the truth. Her nostrils flared, pouring more wine into her goblet and drinking under his disapproving frown. She turned her back to him, facing Joseph, whose cheeks had sunk.

"I did not intend to bring the castle back. At least, not at first." He seemed to deflate a little. "There is a device which makes all of this possible. It comprises of Crystal wands, five to be exact." Gin's eyes darted to Col at the mention of Crystals. He leaned his elbows on the table, hands clasped in front of his jaw as he peered smugly down his nose at Joseph.

"I stumbled across the device some 20 years ago now. The ruins of this castle were a stomping ground of mine. I knew every crumbled stone like the back of my hand. At least, I thought I did." he said, with a little shake of his head. "I usually took what was left of the most well-preserved stairs down to a small nook where it gave me the perfect amount of privacy to study. It was a dead end as the river ran past it, so no one bothered to venture down. It was peaceful."

Gin knew the exact steps and nook he spoke of. Many of her younger childhood memories were those of playing in the park and the castle ruins while her mother sat watching her from the highest point. Funnily enough, that little nook he referred to was one of her favourite places. She could vividly recall the smell of the river water, the earthy scent among the long grasses and wildflowers on the lazy breeze of a warm day. It was her own little hideout, away from the choking stench of her mother's chain smoking. It was strange to hear someone else speak about it.

"Anyway, this particular evening I dropped my pen. It rolled off into the long grass on the hillside and as I parted it with my foot, it collided with something half buried in the earth. A wooden chest, one end wedged into the soil. I spent the evening digging it out. No small feat when your only tool is a pen, which I found not far away."

"It was almost dark by the time I had it out, so I took it home, broke the padlock that secured it and inside, Gin... inside was the most amazing artefact. *The device!*" The whispered excitement in his voice glowed in his eyes.

"It looked like a glass trinket box, but after reading through the notebook inside the box, I found out it was actually Crystal."

"Reading through the notebook should have made you put the damn thing back where you found it." said Col, lowering his chin. Lady flora stroked his arm soothingly, a fine line wrinkling the porcelain skin on her brow. He seemed not to notice though, intent on Joseph, who was looking down at his hands, his steely glare not meeting Col's.

"There was one Crystal already in the device. The most incredible thing of beauty."

"Like the galaxy itself, right?" asked Col, standing and pacing a little, hands casually sunk into his pockets. Lady Flora looked on with concern.

"Indeed." said Joseph, finally acknowledging him but still not looking at him. Gin eyed them, the tension palpable. Even those around the table were giving each other furtive glances.

"There were four other Crystals and space for each to be placed. But, the problem was, according to the notebook, they scatter after each activation of the device and are well hidden."

"Not well enough, apparently." said Col, looking upwards with a shake of his head. Joseph's knee bounced up and down, his eyes narrowing as if trying to shut him out.

"It needed all the Crystals to activate. And when complete... *it would send you through time!*" Joseph almost convulsed in excitement. "Now, it said it can only go backwards in time, to when it was last activated and forwards to any time frame you could dream of. But it would alternate between the direction of travel. Of course, I had no idea what time period it came from, but I was so intrigued as to where this device originated, if real at all." he said, biting his cheek. Col let out a mirthless laugh. Lady Flora swivelled in her chair, watching him like a hawk.

"Tell us. Tell us where it took you, Oldman." said Col, stopping in front of the fireplace and running a finger along the mantle. Gin's heart pounded in her ears.

"Where?" she asked, searching his face, thirsty to know more, her drink fuelled confidence letting her guard down.

Joseph stayed quiet for a time. Nobody seemed to move a muscle or breathe too loudly.

"It was... not my fault." he said in a hushed voice.

"Debatable, seeing as my mother clearly wrote a warning in the notebook to not activate it." muttered Col, his back still turned.

Joseph closed his eyes, a heavy sigh deflating his chest.

"Two years of my life, I worked solely on finding the hidden Crystals around the ruins of the castle. I did not intend to use it once I had found them, but... I couldn't just walk away! Just leave them! I had to find them, if just to keep them safe. But I admit, I became too invested... too curious..."

"Too foolish." said Col, finally turning to face him with a stony glare, the muscles in his jaw clenching. Gin's gaze darted between them, drinking in every bit of knowledge she'd craved for so long. Every muscle in her body tensed.

"I'm only human, Col. I didn't know that it would bring me and all of you back to that night. And for what it's worth, I am sorry that you had to witness your father's death," he hesitated, "again."

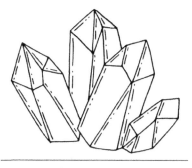

Chapter Nine

The penny dropped as Gin watched Col prowl out of the hall, like a shadow swallowed into the night. She stared at the door as it swung shut with an objecting groan. The silence he left in his wake was thick. It was no wonder Joseph and Col didn't see eye to eye.

"He can never leave the past alone. But now that's out of his system, let's not dwell." said Louis. Gin frowned, his past clearly did not bother him, yet it was his father too. He grabbed a chunk of bread and bit the end off. She was stunned into silence, watching him eat, totally unfazed.

"I'm sorry you had to witness that, Gin." said Joseph, quietly. She ducked her head, nose wrinkled as she met his gaze. "It was unfortunate timing. I stumbled upon the device after Col and Louis's father passed away in a timeline other than his own. When he died, it automatically sent his body home. Their mother hid the device after that, afraid of losing anyone else. I was the first person to come across it since then. So, of course, it continued the algorithm, taking me back to that awful night." His voice was low, sombre. The room had gathered into whispered chatting amongst themselves, leaving Gin and Joseph to finish what she started. But she knew Louis was listening, his deep sigh sweeping past her cheek.

"It took seven years to locate the Crystals again when I travelled back to 1461. Partly because I didn't want to leave as soon as I arrived. It was so *magical*!" Joseph's eyes flickered with a fire, any sign of remorse vanished.

"I had achieved something so beyond the realms of what was thought possible. I had to explore, to make the most of every moment." The fire in his eyes flickered for a moment longer before dimming, along with his smile.

"But that magic soon wore off as the darkness of the time hit me. War, famine, crime. And the punishments…" His face screwed up along with his fist. A shiver tiptoed down her spine.

"I feared for my life every waking moment. Even my dreams were clouded with nightmares. So, I layed low. But searching the grounds took time, and a lot of it." He dragged his teeth over his top lip, wincing. "I managed to find an ally within the castle, who helped me find the Crystals." His eyes flicked over her shoulder. Her gaze narrowed. Louis. He'd gone behind his mother's back. She inhaled a trembling breath.

"After seven years, I finally had them and with help, the device too. We wasted no time in returning to the future I had missed." he said, a small triumphant laugh escaping. But Gin shook her head in horror.

"Excuse me if I don't see the exceptional side of this." she said. Joseph floundered for words as he looked helplessly from her to Louis.

"We're better off here, Gin." said Louis, leaning forward, hands clasped on the table. She clenched her jaw, twisting.

"You mean *you* are better off here." she hissed. "Let me guess. As soon as Joseph learned of the prophecy and connected the dots to me, you had no problem putting yourself before everybody else. No matter the cost of what they would be leaving behind," his gaze narrowed before blinking several times. She raised her chin.

"That's what I thought." she whispered, downing the rest of her wine and slamming it onto the table. Joseph recoiled as she scraped her chair backwards. "Excuse me." she mumbled.

"Gin please," pleaded Louis. But she wasn't stopping, soulmate or not. She needed to get out of this castle and back to Hope. She couldn't contemplate a future here when the people here were not here by choice. They were simply on show for the world, having been forced to leave their lives and those they loved behind. All to fulfil the greed of two men. One who was trying to be the father she

74

never asked for, and one who claimed to be her true love. It twisted her stomach angrily.

The air in the courtyard was cool as it licked her face and the setting sun cast an array of delicious colours, a melting pot splashed across the sky. It felt good to be out of the hall, away from everyone, although the effects of the wine were becoming apparent as she crunched over the gravel. Walking in a straight line took a lot more effort than usual.

Gin stumbled upon a beautiful rose garden, tucked away behind a stone wall that she pressed up against. She let herself linger there, marvelling at the hues of the pink, yellow and red through the setting sun. With closed eyes, she breathed in the sweet honeyed musk aroma from the roses. A deep ache settled in her chest. This was the kind of place she'd longed to take Hope. To while away the hours amongst the winding paths, listening to the beating wings of the bees as they flew lazily between flowers. And she had been so close to grasping it. But that was impossible now. She couldn't be a part of this place. That glimmer of this being a possible future for them had been ripped at the delicate seams. She should never have let herself hope.

Her eyes flashed open with the stab of pain as the realisation hit her. The fog of confusion she'd had all day, finally cleared. She needed to get back to Hope, now.

On shaking legs, she climbed a small gravel path to what looked to be the stables. It was dark now.

The lamps had been lit, and she could just make out a narrow gate in the far left corner. She peered over her shoulder once more to make sure she was alone before making a bee-line for it.

"Come on, please be a way out, please, please." she muttered under her breath. Grasping the metal bars she gave them a shake. Locked. She fumbled in the dimming light, hands searching for a handle or chain or something!

"Come on!" she whispered, heart beating wildly.

Finally, her fingers found the lock and a thick metal chain securing it fast. Gin tutted, tearing her arms away from the gate. She blew escaped locks of hair out of her face, looking up. It was tall, but at a push, she reckoned she could climb it.

She rubbed some warmth into her fingers, before wedging her foot onto a craggy flint in the stone wall next to the gate and pulled herself up. She stepped onto one swirl of metalwork on the gate and hoisted herself higher.

"I wouldn't do that if I were you, Sparkles." came a familiar voice from below. Gin's head whipped down to see Col leaning against the wall, hands in his pockets. His face screwed up in thought as he studied the gate. She nearly lost her footing at his sudden appearance and clutched the bars tighter, ignoring the pinch of her skin between the gate and her many rings.

"It's a good job you're not me then." she said, the dizzying effect of the alcohol coupled with the height sending a wave of nausea to her stomach.

"True. It's just, it's a big jump on the other side."

"I can make it!" she snapped, looking up as she pulled herself higher.

"You didn't let me finish." he purred, pushing off the wall and lazily walking to the other side of her and plonking himself against the bars. They rattled dangerously, and every muscle in her body tightened further. She shot him a flinty glare.

"Well you're not making it any easier."

"Neither is the coil of razor barbed wire waiting for you on the other side." he said, gesturing through the bars. She froze, pressing her forehead against the cold metal, eyes drifting to the ground below beyond the gate. She squinted, forcing it into focus. There, waiting like a crocodile with its mouth wide open, was the razor sharp wire. Her face fell. Of course. Of course, it wouldn't be that easy. She closed her eyes, running her tongue over her dry lips.

"Messy." he mumbled, sucking the air in through his teeth, eyes flicking to her. Gin sighed, letting go of the railings as she jumped to the ground. She lost her balance and ended up falling to her knees. The pain failed to register, the disappointment quietly overshadowing it. A raw sob escaped her as she braced her thighs.

"I have to get out of here." she said, staring at the ground. She ran a hand over her forehead, trying to regain control of her emotions that were sparking all over the place. Col let out a humourless bark of laughter.

"I've been telling myself that for years." He offered her a hand. She looked at it, vision not only blurred from the wine but the tears that had pooled there. Instead of taking it, she pushed herself up, wiping at her cheeks with the back of her hands.

"The idea of running this place doesn't take your fancy, huh?" he asked, looking around the dusty yard. She studied him warily before answering, every instinct telling her to stop talking to him and run. But she found her body betraying that instinct.

"Of course not. I want nothing to do with this place. Not when It was never his to begin with. You can't *own* people." she said, exasperated. It was all she'd ever known, being owned. She wasn't about to become the owner. "How do you do it? How do you stay here, playing out Joseph's fantasy? After... " she looked down at her hands, not wanting to inflict the pain of his loss upon him. Col studied her carefully.

"It's not by choice, if that's what you're wondering." he finished darkly. She glanced at him sheepishly. The darkness had swallowed the usual intense blue of his eyes and the playfulness that laced his face had vanished.

"I'm sorry." she whispered, breaking the heavy silence. "About your father."

Col scratched his cheek with one hand, the other still firmly in his pocket. He didn't speak, only nodded his head, looking down at the cobbles by her feet. Then suddenly he was moving, crossing the yard to a stable door. It opened with a groan and he hooked it back against the wall.

"I guess Joseph didn't mention that he's also the reason my mother was sentenced to hang?" he paused. She opened her mouth to speak but nothing came out, her strangled voice trapped at his words. "Mm, didn't think so." He disappeared into the stable.

Gin folded her arms over her stomach, looking around the empty yard, knowing the sensible thing would be to leave. To go now, find another way out. She had no reason to get involved or to know any more than she already did. But her traitorous feet took her straight towards the stable door that Col had entered. She stared into the moonlit room, the scent of musty hay filling her nostrils.

Col had his back to her as he spoke gently to an enormous horse, his hand running slowly down its head to its muzzle.

She swallowed at the sight of it. His horse had cut an imposing sight in the joust, but seeing it close up was something else. It towered above Col, its thick neck disappearing into the shadows of the stall. A cascade of shivers ran over her scars.

"Easy girl." He lowered his head to its snout as it chuffed. Gin stepped back but stopped as she watched him calm her nodding head into his arms again. She couldn't help but be in awe of his control over such a huge animal. An animal that had been trained for war... now seemingly at peace in Col's hands.

Her chest throbbed wildly as she waited, unsure of what she could possibly say after what he'd left her with. But Col didn't leave her in limbo for long.

"My mother wasn't held in high regard in our time. She was only protected by Lord Lowndes, the owner of this castle, because she could keep him and his knights alive with the healing Crystals. But, as time went by, suspicion grew around her in circles outside of Lowndes's control." he said, his hand stroking along the horse's muscled neck. "After our father's body returned the first time, she buried him and hid the Crystals in fear of what would happen to me and Louis. And Lowndes... well, let's just say he wasn't impressed. He gave her the choice. Tell him where they were or imprisonment." He turned to her then, the moonlight sculpting his chiselled face. Her eyes widened, making no attempt to hide them as she would normally, horrified at what she was hearing.

"Of course, she took prison. And I vowed to help Lowndes find them if he promised her release. Stupidly, I thought I could rely on my brother for help. But Louis wanted nothing to do with the Crystals, choosing his own safety over helping our mother."

Gin's mouth soured.

"Until the day that Joseph turned up, and we all ended up back to the night our father's body appeared." He crossed the room, leaning against the doorframe, half soaked in moonlight. "Only Lowndes thought I somehow found the Crystals without telling him and brought everyone back in time. So he decided to teach me a lesson. Her punishment was more permanent the second time around." Col's chin dipped. Gin hugged her arms tighter, her stomach clenched.

"But Louis helped Joseph find the Crystals. Why wouldn't he help you or his mother?" she croaked. Col met her gaze, one brow arched.

"Wasn't anything in it for him when I asked," he said, pointedly. Heat flooded her body. Her. Joseph had promised him *her.*

"I-I'm so sorry." she began, the room spinning still from wine and dizzying guilt.

"It's not your fault." He took a silver flask from his waistcoat pocket and drank. The thought of alcohol turned her insides as she felt its effects full force in the cold night air. "I'm sure the promise of a soulmate would convince anyone. And in answer to your earlier question, I plan on leaving as soon as I find the remaining two Crystals." He plastered a feline grin onto his chiselled face. "So just as well you don't plan on getting comfortable here."

She inhaled deeply. It didn't matter to her, she certainly would not be hanging around. But part of her was glad that he had a long term plan.

"Do they know?" she asked, carefully. He huffed a laugh.

"It's no secret. But I promised to let Oldman have his fun until I find them. Think he's counting on me being outnumbered by everyone. See, if I leave, the device will take everyone else with it." his eyes flashed. She rubbed her forehead, imagining the chaos that day would bring. A day she reminded herself she would not be seeing. In fact, she needed to leave before Joseph or Louis came looking for her.

"Well... for what it's worth. I hope you get back there. I can't stay here either." she said with a nod, forcing her feet forwards and out into the yard.

"You're not really in the best condition to go anywhere tonight," he said gently. She frowned at the lack of sarcasm in his softened voice this time, her breath clouding before her.

"I don't have a choice! I have to, I need to go." she said, Hope's name dangling dangerously off the tip of her tongue as she forced herself to stop.

"Surely you can wait it out until morning or the afternoon. You're not going to be feeling great anytime before midday, that's for sure." he said, baring his teeth as he pulled his chin in.

Gin put a hand on her forehead.

"You don't understand." she said, more to herself. He spread his arms wide, the drink in his flask sloshing inside.

"Then tell me. Do something everyone here would be appalled by. Trust me." he said, a dangerous smile ghosting his lips.

Gin glanced away, her heart hammering as she wrangled her fear of telling anyone about Hope, about what Slayton might do if she went against him. But her mind reeled in an alcohol infused stupor, panic flowing freely every second that she wasn't closer to her. She squeezed her eyes tight against the non-stop debate in her head.

"Or don't. Either way, I won't stop you from leaving. Just, do it when you're sober enough to see the ground beneath your feet." he said, following her stumbling footsteps.

She didn't want to think anymore, didn't want this burning pain in her chest. She just wanted it to stop. What did it matter if he knew? He didn't care about anything; he would tell no one.

"Hope." she muttered, panting. Col's eyes danced momentarily before narrowing. She clutched her chest, as if she could claw the pain and guilt of leaving Hope from within. Her eyes shuttered. Maybe the words wouldn't be real if she didn't look. Like it wouldn't count.

"She's back there. With a monster... he has Hope... my daughter." she whispered into the night.

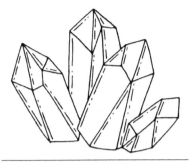

Chapter Ten

Col had been silent ever since he told Gin to follow him, and she had been in a state of panic in turn, nearly jogging to keep up with him through the deserted castle grounds. She'd given in to whatever weakness took over her stupid brain and confessed to Slayton having Hope. She'd told him the whole thing… all except his punishments she'd earned. That was a shame she could barely admit to herself.

His whole demeanour had changed, and she was genuinely terrified of where he was leading her. Her mind delved to many depths. The worst potential outcome being that he was taking her directly to Slayton himself, having been caught out. Her chances of living a normal life with Hope dashed before her eyes. It was a relief when they had ended up in his cottage, where she found it reassuringly just as messy and unoccupied. It hadn't seemed to calm Col though, who continued to pace in front of the empty fireplace, face like thunder. Her nerves were as good as shot. She held her tongue for as long as she could, perched on the edge of a wooden bench.

"Col, say something." She wrung her hands in her lap, legs bobbing restlessly.

Col ran a hand through his flop of black hair before finally stopping. He rested his palm on the mantle.

"Right now I'm fighting the urge to get my brother," he said through a strained voice.

"But you promised you wouldn't tell!" she all but shouted.

"Which is exactly why I'm fighting the urge, Gin!" he gritted out. He tipped his head to the side, releasing a breath as he met her worried eyes. "Look, I gotta tell you… If I'm feeling this much anger towards this Slayton, I can't imagine what Louis would feel towards the love of his life's child's kidnapper and all round asshole."

She grimaced and put her head in her hands.

"He should know," he said carefully, as she shot him a look of bewilderment. "Not for his sake. For yours. Having the support of your bloody soulmate would probably be in your interest right now. I say we get Louis, grab our weapons and go get Hope ourselves! I'm more than happy to pummel the guy."

"No, Col. No." she groaned, looking up as she dragged her fingers down her cheeks. "You *can't*. You don't know what he's capable of."

"You saw me stab my brother with a lance today, right?" he asked.

"Yes, and you also knew you were going to heal him."

"Doesn't make it right." he countered.

"Are you really trying to get me to hate you right now, after just confessing something I should have taken to my grave?" she asked, bracing her knees.

"Not to mention the battles I've fought in, the men I've slaughtered with absolutely no hatred, just orders from a power hungry king." he continued casually, looking to the rafters.

"This isn't the 15th century Col, there is no battlefield. You can't just kill someone without going to prison for the rest of your life. And seeing as you don't age here, that's a very long time." she pointed out. Col scowled, sucking his lip between his teeth.

"I should have stayed. I shouldn't have left her alone with him. Instead, I just froze up. I let him give me over to Joseph." she said, shaking her head in disbelief. Col stepped towards her slowly and crouched down, resting an arm on his knee.

"Don't do that, don't blame yourself. Now, I don't know the guy, but I'm sure your fears are jumping ahead of themselves. When it comes to those we love, we always fear the worst." he said, glancing down.

"But you know firsthand that sometimes, the worst happens." Their eyes met. His mother was a prime example.

"It was a very different world back then. People had little to no moral compass. Me, being a shining example."

Gin's eyes glazed over in thought.

"You haven't met Slayton." she said quietly, hunching her shoulders, almost feeling the bite of his belt on her back. "He's always seen as a shining beacon of light, helping the sick, giving the vulnerable a home and safety when really, he hides his darkness in plain sight. And no one will ever see it apart from the ones who are trapped behind those walls."

"Don't you think it's time?" Col scowled, "To let the world see behind those walls?"

The pit of fear in her stomach almost swallowed her up. It seemed impossible to make the world see what they've been blind to. She ducked her head.

"It wouldn't make a difference. He has too much power on his side, I've seen it. He can make bodies disappear with a simple call to the police. I have to do this alone. I don't want to drag anyone else into it."

"And what exactly are you going to do?" His piercing eyes narrowed. He was quiet, expectant for an answer. An answer she knew she didn't have. Heat rose in her cheeks as she racked her brain for a plan.

"I'll tell you what you'll do." he said, as the silence hung between them. "You'll march over there, if you can find the place through the alcohol fog, barge your way to Hope, which won't do you any favours for her sake, may even terrify her! And if Slayton is the monster you say he is, then you'll probably suffer a fate that I don't want to contemplate having to explain to Louis. You would know better than me, but I'm guessing it wouldn't be pretty." His voice was a rumble through the darkness. "Then Louis would stab me right through the heart for not telling him and we both know he doesn't *do* healing." he smiled flatly, eyes flashing.

Gin pressed her lips together as a tear rolled down her cheek. He was right. She wouldn't stand a chance.

"I'm not getting her back, am I?" she said weakly, pressing her palms together in front of her face. The realisation hit her hard in the gut.

Defeat. This gut wrenching feeling was *defeat*.

He tipped his head back slightly, surveying her. After what felt like an eternity, he inhaled a long, sharp breath and rose, pacing once again.

"I'm going to offer you a proposition." he said, folding his arms. Gin blinked, not expecting those words at all.

"I'm no people person, if you hadn't noticed. Keep myself to myself, look after my own horse, shovel the shit, clean my own armour. I have no need for an annoying little squire." he said, pausing to survey her. "But I think you could do with being just that." Gin's eyes narrowed.

"To be your squire?" she spluttered.

"Yep."

"You can't be serious?"

"Serious as a heart attack." He flashed her a smile that disappeared in seconds. "If you let me train you, I'll make you strong, both physically and mentally. Stronger than that weasel back at the Hospice. I promise you. He won't know what's hit him when you return for your daughter." he said, fixing his dancing blue eyes on hers. She shook her head, the idea so ridiculous. Rubbing her temples, the dizziness subsided, giving way to an angry headache. "No. Besides, I'm sure Joseph would keel over if you were to take me under your wing." she said.

"One can hope." he said darkly before checking himself after she shot him an icy look. "We'd get around that somehow." he bit his cheek, trying to reel her back. Gin scowled.

"I've told you, I'm not staying here. I don't want or *need* any of this. All I want is my future with Hope, far, far away."

"And that is what you'll get *if* you do this properly. If you leave now, where will you go?" he asked. She looked away, ashamed to admit she had no clue.

"You might not want this, and that's fine. You don't have to. But it is your best bet at getting what you *do* want. You play it smart. You find his weakness. Hell, everyone has one. And you *break* him." He knelt before her again and she slunk back a little as something in her chest fluttered. "Let me help you." he seemed to sag, pleadingly. Her heart thrummed heavily as she danced on the precipice of staying.

"Why? What would you get out of this? Apart from grating on Joseph and Louis some more." She pursed her lips.

He sighed through his nose, weighing her up carefully.

"My mother cared about this family. Cared about our futures enough to sacrifice her freedom. If I can do something to help the woman who she saw to be an important part of Louis's life, then I will. Just don't tell him I said that." He stalked into the kitchen, leaving her in the gloomy room, alone with her whirlwind of thoughts. Her lips parted as she let the air fill her lungs. She could scarcely believe she was actually contemplating this idea. But her options were thin. If she left tonight he was right. She'd have no place to go except back into Slayton's trap. And what good would that do? She'd be risking Hope's future and couldn't help the other patients through fear again...

Something clicked in her brain.

It ignited a buoyant feeling within her.

Her options may be limited, but Col wasn't the only one who could bargain. She pushed her shaking legs to stand and followed a fizzing energy that came from the kitchen. Where she knew he kept the Crystals. Their energy palpable.

Col stood at the kitchen window, swigging on a bottle of dark amber liquid. When she spoke, he cocked his head, looking over his shoulder, his angled features silhouetted against the moonlit window.

"Ok. You win." she licked her lips. "On one condition. You also train me to heal with your Crystals." she said. He turned slowly and she raised her chin. Backing down was not an option. It was time for another painful truth.

"I have let everyone at the Hospice down. I haven't helped anyone since the birth of Hope and... I *owe* them. If you'll let me." she trembled as she awaited his answer.

His eyes raked over her as he drew nearer, his dark brows set firmly. Shame prickled her cheeks at what he must think of her. But she held her place.

"Now, why would I let you do the very thing that got my mother killed?" he mused, tapping the neck of the bottle at his side. She blinked.

"Because you know that I'm a powerful healer. You said as much this morning." she said, clutching at straws as she lowered her chin, fixing her eyes on his, her chest rising with each breath. His eyes narrowed. "Your mother must have known it. It's what I'm meant to do."

A muscle in Col's jaw feathered before his eyes fell to her mouth for a split second and a swathe of goosebumps erupted over her. But they swiftly vanished when the front door burst open. She blinked furiously, jumping on the spot, but Col hadn't budged an inch.

"You know it's polite to *knock* before entering, brother." he said, not tearing his gaze away from her for a second.

"Gin! We've been looking all over for you." Louis panted, ignoring Col's remark and marching into the kitchen.

She stepped backwards, undoing the spell she had seemingly been under moments before. "Why are you *here*? What did he do?" he spat as he searched her for any sign of harm.

"I'm fine. He's done nothing." she said, her nose wrinkling. Her defensiveness surprised not just her, but all of them. Fortunately, it was dispelled by the arrival of Joseph. He burst over the threshold and stared at the three of them in disbelief.

"Seriously. Knocking?" said Col, twisting on the spot this time.

"What's going on? Gin, why are you here?" he asked, ignoring Col again. Col rolled his eyes. She crossed her arms as she looked between the two new arrivals. How was she going to explain herself?

"She was just telling me how much she wants to be my squire." said Col, before tipping the bottle to his lips. She spun, gaping at his playful grin. Louis and Joseph snapped their heads towards him.

"Oh, good, I'm not invisible." he said.

Gin released the breath she'd been holding. He gave her the smallest of nods as he pursed his lips. A shiver of hope bubbled in her chest, and she had to clamp her teeth onto her lower lip to stop the smile that threatened to spread. She'd just made a deal that was going to get her daughter back *and* heal those she'd abandoned. Albeit a deal with the so-called devil.

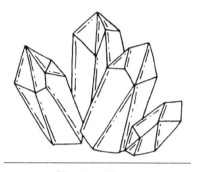

Chapter Eleven

Gin fell into dreams about Crystals and blood… so much blood. When she awoke abruptly in the small hours of the morning, a shadowy figure sat in the window seat, feet resting on the table, an unmistakable flask hugged to his chest.

She sat bolt upright as Col turned to her.

"Morning Sparkles. No such thing as a lie in for squires." he said, taking a swig of alcohol and rising. Recollection etched its way through the haze of sleep of her arrangement with Col. The sound of his boots on the stone floor was amplified by the peaceful early hour and the stark emptiness of her room.

She pulled the blanket up that had been draped over her at some point, probably by Daphne after she'd collapsed last night. He paused when he noticed this protective move and threw a bundle of clothes onto the bed from where he stood.

"I'd say no more pretty dresses, but if Daphne failed to wrangle you into one, then I'm guessing it won't be a problem." he said.

She squinted through the murky dawn light at the clothes at the end of her bed; black leggings, a white linen shirt, green hooded tunic and brown leather belt.

"Ugh. I am never drinking ever again." she groaned, rubbing her forehead. It pounded ruefully. Col smirked.

"And here I was, about to offer you some breakfast." he said, looking at his flask. She wrinkled her nose.

"Boots are by the door. I'll wait in the hall for you. The civilised breakfast should be ready for the knights and their squires if I remember correctly. Been a while since I've joined them." he said, lingering for a moment before tucking his flask in his jacket and leaving her to dress.

She listened to his footsteps drift away before hopping out of bed, eager to get started on her training. Despite her dreadful headache and the early hour, there was a buzz in her chest, a feeling she'd not felt since the days of being useful, helping patients. She had a purpose. Goals. She would make a difference again.

Gin washed quickly, admiring the roses that Daphne had cut for a small vase on her side table, dressed in the clothes Col had left for her and stuck her hair up into a messy bun. She inspected her reflection in the full-length mirror. She was pleasantly surprised. The outfit was comfy, simple and, most importantly, it covered her scarred back.

Just one more touch, she thought, looking at the bun upon her head. She reached for her mother's well loved red ribbon she'd hung over the mirror the previous day and wrapped it around the base of her bun, finishing it with a bow. She smiled gently at her reflection.

"OK, Let's do this."

Her knee high leather boots clopped down the stairwell, even as she tried to be quiet. The halls were silent, bar a few maids scurrying off to rooms with hot water and bedpans. And it was *cold.* Goosebumps pricked her skin as she caressed her arms to rub some warmth into them. If this was a summer morning in the castle, she dreaded to think what a winter one was like. But she was hoping to be long gone by then to have to find out.

A voice drifted up to her from the Great Hall as she approached.

"You're full o' shite, lad. The day you take on a squire'll be the day I kiss your crease!" said the lilting voice through guffaws from others who joined him.

Gin made her way down the steps, the table falling silent as all eyes turned to her in full squire attire.

It had been Sir Alistair who'd spoken, a slightly older knight with greying hair slicked back into a ponytail. He almost choked on his drink, his gaze the last to settle upon her as he stifled the last laugh.

"Well, pucker up, my friend." said Col, clapping him on the shoulder, giving Gin an approving nod. Her ears burned under their scrutiny as she found Louis amongst the gathering of knights and their squires, eating what looked to be steaming bowls of porridge.

He rose from his seat and shoved past Col, who'd been standing, and made his way to meet her at the bottom of the stairs. He hadn't been happy when she left the three men at Col's cottage last night, and she hadn't stayed to hear the end of the heated discussion about her new role that had broken out. Thankfully, neither she nor Col mentioned her studying the healing Crystals. She had a feeling that would have been a complete no from Louis, given his thoughts on them. She didn't want to give him or Joseph the opportunity to ruin this beacon of light for her. But she was here for now and she was going to have to face him, in all his agonising worry that he was trying to hide. The strained smile he wore below his high cheekbones gave him away. She inhaled slowly and braced herself.

"Good morning, Gin." he said, blinking several times. She returned his strained smile with her own.

"Listen, it's been a whirlwind since you arrived and we haven't had a moment's peace. Would you allow me the opportunity to speak with you? Alone?" he asked, brows squished upwards. His eyes were greyer than the intense blue of his brothers, and his lashes were coppery brown. He was handsome though, and she could see the fascination people had with them. Real life knights, straight out of an epic tale, living and breathing before them. There was a certain thrill that they brought to the atmosphere that she could appreciate now that her initial shock had subsided. But it didn't change anything. Her heart didn't belong to him.

She tugged her jacket, risking a glance over his shoulder. All eyes were trained on them except Col's, who had taken an intense interest in the cuff of his shirt.

"Um." she began as Louis licked his lips with cautious hope. Her chin dipped as her stomach writhed uncomfortably. Despite her resentment towards him, she couldn't help the squeeze of sympathy she felt. He'd waited for goodness knows how many years for this, hoping for the chance of his mother's prophecy. She knew what waiting felt like. Even if she couldn't fulfil it in the way he hoped, she could at least give him the chance to talk to her seeing as she was staying a while. She twisted to the side and cleared her throat.

"Ok, sure." she said.

"Wonderful." he beamed, wrinkles fanning out around his eyes. She chewed her lower lip, already second guessing herself.

"Shall we have breakfast in my quarters? Daphne will be more than happy to bring it upstairs." he suggested. Daphne, who had just finished setting the places for others to arrive, glanced up, about to speak.

"Actually, we've only got time for a quick breakfast," said Col, pulling out the chair next to him, tipping his head for Gin to sit. Daphne pressed her lips flat and Gin felt the air thicken.

"Being Gin's first day as my squire and all, our schedule is full."

Louis let out a humorous laugh.

"Well then, she needs enough time to eat a substantial breakfast." he said, turning to a pale-faced Daphne. "We'll be upstairs, Daphne. Please see that plenty of food is brought up."

Daphne hesitated before nodding, her gaze darting warily between the brothers. Gin didn't miss the look she levelled at Col that told him to stand down. His eyes widened momentarily before settling on her.

"We head out at six thirty." said Col, resigned. "Have my squire down here by then."

Louis didn't answer as he held out his arm for her. Again, she didn't accept, but nodded to Col, whose gaze burned into her back, all the way up the stairs.

They walked past the set of spiral stairs that led to her room and down a narrow hall with only enough room for single file walking. She crossed her arms as he stopped at last by a door at the end of the hallway.

"Please." he said, motioning for her to enter first. She inhaled slowly and walked into a much larger room than hers. The curtains over the bed were deep blue, embroidered with gold. She averted her eyes quickly, finding something else to inspect as he stoked the smouldering fire.

The room couldn't have been more different than Col's. Not an empty bottle in sight or a discarded piece of clothing to be seen. A sheepskin rug was thrown over the back of a chair, which she stroked absently, watching Louis's broad shoulders as he lifted another log into the hearth.

"So. You haven't changed your mind about squiring, I see?" he said, pushing himself up and taking the seat next to the one she stood by. She looked at her hands, straightening a ring, as he studied her uniform.

"Nope. I haven't. So if that's why you want to talk, then I may as well save you the trouble."

"No... no." he cut in, sitting forward. "That's not what I want to talk about, Gin. You know, I think it's absurd and a ploy of Col getting under my skin. But I don't want to argue with you. I've only just found you." he smiled weakly. Her shoulders slumped as she lowered her defence a little. "Please, have a seat."

She took it gingerly, staring at the fireplace. If he didn't want to talk about that, then she knew where this was going and it wasn't much better.

"Gin, I can't even begin to tell you how relieved I am now that you're here." he said, carefully. She suddenly became very aware of her breathing as she shifted in her seat. She couldn't bring herself to look at him.

"But I never doubted it would happen. Never lost hope."

She had to say something, and quickly. She couldn't pretend this was going anywhere. For her sake and for his.

"Sir Louis... "

"Louis, please." Her eyes flicked to his, and she wished she hadn't looked. His face was so full of warmth she knew she was going to douse any second.

"Louis." her brows knitted as she reached for words. "This soul connection, the prophecy, if it's real... " she winced as the corners of his mouth fell ever so slightly. "I can't give you what you're looking for." she said. He nodded slowly in the silence that followed, lips pressed flat.

"You don't have to worry. I'm not expecting this to happen overnight. You've just got here and your life has changed, for the better, and well, I'm a patient man, Gin." he said, touching his fingertips together. "I've waited more than one lifetime to find you. I'm not about to give up now." His voice was almost a whisper, and her stomach knotted with a sudden regret of following him up here. She swallowed heavily, wishing Daphne would hurry so that she could eat and leave.

"How can you be so sure it's me? Or that love is what you'll find?" she asked, nose wrinkled. He paused, his eyes lingered on her before smiling softly.

"Because I have loved you all along." he said, as if that was enough of an explanation.

"I get it, you've waited a long time, but," she bit her cheek. His presumption drove her mad. And her inability to tell him to stop hoping for her to fall in love drove her even madder. "I've got a lot of unresolved things I need to take care of."

"And I'll be by your side to tackle them with you," he said. She ground her teeth, clearly failing miserably. Thankfully, a tap at the door was followed by Daphne waltzing in with their breakfast. Louis delved in, prompting Gin to do the same, but somewhere between agreeing to speak with him and here, she had lost her appetite. She scraped around the edge of her porridge as he made small talk. All the while, all she could think about was getting back downstairs to begin her training. Not that she had any idea what that entailed. But anything was better than sitting here.

When he finally looked at the clock on the mantelpiece and acknowledged it was time they headed down, she practically jogged along the hall and down the stairs. Col waited by the door, leaning against the doorframe with Lady Flora talking heatedly at him. She slowed and hovered at the bottom of the stairs when Louis finally caught up. Col looked over Lady Flora's porcelain shoulder at them.

"Thank you, Gin." said Louis. She dragged her eyes from Col and nodded.

"No problem." she replied, tucking her hands under her arms. Louis stepped closer and scooped her hand out and brushed a kiss upon the back, sending a jolt of ice to her core.

"I look forward to our next meeting." he placed his free hand on his chest.

She withdrew as the hairs on her neck stood sharply and her scars tightened on her back. Her eyes were wide as Col made an appearance over his shoulder, eyes narrowing at her hand.

"Alright, lovebirds. Time to break it up." he said, slapping a hand on Louis's shoulder who jerked a little under the weight. Louis's lips flattened as he turned to face him.

"Don't do anything stupid today. She's not a toy for you to play with. If she ends up needing those Crystals of yours, I imagine Joseph will be quick to whisk her out of your ranks." he warned, quietly, but Gin didn't miss a syllable. Col gave him a flash of a smile under lowered brows. Louis bowed deeply to Gin and disappeared into the courtyard.

She let out a shaky breath as she stared at the big oak doors. She'd never been kissed by anyone but Hope before, and the skin on her hand tingled uncomfortably.

"You alright?" Col asked, lowering his chin.

"Uh-huh. Ready to go and thrash a sword around." she bristled. Col smirked.

"Easy there, Sparkles. We've got a long day ahead of us."

"I'm counting on it." she said, welcoming the distraction. "Do me a favour. Don't go easy on me just because Louis and Joseph are breathing down your neck." Col raked his eyes over her face. She could see the uncertainty behind his eyes.

"I can take it, ok? Don't treat me any differently than you would a normal squire. Just because I'm a girl and part of your mother's prophecy." Her eyes skipped around the room before settling on Col again. "Unlike you, time is not something I can play with. Every day counts towards getting Hope out of harm's way. Promise you'll be as tough as you would on anyone else."

Col chewed his cheek and rocked up on his feet, considering her. She tilted her head, inwardly pleading. She needed this. He cast his eyes skyward, mumbling something she couldn't make out.

"Ok. Alright. But a certain lovesick knight won't be happy." he said, brow wrinkling.

"I know. I'm sorry." she grimaced. He puckered his lips and nodded towards the door.

"Come on. Let's go ruffle some feathers."

Gin bit her lip as she followed him into her first day of training.

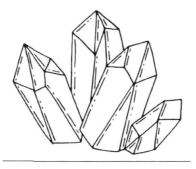

Chapter Twelve

The stables were a hive of activity, a stark contrast to the sleepy castle. Squires hurried about, mucking out the old straw and tending to the horses. The clang of armour being moved emanated from the depths of the stalls, being polished to a shine, ready for another bustling day.

Col sauntered over to the stable in the far corner and unbolted the heavy metal lock. He held the door open for Gin to enter, but she hung back. She knew what awaited within and she wasn't going to be the one to wake it.

"Come on, you tell me not to go easy on you and you're afraid of the horse?" he asked, shifting his weight.

"I saw how big your horse was last night."

"Thank you." he smirked playfully. She squinted in disgust and shook her head.

"I just don't want to be eaten alive before I've had the chance to train."

With a deep chuckle he disappeared into the gloomy stable. She waited, straining her eyes beyond the threshold, when the top half of the double barn doors to her right swung open with a thud. Col braced his hands on them casually and cocked his head back for her to follow. Just as she was about to make her move, Daphne appeared at her side.

"I thought I'd find you down here dearie, I couldn't let you start your first day without checking on you, and you know... that you're sure you're still certain to go ahead with this." she lowered her voice, glancing over her squire attire.

"I'm fine, Daphne, thank you. I was just about to meet Col's horse."

"Ah yes, the beast." she said, eyes darting to the stable.

"I'm sorry, are you calling my sweet Cora a *beast*? Because she would be most hurt to know that her apple bearer thought of her in such a manner." said Col from the window.

Daphne clicked her tongue and turned to face him. Slipping her hand into the deep pocket of her apron, she tossed him two crimson apples, which he caught with a practised hand.

"I'm quite sure she'd eat the apples, hurt feelings or not." she said, crossing her arms.

"It would be emotional eating, Daph." Col remarked, pouting as he slunk out of view. Daphne shook her head, but Gin saw the smile behind her eyes. She gestured for her to go in.

The dust danced in the rays of morning light that seeped through the open door. She headed past the first stall to the darker end, listening for any sign of hooves. But a swathe of warm breath sent a shiver down the back of her neck. She twisted so sharply, throwing a hand to the back of her neck, that she backed up into Col, who had emerged from the shadows. He steadied her gently, placing his hands on her shoulders. Her heart rate rocketed at the overload of sensations, the feeling of his hands on her shoulders, so close to her scars. She whirled, not knowing where to look, the *beast* or the warmth of Col's body that she had stepped away from.

"Whoa, easy." he breathed, his hands moving to stroke Cora's mane.

Gin's heart was still beating furiously at her ribs as Daphne settled beside her.

"See? Beast." she whispered, leaning her head towards Gin's.

"Does she go for the neck of everyone she meets?" asked Gin, hand still clasped behind her neck.

"It's rare that this *beast,*" he threw a sideways glance at Daphne who rolled her eyes, "comes to greet anyone. She likes you." he said, eyeing her from the side.

"I'm flattered." Gin lied.

"You should be." He lowered his forehead to her mane of black hair. It caused an ache to surge in her chest as she thought of Hope, how she used to press her forehead to hers when she'd clamber onto her lap for a cuddle. It was short-lived though as Cora began kicking her hooves against the stable door, pawing the cobbles. Gin held her breath.

"Cora can't help the way she is. She was trained for war. She's seen more horrors on the battlefield with me than anyone should have to. That's going to leave its mark." There was sadness in Col's voice. He whispered to Cora, using the calmness of his voice to soothe her, running his hand down her long neck that was swallowed into the darkness. She bucked her head a few times, but the snorting soon turned to soft chuffing as he moved his hands to her muzzle and spoke words that Gin couldn't make out. The way he handled her caused a swell of warmth in her chest. He was lost to her. There was more to their connection than just a fighting machine. They had been through war together. Seen the devastation of it all but survived, together. And as Gin watched the pair, she saw a beauty to their bond.

Gin suddenly felt rather foolish to have judged Cora so harshly. She pushed past the knot of nerves in her stomach and took a tentative step forwards.

"You're right. Cora's not a beast. She's adapted to the nature of her world." She felt Col's eyes shift to her.

"The fact that she is still here, fighting every day for her life, is a miracle itself." said Col, quietly. "She just needs to understand she's not alone. That she's come out the other side stronger than ever." he said, lifting his chin a little.

The pair lingered, held in each other's gaze. She hadn't just been speaking about Cora. She'd had to adapt to living in the danger of Slayton's Hospice, adjust her life to survive. And she wasn't sure Col had been talking solely about Cora, either. But as quickly as the thought entered, it flitted away with the cool breeze that floated in through the window. As the heat rose in her cheeks, she struggled to tear her eyes away. She'd normally be running a mile under this scrutiny by now, but she wasn't. She was seemingly rooted to the spot. Relief flooded through her when Daphne broke the heavy silence, her shoulders slumping out of the tight hold she'd unknowingly held.

"Yes, well, that may be so, but I still have no desire to go near her. She's a loose cannon, Col, and you should be careful. Some pasts cause too much damage to repair."

Gin noted the flare of Col's nostrils at this, and her eyes suddenly fell away from his grip. Her stomach sank. What if she was right? Was she too damaged to make a difference? What if she was destined to end up like Cora, stuck in her fear forever?

"That's not what you normally preach to me," said Col darkly. He turned away from them and threw open the top half of another stable door with more force than necessary, letting more light dissolve the shadows.

Gin glanced at Daphne, who was flattening the front of her apron, her cheeks a shade of pink that didn't normally grace her pale skin. She got the feeling they were now speaking about something completely different, the air suddenly heavy again.

"I don't preach to you about your horses, Col." she said finally. With a darting glance at Gin, she flashed a tight smile that was definitely not her own.

"Right, well, I'll leave you both to it. I'm sure you've a lot to get through, and I don't want to get in the way." she said, waving over her shoulder as she scurried into the stable yard.

Gin watched her go, not stopping to talk to the stable boys and squires milling around who tried greeting her.

She bit her cheek and turned to look at Col, who had busied himself with preparing hay and grains. Whatever had passed between them had cut deeply and she wasn't going to pour salt into the wound.

She slinked to his side and helped to break up the hay into the bucket he was filling, working silently and following his instruction when given.

This quiet brooding Col unnerved her, and when he announced he was going to take Cora out for a ride before gates opened, she was left both relieved and troubled. She had wanted to say something to make him laugh or for him to make a sarcastic comment to her on his way out. But he left in the same silence as they had worked in.

Gin had been left to muck out Cora's stable for what seemed like hours. Her back ached, her clothes were filthy, and she couldn't even detect the smell of manure anymore, her senses so used to it.

It wasn't quite the morning she'd envisioned, and she failed to see how shovelling horse muck would help her on her journey to becoming stronger.

By the time the gates opened and the first visitors trickled into the yard, her mood was anything but ready for the onslaught of public eyes. She made quick work of wheeling the barrow she'd just emptied back into the stall to fill it once again. But the eyes that greeted her were almost as bad as the ones she'd been eager to escape.

"So tell me, Gin," said Lady Flora, her crimson lips pulled back in a snarl, "was it not enough to have my castle and an honourable knight tied to your very soul, that you also felt the need to have *my* knight bending to your every whim, too?" she sneered, tilting her head so that the sunlight illuminated the fiery red curls over her shoulder.

Gin's jaw clenched, and she dropped the wheelbarrow, sending dust swirling into the air. She sighed heavily. A bitter lady of the castle was not what she needed on her list of worries.

"I don't want your castle or *any* knight, honourable or not. So please, let me get on with my squire duties, and you can get out of this dusty stable that is ruining your beautiful dress." She nodded to the wet and mucky hem of her skirt. Lady Flora adopted a hard smile and glided towards her. Gin drew her chin up, heart pounding as she met her sharp eyes. Lady Flora may have looked like a delicate porcelain doll, but she was anything but.

"I know this must all be rather overwhelming, trying to fit in amongst such wealth and privilege after your... *limited* experience." she said lazily, inspecting her nails. "There are some things you should know that will help you transition." Gin watched her circle the room slowly, dragging a finger along the wooden gate to Cora's stable, sneering as she inspected the dust on her fingertip.

"Joseph would never have the guts to tell you himself. He values you too much. I, on the other hand, don't have that affliction, and protecting what is mine is of utmost importance. So listen and listen carefully. There are certain people and areas of the castle you should avoid." she said, locking eyes with Gin, whose heart was now trying to escape through her throat. Her toes curled in her boots.

"We have peace here, stability; something we've never had before and I don't intend on losing that. Joseph may have promised this place to you, but he forgets I am the rightful heir. I will not have it snatched from me by an orphan." she spat.

"Like I said, I have no interest in your castle. It's all yours." said Gin, through gritted teeth.

Lady Flora was still for a moment, scrutinising her down her long, delicate nose until she finally decided that perhaps half the battle was won.

"Good." she said at last, eyes narrowed. "Now, I don't know what your little game is *here,*" her eyes travelled around the stable, *"but Sir Col is promised to me."* she almost snarled the last word, teeth bared. For reasons unknown to her, a flash of something hot and angry surged through Gin's chest. It was fleeting, but it did not go unnoticed, confusion fogging her brain. Admittedly, she couldn't imagine Col being anyone's betrothed, and she tried to swallow the laugh that threatened to break.

"I've no interest in Col-"

"Sir Col to you." she interjected, leaving Gin gaping. She took a deep, steady breath, willing her tongue to hold. "My reasons are my own, but I assure you, they were not to do with winning the affections of *Sir Col.*" She had to freeze the eye roll that begged to be released as Lady Flora's vehement gaze bored into hers. She couldn't imagine anything so ridiculous.

"I certainly hope so, Gin. Or this charade will be unnecessarily painful for you and most inconvenient for me." she said, lingering on her silver eyes, her brows twitching towards each other a little. Gin blinked and looked away, heat flooding her cheeks.

"Whatever freak of nature you are, your time here is limited. Sir Louis will follow you like the lovesick puppy he is, and you'll stay well away from my home. *My* people. Joseph won't live forever. But I will." she clenched her jaw, staring still into the pools of Gin's starlit eyes but not seeing. "I will have the castle back, with Col by my side." her eyelids fluttered as she drew a sharp breath. Disgust rolled back onto her face as she realised she was face to face with Gin.

"You are to stay away from the dungeons whilst here too, that is of utmost importance, do you understand?."

"There are dungeons?" asked Gin, her interest suddenly piqued. She'd seen no sign of them on the map of the grounds and nobody had mentioned them.

"No. So should you stumble upon them in your time here, turn around and forget you ever saw them." She spoke quietly. Gin's chest tightened, wanting to know more. But at the red hot point of Lady Flora's threat, she knew better. She bit her cheek.

"Like I said, I will stop at nothing to protect what is mine. Should knowledge of the dungeons get out, then *everything* we have built here will be finished." There was a flash of worry behind the threat and it made Gin's insides churn. What was she hiding down there? Gin didn't reply, letting her hard glare speak for her.

"I'm glad we had this little chat." said Lady Flora, pushing past her. Gin held her footing, not wanting to give her the satisfaction of watching her go. She knew she'd now have her breathing down her neck.

"Let's just not make a habit of it." she added, her footsteps falling away, along with the voices of a throng of guests who followed in her wake.

Gin stared at the ground, lost in thoughts of anger and intrigue. The anger of adding a Lady Flora shaped hurdle to her mounting runway of obstacles. The anger of being stuck in here, mucking out stables instead of real training, getting stronger for Hope. And the spark of frustration at being forbidden from knowledge of what was in the dungeons. She clenched her fists by her side and kicked the wheelbarrow over, watching it skid across the cobbles and hit the wall with a resounding thud.

"Should I even ask what it did to deserve that?" came Col's voice from behind her.

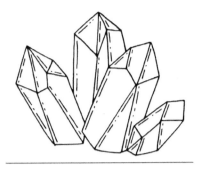

Chapter Thirteen

Gin whirled, her body trembling at the sight of Col returning from his ride after she'd been literally shovelling crap for what seemed like hours. Cora stood tall and proud behind him, her black coat shining in the sun. It looked like velvet, though Gin noticed that there were scars upon her legs and sides. A physical remnant of her past, just like her own marred back. Only Cora seemed to wear hers proudly, no shame in who she was. She checked herself, looking away, feeling foolish to be jealous of a horse.

"I'm done here." she said, throwing the shovel to the ground and marching towards the door. Col's head bobbed backwards.

"Hey." he said, holding his hands up tentatively as she approached. She stopped, nostrils flaring as she stared out into the courtyard.

"Spill it, Sparkles. What happened?"

She reeled, whipping to meet his gaze.

"What happened? You mean, while you left me to clean the shit up?" she asked, brows raised. His lips puckered. "Did I mention my daughter is human? Not a horse. And this is completely pointless?"

"You do know what a squire is, right? Shovelling shit is a rite of passage." he said carefully.

"Yes, but the whole point of *me* becoming your squire was for you to train me, get me strong, and be able to stand up to fight for myself. Not to clean the stables while you ride off the steam that you were harbouring after Daphne left."

Col's eyes narrowed as he looked down.

"Look, I shouldn't have left like that." he said, nodding at his feet. She eyed him sideways, bottling the anger that flooded her chest. He looked up, the muscle in his jaw feathering. "She hit a nerve that I usually guard better. I'm sorry."

Gin inhaled slowly, her chin dipping as she released the anger through her nose.

"There are things about my past that are best left there. I don't like to be reminded of them. But I promise I'll do my best not to let it get in the way here. With you." he added, eyes dragging down to her lips and back. She felt a shiver along her spine. Why did she seem to crumble every time he did that?

"I'm not asking you to let me into your past. But there is only one way I stand a chance of getting Hope out of that place. So I'm asking you to make me strong, to teach me how to fight... and fight dirty. I'm pretty sure you know all about that." The words left her mouth so quickly she almost surprised herself. She blinked, swallowing as he grimaced.

"Well, I am ever the black sheep." he said darkly, leading Cora into the clean stable. She closed her eyes, regretting her choice of words, but it was too late and perhaps too honest to take back.

"You want to learn to fight dirty? You got it, Sparkles." he said with his back to her.

She turned, eyes wide as she watched the muscles in his back work and he swung the stable door closed, bolting it securely with a force that wasn't needed.

She wriggled as her chest tingled, anticipation bouncing off every nerve.

"Meet me in the arena in half an hour."

"But that'll be just before the joust starts. The stadium will be filling up. Joseph won't let whatever it is you're planning slide. Not after yesterday." she said, brows squished over her bright eyes.

"Lesson number one in playing dirty." he said, prowling towards her. "Don't care what others think." He stopped before her, her mouth dry. The light that usually gleamed in his eyes was darkened under his brows. Her chest constricted, knowing full well her words had caused that dullness.

"We can do it somewhere else. You don't need to get yourself into Joseph's bad books any more than you already are." she said, the wind leaving her sails.

"I'm pretty sure that book is full, anyway. Let's start a new one. Unless you're not up to getting as dirty as you talk." he said, quirking a brow.

She studied him, eyes narrowed. There would be no going back from this. Joseph would be livid and Louis not far behind. But she'd deal with them later.

"I'll be there." she said, turning her back as she hurried through the courtyard before she lost her nerve. Her bluntness seemed to have paid off though, even if guilt still sat like a rock in her stomach.

Half an hour later, Gin stood at the top of the hill that overlooked the arena. The first of the crowds had already trickled in, ready to take their seats for the tournament. She blew out a long breath as she prepared to face whatever Col had planned. Perhaps it was foolish, but she wasn't scared. Even after seeing what he did to his own brother, he knew he had the power of the healing Crystals. Although she hoped it wouldn't come to that. But she was ready to take whatever he was about to throw at her... and whatever came after from Joseph and Louis. Her goal was bigger than any of them, and she wasn't about to let them stand in her way.

"Ah, Gin."

She spun, faced with Louis coming down the long path, Podraig leading his horse behind. Both knight and steed were fully armoured, with a swarm of excited guests surrounding them. He smiled broadly, signing photos that were being shoved in front of him and waving to those who called his name. She half wondered about marching off ahead while he was occupied, but he was going the same way she was. So she stayed put, biting her cheek as he slowly made his way through his fans.

He halted before her, ignoring all others now that she was before him. His Adam's apple bobbed.

"No Col?" he asked.

"He's meeting me at the arena." She hugged her arms as he nodded, glancing over her shoulder.

"May I escort you to the arena stables, then?" She opened her mouth to reply as a mass of blond hair swished in front of her. She stepped back, wafting floral smelling hair from her face.

"Oh my gosh, Sir Louis!" Squealed the lady, bouncing on the balls of her feet. Louis went rigid, his face pinched as he glanced apologetically at Gin. She held a hand up, smiling, not too sorry for the interruption.

Podraig rolled his eyes as she glanced at him. She meandered over to him while Louis cleared his throat and smiled kindly at the lady who held his coloured favour out for him to sign.

"You get used to it." said Podraig, adjusting the reigns he held. "People literally come from all around the world to see them. I mean, the castle is impressive and the rest of us mere time travellers aren't so bad. But the knights… they're the ones who really draw the crowds in."

Gin scowled, looking at Louis as he posed for a photograph with the lady. She had now wrapped her arms around his neck as he stood stoically.

"Is that why Joseph puts up with Col?" she asked, unable to keep the bitterness from her voice. It was becoming clear that money and fame were the driving force behind Joseph's venture. He'd shown little to no care for anyone so far, herself included. She was simply a tool to secure his legacy.

Podraig eyed her sideways.

"The people love them, romanticise them, even. They're intrigued by their power, their courage. Even their danger. Joseph knows that."

Her eyes met his. He couldn't have been much different in age than her and yet his years had a lifetime of knowledge on hers.

"Does it bother you? The attention they get?" she asked. He was silent for a moment before looking at his knight.

"No. I guess you can say they've earned it. The amount of battles they've had no choice but to lay down their lives for. Not such a bad retirement." he smiled crookedly.

"I apologise. Never a moment's peace." said Louis, returning, his cheeks flushed slightly. "Shall we?" he motioned towards the arena. She cleared her throat and nodded, walking side by side, his armour chiming gently with each step.

They soon found themselves at the back entrance to the stables behind the arena, under the shade of billowing trees that swayed high above. The guards let them through and he waved goodbye to the gathered crowds that had followed them down.

Gin wasn't sad to see them shut behind the large oak gates. The drums beat softly from within in anticipation of the joust. Podraig led the horse towards his holding pen, but Louis lingered.

"Has Col treated you well this morning?" he asked, brows knitted over grey eyes. She opened her mouth, nodding even though she wanted to complain. She caught herself wondering what she'd be doing if she'd been Louis's squire. But she was sure he'd rather wrap her up in cotton wool than have her spend a moment in these boots.

"You know, I wouldn't have taken this on if I didn't want to. You don't need to worry about me or how Col is training me." she paused, his eyes dropping to the ground. She could see genuine concern in his face, the same concern she felt for Hope every day. He dragged his head up again, muscles twitching in his jaw.

"I will never not agonise over your wellbeing, Gin." his voice was strained, and she felt a heat rise in her chest. She couldn't fathom how his heart was so open to hers. It was something she didn't think she'd ever understand. Suddenly, a bubble of nerves erupted in her tummy. She bit her lip as she glanced over his shoulder. She was about to put him through even more torment the moment she stepped through that gate.

"Listen, I *am* ok. I'm doing this for reasons that I can't explain right now. But if you really mean what you say, that you care about me, then I need you to accept that I am capable of this." she said.

"It's not you I doubt." he said resentfully.

"He's... he's not that bad." she stammered. She meant it too. She didn't think badly of Col, despite other people's opinions. Her knowledge of people was limited and overshadowed by Slayton, but she couldn't explain the feeling she got from him.

Louis baulked, running a hand over his stubble.

"Oh Gin." he sighed, a mirthless laugh escaped as he weighed her with his gaze.

"You don't know him. What he's done. What he's capable of."

Her brows drew together as her heart thrummed.

"What does that mean?" she asked flatly. Louis licked his lips, shaking his head.

"Oh, come on, you obviously have something to say. So say it." she said, crossing her arms. "You betrayed him to get here. Helped Joseph behind his back. What terrible thing has he done that would drive you to deceive your own brother?" she asked, brows raised. He stared at her from under his copper brows, his lips parting as he turned over her words.

"Do you know we have a dungeon here?" he whispered, with a calmness that iced over her chest. Her shoulders rose noticeably, her senses alert as she remained silent. She blinked, looking away.

"I'm not the first to warn you, am I?" he asked, eyes narrowing. Her nostrils flared as she recalled Lady Flora's visit.

"So what? What does it have to do with Col, anyway?" she asked as her stomach hardened. She had been sure it was Lady Flora who was hiding secrets down there.

"Everything." Louis whispered. She didn't know what to say, how to respond as the ice in her chest spread greedily through her body.

With a thud, a side gate swung open against the wall and jolted her out of her racing thoughts. Their gazes fell upon Col, frozen in the doorway as his eyes darted between the pair.

"I feel like I've interrupted a moment." he said, tipping his head back as he shut the gate on the screaming crowd outside. Gin shuffled her feet, rolling her lips as she shook her head.

Louis chuckled darkly, eyes cast to the sky.

"Please, don't stop on my account." he said as he sauntered off to his stable. Gin watched him go before lowering her voice to Louis.

"I can't do this now. I have to get ready." she said. Louis pressed his lips together and nodded slowly. She swallowed the dryness in her throat, pausing with a heavy sigh. It was proving harder than she thought, having people in her life that cared about her. Her natural urge to look after people brought about the need to reassure him.

"I've dealt with far worse people in my life." she said to his furrowed brow. "I don't fear Col." she turned, crossing the yard to Col's stable. She could feel the burn of his gaze on her back the entire way.

She found Col weighing a sword in his hand. It was no small trinket, the blade sharp and angry. His lips puckered as he examined it, head cocked.

"Ready to give them something to talk about, Sparkles?" he asked, sky-blue eyes meeting hers. Her stomach flipped. Whatever secret he hid in the depths of the castle, now was not the time to ask. She only needed his training, not his past, she reminded herself.

She eyed the sword with a stillness in her body that her beating heart did not mimic.

"Ready."

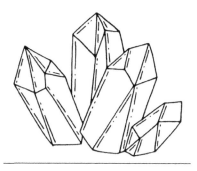

Chapter Fourteen

Gin kept her eyes down as she followed Col out of the stable. The weight of her sword sheathed at her side felt completely alien. The cold metal of her shield bit into her arm and clanged against her metal breastplate. It wasn't the best fit, having belonged to one of the squires, but it would do the job.

"Gin!"

She closed her eyes, ignoring Louis as he called. He would have nothing good to say.

"Gin, stop!" His armoured footsteps thudded on the gravel. He was running.

"Don't waste your breath, brother." said Col, trudging towards the large wooden gate of the arena. The trumpets and drums coursed through the air. "This lesson doesn't involve *caring*."

Gin tightened her grip on the shield, as if it would deflect Louis's words.

"Don't be an idiot, Col. Don't play with her just to piss me off." he said, finally catching up with them, grabbing Col by the arm, the metal groaning. Col's lip curled and the look of pure anger made Gin's scars prickle.

"Believe it or not, brother, not everything is about *you*." said Col. His voice rumbled like thunder as they stared each other down. Neither wanted to break first.

"You're telling me that whatever you have planned with those swords is in her best interest?" asked Louis, shoving Col backwards as he released his arm. Gin's gaze darted between them, her chest restricting as she struggled to get a hold of her voice. She didn't want to be the centre of this argument, another wedge between their already fractured bond.

"Actually yes. Seems I don't need a soul connection to give her what she desires." Gin winced as she watched the corners of Col's lips curl up, his words hitting Louis with perfect aim. Louis snapped, closing the distance between him and his brother, pushing him against the wooden gate, the drums eating up the thud of metal against wood. The smirk never left Col's face, even as Louis held him by the neck.

Gin's arms slumped as she dropped her shield, grabbing Louis by the arm that held Col.

"*Enough!*" she cried, fixing Louis with the full intensity of her silver eyes, the sun illuminating their depth. Louis blinked, scowling as he released Col, licking his lips slowly. She kept her gaze firmly upon Louis, holding her palm up to him as he looked between them.

"I am not a weapon for either of you to use against each other. I will not be told what to do... not anymore." she said, panting. "I *want* to go out there, Louis. My past hasn't given me the luxury of moving on. I have to stand up and fight now." She swallowed the pain in her throat. Louis rubbed the back of his neck as he looked on hopelessly. She let her eyes fall. It was becoming increasingly more difficult to keep her past from him. She was beginning to wonder if their soul connection had anything to do with it. As crazy as she knew that sounded.

"I realise your past has been tough but you don't have to fight for yourself to prove anything, Gin." he said, quietly. Her mouth twisted sourly.

"I'm not fighting for myself, Louis." She picked up her shield and faced Col. His features had softened as she found him watching her. He offered the smallest smile. It was enough to know he understood. She was absolutely ready to start fighting for Hope.

Col whistled to a confused guard who had been watching from the sides. Despite his obvious doubts, he obediently unlocked the gate.

"Like I said... not everything is about you, Louis." said Col before he pushed open the gate and walked into the thick fog.

Gin watched, open-mouthed, as the crowd cheered loudly through the mist. She glanced back at Louis, still scowling after his brother with vacant eyes.

"Be careful, Gin." he said, shaking his head slowly. "I'll be here. You say the word and I'll get you out of there."

She gave him a small nod, knowing she'd not need his help but giving him the reassurance he needed. Tightening her grip on the shield and inhaling deeply, she prepared to walk through the fog.

It felt like an eternity, treading the ground blindly as she made her way into the arena. But finally, the air cleared, and the enormity of the arena greeted her. The seats were practically full. And there, in the centre, twirling his sword high in the air in one hand and surveying his audience with a playful smile, was Col.

"My Lords and Ladies! I welcome you with open arms to what I promise will be the highlight of your day." he said, lavishing in his captive audience's attention.

Gin peeked at the viewing platform where she had sat yesterday with Joseph and Lady Flora. The curtain was still drawn, much to her relief. With any luck, it would be over before they arrived.

She lingered at the end of the arena, waiting with bated breath for the moment she would be called upon. For now, all eyes were upon their knight.

"Jousting, as exhilarating as it is, is nothing compared to hand to hand combat. Where you are no longer upon the back of a powerful war horse, but face to face with the enemy. Duels... that's what gets your heart pumping."

Gin's hands were slick with sweat, and not from the heat. Thoughts of being out of her depth constricted her stomach, but there was no turning back, no running. This wasn't about her. This was about vengeance and justice. Words she had only ever dreamed about that were now something tangible. She wiped her free hand on her thigh.

Col paced the length of the tilt, scraping his blade along the wood.

"Duels come in many forms, but I'm not in the business of boring people. So let's skip to my favourite. The Duel of Honour. Not in the least bit chivalrous, almost always carried out in private and *absolutely* illegal." He spun on the spot, eyes falling upon Gin. Her back prickled as goosebumps erupted. Col walked to the centre of the tilt, beckoning her to do the same.

She breathed deeply and began walking, feeling the burn of all the eyes in the arena. Then a second pair of footsteps joined her. Louis walked along the edge of the crowd. He fixed Col with a flinty look, hand upon the hilt of his sword that now rested at his hip. He stopped, feet planted wide. Gin ground her teeth. It was clear he was going nowhere, ready to step in if he deemed it necessary.

Col threw a sideways smirk at his brother before halting a few paces from Gin. Chin raised, he scoured her face and spoke quietly enough for only her to hear.

"Still time to back out, Sparkles." he said, brows knitted.

Gin's nose wrinkled, her hand reaching for the handle of the sword by her side.

"No, there isn't." she heaved it from its sheath, the weight of it searing through her arm, dragging its tip to the ground. Col's eyes flicked from the gleaming metal blade to her. She readjusted her grip and lifted the sword in trembling hands, hoping he wouldn't notice the shadow of doubt in her eyes. If he did, he kept his tongue still. The sting of Louis's watchful gaze continued.

"No referees in these duels, no rules to follow." Col's voice turned back to the silent audience. "And today, I challenge a worthy opponent. I challenge my very own squire." Murmurs broke out in the stalls as he drew his own sword, chin dipping. Gin's jaw was aching, every muscle taught.

Col threw his shield to the ground. She watched as it landed in a cloud of dust as he held out his free hand, waiting for her to shake it. Gin lifted a brow. His only reply was the cock of his head, eyes narrowed. She placed her own shield down, caught up in his gaze, and held out her hand, trying to keep it steady. She was following him blindly in this lesson, hoping he'd follow through with his promise.

But in a flash, Col had seized her hand and spun her back to his stomach. Their armour smacked against each other, his sword raised across her chest as the audience gasped. Gin's mouth fell open as she gasped for the air that was knocked from her chest. Her back protested at the contact with a streak of heat.

"Lesson number one! *Never* shake the hand of your opponent if they have their sword drawn. You don't want to end up impaled before you even have the chance to raise your own."

Gin now faced Louis's blazing wrath, his contorted face frozen under heaving shoulders. It would take but one nod from her and he'd swoop in. So she lowered her eyes, trying to ignore the heat of Col's breath on her neck, sending an inexplicable shiver down her torso.

Laughter met her ears as it rippled through their audience, her naiveness, their entertainment. Heat scorched her cheeks as she pushed away from Col, whirling on the spot. She blocked out their amusement. With a heavy blink, her vision cleared. Col ran his tongue over his lips before giving her a tiny affirmative nod, stirring the fire within her belly, and she remembered why she was in the arena. She rolled her shoulders as she found her footing.

"As the challenged opponent, you are entitled to the first strike, while I will attempt to block it." he said, lazily getting into position, shield back in hand.

Gin wasted no time, raised her sword with all her might and brought it down upon him, clashing with his shield. It vibrated up her arm as he blocked it by the skin of his teeth. She had no idea what she was doing, but revelled in the look of surprise that swept over his face. A small smile tugged at her lips as she staggered back a few steps from the impact.

Col twisted his neck, sniffing as he recovered from the blow.

"My turn." he said, circling each other. Gin caught sight of Louis, gesturing to her shield that still lay upon the ground, and raised his arm to his chest. She instantly lunged for it, bringing it to her body and bracing it hard.

Col made swift work of lifting his sword, bringing it down upon her shield as she held it above her. The force brought her to one knee, cracking against the dry summer earth. Tears stung her eyes as she rose, ignoring the urge to rub it. Instead, she channelled the pain into the swing of her sword, crying out as she swung it at him. This time she missed, Col sidestepping in the blink of an eye.

"Lesson number two, footwork. Be light and nimble. Not a sitting duck." he cried, eyes alert. She swallowed but her throat protested, too dry to follow through as she tried gripping her sword tighter in her sweaty hands. They continued to circle each other, like some sort of twisted dance. Her arms already sang with the ache of their heavy load and he was dragging out his move, driving her nerves skywards.

Finally, he made his lunge, which she pushed aside with her shield as she flinched in the opposite direction. Col raised an eyebrow and opened his mouth to say something just as she lunged right back at him, the element of fast reaction seeming to work. He didn't have time to position his shield, blocking it with his sword instead. She cocked an eyebrow at him as a few gasps whispered around them amongst the ongoing cheering for Col.

His eyes danced with approval and he slowly loosened the strength of his sword against hers, bringing her face inches from his, whether she liked it or not. Gin's pounding chest leaned into his, their eyes locked as they caught their breath. This time, she found her eyes falling to his parted lips. They curled slightly at the corners.

"Careful, Sparkles. Your soulmate's watching." he teased, before the metal of his sword against hers screeched, and he sent her stumbling backwards. She couldn't help but smile to herself as she regained her footing.

"Was there a third lesson yet?" she yelled, as laughter broke out around them. Col sucked in his cheeks and studied her. He smirked, enjoying this new and fierce version of her. And she couldn't help but admit that she, too, was enjoying it. This deep down version of her he'd pulled to the surface and laid bare for all to see. It was electrifying.

He didn't speak, only continued to drink up the sight of her power play with hunger in his eyes. Then, to her surprise, he chucked his shield to the ground once more.

"We've covered that lesson." she said, eyes flicking to the discarded shield, watching it skitter along the dry ground. She'd taken her eyes off of him long enough to miss his free hand reach into his pocket. He let out a cry and her eyes shot to him, the warning shout from Louis falling short. But it wasn't his sword that was raised. Instead, he flung his clenched fist towards her, releasing his fingers, sending what felt like a thousand needles into her eyes.

She dropped both her sword and shield as her hands flew to her scrunched up eyes, shock rooting her to the spot. The silence after the gasps that filled the arena was almost deafening.

"Lesson number three. Always carry sand in your pocket."

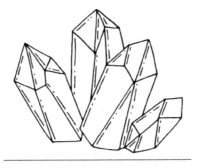

Chapter Fifteen

Gin pressed the palms of her hands into her eyes and dropped to her knees as a guttural roar sailed past her, followed by a thud and a muffled groan. Grit scratched at her eyelids with every movement. Try as she might, she couldn't will her eyes open, only hearing the scuffle that played out feet away.

"Argh, the longer you hold me down, Louis, the longer I can't heal your girl." Col growled. The moments passed agonisingly until she found her strangled voice.

"Let him go, Louis!" she cried. It was with a seething huff that the sound of Louis rising had her reaching blindly for Col. He met her without hesitation.

The crowd hummed with frantic whispers, noise whirling around her as she knelt motionless on the ground before being grasped around the shoulders, hoisted up and walked a short way. She was lowered onto a stall and the crowd quieted as a door slammed shut.

"Do *not* rub your eyes." came the sound of Col's voice.

"She wouldn't have to if you hadn't pulled that stunt." said a second voice. Louis had followed them into wherever they were. "Jesus, Col. Just because you have the ability to heal people does not give you the right to treat them like toys!"

Gin's breath came in gasps as she tried not to rub them, scrunching them as tightly as she could instead. Her knees bobbed up and down at the sound of water being poured.

"That stunt was exactly what she asked for. In not so many words."

"Are you *completely* out of your mind, Brother?" Louis's voice came from beside her now.

"No, but your hero move out there made her suffer a hell of a lot longer than needed." Col was before her now, his voice close.

"I *care* about her safety. A quality you wouldn't understand." said Louis, darkly. She felt the words hit her stomach like a rock. Guilt pricked her cheeks for asking this of Col, knowing Louis would place all the blame on his brother.

"Then you should try asking her what she really needs, instead of assuming you're the solution to her problems. Now quit wasting my time so that I can heal her, damn it!"

Gin shook her head in her hands, wishing for their bickering to end.

"Just *go*, Louis. Please… let him heal me." she pleaded before clamping her lips shut against the sting. "I'll find you after, I promise." He didn't answer, but after a moment, soft footsteps padded away. Before he left, he muttered to his brother.

"You're dangerously close to turning her into another Brandon, Col. That dungeon is taken." Louis slammed the door, leaving them in silence.

Gin froze, wishing she could see Col's face at the mention of this warning. Now this dungeon had a name for its prisoner. An actual prisoner. The thought unsettled her deeply.

"I need you to lean your head back into my hand. Ok?" he asked calmly, not addressing Louis's parting words.

She couldn't bring herself to talk or question him, the discomfort taking control. She nodded, holding her breath as she battled with her inner thoughts of not wanting to relinquish herself to anyone. Especially blinded.

She felt his hand cup the back of her head and her whole body went rigid as he lowered her back.

"I'm going to wash your eyes now, but you've got to try to keep them open for me. We need to get the sand out before we can heal any damage."

Gin scrunched her nose up, lowering her hands as she braced herself.

"On the count of three… One… two… three." he said, pouring the cold water into her already streaming eyes. She blinked furiously, the water trickling into her hair and ears as she let out a cry. The sand clawed at her eyelids, trying to hold on as the water seeped in. She flinched against his hand but he held her steady.

"That's it, you're doing great." he said, the constant stream of water fighting against her battling eyelids.

"You're an awful liar." she choked, opening her eyes a little wider as he paused. Col huffed a laugh.

"Of all the times to be sarcastic, you choose now?" he asked, his voice quiet as he concentrated on rinsing.

"Learned from the best, I guess." she said. Col was silent, letting her clear her vision between pouring. It still felt as though her eyes were full of sand, even after multiple jugs of water.

"How's it feeling?"

"Like I just got a handful of sand thrown in my eyes, followed by a gallon of water." she said, blinking against the burning sensation. She squinted up at him, his face blurry around the edges. There was no amusement in his eyes as he grabbed the cloth that draped over his shoulder and dabbed her eyes gently. She pushed her face into it, letting it soak up all the water and tears. When she emerged, Col was stony faced, staring into his hands.

"What's wrong?" she asked, pinched brow. He didn't look up as he spoke.

"I'm just sorry for doing that to you." he said, a muscle feathering his jaw.

"No. You don't get to be sorry, Col. I asked you to show me how to fight dirty. And you didn't let me down." she dabbed her eyes again. Col winced.

"Yeah, well, just because I'm the bad seed doesn't mean that felt good."

Gin's eyes snagged on his, caught up in a tangle of something that stirred in her chest, suddenly very aware of his fingers entwined in her hair. She forced herself to look away.

"Sand in my eyes is nothing compared to…" she cut herself off, hauling herself back on what was about to escape her mouth. She gaped up at his searching gaze, eyes narrowed.

"Compared to what?" he asked. She cleared her throat and pushed herself up and out of his hands.

"Can we just get to the healing part?" she fiddled with a thread on the cloth, stiffening under his careful gaze. He contemplated her for a moment before speaking.

"Sure," he said, not pushing her further. But the shadows in his eyes danced with disquiet. He fished a flask from his pocket. She raised a brow, to which he smirked.

"Don't worry, it's water. Charged with aquamarine. It'll heal the scratches and soothe the nerves."

Gin took the flask, drinking deeply. After spending her energy in the arena, she didn't realise how thirsty she was. She drank every drop, feeling it go to work immediately. She didn't think she'd ever tire of the magic. Feeling it flow through her was like soaring through the stars, weightless.

"Thank you." she said, handing him the flask. He took it with a strained smile, but the line between his brows remained. His usual cockiness had evaporated and it unsettled her.

"Listen. I meant what I said. Don't do a Louis and get all soft on me now." she said, nudging him with her knee. He cocked a brow. "I'm preparing to take on someone who has never been challenged before. Someone who hasn't had to fight for a thing in his life. Who always wins because the people around him are so terrified of him, while the rest of the world worships at his feet. Don't go feeling bad. This is on me." she said, eyes fixed on his. They lowered as he sucked his cheeks in, then rose again. He gave a small nod.

Trumpets blared through the speakers from the arena. Col sighed.

"Damn it. I need to get Cora in her armour." he said, standing and stalking past her. She had only just realised they were back in the arena stable. Cora was in her stall at the back, head ducked and her broad back visible over the top of the gate. Gin swivelled, glancing over her shoulder.

"Can I help?" she asked. She felt bad for getting mad about having to clean the stable this morning. Col was making the effort for her. The least she could do was reciprocate with her squire duties.

"Shouldn't you be finding Louis?" he eyed her with a lopsided smirk.

"I will. Later." she said, not wanting to face him yet.

"OK." he said, after a moment. Col disappeared behind the partition. Gin followed.

Cora's armour sat upon a stand. She ran her fingers over the black velvet coat that boasted silver stars and little explosions of light that were carefully embroidered onto it, matching Col's own.

"I didn't notice the stars yesterday." she mused, watching the ripple as she fingered the silver fringing.

"That's our family heraldry. My grandfather designed it after my grandmother discovered the Galaxy Crystal. She wanted it to centre around some bizarre aquatic, dragon-like creature she claimed to have envisioned from the Galaxy Crystal. But my grandfather thought it wiser to symbolise the stars and the Galaxy with our family. People thought she was crazy enough without stoking the fire. My father wore it after him and so it went, passing on through the generations." he trailed off, his voice distant.

"Will you pass it on too, if you have a son?" she asked. He sniffed sharply, tugging the coat from the armour and handing it to her.

"I wouldn't burden a child with me as a father." a flash of a smile that didn't reach his eyes graced his lips, vanishing as quickly as it appeared. He heaved the armour from the stand. Immediately, Cora shifted her weight as Col placed it beside her. Gin frowned and walked cautiously around the edge of the wall, not sure she wanted to get too close now. Cora pulled back on the reins that held her steady.

"Shh, hey, hey. It's alright girl, it's alright." he said, holding the leather strap that ran the length of her cheek, stroking her nose slowly.

"She doesn't like the armour?" asked Gin, inching forwards ever so slightly, tucking a loose piece of hair behind her ear protectively. Col continued to calm her, taking his time to bring her temper down.

"Not so much the armour, but what it means." he said darkly. Not taking his attention away from her or breaking the calmness of his voice.

"Battle." said Gin, wrapping an arm around her tummy, knowing exactly what it meant for her. The same feeling that the click of Slayton's lighter had meant for her. Preparing for the onslaught. She noticed Col had turned his attention to her. She shrunk under his gaze, afraid he could read her mind and see her weakness, crumpled by the memory of a simple click of a lighter lid.

"Right." he breathed, turning back to Cora, who had stopped fighting against her reins but continued to chuff. "It changes her mindset. The moment I bring it out, she becomes the war horse. Which is why I always dress her last, so she doesn't have to be in it a moment longer than she needs to be." he said, looking out at the other knights, their horses fully armoured while they were still being dressed and preened to the shining knight dream.

Gin smiled. Not the warm kind, the sad melancholy smile that comes with understanding.

"She's a lucky horse. To have you caring for her." she said, watching the pair. They seemed to settle each other's nerves, the give and take mutual. Col let out a soft, breathy laugh through his nose and shook his head slowly.

"I don't think you give yourself enough credit." she said, shaking her head. He looked at her, brows raised. "You say you would burden a child, but you have heart. You may bury under a mountain of sarcasm and tough skin... but you care." She wasn't so blinded by his hard exterior. Somehow, she could see past it. They locked eyes long enough for Gin to feel a deep swirling in her stomach. She flinched, remembering Lady Flora's words. *He's promised to me.*

"Well, all I mean is, should you and Lady Flora ever decide to have a child, you wouldn't be burdening them." she said, edging closer to Cora now that she had calmed. She ran a hand along her neck, her muscles firm under her fingers.

"Flora?" he laughed. "What in the name of hell makes you think I'd consider raising a child with that siren?"

Gin threw him an eye roll.

"My eyes may be abnormal, but my vision is fine." she smirked. Col tipped his head back slightly, eyeing her. "Oh, come on. She was practically sitting in your lap at dinner. She didn't need to warn me to know that you two are a *thing*."

"She warned you?" he asked incredulously, handing her a small brush and using one himself to brush Cora. Her eyes widened as she followed his lead, running the bristles over her gently. Realisation hit too late that she probably shouldn't have said that.

"She just mentioned something in passing, that's all. And that I need to..." she trailed off, realising she may be stirring a bubbling pot. Her eyes darted to his.

"Gin," he said, freezing. "What did she say?"

Her mouth moved, but no words came out as she concentrated on the flow of Cora's mane. He prowled around Cora, following her as she tried to slink away. Gin took a deep breath and turned her body away slightly.

"I think she just got the wrong end of the stick, that's all. She told me you are promised to each other and that I need to... to stay away from you." she said, unable to look at him. "But you know my interest is purely for training, and Louis would literally kill you, so don't worry." She felt the heat in her cheeks betray her, feeling foolish for even suggesting anything else. But Col stilled beside her, his silence unnerving. She turned unwillingly. He stared down at her, the sun behind him, casting his features into shadow.

Finally, he broke the silence.

"She *was* promised to me. By her father." Gin felt a crushing in her stomach, not sure why this hit her gut like it did, coming from his mouth. "But she knows it'll never happen. Or at least she should. Thing about Flora is that if she wants something, she expects to get it, no matter how long it takes. She sees it as hers. But I'm not. Only in the words of her father's blessing, a man that means very little to me now." He leaned back against a bale of hay, shoving one hand in his pocket. He wet his lips. "I've probably had a hand in giving her the wrong message over the years," he winced. Gin chewed the inside of her cheek, not wanting any more elaboration.

"Thing is... I *was* married." his stilled, lost in a distant memory. Gin's brows rose as she searched for words, but they failed her. He was married? It seemed so opposite to everything he was.

"For five years. Then she died." She watched him in stunned silence as he tapped the toe of his boot into a dusty crack on the floor. Her jaw hit the ground as she realised this was yet another death he had to bear on top of his parents.

"I am so sorry." she whispered, frozen to the spot. He looked up at her, shaking his head.

"I rarely delve into my past, Gin, so if I do, it's never because I want your pity. It would be for you to understand who I am today." he said, his voice stronger than before.

"Ok." she said, still but a whisper. Col was quiet for a moment as he weighed his next words.

"I don't know. I think Lord Lowndes was feeling like shit for his part in my mother's death and he'd been close to my father. So when I was ready, he would see I married his daughter. I agreed because I was probably too drunk to see sense, to be honest. I was not in a good place. But I have no intention of marrying again. So it's just been an empty promise, hanging in the air all these years."

Gin pressed her lips together as she thought of the way Lady Flora had been acting around him at dinner. How he'd not returned the affection, yet neither did he push her away.

"She loves you." she said, their gaze lingering in silence until he sighed and looked away.

"I know." he scowled.

"Do you love her?" she asked, surprised at her own boldness. His head whipped up, and she wished she could take it back immediately. "Sorry, you don't have to answer that." she added, cheeks flushing as the room seemed to get smaller and smaller. But he gave a faint laugh as he contemplated her.

"No, it's ok. Just add it to my never ending list of failings. Honestly, no. I don't. And she knows that, which makes me an ass for entertaining her when it suits me." he looked away, which she was glad of, her cheeks getting hotter by the second. This entire conversation had taken a road she was keen to get off.

They continued to dress Cora in silence. Only Gin's mind was anything but. The question of Flora's other warning about the dungeon, backed by Louis's own caution, simmered with an excruciating desire to know more. But he'd just opened up in a way that made her want to keep him safe from her impulsive questioning. Despite having said she didn't want his past, she felt a warmth in her chest for his trust in her.

She'd hold her tongue.

For now, at least.

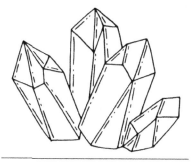

Chapter Sixteen

The Great Hall was buzzing when Gin came down for dinner later that evening. She'd spent the afternoon away from the tournaments and shows, avoiding Louis and Joseph. Having spent most of her life seeking the shadows, going unnoticed came easy to her.

She had yet to find out if news of her earlier antics in the arena had reached the ears of Joseph. But as she descended the stairs, hair freshly washed, hanging in soft curls over a baby blue and white striped sweatshirt, tucked into light blue skinny jeans, she got the feeling there was something else that held their attention. The air seemed electric with excitement as people spoke in frenzied whispers.

Daphne spotted her and left the curly greying haired man, Tom, an archer she'd been talking to, and sprung in her direction. Her face was pinched with delight.

"What's going on?" asked Gin, scanning the table as Daphne sidled up to her.

"I can't say, only because I don't know, and there's not a whisper here that I don't catch onto. So it must be big. Joseph is going to announce something at dinner. Everyone is speculating, of course, rumour spreads like wildfire!" she almost squealed before taking a deep breath and glancing over her shoulder for any sign of Joseph.

Gin wrung her hands, her stomach quivering slightly as the thought crossed her mind of his announcement being the hanging of Col having found out about their duel. She thanked the heavens that they weren't in fact in the 15th century.

As she scanned the room, two figures appeared from a door to the far right, their heads bowed in conversation. Joseph and Louis were greeted with several cheers from the table. They grinned, quelling their discussion. Joseph clapped him on the back and they stood behind their seats.

Louis did a double take as he spotted Gin, his face softening as he pulled out the seat next to him, motioning for her to sit. As she pushed past the unease of what was to come, Col entered. He sauntered across to Gin, who was midway to Louis. She paused, glancing between the two.

"Ready for the big announcement?" he asked, eyes widening for a second.

"Whatever it is, Louis is obviously already privy to it. They arrived together, *whispering*." she mumbled. Col pursed his lips, brows lowering.

"Mm, maybe you're getting a sibling, one he can bend to his will." he jested, to which she smirked. But Col's face hardened, as he leaned in to speak.

"Hey, I need to tell you something-"

"Gin?" called Louis, cutting his brother off. Col hesitated, running his eyes over Louis before stepping aside for her to pass. Louis was still holding her chair out for her, Joseph's narrowed gaze flitting between her and Col.

"Shouldn't I sit with you? All the squires are sitting with their knights." she observed, as she watched them pour their knight's drinks.

"Technically, they're sitting with their *Masters*," he said, lazily, prompting a raised brow from Gin, "But don't worry. I think soulmate trumps Master." He held her gaze long enough for that stirring in her chest to begin again.

"I hope you don't expect me to call you *Master*." said Gin, crossing her arms over her chest to quell the hive of bees that had apparently taken up residence.

He narrowed his eyes, a lopsided smile spreading onto his lips.

"Special occasions?"

"Nope." she said incredulously.

"In private?" he whispered playfully. She gaped, trying to swat his arm before he bit his lip and bowed out to take a seat. She watched him go, laughing to herself before her feet dutifully took her to Louis.

Louis relaxed into a smile. She took her seat with a glance across the table to where Col sat with Daphne. Lady Flora was making her way down the stairs gracefully, her forest green dress billowing at her feet. She noted the empty chair next to hers and then scanned the table until she found Col. Her mouth parted slightly, her wandering gaze unable to settle. Col had not taken his seat next to her this evening and the displeasure was written all over her face. She couldn't help but wonder if her earlier conversation with Col had anything to do with it. Was he trying to put space between them? Not that it was any of her business to wonder.

Gin tucked herself in, peering at Col, who had already started eating the grapes from the fruit bowl in front of him, either unaware of Lady Flora's flaring nostrils or outright ignoring them. He poured Daphne a drink before seeing to his own. Daphne smiled tightly, *not* oblivious to Lady Flora's displeasure.

Gin pressed her lips together, suppressing the smirk that threatened to break.

"Gin, how are you?" asked Joseph, drawing her attention away as the table settled.

"I'm fine, thank you." she said, quick to answer.

"Good, good. I wonder if I might have a word after dinner?" he beamed, taking a sip of wine and checking his phone with his free hand. Gin's eyes slid to Louis's outstretched hand, finger tapping the table as he shot Col a glare. Her stomach hardened. There was only one thing she thought this talk would be about, willing herself not to look at Col as well. The arena duel wasn't being blamed on anyone other than herself.

"OK." she raised her brows, plastering a smile upon her lips.

"Excellent! Good to see everyone," he said, his voice raised to the table at large, "No doubt eager to hear the news I have!" He handed his vibrating phone to Louis, the screen alight with an incoming call. Louis took it swiftly.

"Excuse me, Gin. I won't be long." he said, standing. She waved a hand, needing no apology. In honesty, an empty chair beside her would have been her preference.

Col watched his brother go over the brim of his cup, one ankle draped over his knee.

"As I'm sure you're aware, Gin came to us from the fine upbringing at Slayton's Hospice." he began, her heart sinking to her gut as all eyes shifted to her. Her chin dipped as she gripped a cup of water tightly in her lap.

"I've known Slayton for many years and admire all the fine work he does. Not only at the Hospice that he took over from his late father, but for the many charities he supports and runs. He is simply a hero to so many people. And closest to us, our Gin." Her gut twisted into a knot that threatened to shatter her from the inside as he gushed over the very man who made her life a living nightmare. She daren't look at Col, her cheeks already burning with the feel of his gaze. She just hoped he would keep his mouth firmly closed.

"He is nothing short of a miracle. And I have been lucky enough to strike up a very exciting opportunity with him. I can't tell you how thrilled I am to tell you all the good news." He paused and Gin looked up at him, eyes wide, certain she was not hiding the fear that brimmed behind them.

"Between us, we have come to the arrangement of hosting a charity Halloween Ball, here, at the castle!" he waited, taking in the delighted gasps that rippled around the table and the excited murmurs as he revelled in his news settling. Gin, however, felt like the whole room went dark around her, like she had floated out of her body, nothing tethering her down.

"I, of course, needed no encouragement when he suggested it. We hope to raise more awareness for those who are vulnerable in our society. To raise the funds needed to support his many ventures by selling tickets to the public, to what is sure to be the most spectacular event of the year. His presence here alone will be something that will bring all eyes on us and draw in crowds." He drew a deep, satisfying breath, chest puffed out as he rested a hand on his hip before looking down at Gin. Her heart raced as numbness swept through her body. She was suddenly aware of Col's hand on the back of her chair as he slid into the empty seat beside her. She released the breath that had caught in her throat as the warmth of his knee pressed against hers.

"Come on, a man of such wealth and prosperity needs no extra help to raise money." said Col casually, leaning back in his chair, the front legs lifting slightly.

Gin shook her head slowly, knowing full well that he wasn't doing this for money or any charitable reason.

Joseph tried to smile, but it faltered into more of a sneer.

"Every little bit we can do to help is worth it, wouldn't you say? Without Slayton's Hospice, your Squire might not even be here today." he said, trying hard to keep the cheer in his voice. Col took a sharp intake of breath through his nose and she knew if she didn't say something, he was likely to say something that overstepped the mark.

"I-I think he has a point… Slayton's wealth goes beyond his own, his father's legacy is overwhelming. He doesn't need to raise more money." she said, trying to keep her voice even as her heart thrummed wildly. The thought of him here, in these walls, a place where his darkness hadn't overshadowed.

Joseph cocked his head.

"Don't you see how important this is? Not just for those he helps, but for us, too? To be part of such a noble cause, it will do wonders for us as well." A nervous laugh escaped him as he looked for support from others around the table. Gin could see the instant excitement had an edge of doubt now that she was voicing her opinion. Daphne's brows sat low, her lips a thin line. Her earlier elation had vanished.

She pinched the bridge of her nose, realising for Joseph this was just a lucrative opportunity to be seen mingling in Slayton's circle. She could tell him how gold practically flowed through Slayton's veins until she was blue in the face. It wouldn't matter. Joseph's ego wouldn't lose this opportunity for anything.

She glanced at Col, his knuckles rapping lightly on the back of her chair. There was a burning desire in his eyes to tell Joseph the truth, to get him to stop this madness. She gave him an imperceptible shake of her head and ran his teeth over his lip, as if trying to quell the urge. Joseph was the last person she wanted to tell. He was so wrapped up in his own world that she doubted it would even permeate the surface of his bubble.

"Well, I for one think it's a tremendous idea, Joseph." chimed Lady Flora, raising her chin, placing her hand over Sir Tarrick's, who she'd sought the company of in

Col's wake. "What better way to give back to the foundation that takes in the outcasts of the community?" she smiled bitterly at Gin. She let the insult slide, her mind racing with the bigger issue of Slayton coming here.

Col, however, was restless beside her, his knee bobbing up and down against hers. She could almost feel the anger rising in him.

Joseph started talking again, although it was distant, as she was frozen under Col's gaze.

"Gin?" asked Col, the low rumble of his voice reaching her and jerking her out of the ringing silence in her ears. She squeezed her eyes shut and clutched at her stomach, nausea shuddering through her body as she listened to Joseph's rambling.

"So much good will come of this, not to mention a bloody good night! And you Gin," he said, pausing to look down at her, lifting his heels as he locked his arms behind him, "You are the inspiration behind it!" he beamed.

Gin couldn't meet his eyes for fear of throwing up.

"You haven't had it easy growing up without a mother... or father figure." he said, clearing his throat as he stumbled over his words. "But you have had first-hand experience of Slayton's fine care and no doubt turned out stronger and wiser and more caring than you would have in a typical family home."

She clamped her tongue between her teeth until she tasted blood. Until the ludicrous story he had built in his mind of her life had stopped spilling from his lips.

"What makes you think-" blurted Col, lips pulled back, before Gin brought him into a swift silence as she placed a shaking hand on his knee under the table. He stilled instantly under her wide eyes. A muscle twitched under her fingers. He gaped at her for a moment, but she didn't move. She wouldn't let this be the moment Joseph and the entire castle found out about her shameful past.

Col's eyes slid to her trembling hand on his knee and she snapped it back to her cup, sending her water splashing dangerously.

Joseph took a deep breath, pushing past the interruption.

"In fact, Mr. Slayton and I both agree that there would be no one better to make a speech to our guests than you, Gin. To encourage them to dig deep into their pockets. It would be an honour to hear your story, and bring it to life for all to connect with." he said, drawing himself up proudly.

Gin swallowed the nausea that now intensified, all eyes intently trained on her. She heard Col shuffle in his chair and mumble something into his fist, elbow resting on the table. She placed her cup on the table before her shaking hands spilled it all over the place.

"Uh, I'm... I'm really not much of a public speaker." she choked out, her throat constricting as she wiped her sweaty hands along her thighs.

"Nonsense." sang Lady Flora from the far end of the table. "You absolutely must. People lap up a good sob story. I can see it now... the girl whose father failed her, mother too sick to care and Slayton salvaging what little was left of your life." she crooned, watching the liquid in her goblet as she swirled it gently. "They'll be throwing cheques onto the stage." A twisted smile crossed her lips before she took a sip. The snap of her eyes to meet hers sent a shiver down Gin's spine. She refused to rise to the bait. But again, she felt the anger ripple out from Col. It was like sitting next to the burning log fire in his cottage. But before he could respond, Joseph spoke, his laugh tinged with annoyance this time.

"I'm quite sure Gin's story won't be as tragic as that, Lady Flora. The point of the speech is to highlight the *fine* care that she and her mother were lucky to receive at Slayton's." he said, his voice trailing off as he picked at the wood on the table.

"Of course. And what about her absent father? Abandoning her at her most vulnerable. *That* will captivate the guests, be sure to include that in the Speech, Gin" said Lady Flora, tipping her drink towards her. Gin buried her mouth into her clenched fist, trying to shut out their voices as Joseph stammered over his reply.

"ENOUGH!" Col exploded, startling everyone in the room. Even Daphne froze, wide eyed, at his outburst as she passed a tray of steaming buns around the table. Lady Flora's cheeks flushed at being silenced by him as she looked down, fiddling with a ruby red napkin.

"She'll do the damn speech if she wants to and say whatever the hell she wants to say, *if* she chooses to." he said, looking from Lady Flora to Joseph, his shoulders hunched with pent up anger.

Gin squeezed her eyes tighter than ever, as if she might just disappear if she tried hard enough. The noise was too much.

"Fine, it's not compulsory, I'm sure Mr. Slayton can do a perfectly impactful speech alone... but, Gin... If you would just think about it? You won't have to write it alone, we shall help you." he said, rounding on her.

She looked up finally. He was holding his breath, waiting for her to speak, the hope in his eyes pleading. She couldn't bring herself to let him down or agree. He turned back to the table, plastering his showman smile.

"We can discuss the details tomorrow, Gin. Now, let's fill our bellies. It's been a busy day and we have a *lot* of planning to get under our belts before Halloween."

Gin pushed her chair back as he took his seat. She needed to get out of the hall to find peace. To breathe. He barely noticed her leave, but all other eyes were on her. Daphne made to get up, but Col raised his hand to stop her. Whispers followed her as she stalked out of the big oak doors, letting them swing shut behind her.

She didn't have a coat and the cool evening air should have clawed at her skin, but she was numb to everything. A moment longer under the scrutiny of the table and amongst the talk of Slayton or the Ball, and she was certain she'd throw up.

She ran her hands through her hair as she crossed the courtyard, barely registering the heavy footsteps behind her.

"Gin, wait!" Col was jogging to catch up, but she wasn't stopping for anyone. Not even as the urge to stop and scream all her fears at him pulsed through her chest. She pushed it away, keeping her eyes down, the wind streaming in her ears as she reached the bridge over the empty moat. But Col was fast, his stride longer than hers, and he cut her off. She halted at his chest, refusing to look up at him.

"Gin. Talk to me." His voice was strained. She breathed deeply, taking in the sweet-musky scent of the trees that swayed around them. The rustling sound sang loudly in her ears.

"Don't close up on me. Not now." He winced and moved a step closer. The panic and fear began to break the wall she had tried to keep up. Her body shuddered, tears rolling down her cheeks as she braced the damp mossy wall of the bridge.

The next moment, Col pulled her in, enveloped his arms around her shoulders, and she was crying against the warmth of his chest. She didn't pull back, even though instinct would normally have her doing so. Her body wouldn't budge. No one had ever held her, comforted her. She'd held Hope, of course, but she was so small and she'd been the one doing the comforting. This was different. *She* was wrapped in powerful arms, clutched to his chest as if he was afraid she'd crumble if he let go. Something swirled in her chest, warm and intoxicating. Feelings she'd never navigated before. But she let herself just breathe in the sweet, leathery scent of him.

"It's ok. It'll be ok." he muffled his words into her hair. She shook her head.

"How? How is this going to be ok? He's coming *here!* I'm not ready to face him yet. He'll win, *again.* God, *why* won't he just leave me alone?" she asked, pulling back, steadying herself on his arms.

He grimaced, searching her face with the intensity of those blue eyes in full force. He chose his words with care.

"*Because*... that weakness we needed to find to break him. It's you, Gin. His weakness is *you*."

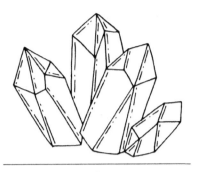

Chapter Seventeen

Gin stared blindly at the wet patch on his shirt where she'd sobbed, and it hit her like a thousand bricks raining down.

"I'll never be free of him." Her hollow voice seeped into the silent grounds. Col lifted his chin. No hint of sarcasm danced within his eyes now.

"I promised to help you get Hope back, to be able to go on with your life without the fear of Slayton on your back. And I don't waste my time making empty promises." he said, sweeping the strands of hair from her cheek that had stuck to her tears. Gin held back a shudder from his touch. To her surprise, it was not unwelcome.

"This speech they want you to make. I know it's a big ask. I know you don't want to do it. Hell, I was against it too, but hear me out." His cautious tone had Gin backing up, trying to process his words.

"No. Don't. Don't ask me to stand up there and tell the world he's the hero they all think he is." She raised her palms.

"I'm not." he assured her, closing the step she'd taken back. "But the more I think about it, a room full of wealthy high-class people, reporters, photographers… it's the perfect time to make your move." She cupped her elbows, nose wrinkling, unable to see his point. Col straightened, sinking his hands into his pockets.

"You let them come up with their version of the speech, praising the hell out of Slayton, while you write your own. One that will destroy him. Take him down in one swoop." he said, fire in his eyes. She squinted, letting his words sink in. She wanted to ruin him, but she never imagined it being a public event.

"I-I can't… what if they don't believe me? What if Slayton gets away again and punishes Hope because of me?" her hair swayed around her face as she shook her head, mind racing with reasons not to go through with it. Col dipped his head, tilting her chin up, bringing her out of her thoughts.

"He won't. By the time he walks through those gates, you won't have a single doubt in your mind about what needs to be done. You will stand up there with the strength and courage of *every* person he has ever hurt in your heart. And those voices are going to replace his poison. He expects you to still be under his spell and tell them how fucking great he is. But he's unknowingly given you the *best* opportunity to bury him. He'll never see it coming," he cocked his head, *"Trust me."*

Gin's chest caved as the insanity of what he was saying made more and more sense. Slayton would have no way to take back her words once they left her damaged soul. There would be too many people in one room, too many to scare all at once to keep their mouths shut. The reporters would have no choice but to run the story with so many witnesses.

She sighed heavily, leaning over the edge of the wall.

"I always imagined someone else exposing him for what he is. We'd just get to live in the glory of their triumph." she said, playing idly with the moss that sprawled over the stone wall. Col joined her, arms resting on the cold stone. He hung his head between his shoulders and fixed those sky-blue eyes on hers.

"Lesson number four; be your own goddamn hero."

A buzz thrummed through her chest as her heart pounded at the thought of being the one to expose him in front of the very people that love him. The corners of her mouth turned up. Maybe she could do this.

"Thank you." she whispered. He tapped the wall and looked away.

"Don't thank me yet." he sucked the air through his teeth.

"What?" she asked flatly. He puckered his lips, choosing his words with care.

"Well… I think you should tell Louis," he said. Gin straightened. She took a moment to reply and in that time he had slid a sidelong look her way.

"What does Louis have to do with me being my own hero?" she baulked.

"Absolutely nothing." His brows rose.

"Good, because I already have one pushy knight looking out for me." she said, lips pursed.

"And I'm not going anywhere." he said, lifting his chin. "But. Louis does care, in his own annoying knight in shining chivalrous pants way. I know how long he's cared. He never stopped, never gave up hope of finding you." His brows lowered along with his eyes before returning. She swallowed. Discomfort writhed in her stomach as he spoke of Louis's feelings. "This is going to be a monumental moment for you. And even though you don't want this soul connection, it *will* get stronger, bit by bit. Even if it is just friendship. Or… if it develops into something more." She watched his throat bob. "You deserve the gift of having a soulmate by your side in this." he paused, unable to quite look her in the eye.

Gin's stomach dropped, her mind wrestling with uncertainty. She had no intention of staying here after Hope was by her side and hadn't even considered telling him about her. As much as Col said her soul connection was ever growing with Louis, she didn't want to let it. She didn't want Louis leaving the castle and galloping off into their precious future with them. Maybe that was selfish, but she didn't care. She'd waited years for the opportunity to build a life full of truly living, with Hope and Hope alone. But then, like Col said, the prophecy didn't say they were bound forever in love. If she really didn't have a choice in what her soul desired, then she'd take friendship if she had to take anything. She rubbed the back of her neck, sighing.

"Say I tell him. What's to stop him from telling Joseph? He seems to be in his pocket most of the time. One word to him and we're screwed."

"He may be a goody two-shoes, but he isn't stupid." said Col, brushing her fears aside. Gin frowned, looking down as she twisted one of her rings.

"Ok. I'll tell Louis." she conceded.

"Tell me what?" came a voice from behind her. The pair's attention shot to Louis, pressing a button on the phone Joseph had handed him. The screen went dark, and he was left eyeing them suspiciously. Gin's body went rigid. She thought she'd have at least the night to think about how *exactly* to tell him. She blinked rapidly, scraping a hand through her hair.

"Uh... Louis." she stammered.

"Care to join us for a nightcap, brother?" Col plastered a smile upon his lips, hands wedged in his pockets.

Louis angled his body away from them, eyes narrowed as he studied them.

"Sure. Let me return this to Joseph and I'll be with you. Meet me in my quarters." he said, walking around them. Gin turned, eyes trailing him.

Col took a flask from inside his jacket pocket and paused, tipping it towards her.

"You still never drinking again?" he asked. Gin dragged her eyes from watching Louis disappear into the courtyard, to the flask. She was close to accepting, but she needed to be careful with what she gave away this evening. She needed control. No more information than necessary. She rolled her shoulders as she felt a shiver run over her scars, as if they were reminding her what was at stake. With a small shake of her head, they made their way to Louis's room.

*

Gin watched Louis like a hawk as she sat across the table from him in his ordered room. The fire was roaring in the hearth, already lit for the night. The silence was seemingly endless as he processed everything she'd just told him. Everything except the way in which he punished her. There was no need to add fuel to a fire that was simmering in both brothers' heads.

Col was leaning back in his chair between them, ankle draped over his knee that supported his flask. His nostrils flared as his eyes danced over his brother.

"This is the part where you tell Gin that you're one hundred percent behind her all the way and vow to do everything in your power to help reunite her with her daughter." he said, leaning over his lap.

Gin couldn't peel her gaze from Louis, her heart hammering at her chest. What if Col had got it wrong? What if he was going to run straight to Joseph and give it all away? One word to Slayton and she'd never see Hope again. The knot in her stomach tightened and twisted. She wetted her lips swiftly, only for them to dry again instantly as her breathing intensified.

"Louis?" Her voice was barely a whisper. Col frowned between them.

Louis cleared his throat.

"Bloody hell, Gin." he said, running a hand down his face. She swallowed. "Why didn't you tell me?" he asked, his face pained. She pursed her lips, weighing his words. She couldn't lie to him.

"Because I had planned on being long gone before having to tell you about the darkest part of my life." She didn't miss the flash of hurt that etched his features. She closed her eyes, scolding herself for the harshness of her words. She dug deep for the pain that she was suppressing, the reasons for keeping it buried.

"I've spent years going over everything I could have done differently. How I could have done more to save my mother from his neglect. How I could have insisted Slayton get outside help for Hope's birth mother. I could have been stronger for everyone at the Hospice. Found a way to continue helping them after Hope, instead of leaving them at Slayton's mercy. And every time I even let myself think about it, another piece of my heart shatters. So instead of trying to fit the broken pieces of every one of my failings back together, I left them on the ground. And telling Col, you or *anyone*, only drags those shards back with searing pain." she said, staring into the fire. "I don't have people in my life who care... at least I didn't." she glanced up at last, her eyes landing on each. Louis shot Col an annoyed glance. "So I'm sorry if my decision to keep it from you hurts. I never meant to tangle up anyone here in my past."

Silence. She could feel the burn of their gaze. She had nothing to do but wait now, cards on the table, vulnerable to Louis's next steps.

Louis rose, bringing her attention with him. He moved his chair around the table, placed it next to her, and sat, elbows on his knees. Her pulse quickened.

"Do not apologise." he shook his head in disbelief. "I am the one who must. I am truly sorry. My senses left me the minute you walked into the castle. Understand, I only mean to help you, protect you." Gin's shoulders rose, inhaling a shaky breath.

"You, of course, have my express support. I will not rest until we reunite you with Hope." he said. She released the breath she'd been holding. He would not tell Joseph. They were safe. Her eyes fluttered heavily. She couldn't help but feel a bubble of warmth towards him.

"Thank you."

He turned to Col, who stood.

"Thank God your senses didn't abandon you completely, brother." he said, grabbing a bottle of wine from a shelf of neatly placed bottles, and uncorking it. "This calls for a toast." he said, pouring the deep red liquid into three cups. "And Gin, you can pretend." he said, sauntering back with their drinks. Gin took hers with a suppressed smile.

Louis studied them as he took his cup, lips pressed together.

"I uh… I think I see at last, why you train with my brother." he said, brow wrinkled.

Gin exchanged a fleeting look with Col, her cheeks prickling with heat. "Seems I owe you an apology too." he said, tilting his head up at Col.

"I wasn't just being a dick as usual, you mean?" asked Col, with a crooked smile. Louis chuckled softly.

"Quite. You really were trying to help." he paused, then raised his cup. "To new beginnings. For all of us." he said. Gin looked between them, her chest squeezing with something new. Something warm. These two brothers were taking their first steps to putting their differences aside, in the face of defeating her nightmare and that of so many. She raised her cup, nose wrinkled as a genuine smile crept onto her face. The first in a long time.

As Gin and Col meandered down the path to his cottage, they spoke about the healing Crystals and what Col wanted to teach her that night. With the ball looming, time was not a luxury. She wanted to soak up as much as possible about how to heal the patients she'd left behind. And the most peculiar thought crossed her mind. Instead of pain and regret, her heart felt lighter than it had. It was not weighed down by misery, but the promise of a future with two people backing her up. People who made the thought of facing Slayton possible. As much as it terrified her, she had people on her side for the first time. They didn't come in the form of a typical mother or father. They weren't even of this world. But they were here now, and she would appreciate their presence whilst they were. And when the time to say goodbye comes, she'll let them go with the grace that they'd shown her, hoping that Louis would understand her choice to do right by her daughter. She would have Hope and her own future to build.

That warm feeling followed her all the way down to Col's cottage.

And that's where it ceased.

Gin walked straight into Col's back. He'd stopped at the little gate to his overgrown garden, staring, mouth open. She followed his gaze down the lamplit cobbled path, overrun with weeds, to the door... it had been kicked down.

Papers from his notebooks fluttered about the ground, getting caught up in branches of the shrubbery. Tiny glints of colour flashed on the pathway.

His Crystals, notebooks... his life's work scattered in ruins.

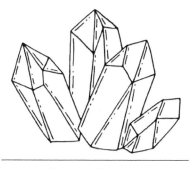

Chapter Eighteen

"Stay here." ordered Col, pushing open the gate and stalking off down the paper and Crystal strewn path.

"You're kidding, right?" She scurried after him, careful not to kick any of the Crystals. Col didn't try to stop her, lost in the carnage.

The moment she entered the cottage, a feeling of despair ripped through her. It started in her chest and rippled out like a pebble dropped into calm waters. She cupped her mouth, taking in the scene. Crystals lay shattered on the floor, notebooks ripped to shreds. This was not a simple robbery. This was an attack on Col.

Her eyes fell to him, searching with frantic speed for something in the kitchen where the damage was worse. Treading carefully through the living room, minding what she could, the pressure of distraught energy mounted as she neared the kitchen. She tensed her body against it, trying to block it. She needed to stay calm, focused.

"Argh!" he screamed, his fists thudding on the kitchen table, making her flinch. He brought a hand to his brow and let out a heavy sigh through his clenched teeth.

Gin clutched her middle, the horror-stricken energy clinging to her like a magnet, drawing the frenzied pain.

Col whipped his head to her, and his face softened slightly.

"You need to leave. I'm able to control their energy better than you are. Don't put yourself through this." he said, scanning her crumpled face. She closed her eyes and shook her head.

"This is *them* I can feel?" she marvelled. He gave a grave nod.

"And this amount of combined energy… it's powerful. Go." he said, sternly.

"No." She levelled him with a hard look of her own. She wouldn't leave him in this alone. Nothing could drag her away. Col narrowed his eyes.

"I need to be here." said Gin, almost surprising herself. She glanced at his furrowed brow. "I can't explain it... other than a feeling that I *need* to be here." She looked around at the lucky Crystals that remained whole amongst the fragments.

Her anger was dissolving, but in its place was a gaping hole filled with sadness. She could feel their loss like it was her own. If anything was going to convince her of the soul connection through these Crystals, it was this pain.

"Hey." said Col, stepping closer, hands hovering by her arms.

"They're grieving, Col." she said, not meeting his gaze.

"Which is why you should leave. Being so new to the connection, their energies will hit you hard." he said, his brow wrinkling.

"I can't. I can't leave them... not like this." her shoulders slumped, the burden now fully in her heart too. Col was silent beside her. After a moment, he released a sigh.

"And you doubted you're the Silver Soul." he said, observing her.

Gin winced, watching him run his hands over his hair until they met at the back of his head, clasping as he stood and took in the destruction. She grieved for him too. His life's work and future shattered around him. She gritted her teeth against the urge to put her arms around him.

And suddenly a pit burrowed further into her stomach. What would this mean for healing those at the Hospice? That bright candle of hope in her chest gave way to darkness again. How many more ways was she going to let them down?

She walked around the kitchen table to where he kept wooden buckets by the back door. She grabbed it and began collecting the Crystals that were salvageable. And finally, the shards that were past saving went into a second bucket.

They worked in silence until all that was left was to sweep the shards that were too small into a pile.

"What do we do with them?" asked Gin, looking downcast at the most beautifully devastating heap. Even in the immense sadness of it all, she couldn't help but think it was the most stunning wreckage she'd ever seen.

Col stared at the pile a moment longer with clouded eyes. She could feel the decision weighing on him heavily. He threw the broom against the wall blindly.

"There's nothing to be done with them." he said, miserably. She frowned, squatting to pick up a larger shard of lavender coloured Crystal from the pile.

"You can't just throw them away. They're a part of you, Col, a part of your history… your mother." she said, refusing to believe he could disregard them so quickly.

"What am I going to do with them? I don't need another grave to mourn." he offered her a fleeting glance before grabbing a wooden bucket that had stood near the fireplace. She grimaced as he scooped them into it, blinking as the pieces struck the bottom. She swallowed the lump in her throat.

"Who do you think would do this?" she asked hopelessly.

"How long have you got? I'm not exactly knight of the year, could be any number of people." He turned to her, scuffing his boots. "You and I have something to do."

"What is it?" she almost whispered, feeling the nerves pulsating from him. He headed for the door with heavy footsteps.

"You'll see."

Gin followed Col briskly through the dark grounds, the sombre mood weighing on them in heavy silence. They reached the Great Hall where people were still milling about with after-dinner drinks, engaged in conversation. A merry tune rang through the cavernous room, contrasting everything about the evening.

Lady Flora ceased her conversation as the pair marched in. Gin walked behind him as he headed straight for Joseph, who was in deep discussion with Daphne. All heads soon swivelled, watching Col lean in between them.

"I need a word." he said to Joseph, drumming his fingers that he braced on the table.

Daphne glanced at Gin, startled, but Gin looked away, unable to explain even if she could.

"Can it wait, Col? I was just-"

"It can't." Col interrupted, pushing himself away from the table, and paced in front of the sputtering fireplace.

Gin clenched her sweaty hands. Surely he didn't think Joseph was responsible for the destruction? She knew they walked a narrow ledge, but she wasn't convinced Joseph would stoop to that level, destroying the very things that made his castle a reality.

Joseph muttered an apology to Daphne and rose with slow defeat.

"What do you want, Col?" Col stopped pacing, his face pinched.

"I need to see it." was all he said. Joseph gave a cautious sidelong glance at Gin. There was reluctance in his eyes as he hedged to answer, wetting his lips before finally speaking.

"Is this really necessary?"

Col cocked his head.

"Someone broke into my house, smashed most of my Crystals and tore up my notebooks. What do *you* think?"

Joseph's brows rose as he blinked. He didn't protest nor did he respond, but he made quick work of disappearing through a door to the right, quickly followed by Col.

Gin clenched her jaw, doing a sweep of the eyes that had fallen to her in their wake. Lady Flora's throat worked before she composed herself and swept up the stairs. Gin swiftly followed after them, out of the Great Hall and down a long corridor. At the end, there was an enclosed staircase, with steps leading both up and down. Joseph led them spiralling down, seemingly well below the castle. The air got noticeably colder the further down they went and the walls damp beneath her fingers as she steadied herself.

"Watch your step. They're uneven and can catch you off guard." said Col, pausing to check on her. She nodded, not that she felt at all sure about where they were heading. They carried on down the tricky steps, some deeper than others, some narrower, some with a double step on one.

"Where does this lead?" she asked, craning her neck to see past him, but the spiral staircase wound further still.

"To something I sure as hell hope is better guarded than my house." said Col. Gin's stomach flopped nervously. She didn't think either of them could take another hit today. First Slayton, then the Crystals. It was almost enough to make her reconsider that flask in Col's pocket.

"You had better hope your protection Crystal works as well as you say it does." said Joseph.

"They never let me down before."

"Then why insist on coming all the way down here to check?"

There was a pause, and Gin's stomach quivered. Joseph had a point. Col inhaled deeply.

"Because it seems the universe likes to surprise me lately." he said, finally, as they reached the bottom of the stairwell. Gin leaned on the wall. The cold damp bit through her thin sweatshirt.

Col took a lantern from the stairwell and walked slowly towards an arched door. Gin squinted as the new light revealed a strange embossing upon it in an oval shape. In the centre, the light reflected on what looked like a pool of black glass.

"We got it from here, Joseph," said Col, eyes trained on the door. Joseph drew his shoulders back, staring at Col's outstretched palm.

"You'll have to forgive me if I don't feel entirely comfortable leaving you alone with it."

Gin watched the back of Joseph's head cock to the side, intrigue burning in her belly.

"I'm sorry, you make it sound like I'm supposed to care how you *feel*." said Col, twisting to face him, still expectant. Joseph's shoulders heaved upwards before releasing a sharp breath, passing something from his pocket to Col's palm.

"I'll be waiting for that back, so don't go trying anything stupid." Col's only reply was a sharp smile that vanished as soon as Joseph turned his back.

Joseph paused as he approached Gin, his brows dug in.

"This place is off limits to everyone. Please, speak of it to no one." he said. She cocked an eyebrow but nodded. She had no desire to talk to anyone in general, so it didn't bother her.

Col watched him leave with narrowed eyes.

"C'mere." he said.

Gin stepped onto the uneven ground, dodging pools of dark water. She dreaded to think how far below the castle they were. The small arched walkway to the door seemed too small and suffocating.

Standing by Col's side made it ten times worse, their bodies mere inches apart. She kept her eyes firmly on his hand, resting by his stomach, clutching whatever Joseph had grudgingly handed over.

"This is Black Tourmaline." Col spoke quietly, unfurling his fingers to reveal a jet black Crystal, the light from a torch on the wall flickering on its glassy surface. "The other half of the one in the centre of this door."

She looked sideways at the door. What she had mistaken for glass was indeed the same shape as the oval tourmaline in Col's hand.

"If it's done its job correctly, the door should be sealed shut." he said, patting the pocket of his trousers gently in hesitation before closing the distance between him and the door.

Gin held her breath as he reached out a hand and pushed. Nothing happened. Not even a budge. Col's head dipped as he pushed himself off, his mouth parted as he released a carefully held breath.

Gin shuffled her feet, numb with cold, as she met his eyes at last.

"So, what are we so relieved about still being locked away behind there?" she asked, crossing her arms to fend off the chill. He tilted his head back for her to come to him. She trod carefully. When she reached his side, he held the Crystal out for her. Her brows rose, pulse quickening as she hesitantly held out both hands. It was warm. Abnormally warm. In fact, it was almost hot as it lay cupped in her chilly hands. She blinked several times.

The faintest smirk played on his lips. She felt her own face relax at the sight of it. The evening had been fraught with sadness and disappointment. This tiny flicker of his usual self eased the heaviness in her chest.

"When they're placed together, the door unseals itself. If that Crystal was ever lost, my chance to ever go back would disappear with it." he said, rubbing the back of his neck. "A fact Oldman *loves* to remind me of."

Gin swallowed. She cupped it tighter, its worth now felt like gold and suddenly she realised what rested behind that door. The device.

"And you let Joseph look after it?" she said, nose wrinkling.

"It's part of our... deal, if you will, while I work for him at the castle until I find all the Crystals." he said, sourly. The thought of him leaving sat oddly in her tummy and she was keen to get off the subject.

"Take the tourmaline in your left hand." he said with a small tight smile. She did so carefully, glad he hadn't pursued the topic.

"Now, put your hand in mine." he said, holding out his palm. Her eyes darted to his, the breath stolen from her lungs. She saw his throat work as he held his hand out for her, eyes shuttered behind thick black lashes. He waited with confidence and patience, not pestering her to comply. Gin's stomach fluttered as his cold rough hand cupped hers, warm from the Crystal's inner heat. It was a strange sensation, one that she didn't dislike.

"Hold it tight." he said, raising their hands to the other half of the Tourmaline in the middle of the embossing. He guided her hand to the dark shimmering Crystal and together they joined the two. Her heart was pounding wildly, as she didn't dare move in fear of letting it slip to the ground.

"It will get hotter, just below burning. The heat should transfer through your hand to mine, which will halve the impact on you." he said, calmly.

Gin looked at him, wide eyed, holding her breath and bracing for the heat. His gaze was firmly fixed on her.

"I've got you, Sparkles." his voice was quieter, slightly broken, and it sent a shiver of goosebumps over her body.

After a moment, she felt the heat intensify, as if she were holding her hand too close to the flame of a candle. Col tightened his grip on her hand, and with that she felt the heat ease a little as it passed through to him.

"Are you ok?" he asked, his brow furrowed, examining her face. She was about to say yes, but another wave of heat spiked through her hand. She gasped, hearing a clunk and the Tourmaline plummeted to an icy cold temperature, cooling their hands.

They basked momentarily, enjoying the cooling sensation that flooded through their hands. It was only then that she realised his fingers had slipped between hers in the process and she had curled hers around his. Their eyes met and lingered for too long. A rush of heat, different from before, spread out from her stomach as his eyes lowered to her lips. She loosened her grip, looking away, and he let go, clenching and releasing his hand several times. It took her by surprise, an all-consuming heady feeling. She scuffed her foot on the damp ground, all too aware of her body. She handed him the now cold Tourmaline, eyes cast down. Col cleared his throat.

"Give it a push." he said, nodding towards the door with a hard stare. Gin refocused, bringing her thoughts away from the swirling madness within.

Her fingers were ice cold now with the remnants of its sudden biting blast. She stroked her palms, trying to get some warmth to flow again as she stepped closer to the door.

Her heart was in her mouth as she reached out. Bracing her hands on either side of the embossed centre, she took a deep breath and pushed.

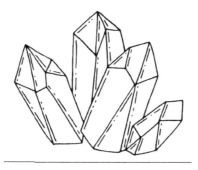

Chapter Nineteen

The door swung back without so much as a creak and eight lanterns burst into life on the walls, illuminating a small octagonal room within.

Gin stumbled back a step at the unexpected explosion of light. Col placed a hand on the small of her back to steady her and a shiver tiptoed up her spine, prickling her unyielding, scarred skin. But as her eyes fell upon what stood proudly in the middle of the little room, she had little time to think about it.

Nestled atop a white marble podium was the device. More beautiful than her imagination could have conjured. The flames from the lanterns on the walls licked its Crystal walls and created a glowing moonlight lustre about it. Silver edging hugged the corners and glinted in the flickering haze.

Flares of blue and green light shimmered from the two Crystals within and cast an ocean like ripple of colour on the white marble podium. The total effect was like a moonlit sea.

Gin's hands were clutched to her chest, rooted to the spot, spellbound by the beauty of it.

Col sighed from behind her, his breath warm on her neck against the cold damp air of the stairwell, bringing her out of her daze. Shifting his feet, she felt the relief flood out from his chest. She, too, could feel it. His way back was safe.

She smiled, watching the wrinkle on his forehead dissolve into his tan skin. It was the small sort of smile that was tainted. She desperately wanted to feel complete happiness for him, for his security in knowing he'll be able to go back one day. But her happiness was edged with the strange sensation of loss.

She swallowed hard, having to remind herself that he wasn't hers to lose in the first place, and scolded herself for being so ridiculous. She had her future mapped out, and so did he. This odd friendship they'd seemed to kindle was something she would have to let go of. She never wanted this anyway, needing no one but Hope. This whole squire business had really gone to her head.

"After you." he said, his voice hoarser than usual.

The air was thick with a vibrant earthy scent, as if the walls were teaming with life, like a forest floor. The moment she entered, her energy shifted along with a weight in her chest. She rubbed her palm over her heart where the ache was heaviest.

Col was at her side in a second, looking from the device to her and back again. "You feel it, don't you?" he said, not really a question at all.

"What is it?" she asked, nose wrinkling as she felt her senses dulling to everything around her, apart from this ache in her chest.

Col dug his hands into his pockets, a distant, empty look on his face as he rested a foot on the step to the podium.

"Longing. Pining. Heartbreak… the four element Crystals are connected, much like your soul connection with Louis." he said with a darting glance at her. "When they're apart, they yearn to reconcile. The bond never breaks, no matter the distance. And they *feel* it."

Gin's lips parted. The anguish they felt at being parted from their soul connection was almost too much to bear. She didn't want to imagine ever feeling that way about Louis. Not that she could imagine a future where she would. But a fear flashed white hot across her. What if he was right and she would grow to love him, even as a friend?

Was this what awaited? Her breathing grew heavier as she quelled the lump that was forming in her throat.

"Can't you heal their pain? Can't you help them?" she asked, brows knitted. Col winced, looking down.

"Even if I had all the healing Crystals, wounds of the heart and soul are not like physical wounds. They go much deeper, beyond the power of the Crystals. I can force nothing upon them. The heart and soul... they're a force of their own." His voice echoed softly around the small, domed room. It was the answer she feared. Louis was bound to her soul, no matter how much she fought it. She clung to the hope that through his leaving one day, he would find happiness back in the life where he belonged. And she and Hope could do the same in a life without the shadow of Slayton looming over their backs.

In an attempt to change the subject, she stepped closer to the device, leaning in to better see the two Crystal wands.

"Which two are these?" she asked, peering over the top of the device.

"Malachite is the deep green wand, and Azurite is the blue one." Col tucked his hands into his pockets.

"But you said you only had two more to find?"

"Uh, yeah... Aqua Aura and Sunstone." he said, jaw clenching.

"But then, shouldn't the Galaxy Crystal be in here?" she cocked her head. Col laughed but there was little humour in it.

"You don't miss a trick." he mused, scratching his smooth cheek. "*That* stays with me."

Gin bit her cheek, a nagging worry squeezing her chest.

"Don't you think it would be safer here? I mean, after tonight... the break in." She trailed off.

"You mean trust Oldman with it? Come on Sparkles, you know that's not going to happen. Besides, it's safe. Trust me. Some things need far greater protection than even this room can provide." he said, straightening his shoulders. "Plus, I'm just selfish." His grin slid to one side. She pressed her lips into a fine line. She wouldn't trust Joseph either, but surely it was riskier to be left unprotected, now more than ever.

"The Galaxy stone is the driving force behind all the magic, if you will." his tone turned serious. "But the four Crystal wands are what makes time travel possible. Their collective power. If just one is missing, then they're incapable of making the shift." he hunched over the device. "See, each of the four wands represent an element of nature. The tall green one, Malachite, is the earth element. It also aids in protection while travelling. The blue and white marbled Crystal is Azurite, for air. Its properties repair and maintain the ageing process. Hence, my youthful good looks." he said, shrugging his shoulders. Gin raised an eyebrow.

"How old are you, exactly? I mean, the age that you're stuck in, not the ancient relic that you are." she asked, tilting her head. Col slapped a hand to his heart in mock hurt.

"I'll have you know there's life yet in these old bones. They've barely grown into their skin in their twenty-six years." He said, looking down his nose at her as he drew closer. She crossed her arms, turning her attention back to the device.

"So, if Earth and Air are here, you're missing Fire and Water?"

"Correct. Sunstone, formed within lava itself, it's the very essence of fire. Promotes living in the moment, without fear. And last but by no damn means least, Aqua Aura. This one's fascinating." he said, eyes narrowing. Gin raised her brows.

"And the others weren't?"

"Oh, they all are in their own right. But this one, it has something unique. The last element, water. It literally rewrites the rules. There are no boundaries with this Crystal. The possible outcomes it can create are infinite."

Goosebumps pricked her skin, and she ran her hands up her arms.

"What if a visitor was to find a Crystal?" she asked, brows knitted. "You'd be looking forever in vain."

"The Crystals can't leave the grounds. Their gravitational field is tied to the device. If anyone tried to sneak one out, the pull of the Galaxy stone wouldn't let them past the gate." he said.

"Smart." she said, running a finger over the top of the device. It hummed beneath her skin.

"It's nature. The smartest thing ever to exist." his gaze hovered on the device. "Everything is energy, Gin. The universe and all it holds, down to the particles we can't even see. The flow of the universe's energy runs through the Crystals, just as it runs through you and I. Being connected to the universe is the key." Gin watched him idly for a moment, letting his words sink in. It was a concept she had started to see for herself. Just being in this room, surrounded by Crystals, she could feel the energy teaming around her. They were alive. They were connected to her.

Col pinched the bridge of his nose, closing his eyes with a strained sigh. It pulled her out of the questions that riled in her mind. After the devastation of the morning, his senses were probably more vulnerable than he liked to let on.

"You should get some rest, Col. Get a clear head before thinking about who could have broken in."

"Hm, I don't think I'd be able to sleep if I tried." he grunted.

"Well, there must be a Crystal that can help you? Something to aid rest." she said, eager to help.

Col rubbed the back of his neck and winced. She could tell he was preparing to put his guard up. She'd done it enough herself.

"Let me help you, Col." she said, clasping her elbows to her sides as she twirled a silver ring around her finger nervously.

Col studied her for a moment, from under a knitted brow.

"Well... there is something, but whether it's smashed to smithereens, I don't know." he breathed a sigh that held the weight of both their problems.

"There's only one way to find out." she said, turning on her heel and stepping out of the room, the thick feeling of heady pining melting away like frost in winter's sun.

Col raised his brows as he watched her, hesitant to leave. He took one more glance over the device, safely nestled within, before following her out and closing the door behind him. A sound like wind blowing over the top of a glass bottle rang softly through the alcove. The device's sanctuary was safe once more.

Col searched silently through what was left of his collection, nostrils flaring now and then, until he found what he needed.

"Amethyst." he said, finally turning to her, holding out the many pointed Crystal, its vibrant purple hue glowing in his palm. "Its properties are excellent for balancing energy and helping insomnia. If anything is going to work, it's this. We also need lavender." He said, nodding to the herbs hanging by the window. Gin was on it, collecting a few stems of lavender, while Col tore a piece of cloth from a rag.

"You need to wrap both the Amethyst and Lavender inside the cloth and place it under the pillow. Bedroom's this way." he said, eyes down as he handed her the items. She took them, catching his gaze as his fingers brushed hers. Her heart thrummed in her ears as heat rose in her face. The thought of his bedroom suddenly left her feeling unbalanced for some reason.

"Right, uh, yes. Well. After you." she said, stumbling over her words. Col gave the tiniest pinched smirk before he padded off into a room just off the living room. She screwed her face up behind his back, cursing herself for being so immature.

His bedroom was lit through a small window, shuttered with thin sheets of animal horn, creating a dappled moonlight through the overgrown ivy that caressed the walls outside. Unsurprisingly, the bed was unmade, like the rest of his cottage. The only other piece of furniture in the room was a chest beside his bed. On top was a lantern, a few scattered Crystals and a little figurine of a wooden horse. She lingered on it, which did not go unnoticed. Col cleared his throat and stepped in front, blocking her view.

"You can just place it under the pillow. I don't think Louis would approve of you tucking me in." he said, hands in his pockets, a wry smile on his lips. Gin pursed her lips and began wrapping the Amethyst and Lavender up carefully. She was trying her best not to care what Louis would think.

"If you think I'm leaving without witnessing you laying your head on that pillow, you can think again." she said, stepping around him and placing the neatly wrapped parcel under the fluffed pillow. She put her hands on her hips as he narrowed his eyes.

"Fine." he growled softly, slinking up to the bed, inches from where she stood. She caught the sweet, leathery scent as he bent down to untie his boots, standing up tall again and meeting her gaze as he kicked them off. She swallowed all too noticeably, his eyes dragging down to her throat.

"Do I get a bedtime story?" he asked with a feline grin. Gin blinked up at him, holding back the urge to smile.

"Don't push it." she replied, as he pouted.

Finally, he lowered himself onto the bed, swinging his long legs round and placing an arm behind his head as he lay on the pillow. He never broke eye contact and to her surprise, neither did she. Until her gaze settled on his shirt, hitched a little over one hip as he stretched out.

"You happy now?" he asked, raising a brow. Her cheeks heated, and she forced herself to look away, tucking her hair behind her ears.

"Yes. I'll let you sleep." she mumbled, turning towards the door. But before she could leave...

"Hey, Sparkles... Happy Birthday." he said quietly, as if sleep was on the horizon. The breath was knocked from her chest. No one had remembered... except Col. She pressed her lips together, closing the door behind her. She blew a strand of loose hair from her face and leaned back against the wood. Her world was becoming a confusing madness because of these two knights.

Pushing herself off the door, she traipsed through the living room, pausing as something tugged at her, like Hope used to tug on her sleeve for attention. It was drawing her to the bucket of broken Crystals by the back door. It seemed such a terrible waste. The indispensable power that could have done so much for so many people at the Hospice, diminished to what little was left.

As she peered down at it, an idea came to her. She couldn't leave the remnants of these beautiful Crystals to be thrown out. She scooped it into her arms, gripping it as she made her way out of the cottage and up to her room. Inspiration had struck, igniting the creative spark that had laid dormant since leaving her little room of treasures with Hope. She couldn't fix them, but she *could* create something for Col to keep and cherish in a new light.

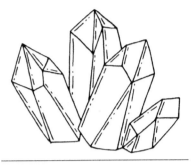

Chapter Twenty

Gin spent her restless hours of the night playing with the shards of Crystal, fashioning them in every which way until they resembled some kind of colourful nebula.

With her ability to seek the shadows, she snuck out and took a perspex sign from outside the gift shop and removed the large poster within. She then slid the shards of Crystals into the base, one by one, until they filled the entire thing, like a stained-glass window, only a million times more magical. She sealed the bottom again and placed it on the table by her window.

The world was waking; the moon hunkering down to make way for the sun. Soft tendrils of light stretched out and illuminated the Crystal window with the most ethereal light, casting hues of every colour on the bare stone floor and walls. She smiled as she stared at her work. It felt good to create something again, to work with her hands and she had to admit... this was the most beautiful thing she'd ever made. She could see the wonder in Hope's eyes now. She would have loved this. A little lump stretched her throat, and she swallowed it down painfully.

She ran her ring clad fingers over one corner when something caught her eye out in the emptying courtyard. There, in the far right corner behind a row of bushes and trees, was a part of the castle she'd not noticed before. She supposed she'd never taken the time to really look, but it seemed plain as day now, with the aid of Louis.

He was locking a narrow wooden door that was inset down a few steps. When he turned to come up, he hung the key that was attached to a large round metal ring onto his belt, amongst the other personal items that swung at his hip.

Gin stepped carefully around the Crystal window to get a better view. She sat on the edge of the window seat, peering down, eyes narrowed.

Louis stepped out from behind the bushes and hurried towards the castle. She noticed a jug in one hand, empty apparently from the way it was swaying with his light footsteps. As he disappeared under the covered steps to the entrance, she drew her eyes back to the door he had come out of. It was well camouflaged behind the foliage and being set into the wall below ground level. It was no wonder she had not seen it before.

Then a thought occurred to her as she bit gently on her long thumbnail. Her heart pumped faster, realisation dawning upon her.

"The dungeon…" she whispered. She hadn't gone searching for it because of the warnings she'd received, despite her intrigue. But she couldn't deny the possibility of this being the doorway, concealed from the main path and locked.

Then another thought occurred to her, which sent her swiftly across the room to the map that hung above her fireplace. It was too high for her to see the details as she peered up at it. She clocked the stool that stood at the side of the wardrobe, fetched it and stepped up carefully; the legs wobbling on the uneven stone slabs. Grasping the shelf over the fireplace, the grit and dust scratched her fingers.

The ancient map had been drawn on parchment that was placed in glass since its arrival here.

She traced a finger from the entrance of the castle, the spidery writing marking it, all the way along the path that hugged its walls in the courtyard. And there, tucked beside the row of bushes and trees, were the words, "Dungeon and Oubliette".

Her mouth fell open, disbelief in it being shown here all this time. Though she hadn't a clue what 'Oubliette' meant. She swallowed, not entirely sure she wanted to know. Something unsettled her stomach when thinking about what was down there. What Col was hiding. And what business did Louis have going down there?

A sharp rap on the door jolted her out of her thoughts. She ran her sweaty palms over her thighs before throwing a blanket from the bed over the Crystal window. She crossed the room and opened the door, expecting Col, waking her up early again for squire duties. But Daphne came bustling into the room with armfuls of different fabrics.

"I'm not disturbing you, am I, dearie?" Gin opened her mouth to reply as she peeled herself from the wall that she'd sprung to in Daphne's haste, but she was not quick enough. "I know it's early, but the day always runs smoother with a prompt start! And with the Ball coming up, I thought we should make a start on planning your dress! I have some beautiful fabrics, and well... between you and me, *I wanted you to have the first pick before I show Lady Flora.*" she said in a hushed voice, placing them on her bed and twirling around to face her, inhaling all the breath she'd just expelled.

Gin eyed the massive pile of richly coloured fabrics that flowed like a river, layer upon layer of rippling material. She had avoided Daphne's attempts to get her in a dress so far, but she had a feeling the Ball was going to be harder to get away with wearing her own tired clothes. With a cautious glance at Daphne, a sparkle of excitement glowed on her face.

She couldn't bring herself to agree or disagree, instead gave a wavering smile as she repressed the rising sigh that filled her chest. It seemed to appease Daphne as she spun around, spreading the fabrics across the bed. Reaching in the folds of her apron, she retrieved a rolled up parchment.

Gin peered over her shoulder at the luxurious fabrics in hues of reds, blues, golds, emerald greens and violets as they swept over her bed. They were colours of Autumn at their most opulent.

Daphne unravelled the parchment, arms wide as she held it open.

"I've been saving these designs for an occasion fit to bear them. I think this might be just that!"

Gin's eyes roamed over the intricately sketched designs. One had long fluted sleeves, trimmed with lace that hung down like delicate webs. The neckline scooped down with matching lace trim; the body fitted before an explosion of skirts cascaded to the floor.

Another had puffed off-the-shoulder sleeves that tapered into fitted sleeves to the point of the knuckles. The bodice of the dress was corseted with a two layered skirt. The outer skirt was plain and parted in an inverted v shape, revealing layer upon layer of the frilled inner skirt. Both were fit for a mediaeval ball, extravagance bursting at their seams. Her nose wrinkled behind Daphne's back. They were the exact sort of thing Lady Flora would revel in, all the while stunning everyone. But on her... she had the feeling she'd look like a clown's daughter.

Then Gin's gaze found the last design. She tilted her head as she studied its simpler, more elegant lines. It didn't look mediaeval at all.

Daphne's head twisted cautiously, eyeing Gin from under raised brows.

"This one." said Gin, placing her long chipped nail polished fingers over the third sketch. "It's so different from the others." she mused.

It appeared to be satin, the drawing positively glowing from the page. The figure hugging silhouette fanned out softly at the thighs. The squared neckline dipped down under the arms. It was held up with white bead straps, four on each shoulder, that draped down to just above the elbow. The beading continued around the neckline, almost like scalloped lace. The way the skirt fell to the floor and flowed behind made it look like a waterfall spilling out into a river. A pulse of excitement ebbed through her chest. It was beautiful.

Daphne laughed softly.

"Yes." she lowered her arms and gazed down at it, a slight smile skimming her lips. "It's one that has a special place in my heart. I was in two minds whether to show you, but, well..." she glanced at Gin, pausing for a moment, "It just seemed *right*. I don't know. It's silly, it's just a dress, for goodness' sake, and here I am getting all sentimental about it. I know it's different, perhaps *too* different?"

"No, no, I... I like it." said Gin, meeting Daphne's incredulous look with her own. The desire to wear a dress had never been so strong in all her life. It seemed to pull from the page.

Gin smiled softly, to confirm to Daphne that she really meant it, the shock still plastered on her face.

"Right! Well, I mean, in that case, let me show you the rest of the sketches for it!" she said, waving the parchment aside and reaching into her other apron pocket for a small wad of papers.

"Forgive me, I have to concede, I did not expect it to be such a simple decision for you... I'd come prepared for battle." she smirked. Gin jerked her head back.

"I'm sure I have no idea what you mean." she said airily, taking the new sketches from Daphne. A sly smile played on her lips. She had expected it herself.

But Gin's smile slipped, her body paralyzed, as she looked at the top drawing. Daphne's voice became an echo in a far-off room as she gushed over the design. Gin gripped the papers so hard that her knuckles turned white as an icy shiver ran down the nape of her neck.

It was backless.

Completely open.

The material came to a point in a V shape, at the base of the spine, the beaded trim joining onto four beaded straps, two of which crossed halfway up.

She swallowed involuntarily, opening her mouth to speak, but nothing came out. Daphne had finally stopped talking and had to double take at Gin's ashen face.

"Are you alright, dearie?" she asked.

Gin tried to speak again, but the fear that gripped her held fast. She couldn't possibly wear this. It was out of the question. The entire world would see her scars in front of the very man that gave them to her.

She shook her head, thrusting the papers into Daphne's hands.

"I uh... I need to think about it, that's all." she said, frowning as she did her best to keep her hands from trembling. Daphne looked from the papers to Gin, blinking rapidly. Gin clamped her lips, placing her hands on her hips as she waited for Daphne to leave. She couldn't look at her. The design had meant so much to Daphne and she'd dashed the excitement from under her. She cursed herself for it.

"Of course, of course, dearie." She said, trying to stabilise a faltering smile. "You take your time. I'll leave everything with you and you can ponder over them in peace. They're all so lovely after all. You must be certain of your choice!" Gin forced a smile as she tried to give a small nod.

"Thank you, Daphne." she said, listening to her footsteps scurry across the stone floor before they slowed.

"If I may just say something, which I know is none of my business, but it's been on my mind the last couple of days…" Daphne paused at Gin's questioning brows. "Well. I really wanted to apologise. I may have been a little quick to judge your decision to be Col's squire." She twisted her hands. Gin blinked. She knew she didn't approve, along with everyone else in the castle, but she had a feeling she had more of a soft spot for Col than she dared to let on, especially in front of Joseph. The fact that she brings Cora apples every morning spoke more than any words. And Col's absence from eating with everyone in the Great Hall meant he must rely on Daphne saving him food.

"It's ok, Daphne, really." she said, waving away her attempt to apologise. Daphne's brows knitted as she shook her head.

"No, it isn't ok. I should know better than to get swept up in the politics here. Josephine would be turning in her grave." she said, eyes on the high ceiling. Gin's head tilted.

"Col and Louis's mother?" she asked, recognising the name. Daphne pursed her lips and nodded slowly.

"See, Josephine and I were good friends. She was a ray of light in the darkest of times, she really was. Always had time for any soul that would accept her help, putting herself in danger in order to heal people. Fighting to get her craft to everyone she could. And Col," she almost whispered, closing her eyes, "he used to be so much like her. He followed her in all her plights."

Gin's mouth parted, not entirely sure she'd heard her properly. When Daphne opened her eyes again, they were unfocused.

"But life dealt them both a hand that crushed him. When Josephine was taken to the dungeons, I promised her then that I'd look out for him, but…" Daphne's eyes darted to Gin's, her attention back in the room. The pain behind them made Gin's chest cave as she watched her struggle to find the words.

"Life never got easier for him. It almost seemed as though bad luck followed him like a shadow. There's only so much you can do for someone who hasn't decided to fight back against the darkness. Someone who let that darkness take them completely... to the point I had to use the Crystals to bring him back." Gin swallowed, a cold wave of horror hitting her core. Her eyes prickled as she listened. Was she really saying that Col had tried to end his life?

"And as hard as I've tried, I haven't been able to break the armour he shrouded himself in. But you Gin... in the short time you've been here, I've seen a flicker of light in him again. It's been a long time since he's made an effort with anyone." Gin inhaled a shaky breath, averting her eyes. In her mind, Col was the one who was changing her. The notion that she was having any kind of effect on him seemed crazy.

"I know you're destined for Louis... but you're also casting light on parts of his brother that he'd buried long ago."

Gin remained silent a moment longer, unsure what to say. But in true Daphne fashion, she did not keep her in silence for long.

"I've absolutely gone and said too much, but with your presence here, I almost feel as though Josephine is reaching out to us all. Like she's found peace through you. I... I'm sorry. I don't..." she blinked heavily, brows raised as she floundered for words. Gin stared at her, waiting for her to speak, the early morning birdsong filling her ears in the quiet. She cleared her throat, the ache shifting as she found her voice.

"It *is* ok, Daphne." Daphne blinked, meeting her gaze. "You don't have to apologise. For *anything*." she said firmly. She didn't know what else to say, but she felt her sorrow like a deep well of cold, forgotten water. Daphne hesitated, before nodding, trying to hold on to a faltering smile.

"Breakfast! I, uh, I must get back to the kitchen. A castle full of hungry bellies awaits!" she said, scuttling from the room.

Gin was left gaping in her wake, her mind stumbling over everything. Col hadn't always been the black sheep. He'd cared about others. He'd fought to heal them. Like his mother. She couldn't imagine the pain he kept locked away that warranted the taking of his own life. A shudder scrambled down her spine at the thought.

She dragged her hands down her face, fingertips stopping on her mouth as her eyes flitted to the image of the backless dress on the bed. It conjured up that fear again, gouging at her stomach. An image of her in the middle of the room, the horrified faces of those around her as they gaped at her back, seared her vision. Louis and Col's twisted looks of disgust. Lady Flora's red lips parted beautifully in laughter. Joseph pushing her back into Slayton's poisonous web, ready to make sure she never sees the outside of the Hospice again.

Her face contorted, frustration ebbing through her veins like molten liquid. She reached a hand over her shoulder and into the neck of her top, letting her fingertips trace the tendrils of scarring that stretched to the tips of her shoulders. The permanent reminder of her weakness.

She gritted her teeth, eyes flashing open in a burst of anger, for it also carried a different meaning for her now. She dragged the tips of her nails along the painful scar tissue that had developed new nerves over the years, hitting a new nerve within her that had developed since coming here. Her desire to hurt Slayton, like he had hurt her. Not physically. Pain to him would not come in physical form. He was far too numb for that. It would come with the falling of his empire, his reputation. And the whisper of an idea came to her, connecting the cracks of her fractured past.

She marched over to the sketch that lay on her bed, staring down at it with her chin held high as the thought seized her mind. Maybe it was time to swallow her pride. To face the darkest part of her at the same time as the world.

Her chest filled with the beat of a thousand wings. Perhaps her weakness was her strongest weapon against Slayton. Showing the world how his true self was forever marked upon her would surely be the brick to pull in order to send his walls tumbling down. It was the last thing he would think she was capable of. That's why it was the one thing that she had to do, no matter the shame it would bring upon her.

She ran her fingers over the sketch of the backless dress, goosebumps rising on her arms. She knew this really was the one. It called her for a reason.

Gin bit her lip, looking over at the Crystal window she had spent the night pouring herself into. She thought of Col and the hurt that he'd had to deal with yesterday.

Desperation flooded her veins to return his Crystals to him, to confess to him about the scars and how she'd use them against Slayton. She would need him to push her forwards if she was to back down and lose her nerve. She'd tell Louis afterwards. With any luck, he'd be so repulsed that he'd back off.

Her mouth twisted sourly as she prepared to reveal the darkest part of her past to the person she was apparently bringing back into the light.

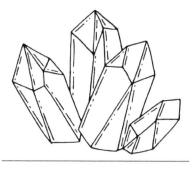

Chapter Twenty-One

The castle was an inhospitable place before the fires had been lit in the morning, but it wasn't anything she was unaccustomed to. The only rooms that had been lucky enough to have heating switched on at the Hospice were Slayton's quarters and the communal areas. Her room had always been encased in a chill.

She closed the door to the Great Hall, leaving the chambermaids to scurry about with logs for fires, and out into the fresh morning air. The light breeze blew through her warm brown hair, sweeping it over her shoulders as she hugged the Crystal window to her chest, still covered with a blanket.

Her footsteps tapped gently across the wooden bridge to Col's cottage. The sound of the small water cascade just beyond the castle kitchen that was usually drowned out by the noise of the crowds was trickling gently in the distance. She squinted through the fog that clung to the water like thick cotton, illuminated by the rising sun. But the chill that clung to the air bit greedily at her fingers. She tightened them around her swaddled gift as she blew out a scant breath of nerves. The possibility that it would just remind him of all he lost was ever present in her mind. But she had to attempt to heal some of the pain in the only other way she knew. By creating beauty from broken, discarded things. Just like she'd do with Hope, to make their day a little beautiful.

There was no light coming from the little windows of his cottage, so she opened the door gently, hoping not to wake him. But as the door unfurled, the unmistakable smell of alcohol pummelled her senses.

"No." she whispered, stomach clenched as she paused in the doorway. The fire had long since gone out and no lamps remained lit.

She rested the window pane against the wall and stepped in, searching in the gloom for where he normally kept a tinderbox topped with a candle on the windowsill.

Her fingers found the cold metal, and she wasted no time in getting the box open. She had tried her hand in lighting the tinder before, and it was not a quick process. After several attempts at striking the piece of flint against the steel, she finally created enough little embers that showered the char cloth in its small compartment. Blowing gently, she held the sulphur tipped wooden splint into the cloth and watched as the glowing sparks ignited it.

With the candle lit and replaced on the round tin box, she held it out to guide her way. It didn't take long until her foot collided with a glass bottle, sending it sliding across the stone floor and into another bottle. Holding the candle down, it was clear that both were empty.

With a heavy sigh, she shuffled towards the kitchen, following a devastating trail of more empty bottles, some in pieces as they'd smashed to the ground. Now she just needed to find their victim. And it didn't take long.

Slumped over the table, head in one arm, bottle in the other hand, dangling to the floor, was Col, completely out of it. She sagged against the archway, tipping her head back as she closed her eyes. Perhaps when she opened them again, it would be a trick of the low light and the bottles were, in fact, something else entirely, and Col was still tucked up in bed. It was a fool's hope.

Upon looking down, there he remained. She closed the gap between them, plonking the candle on the table.

"Col. Col!" She braced his shoulder, torn between a pang of guilt for leaving him all night and frustration at his recklessness. Daphne's words came flooding back to her.

There's only so much you can do for someone who hasn't decided to fight back against the darkness.

She gritted her teeth, nose wrinkling as she tried to push the words away. A swell of panic rose in her gut. He wasn't giving up on her now, not when she'd finally put her trust in someone for the first time. The thought stung, and she fisted his shirt against the pinch in her chest.

"Col, wake up! Before I throttle you myself." she said, snatching her hands back. Col gave a throaty groan, making no effort to move.

She stared wide eyed at the mess he'd got himself into. She knew he drank too much, but it never seemed to affect him. This time was different and it scared her. She didn't want to think about how much alcohol was swimming through his veins.

Her nostrils flared as she looked around the room, more and more empty bottles appearing as her eyes adjusted, until her gaze fell upon a bowl of water under the kitchen windowsill. She glanced back at him, and the empty bottle that dangled from his slack arm, snatched it up and marched over to the bowl. Air bubbles broke to the surface as she filled it with cold water.

She didn't hesitate in tipping it slowly over his head. She wanted him to feel the ice cold burn that stabbed at her chest.

Col started, grimacing as the water trickled down his face.

"What the-" he slurred, squinting up, eyes falling upon Gin, her arms now folded with the empty bottle in her hand. "Argh... your aim is way off, you know." he said, motioning to his mouth.

"I think you hit the target enough times yourself." she said coolly. He seemed to shrink a little under her hard gaze. "Tell me, how long did you leave it before getting up for your first drink after I left you yesterday?"

He frowned, running a hand through his wet hair.

"Well, technically, I didn't get up at all. The first was under the bed." he said, with a smirk before realising Gin was not amused in the slightest as she turned to leave.

"Hey, I'm sorry. I'm sorry, please... don't go." he said. She would have kept marching out of there if it hadn't been for the slight wobble in his voice as he asked her not to go. She turned slowly, wrapping her arms around herself.

"Why, Col? Why did you do this to yourself? I mean, I get that you're angry about the Crystals, it was terrible and you *know* I felt it too." her shoulders slumped, recalling the desolate pain she experienced, knowing it must have paled in comparison to his, "But why put yourself through *this?*"

Col took a deep, slow breath, eyes fixed upon the table and the bottles that lay there.

"Because it numbs the fucked up world, Gin."

"Until you sober up, then what happens?"

"I get yelled at apparently." he mumbled, rubbing his forehead. Gin was bubbling with frustration. She felt her body shaking as he refused to acknowledge the truth.

"You're killing yourself!" she shouted, unable to keep a lid on her emotions. Col faced her now, a low humourless laugh on his lips. She recoiled slightly, jarred by his reaction and the bloodshot whites of his eyes that replaced the sparkle.

"What could possibly amuse you about drinking yourself to the grave?"

Col's smirk slipped away, sourly. She had hit a nerve, and she relished at sparking something other than sarcasm from him.

"You haven't the first clue." he said, their eyes meeting, steel against steel. Her heart skipped as the heat rose in her cheeks. "You don't know the parts of me that I chose to leave in the past, and yet they still haunt my every waking hour and follow me into my nightmares. Why, in answer to your question, I choose to put myself through this... should be the other way around. Why do I put myself through every sober minute of the day?" his voice raised, nostrils flaring as he broke eye contact.

Gin hesitated, blinking away her blurred vision of cross tears. Her anger lifted a little as she looked at him, hunched over and full of invisible pain he shut her out from.

"Then let me in." she whispered, but he shook his head softly. Before she knew what she was doing, she had taken up the seat beside him, determined not to waste this moment of honesty he was teetering on the brink of. "You were the first person who I trusted enough to let into my past. And that is not a place I visit willingly. Please... trust *me* this time, Col. Let *me* in." Her voice was barely audible as she reached out to place her hand on his. Her fingers brushed the scars that marred his hands from battles, long ago. She swallowed nervously as she watched his jaw clench, his eyes sliding to their hands. It felt alien and easy all at once. The act of holding someone's hand, so simple and yet so outlandish. It wouldn't have taken much for her to pull away, but in this moment, she didn't want to.

"You don't want to see that side of me. You won't like who I am after... and you're pretty much the only person I don't want to scare away." he said, not meeting her gaze, his body tense. An ache settled in her chest at his words. He cleared his throat. "Louis would kill me," he added. She gave a tight smile, tightening her grip on his hand.

She was not letting up, even as her stomach roiled at what secrets he was keeping. She dug deep for words that would normally have stayed buried.

"The prophecy may tie my soul to Louis, but I'm *your* squire. You don't have to wear the same armour for me that you wear out there." she said. Even as she spoke the words, she couldn't believe the honesty that propelled them. She didn't want the knight that everyone else queued up to see. She just wanted to bring light to his shadows and it terrified her. But she couldn't sit back and let him ruin his life, for his sake and for hers.

Col sat with her words for a minute, shoulders curled, until finally he looked at her. His vulnerability was unfurling, she felt it somehow.

"I've never spoken about this to anyone. Not since it happened." he said, his voice fragile and husky. "I've never even had to speak these words before." Retracting his hands from hers, he tucked them into his arms.

Gin hardly breathed, paralysed on his precipice of letting her beneath his shield. He was trying to form the words in his head that were clearly eating him up inside. She wanted to reach in and say them for him as she sat with patience, his shallow breaths on the cusp of grasping them.

"I uh... I used to have a son." he said, his eyes dulled by an otherworldly sadness. Gin swayed slightly in her chair. Her body was numb with a cold shock that took root in her core. Two words resounding in her head. *Used to.*

Col frowned, swallowing hard.

"Max. My whole world squeezed into the five meagre years I had with him. He had the most unruly head of curls you'd ever see… as black as coal." his gaze wandered off to a past being uncovered for the first time in who knew how long. She almost felt him shift in time and space.

"People would tell me time and time again that he was the very image of me. Except for his smile… that was his mother's." he added, his expression turning sour. She could almost taste the bitterness in the back of her throat.

"His mother had never been the biggest supporter of my mother's gift. Afraid of what would happen if the wrong people found out. I don't blame her for being scared. If Lord Lowndes reconsidered, she would have been tortured into confessing witchcraft. And if she survived, she'd have been hung or burnt to her grave, anyway. Ironically, the very fate that she was destined for, thanks to the arrival of our very own Joseph Oldman." his nose scrunched up and Gin's heart plummeted, remembering Joseph's part in all this.

"There was no way Lord Lowndes could appease the people without giving them a public execution of my mother. And to make them see he was truly sorry for lying to them, I was made to watch... along with my wife and son. Then she left, taking Max, without a word. They were gone before I even had a chance to talk her round." He shoved the words out now. "I tried to make a better life for them after, but she could never forgive me. And she messed up. Made a deal with some crook for all the money she needed to start a new life in exchange for the Galaxy Crystal. When she couldn't find it, she took a few Crystals and a random notebook, thinking it would be enough to please them." His eyes darted to the ceiling as he rubbed his hands through his hair. "It was a mistake that cost her life... and Max's. And Lord Lowndes thought he could buy my forgiveness for his part in all the death of my family with the hand of his daughter..."

Gin took a deep breath as she clasped a hand to her mouth.

Col's chin quivered slightly as he continued to stare up at the ceiling.

"That's why I have to go back. I have to bring justice to those behind Max's death. I *have* to find out who was behind it." His jaw clenched and so did Gin's stomach.

"I'm so sorry, Col." her words felt so pathetic, so weak. But she failed to find anything to say that would be adequate to grieving the death of a child. She wouldn't know how to go on, knowing Hope was no longer of this world. His dependency on drinking to numb the pain suddenly became clearer. She found herself wishing to unload his heartache. But she knew that was a burden he would always carry. Gin pulled her chair closer to him, the legs scraping along the stone floor.

"Look at me." she said, softly. He lowered his arms, letting them slump to his lap, and looked up. "I know nothing and no one can ever replace Max. That place in your heart and soul is untouchable. As it should be. And drinking will numb the pain for a moment... but at a cost. And you know what?" She looked down at their hands. She thought of the reason she had come here... to show him her scars. They seemed like scratches in comparison to what she knew now. And then she thought about what he might do if he found out about what Slayton had done. He'd been more than willing to deal with him himself before. Who knows what he'd do if he knew the suffering he'd inflicted upon her. She couldn't risk him running into danger, losing his chance at finding justice for his own son.

She hesitated, blinking several times.

"I need you. For as long as I can have you." she said, her voice on the verge of breaking.

Col's eyes danced, narrowing and flashing with intensity before he held her hands, placing his forehead in them.

"I'm sorry. For being such a shitty human being."

"You're not-"

"I have been. I've been weak when you need me to be strong... and *that's* shitty." he said, looking up and resting his smooth chin on her fingers.

"Col, please-"

"Just... just let me finish." he pleaded. She was almost certain he could feel her heartbeat vibrating down to her fingertips. "I have to come clean about one more thing and before I do, I want you to know that since you came here, I've felt alive again. I've felt a sense of something that I didn't think I'd ever feel again. Feelings that my selfish ass certainly doesn't deserve. And you *do* have me... for as long as you need me." He wrapped his lips around his teeth as she smiled, her chest swelling with warmth. "But I will not hold it against you if, after what I have to tell you, you want nothing more to do with me. I will protect you, to the ends of the earth. I will get Hope back for you and see that Slayton is no longer a concern for either of you. Hell, I'll even make damn sure Louis is always the best man he can be for you." He looked away, as if the thought grated on him. "But I can do *all* that without you having to even look at me."

Gin swallowed nervously as her smile faded. The air seemed to chill around them, bringing a fresh wave of goosebumps along her arms. She wasn't sure she wanted to know what he was about to tell her, but the importance he put on it gave her no choice.

"Col, what are you talking about?" she asked, tilting her head. He cleared his throat. When he spoke, his voice was raspier than ever.

"One man involved *was* caught. The one who carried out my wife and sons murders. And Lord Lowndes appointed me to choose his fate."

Gin straightened.

"That's good. That at least one of them was held accountable." she said, cautiously.

Col closed his eyes.

"You don't know what fate I gave him yet." he said darkly. Gin gritted her teeth. He was right. And she wasn't sure she was ready to find out.

Col stood on wobbly legs, peering towards the living room window.

"Come on," he said. Her breath hitched in her chest.

"Where are we going?" she asked, afraid of the answer she'd get. He was quiet for a moment. Too quiet.

"To show you something I leave my brother to deal with because I'm too ashamed, angry and selfish to do it myself. You asked me to let you in, Gin... so this is me, letting you in on the darkest part of me." He walked past her, towards the front door, leaving her rooted to the spot, ice flooding her veins.

When she found the strength to stand, she followed him out, walking blindly past the Crystal window that still sat covered by the windowsill. Towards whatever darkness he concealed.

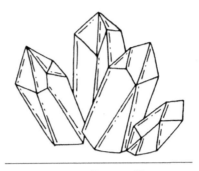

Chapter Twenty-Two

The smell of cinnamon and honey porridge drifted through the kitchen door that was left ajar, as Col led Gin along the narrow gravelled path. She paused when reaching the steps up to the kitchen, surprised to see that Col hadn't. He continued walking down a path that went seemingly nowhere, only to stop when he realised, she was no longer following.

"I'd quite like to keep all my limbs, so that involves keeping Joseph out of what I'm about to show you. Can't risk being followed." he said, answering her puzzled look. She nodded briskly and joined him.

The path narrowed as they followed it around the circular wall of a tall turret that jutted out. She looked up, tracing the dark stone with her eyes as it disappeared into the sky.

"Be careful down here. It's slippery." he said, edging down an uneven verge as the path tapered off into the grass. He turned, holding out a hand to help her. She thought back to when she first arrived here and how she was quick to brush the offer away. Now, though, as she slipped her hand into his calloused fingers, it felt... comforting. She caught his gaze as she hopped down, a jolt of energy surging through her chest. *That* was definitely not as comforting, the feeling of nervousness that she would get sometimes around him. But she found herself wanting more of it, searching for those little bolts of energy. It caused a confusion within her she was still trying to figure out.

They stayed close to the curving wall, following it all the way to the back, to where it should meet the castle wall. Instead, she was surprised to see the bottom of a staircase spiralling up through the turret.

"It's only five hundred and forty-two steps to the top." said Col, to Gins raised brows which instantly lowered with narrowed eyes. The corner of his mouth quirked briefly before the shadow of whatever he was preparing to reveal to her returned.

"You go first. Watch your step. They get pretty steep and narrow and can change height and depth on you. I'll stay close behind." he moved back for her to pass the little doorway. The smell of damp stone was heavy in the air and as she began climbing, she could feel it clinging to her skin, like a cold mist.

It didn't take long for her legs to feel the ache of ascent, the continuous spiralling movement dizzying. With a misstep on a step that was lower than expected and slippery, she backed into Col's chest. He caught her with a speed that had told her he'd been expecting it, his hands gripping her waist.

"Sorry." she said, cheeks heating as she cursed her clumsy feet.

"You're good." he said with ease, though he swallowed dryly as his cheek brushed the side of her neck. "I'm used to pushing men twice your size with the weight of armour weighing them down, up this beast. This staircase leads to the castle's largest defence point. The weapons we had to haul up here, hot oil, rocks... anything that could be used to drop on the enemy was fair game." his voice echoed up to her. The hair prickled the back of her neck, reminded of the horrors he'd seen, battles fought and lives he'd inevitably taken. It was easy to forget, being here in the modern day. Sometimes they seemed like actors playing a role with the attention of their fans, who so desperately wanted the chance to meet them. The way Joseph put them on show didn't sit well with her, as if he owned them. But put side by side with the hardships they left behind, it was hard to tell which was better.

"I don't know how you did it. How you fought in battles." she said, as the top of the staircase came into view finally. Gin took a deep breath of fresh air, leaning on the arch of the doorway, pausing for breath as he joined her.

"It was different back then. It was expected of men. I'm not saying I agree with it or that it wasn't frightening as hell, but it was a case of honouring your lord and family. Wars today are far less personal. Soldiers hide behind guns and tanks. It's an entirely different thing to look your enemy in the eye, watching life leave their faces as you sink your blade into their body."

She watched him in silence as he stared out across the open roof, the soft sunrise warming his face, lost in ill memories.

"What's worse is they aren't even *your* enemies. Just innocent men, often barely out of puberty, used as pawns in men's game of greed." He ran his tongue over his lips and shook his head. "That is something none of us miss. I'll give Oldman that much."

Gin smiled flatly.

Col pushed off the wall and leaned between a gap in the solid stone merlons of the top of the turret. He sagged, shoving his hands in his pockets.

"Some things, however, are impossible to leave in the past. No matter how hard you try." he said grimly.

She joined him, and he moved over for her to stand in front. She frowned, gazing down into the courtyard, trying to see what he saw.

"What are we looking at?"

Col leaned over her shoulder, his familiar scent tainted with alcohol once again. He pointed, and she followed his arm to the corner of the courtyard that she had seen Louis come out from, with his key. She swallowed, a pit forming in her stomach as dots began connecting between what they concealed in the dungeon.

She twisted her head towards him. His normally tanned skin had paled. His eyes were still tired and bloodshot, but there was something else that radiated from his core... a mix of fear and shame.

"The dungeon. That's the fate you gave him." It wasn't a question. She knew the answer before the words left her tongue. He winced before meeting her wide eyes.

"That, and a whole lot more." he said, tipping his head back as he looked down at the hidden doorway to the dungeon. "It was Louis who found him... Brandon." he said his name as if it left a sour taste in his mouth. "In the middle of disposing of my wife's body in the woodland behind the castle... what he left of it, at least." his mouth twisted grimly along with her stomach. "His part in it was purely for the high he got from killing and dismembering. The guards who questioned him were adamant that he knew nothing about who else was involved, who wanted the Galaxy Crystal."

Gin could hardly breathe while he spoke, her stomach hard with a knot so tight it felt like it would burst.

"What about Max?" she asked gently, afraid of the answer but desperate to know. His eyes searched the horizon. He opened his mouth, hesitating.

"I asked the guards to let me question him. Louis was against it. For my sake, maybe I should have listened. But part of me just *had* to face him... to *see* him with my own eyes, to believe such evil really existed. To make him answer to the man whose family he'd slaughtered. Not that it made an ounce of difference to him. Much like Slayton, I guess. Some people are just wired differently."

Gin swallowed, knowing exactly how some people seemed so far from human. Their insides are desolate of any redeeming quality.

"When I asked him where Max was, *where he'd left my son...* his hysterical laughter... over and *over,* telling me I'd never find his body. After what he left of my wife, I don't think I could've faced seeing how he'd left Max." he said. Gin's throat constricted. Seeing him so vulnerable and hurt hit a cord in her for so many reasons. If it had been Hope, life would be completely pointless. The reason that he drank himself numb was glaringly obvious to her now, no matter how much she wished he wouldn't. She bowed her head, sighing.

"I don't even know... what to say." She met his pained gaze, shaking her head softly. "Col..." she breathed, heart hammering in her chest as her hands did all the speaking for her. She reached up to his face, his usually smooth skin rough with the new day's stubble on her palms. That was when he finally looked at her, the world of pain behind his eyes unloading onto her. "Why didn't you tell me sooner?"

"Because you have your own problems to deal with. You didn't need the burden of mine." he said, thickly. A tear rolled into his stubble. She followed it, wiping it away with her thumb. She screwed her face up. He was right. She'd been so caught up in her own problems that she didn't even stop to think about anyone else.

"I'm *so* sorry. I can't believe how awful I've been. So oblivious to anything that didn't involve getting me to Hope. All the while you're dealing with this." she said, looking away, her hands slipping, brushing his chest as they fell.

Col's brow pinched.

"No. No, that's not what I meant at all." he said, chin dipping as he tried to see her face. But she couldn't meet his gaze, for the shame pricked her cheeks. "You have every right to feel the passion you do for getting Hope and helping the ones still there. For you, the heartache is still so raw. I've had a lifetime and more to deal with mine. So, I am here now for *you*." he said, brushing a lock of hair from her face as she looked up from under her brows. The light touch of his fingertips on her cheek left a simmering trail. He blinked, "For you to live out your destiny with Louis, however that may be. Just as my mother foretold." A line appeared between his brow, dragging his eyes from hers. Gin rolled her lips, the subject of Louis bringing an edge to the air between them.

"I realise now I can't be here for you if I'm constantly running from my demons. Demons that if I tell you about may just scare you away forever. But it's a risk I have to take. I want you to understand the parts of me I hide in fear. In shame." he paused, cheeks hollowing.

Gin clutched her arms and pulled them towards her core. Here she was, expecting honesty from him and yet keeping her scars from him. She had been bursting at the seams to tell him this morning, ready to bear all. But how could she tell him now? She dug her nails into her arms until it hurt. No. She wouldn't risk it.

"You don't have to hide from me. Whatever it is. I've lived in the hands of evil. I know you're far from that. You chose Brandon's fate based on the senseless murders he committed."

Col shook his head slowly, his jaw clenching as he scuffed his shoe along a crack in the paving.

"You haven't heard the worst of it yet." He looked back at the doorway to the dungeon, inset down a little stairwell. Gin clenched her teeth, waiting.

"When he started laughing about never finding Max's body, I saw red. I wanted to hurt him in ways he couldn't even imagine until his laughter turned to screaming. But even *that* didn't feel enough." He took a deep breath, and a shiver ran down Gin's spine.

It almost didn't even sound like his voice, etched in so much hatred. She tugged her scarf up around her neck, little beads of moisture clinging to the fibres from the warmth of her breath.

"Bringing him to the dungeon was a way of justifying my actions. It was a place of punishment. In the eyes of the law, you deserved whatever you got down there. So I took him to the brink of death in the most horrifying ways, healing him with the Crystals, only to do it all again... and again and again, over and over until I couldn't even *think* about anything other than how I was going to torture him next. It consumed me." Gin's mouth parted as she watched the anger in his eyes ignite, turning his blue eyes electric.

"I won't lie... I enjoyed seeing the agony on his face, hoping that he would feel all the pain and more that he put Max through. But it was never enough." he whispered, biting his lip.

"Louis kept telling me I wasn't achieving anything, only hurting myself by going down that path of vengeance. And when I finally listened, I couldn't even bear to look at Brandon. I let him sit in that dungeon for the rest of his pathetic life. No human contact, kept alive on the bare minimum, no bed to sleep on. Just four damp stone walls and a gutter to piss in. No matter how cold it gets, he has no shirt on his back, no blanket to warm himself." Gin barely breathed as the images of his fate rolled before her eyes.

"Louis is the only one who goes down once a day to give him what little he's allowed. He doesn't speak to him, doesn't even acknowledge his existence... I forbade it. I wanted him to suffer, Gin. In the most lonely and humiliating way. And from what little I've dared to ask, I succeeded. He is damaged in far greater ways than I could ever have inflicted with my own bare hands. He's not in this world most of the time, living in a world of hallucinations. Sometimes he'll just sit in the corner screaming at nothing Louis can see, yet the tears and sweat that drips from him, even on a frigid morning, is real. To him, it's all real. I broke him... what kind of person does that make me?" he asked, his gaze unfocused.

Gin carved her hand through her hair. She knew he was no white knight, but this? It was unthinkable. But who's to say what insanity would come from having to face your child's killer? It was something no one should ever have to find out.

She opened her mouth to speak, but no words were forming. His eyes slid to hers. "You don't need to answer. You can turn your back on me now with no shame. It's a burden to carry this. A burden that I don't want you to feel you have to hold on to. I can't even go near the place. I'm ashamed of it every single day and yet... I'm pretty damn sure I'd do it all again." he said, bracing a hand against the stone wall.

Gin felt the weight of his sorrow in her bones. But the horror of what Brandon was going through all these years later still turned her stomach. She gritted her teeth and opened her heart to the pain she would have felt if it had been Hope. It felt like it was being ripped from her chest.

"Col, you were put in a situation that nobody should have to face." She paused, closing her eyes, "If it had been Hope... if Slayton *ever* did anything to hurt her..." She focused on him again, his eyes wide, watchful, "I may not have lived through the time of torture and dungeons, but I'd fear the person I might become." Her nose wrinkled as a flash of anger surged her chest. "Our children are the reason we lose sight of ourselves. But they're also the reason we find the strength to find our way again. You're not a monster." she whispered, and she meant it. Col's face softened a little.

The wind atop the tower whipped her hair across her face. Finally, Col gave a heavy nod, the dimple in his cheek appearing. He looked back at the entrance to the dungeon, gaze narrowed.

"I just don't know that I can ever forgive myself. Not when I'd do it all again." he rasped. Gin followed his eyeline, swallowing the sourness that the dungeon door gave her. She thought of those she'd let down at the Hospice in favour of keeping Hope safe, and a tiny piece of a puzzle slatted into place.

"I don't think we always have to forgive ourselves. Maybe we just have to learn to accept ourselves and the choices we made in the situations we were handed." Col gave her a sidelong look. She watched her words sink in. "Let go of what you can't change... before it breaks you again." she breathed. Col breathed deeply, standing taller as he faced her completely. His brows twitched towards each other for a brief second before he looked down to his left hand, still burrowed into his trouser pocket. He was silent for a long moment, deep in thought, before he pulled his hand out, clutching a delicate gold chain. A pendant that swung as it emerged followed it, glinting in the sunrise. Her mouth parted as she watched it spin, gradually slowing until she could make out its form. It was the shape of a diamond, flat on one side but a pyramid on the face. The four faces were inlaid with a different triangular cut Crystal. As it stopped turning, she could make out the colours of each one. One deep green, one royal blue, one peach with golden flecks, and one bright blue. She'd never seen a necklace so beautifully unique. And then it clicked.

"The Crystals. They're the same as the ones in the device." she said, craning her neck a little closer. Col raised a brow.

"You don't miss a thing." he said, tipping his head. "It was my mother's. Only time I saw her not wearing it was when she hung from the rope tied around her neck. I held it so tightly as I was made to watch, it drew blood from my palms. I've always kept it in my pocket, where I can be sure of its safety. Don't think it would suit my rugged knight aesthetic." he said, shooting her a sly glance. "But on you? I think it would be perfect."

Gin dragged her eyes away from the dazzling necklace to him, then back again, mouthing the words she tried to speak.

"Col, I-I can't... it was your mother's, you can't part with it." she said, shaking her head slowly, her hand reaching for the red ribbon in her hair. "I know how special these reminders are."

Col leaned forwards, pulled her blanket of hair to one side, pausing to stroke the ribbon before reaching behind her neck to fasten the delicate chain. She didn't dare move. His face was so close to hers she could feel the warmth radiate from his skin. She swallowed, her heart almost leaping from her throat. He rested it upon her scarf, his fingers lingering on the pendant for a moment.

"I think she'd want her son's soulmate to wear it." he said, eyes lifting to meet hers. There was something sad behind them. She could barely breathe, aware of every muscle in her body as he stood before her. It was as though she was seeing him for the first time. No sarcasm or selfishness. The person he showed the world had fallen away. It wasn't all the broken parts of him he struggled to keep together, day in and day out.

She licked her lips slowly, pressing them together as she glanced down at the stunning pendant, mourning his fingers the moment they fell away.

"Thank you. It's the most beautiful thing I've ever had." she said, grasping for words, failing how she truly felt. But Col didn't seem to notice. He smiled softly down at her, gazing at the necklace on its new home.

"It comes with one more thing. A promise." he said, placing his hands back in his pockets and pulling his shoulders back. "That I won't let you or Louis down again. No more drinking. I will be here and not in my damn past. A reminder, every time I see it around your neck."

This time, Col caught the tear that rolled down her cheek, wiping it away softly with his thumb. A tear she hadn't realised was there until it was gone.

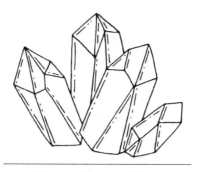

Chapter Twenty-Three

The way back down the spiralled staircase was just as dizzying, but it was at least easier on the legs. About halfway down, Col paused. The sun had risen now, but it was still murky in the turret. She could just about make out his profile as the sliver of light from the arrow slit glowed softly behind him.

"We can go through the castle. Everyone will be down at breakfast by now." he said, reaching towards the wall. Only as she neared the hazy light, she realised it wasn't a wall, but a small wooden door.

"I'll walk you as far as the staircase. You must eat. Gather some strength." he said, as the door groaned open. Gin's shoulders fell at the thought of them parting.

"You must be hungry, too. Won't you come to breakfast?" she asked, knowing it was hopeless to ask. He turned his head. They were the same height for once, as she was still a step up from him.

"I have a lot of cleaning up to do back home." he said, wincing.

"I can help." Her shoulders hunched up, nose wrinkling. He gave her a lopsided smile as he looked back at her.

"Thanks." His gaze was on her nose as he ran the back of his finger down it, her wrinkles sliding away with it. "But it's my mess. You've helped more than you know this morning." he said. She soaked in the softness of his eyes. All the tension that had built up while they were up on the roof, had melted away. Her heart felt fuller than it had done in a long time, knowing she'd done some good for him. A small smile flowered on her lips and remained all the way through the hallways, their footsteps the only noise as they slapped the stone tiles.

She walked a little behind him, watching him as he stalked through. The more time she had spent with him, the more out of place he seemed whenever he was in the castle itself. The opulence and finery seemed too delicate against his rough around the edges aura. His little cottage, full of notebooks and Crystals, what was left of them, and the smell of leather and sweet spice was as much a part of him as the battle scars and calluses on his hands.

When the lull of chatter in the Great Hall reached their ears near her staircase, Col stopped.

"I'll leave you to it." he said, eyes roaming her face. He lingered for a moment, his gaze drifting to the pendant. He smiled warmly before turning, and she trailed him as he left. With a twist to walk backwards on his heel, scraping his teeth over his lower lip in thought, he said, "As much as I was prepared for you to run... I'm *so* damn pleased you didn't, Sparkles." Before she could reply, he had rounded the corner, and she was alone in her whirlwind of thoughts. She couldn't describe the feelings she was dealing with around him. All she knew was that they intensified with each meeting, leaving her deflated as soon as he left.

The breakfast table was laden with food that would normally have made her mouth water. Fresh plump fruit assembled in mounds, bread that was still warm, blocks of cheese, hams and eggs from the chickens in the yard. But instead she sat in her thoughts, idly pushing a grape around on her plate.

Joseph paced at the end of the room, ear stuck to his phone as he bargained with some decoration supplier for the ball.

"We're going to be drowning in pumpkins by the sound of it." came a voice from beside her, pulling her out of her mind. Podraig took the empty seat next to her, eyeing Joseph as he pulled his chair in. She huffed a laugh, glancing at Joseph, squeezing his fingers of his free hand into his little waistcoat pocket, letting out the occasional agreement as he listened intently to whoever spoke on the other end of the line. Her chest tightened as she thought about the ball and everything it would bring with it. Facing Slayton, bearing her scars, collapsing his empire, rescuing Hope... leaving.

Her stomach roiled. She looked back at the grape and continued to push it around gently.

"Is everything ok?" asked Podraig, grabbing a chunk of bread.

Gin nodded quickly, perhaps a little too quickly, as she watched the steam swirl up from the warm fluffy bread.

"Yeah, yes. I am." she said, brow furrowed as if that was convincing enough. Podraig took a slow bite of bread, head cocked as he watched her. She looked from him to the sorry-looking grape several times until he finally raised one eyebrow. She wasn't fooling him, whatsoever.

"I just have a lot on my mind, with the Ball and the speech." she said, shrugging her shoulders.

"So, you're going to do it, then?"

Gin's eyebrows almost disappeared into her hairline as she nodded. Podraig smiled.

"I think it's a great idea. It will help people see past his fame. That there is a real purpose behind it."

She watched him in silence as he piled his plate with slices of apple and cheese.

"Oh, they will certainly see past the fame." she murmured. Podraig nodded, oblivious to the connotation behind what she'd said. His blonde hair flopped forward as he dug into his breakfast.

She watched as one of the castle staff tried to get Joseph's attention, bobbing up and down on his heels over his shoulder. He held a letter, flapping it slightly as he bit his lip. Every time Joseph turned in his direction, he'd wave it a little harder for him to take notice. But it fell on deaf ears every time.

"I think you squiring for Col has been a real eye opener for him, too. Alright, he's not the easiest person to get along with and you're here for Louis," Gin popped the grape in her mouth at last, crunching it with more force than necessary, "but it certainly pulled him back into this reality. I don't know how you did it, pulling him away from his Crystal hunt, which we all know he obsesses over." He shook his head into his plate, huffing a laugh. Gin glanced around the table, heads bowed in conversation and laughter as they ate. She wondered if they knew how close he really was to finding the Crystals. How close they all were to being able to go back. Or if they truly wanted to or not.

"He hasn't given up on his search. I don't think anyone could convince him to do that." she said.

"Well, you've distracted him, at least. Those Crystals are in his blood. He's most likely searched every square inch of this place but he'll continue on."

Gin froze, staring at nothing in particular. A sudden coldness hit her core as a thought occurred.

"Not every square inch…" she breathed, touching her fingers to her parted lips.

"Hmm?" mumbled Podraig through a mouthful of apple.

Gin twisted her head to him, but her eyes remained unfocused. She didn't want to believe it. But the more she thought about it, the more convincing it became.

"Col hasn't looked *everywhere*." she said, fixing her wide eyes on his, as his eyebrows squished together. She glanced around the table, making sure no one was listening, before leaning in.

"*The dungeon…*" she whispered.

She waited for the penny to drop. Sure enough, it came. She watched as it washed over him, like ice cold water. His shoulders rose with a deep breath as he swallowed his food, blinking rapidly.

"He told you? About… *you know*?" he asked, eyes sweeping those around the table too.

"Brandon, yes. I know." she said, heavily. "I also know that he hasn't been down there since coming here. Like you said, he's scoured this whole place. But not there." Goosebumps rose on her arms as the mingled look of horror and realisation devoured him. Podraig dropped the piece of cheese he was holding and clasped his hands in front of his mouth, elbows resting on the table.

"If he goes down there, who knows what he'd do to Brandon… or vice versa." he said, voice muffled behind his hands.

Gin thought for a moment. He was right, it would break him either way. And that was something she couldn't let happen. She gritted her teeth, looking down this fresh path that she knew she had to take. Her eyes shifted slowly to Podraig's and his shoulders slumped.

"No. No. You *cannot* go down there, Gin!" he breathed, wincing. "He was dangerous back then. God knows what viciousness he's capable of now!"

"He'd do it for me." she said instantly, knowing he would absolutely put himself in the path of danger. He'd do it for the sake of Louis not losing her. Podraig frowned.

"Look. If I can get him one step closer to finding all the Crystals, it will be the least I can do. He's done more than I can explain for me." she paused with a shuddering breath. "We both know he can't do it himself. And I wouldn't dream of asking anyone else to do it. It has to be me." She gave a firm nod, drawing herself up as he studied her. She was doing this with or without his approval. The silence stretched out between them. He rubbed his palms down his trouser legs and braced his knees.

"Well, if you're going, so am I." he said, staring down at his hands. Gin's eyes widened.

"No, Podraig. I can't ask you to."

"You're not asking, I'm telling you. What sort of man am I if I let you go into this alone? Besides, if Master Louis found out I knew, he'd never forgive me for leaving you to it." he said, looking at his plate of food and pushing it away gently.

She swallowed her guilt. She'd have to be mad to refuse his offer. It was perhaps one of the most stupidly risky things she'd ever decided to do. Not to mention the wrath she'd face when Col found out. She only hoped that her hunch was right, and finding the third Crystal would distract him from her recklessness.

"Thank you." she said earnestly, hands in her lap. He gave her a small smile and nodded.

"How do you plan on getting through the locked door though?" he asked, crossing his arms carefully.

Gin opened her mouth to speak when the oak doors swung open, presenting the very answer she had in mind.

Louis looked around the room, clocked her, and smiled broadly before heading their way.

"Leave it to me. Meet me in the courtyard at midnight." she whispered. Podraig's brow wrinkled, but he nodded all the same before they fell silent.

Louis strolled over, bringing a powerful scent of lemon and herbs that whipped through the air. His hair was slicked back with the fresh smelling oil concoction, no doubt provided by Daphne and her never ending botanical supplies.

"Good morning, Gin, Podraig." he said, standing between their chairs. Gin smiled up at him, taking a sip of water.

"Good morning, Master. I've just finished, I'll be heading straight to the stables." Podraig said, dabbing his mouth with a napkin.

"Ah, perfect. I'll need you to take the reins there this morning. I am hoping to acquire some of your time this morning, Gin." he said, eyes sliding to the pendant around her neck. Gin smiled inwardly, pleased he'd asked first as she instinctively shifted the pendant along its chain. He must have recognised it, but said nothing.

"Of course." She said, looking over his shoulder at the appearance of Daphne, who had joined the queue of people waiting to speak with Joseph. "Just give me a minute." she said, eyes fixed on Daphne as she rose. She marched over and spoke quickly and quietly.

"My dress. I've decided. I'm going for it. You were right." she said, giving her a warm smile. Daphne's eyes widened and opened her mouth to speak, but Gin turned, a pulse of energy flying through her chest at having taken the first step towards showing her scars to the world.

She eyed the line of people who waited at Joseph's heels. With a roll of her eyes, she closed in on him, to the surprise of those who had been waiting patiently. She was not waiting for his attention to be taken off business this morning. To be fitted into his schedule.

She cleared her throat, causing Joseph to swivel sharply on the spot, nearly crashing into her.

Louis raised his brows and huffed a laugh as he watched her. The look of alarm on Joseph's face melted into a smile as he saw her.

"The speech. I'll do it." she said, raising her chin. She turned to the line of gaping onlookers and caught sight of Daphne smirking in her amazement. Gin twisted back to Joseph, his face a picture.

"These people have been waiting a while now... if you can squeeze them in sometime today?" she quipped. Before he had a chance to process, let alone respond, she had crossed the room to join Louis.

"Col's squire indeed," he said, suppressing a smirk. Her chest swelled as the corners of her mouth twitched. She was seen. She was heard. Not brushed to the side as one of his little projects when it suited him.

Gin pushed open the oak door, the wood groaning under her hands, and let Louis pass. She savoured the silent praise of the eyes that trailed her. She had many hurdles to overcome, and this was just the beginning.

She followed Louis into the courtyard, not caring what he needed with her, eyes locked on the set of keys hung from the belt that hugged his hips. She gritted her teeth. If she was to enter Brandon's cell, she'd need those keys without Louis realising. His disapproval of the Crystals was no secret. He'd do everything to stop her going down there... she couldn't risk him exposing her plan to Col.

She and Louis had been at the stable yard for an hour or so, poring over ideas for her speech and how she was going to approach it. She didn't go into too much detail with him. As much as he encouraged her, she found herself closing up in his presence. She couldn't put her finger on why, but put it down to the soul connection playing with her head. Perhaps it was trying to protect him from doing anything that would put him in danger if he was to find out. She was past trying to understand it. Either way, her speech would need altering away from the brothers if she was to let her scars do the talking.

By the end of the hour, Louis folded his parchment up, tucking his notes in his pocket. Gin sagged her arms over the barrel they had used as a table, hoping this signalled the end of his questions. She still hadn't figured out how she was going to get his keys without him noticing, short of giving him the one thing she knew he wouldn't refuse in order to distract him. But the thought of giving him her first kiss, first *anything,* was not something she was prepared to do yet, if ever.

"I've uh… I've been thinking." said Louis. Gin, still slumped over the makeshift table, looked up. "It's been haunting me ever since you told me about Hope." he said, elbows on his knees. Gin sat up, Hope's name so soft on his lips.

"Go on." she prompted, curiosity picking at her. He studied her cautiously.

"Col wouldn't like it." he said finally, with the weight of a rock being dropped. Gin didn't like the sound of it already. She was doing a perfect job of going behind Col's back on her own. Her silence was enough of an answer as he sighed, frowning.

"What with the break in, I know he's been put through it. And I know you two have… bonded." He looked fleetingly at her pendant, before continuing, "But… I wouldn't suggest it if I didn't think it was an opportunity that we should pass up. I have a feeling you will want to hear this, despite the secrecy. It's your ticket to Hope without Slayton being in the picture." Gin's eyebrows drew close, her heart stumbling over several beats, trying to process what he was saying.

"How?"

"The Halloween Ball." replied Louis, holding a steady gaze. "After your speech. Slayton will be so busy licking his wounds, attempting to fix his image with the press and public, leaving the Hospice at its weakest, his best men by his side. Time that you, *we...* can take full advantage of. We could get her out of there." he said, leaning over the table. His fingers rested close to hers.

Gin scanned his face as she pondered the idea. Despite the logic, it didn't sit well. "It wouldn't be without danger. He'll still have men there. He'd never leave it unprotected." She said.

"Which is why we can't tell Col. He'd never let us go alone. And he has important responsibilities here to be risking getting into trouble. Without him here to get us all back to our time, people's dreams of seeing their loved ones would be shattered." he said, pain streaking his eyes. Gin didn't want to bring up the reason

Col needed to return. Col's vulnerability with her somehow felt like a betrayal to Louis and the soul connection.

"But what about you?" Gin asked, studying him carefully. "If you risk coming with me, then you might lose that, too." Louis's gaze drifted to the window and the quiet courtyard below.

"My dreams are all with you, Gin." His throat worked before he looked at her. She felt her heart throbbing in her chest a million times faster than it should. "I go where you go. Coming back here will not be an option after you have Hope. With Slayton at his most vulnerable... who knows what he or his followers might do to seek revenge."

Gin bit the inside of her cheek as her stomach dropped, the realisation dawning on her. Of course. She couldn't come back here and drag the castle and everyone in it into potential harm's way. She would have to leave. Why did that sting so much?

She glanced at Louis, his unyielding devotion to her shining brightly in his eyes. His fingers brushed hers. She inhaled sharply at his touch. His hands were softer than Col's, no scars marred his knuckles.

"Until we can be sure he and his men are no longer a threat to you and Hope, we'll have to lie low. I know a place. It's not far, but out of the way enough that you'll be safe until the authorities deal with them. Which they will have no choice but to do, no matter his ties... with such a public condemnation, people will not rest until he is behind bars."

Gin pressed her lips together and slowly withdrew her hand from his. His plan to stay with them was too much too soon. And yet his loyalty to her and her daughter tugged at something deep within. It fought with her as she tried to keep it from surfacing.

"Louis, you're setting yourself up for something that I may never be able to give you. Not in the way you want it." she said, unable to meet his gaze. She heard his soft sigh.

"I am under no illusion, Gin. I know you do not feel the same way about us. But I mean it when I say I am ok with that. Love of all shapes takes time. And if all I ever find in you is a friendship that is bound by two souls, then I will be content.

For that in itself is a gift." Gin finally looked up. His face broke into the warmest of smiles. "I will still be there for you and Hope in any way you'll allow." A jolt of energy rippled through her chest. His words stroked that part of her deep down that craved the suppressed idea of being safe. Cared for. She blinked away images of the future he'd put in her mind. She needed to focus on just getting Hope. Her future would not be decided until it happened.

She stared at her hands, thinking over the plan. It would still be risky. But it made sense to strike while Slayton was preoccupied. Col would be by their side in a heartbeat. She had no doubt about that. But that wasn't an option. He needed his freedom and safety to get his justice.

"We keep it between us then." She met his hardening gaze. "We don't tell anyone. Col cannot find out, Louis." she said, making her terms clear. He nodded.

"You have my word," he said.

"And when Slayton is locked away, we come back here?" she asked, tilting her head.

"If you wish to."

"And if Col hasn't left yet, when he does… you'll have to go too." she said, nostrils flared slightly. Louis inhaled slowly, his grey eyes searching her face.

"We could all go," he said after a pause. Her chin lowered, his offer taking her by surprise. Travelling with them had never crossed her mind. What kind of life would she build for Hope if they did?

"It would be too dangerous. I can't bring Hope out of one hell only to live in a new one." she said with a shake of her head.

"Then I will convince Col to stay until you and Hope have lived long and happy lives," said Louis, quick to quell her worries, leaning forward. "Like I said, I go where you go. If only to protect you."

Gin let out a soft, humourless laugh.

"I grew up with a monster. I don't need protection."

"Then I stay for friendship, if nothing else." he shrugged.

Gin's brows bunched together. She couldn't fault his determination to win her soul. Her lips pursed. She wasn't shaking him off yet.

"Fine. I'm in." she said, Louis's jaw clenched before his smile was back.

"OK. Good. We'll need a map of the Hospice, to plan our way in and out with ease. Do you think you can remember clearly enough to draw one?" he asked. Gin nodded slowly. She could have walked through that place with her eyes closed, its secret places permanently etched into her mind from nights spent creeping around in the darkness to help patients.

"Good. Once we have that, you can help figure out the best way in and out." he said.

She nodded again, absently. She wondered if she'd ever be able to return to the castle, even if Slayton had been locked away. What of his loyal men who have stuck by his side? Of his entire network, all the poisoned veins that ran through the country. Would she ever be truly free of him? She wouldn't risk bringing her nightmare to the people here... to Col.

Heavy footsteps entered the stable, pulling both of their heads back into the room. Podraig set down the two buckets of water he'd been carrying, beads of sweat dappling his forehead.

"Uh, I wondered if you were ready to suit up, Master, but I can come back if you are busy." he said, mouth pinched as he purposefully kept his gaze from drifting to her. She knew he felt guilty about going behind Louis's back with her. But it was turning out to be the day for it.

"No, I think we're done for now." said Louis, standing, planting his hands on his hips. Gin glanced at the keys on his belt.

"Yep. Finished." she agreed.

"OK. Come on then, Podraig." he said, leading him into the next partition where his armour was proudly displayed. She chewed her lip, watching them go. If he were to change into his armour, surely, he would need to remove his bulky keys...

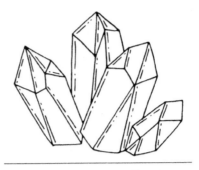

Chapter Twenty-Four

Gin's heart pounded in her ears as she listened to the pieces of armour being donned. The tying of buckles and clanging of metal on metal became more intense as time went by. It was a while later when they emerged.

Podraig gave her a short, wide-eyed look before tilting his head to where they'd dressed, then left the stable. She pressed her lips together, her belly fluttering. The keys were in there.

Louis stepped out in his armour. He really did fit the bill of a gallant knight. Armour perfectly polished, almost as if it hadn't seen a day of battle in its life. She knew differently, of course. He'd seen more than his fair share.

Her gaze wandered over him, and she smiled. He huffed a laugh, eyes darting down.

"It's as if you stepped out of a book of legends." she said, her shoulders slumping and brows raised. He winked before he put his helmet on, the visor left up.

"Someone's been reading the brochures in the gift shop." He frowned but his smile lingered as the trumpets signalled the gates opening.

Gin's stomach did a little flip. She always dreaded that noise. The castle was so much nicer when it wasn't teaming with visitors.

"You're more than welcome to work here on the map for as long as you like. I'll close the doors, no one will bother you." he said, squinting at her.

"Thanks. I'll leave the maps here for you to look over when you're free." she said, forcing a smile. He gave a quick nod and hesitated.

"It suits you." he said, nodding to her pendant. Her heart stumbled to keep pace as she floundered for a smile. But he saved her the trouble, leaving with one of his own.

Gin waited until he'd closed the stable doors, the half-light making the glow of the lamp brighter on the little table where she sat. She listened to his footsteps fade on the cobbles and the soft hooves that clopped behind him. She thought of the promise that had come with the necklace. Louis had no need to worry. Col would not make any move to get in his way. And yet the heat that seeped into her cheeks came with a lashing of guilt that she couldn't explain.

Her eyes fell upon the closed gates to the stall where he'd dressed. She clutched her hands together as she drew nearer, throwing a furtive glance to what she could see of the yard over the stable doors. The odd stableboy busied themselves about the place, sweeping clouds of dust around their ankles.

Gin held her breath and entered the partitioned dressing room, closing the gate gently behind her. She bit down on her lips, having no idea what excuse she'd give if caught rummaging around in here.

The light filtered in through bars that lined the top of the wall, casting linear shafts of light into the small space. The manikin now stood skeletal, no armour to exhibit. She padded the little pile of clothes he'd folded at its base, but no keys.

She frowned, eyes scanning the area for the items he discarded before suiting up. There wasn't a lot in the room, an area where visitors would come to admire the suit of armour.

She braced her hands on her hips, lip clamped between her teeth, when she noticed a small hole in the wall behind a wooden barrel. She closed in on it, clamping her arms around the barrel and shoving it out of the way with clenched teeth.

There, nestled in the little square hole, was a wooden box, big enough for one thing only.

She smiled, kneeling on the dusty cobbles, clasping the box with shaking hands and pulling it out. It wasn't dusty, a good sign that it was something of regular use. There was also no lock, much to her relief. She ran her fingers over the dark wood, turning it to examine. As she did so, something heavy slid to one side of it. She held her breath.

"Please be it, please be it." she muttered, lifting the lid with ease. She let her head tip skyward as its contents was revealed. The chunky blackened key lay inside on its large metal ring. She blew out a sharp breath, grabbing the key from within and placed the box and barrel back neatly.

She held it to her chest. It was heavy, the cold metal biting at her palm. She peeled back her fingers to look at the worn key. Her stomach clenched around a ball of nerves. She had no excuse not to go down to that dungeon now. Tonight, she'd face Col's fear for him. She hoped to the universe that she could get in there without Brandon noticing. Perhaps he'd be sleeping, too weak and tired to rouse. Nausea roiled her stomach as she clung to that hope.

"If you're looking for my armour to polish, you're in the wrong stall." came Col's distinct purr from behind her. She whirled, fingers closing around the key as she shoved her hands into her long sleeves. She tucked a strand of hair behind one ear.

"Col!" she exclaimed, panting, "You scared me!" She laughed airily, her eyes skimming around him. God knows how long he'd been there.

"Sorry," he said, tilting his head back as he leaned his arms across the top of the gate. "After the cold water treatment you gave me this morning, felt kinda good to scare you a little though." The corners of his lips turned up, and she scowled. She made her way to the gate and away from the box she prayed he didn't know was hidden in there.

"Yeah, well, you deserved that, whereas I was an innocent bystander." she said, swinging the gate forward so that he had to move back with it. He licked his lips, stifling the grin that grew.

She stopped where the gate came to a halt, tilting her head up at him. They were inches apart. Her breath hitched in her chest at the realisation. But Col remained as calm and collected as ever.

"I don't know about that. Sneaking around back here, Louis nowhere to be seen." he said, eyes crinkled around the edges as his grin widened. She choked a laugh and looked away.

"I wasn't *sneaking*. Louis caught me at breakfast and suggested we think about the speech." she said, her eyes flicked back to his. The humour that had danced in them moments ago was replaced by a shadow of concern.

"How did it go?"

She looked down, brows lowered.

"Uh… it didn't, really." she said, chewing her lip. "I sort of clammed up."

Col was quiet for a moment, trying to read her.

"It's ok. We can try again later. We have time." he said. The gentleness in his voice pulled a small smile from the depths of her.

"I thought you were tidying, anyway."

"I was… when I came across something." he said, eyes narrowed. He took her wrist gently and moved her to the side, closing the gate. She was acutely aware of his fingers on her pulse, dangerously close to the key she clutched.

"I wanna know why you didn't tell me." he began. Gin's heart was pounding as she tried to keep an innocent face. Did he know about her plan to go into the dungeon? Was he about to rip the key from her hand?

"You've been hiding quite a talent, Gin." he almost whispered, his breath tickling her forehead. She looked down as he bent to lift the cover off the Crystal window she'd made him and forgotten all about. She sucked in the breath that had caught in her throat, closing her eyes momentarily.

"Oh!" she breathed, relief calming her frayed nerves. "I'm sorry, I-I meant to give it to you this morning, but…" she trailed off, the morning's events playing between them.

"Don't be sorry." his voice lifted softly, searching her face like a caress. She blinked it away. "Gin. This is amazing. Not just your talent but your thought to take something weighted in sorrow and turn it into something *so* beautiful."

Her cheeks heated, gazing down at it.

"I just couldn't let you throw them away. I *felt* them… it was the rawest sense of pain. I had to find a way for you to keep them in your life. And to honour them, too." As she spoke, the chaos of her mind was soothed. A calm and warm feeling wrapped itself around her, like a blanket. It was coming from the Crystals, she knew that much. The longer she stared, the more intense it got. Their vibration easing hers. Her muscles loosened, and she found herself smiling a little.

"I feel it too. That feeling of peace." said Col, taking a deep breath. "You did that. You gave them that gift. And me." he added, brows knitting for a second. She reached out her free hand, running it along the top of the frame.

"They deserve peace." she said softly before lifting her eyes to meet his. "As do you."

Col's piercing gaze slid to her lips and her heart somersaulted in her chest. A heady dizziness sent a ripple of warmth through her body, spreading out from her stomach as his thumb brushed over her delicate wrist. She blinked, stepping back slightly. He cleared his throat and covered the Crystals again, releasing her. She held her wrist for a moment, adjusting to the absence of his fingers, wondering if he felt the same frenzy within, around her.

"Thank you. It means more than you know." He cocked his head up sideways, lifting his brows. Gin pulled her sleeves further over her hands. She smiled, but it didn't reach her eyes or her heart. If he did he'd brushed it off with ease.

"Just a hobby. Me and Hope... we'd sit and make things out of anything we could scrounge. Maggie, the carer who helped me when she was born, well, she would save things for us whenever she could." She sniffed, nose wrinkling up a little. "Our room was an explosion of colour," she laughed. "Hope loved it." Gin swallowed, her throat fighting against closing up. "It kept us sane, kept us distracted, always thinking about what we were going to make next. I mean, I no longer had a purpose there when I couldn't help others. It was our lifeline outside of each other." She bit the inside of her cheek, staring down at the covered pane. "And that brought me just as much peace making it."

Col nodded gently as he listened. With anyone else, she'd have felt silly to admit such an intimate detail of her life before. But she knew there would be no judgement from him.

"That hobby? That lifeline? It's a damn talent and I for one can't wait to see your room when we finally get to take Hope back." he said. Gin shifted her feet, coming out of her memories. The guilt that consumed her of having to keep her plan with Louis from him was stifling. But she knew what it was to love a child. She couldn't risk him losing the chance to seek the closure he needed. For she wouldn't rest if it had been Hope whose life was taken, the coward behind the curtain still roaming free.

All she could do was spread a paper thin smile on her face and hope that he would one day understand the reasons behind her betrayal of the trust he so openly gave her.

The peace of the stable was broken. Gin's head snapped to the doorway where Joseph stood, hand on his chest as he cleared his throat. Col didn't look, but somehow knew instantly who was there.

"Oh good, I wondered when we'd have the honour of your company, Oldman." he said, looking at his feet as he scuffed a weathered boot in the dust. Gin swallowed a laugh, keeping her eyes fixed on Joseph.

"I don't have the energy today, Col." he said, pinching the bridge of his nose, "I'm up to my ears trying to sort out the ball and do not need your sarcasm on top of it all. But I do need a favour, if you'll indulge me?"

"Always." said Col, leaning into a twist to face him. He beamed as Joseph stared him down, nostrils flared.

"Tarrick is down, pulled his back out in yesterday's joust. I need you to take his place against Louis. If you think you can manage to not cause too much damage?"

Col puffed out his cheeks and released it, scratching his cheek.

"It's a stretch. But I think I can manage." he mused. Joseph huffed and turned his attention to Gin, offering her a flash of a smile. She could practically feel the annoyance he was bottling. He also hadn't forgotten their earlier meeting by the trepidation in his stance. She lifted her chin slightly, making it clear she would not be walked over anymore. If he thought adoption papers would put a claim on her, then he needed to re-think.

"I uh... I'm glad you're here, Gin, as I was hoping to go over your speech with you, as you have so kindly agreed to it." he said, running a hand over his beard. She felt Col's eyes slide to her without even having to look.

"You want me to joust and yet you try to take my squire away? Who's going to dress me?" said Col, jumping in. She glanced between them, open-mouthed as tensions mounted. "You'll have to see if you can book her into your schedule later, I'm afraid." he said, sucking air between his teeth.

Joseph's eyes narrowed, thin slits piercing Col's.

"You're more than capable of dressing yourself, Col." he said, turning back to Gin and opening his mouth to speak.

"I don't have a squire for aesthetics, Oldman. She's gotta pull her weight." he said, picking at some fluff on his sleeve. Gin snapped her mouth shut as Joseph rolled his eyes.

"Gin, I would really appreciate a moment of your time... when you are *not* busy." he added, looking only at her.

"Of course. I'll come and find you as soon as I'm not needed." she said, lifting her chin. Joseph smiled and pulled his shoulders back.

"Thank you. This speech is important." he said as he pulled out the buzzing phone from his pocket. He looked at them both, holding up a finger as he went to answer.

"Go ahead. We'll see when we can pencil you in." whispered Col, crossing his arms. Joseph, near seething, rolled his eyes and scurried off as he greeted the caller on his phone.

"You think he found anything back there?" asked Col. Gin, looked at him and he rolled his eyes dramatically, mimicking Joseph. She smirked before remembering the key she still had to hide somewhere for the day.

"You should go get dressed! Probably not the best idea to annoy Joseph any more with a late arrival." she said, stepping aside to clear the path to the stable door.

"*Argh, but it's so much fun.*" he whined. Gin puckered her lips to suppress the smile that tugged. "Alright, alright." He looked down at the floor, shoving his hands into his pockets. After a pause, he spoke. "You, uh… you can learn the ropes if you want to." he said, meeting her gaze.

She did a double-take as her heart tried to jump out of her mouth.

"You mean... the armour?" she twirled her finger in front of her, wondering if she'd heard him wrong. Col held her gaze.

"Only if you *want* to. I only said it to get Oldman off your back. I can manage, like Oldman said, always have."

Her toes curled in her shoes as an internal argument played out in her head between being his squire and Louis's supposed soulmate. The thought of being close enough to put his armour on him both terrified and yet intrigued her, more than it should. She'd never entertained the notion that actually being close to someone could elicit such a feeling. Her instincts had always screamed at her to run whenever someone drew near. But now... standing there in front of Col, she wondered what it would be like. She caught her eyes lingering on his chest and hastily looked away, blinking hard. She wanted to run, she wanted to stay, and she had no idea what was going to come out of her mouth as she blindly let go of her instincts.

"OK. Need to pull my weight, right?" she swallowed. But Col was as calm as ever. He flashed her a smile that warmed his eyes and gestured for her to lead the way out.

"Um, actually. I'll meet you in two minutes. Just going to finish up here." she said, running the palm of her free hand down her thigh.

His eyes narrowed ever so slightly, but he left her to it.

In the silence of the stable, she breathed in a shaky breath of musty air as she thought about where to hide the key. In here was not an option. She might not be able to come back for it later. Gin chewed her nail before deciding to keep it on her, stuffing it into the top of her leather boots. She stamped gently, feeling the cold metal slide into a mildly comfortable position, and made her way to the stable door.

She shook her head slowly. She didn't know what had made her agree to dress him. Nor did she know whether to thank or curse it.

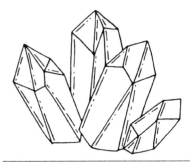

Chapter Twenty-Five

Col had lit a lamp in the cubicle, making it lighter than Louis's. The sun also
licked more of the walls in here. Gin clenched her jaw, wishing for the dim
lighting of before... he was sure to notice her flushed cheeks. Whatever confidence
made her agree to this had apparently bolted, leaving her shaking in her boots.
She loitered by the door, clutching the handle with both hands behind her back.
Col looked up from adjusting the sleeve on his padded jacket. Beside him, his
armour stood proudly on its manikin, freshly polished by her own hands.
He unhooked the lower leg pieces and held them out. Gin stared at them
momentarily before taking them. Her clammy hands left finger marks on the cold
metal.

"This is a first for both of us, so don't panic. We'll stumble through it together,
Sparkles." he said, the smile in his voice clear before she even looked up. Grateful
for his understanding, she returned a small one of her own.

"We'll start at the bottom and work our way up," he said casually. "The greaves
you have there, they protect the shin and can be a little tricky to get on as they are
shaped to fit." he said as she knelt by his legs, her knees wobbling slightly on the
cobbles. She took one greave and attempted to place it around his shin, eyes fixed
on the task at hand and not the lower half of his body that she was now inches
from. She slid the metal down a little until it seemed to fit.

"How does that feel?" she asked, finally risking a glance up at him. She was used to his height by now, but from down here, his legs seemed even longer. The corner of his mouth twitched upwards.

"Not bad," he said, pausing. "Now, just buckle it in the back."

Glad of the excuse to look away, she went about fixing the buckle before moving onto the other greave, her racing heart beating mercilessly in her ears.

She sat back on her heels once done, letting Col shuffle his feet.

"Good. Next, the thigh plates, or cuisse, as they're formally called." he lifted one cuisse from the manikin. It was larger than the greaves, protecting the thigh, knee and just below.

"You'll notice a little peg on the greaves and a hole just under the knee on the cuisse. This joins them securely when you fasten the buckles at the back, stopping them from slipping down." He tapped the cuisse gently and handed it over. She needed both hands to hold this piece, the size making it a lot heavier.

"You ok?" asked Col with a wince as she lifted it to his leg. Internally, she was a thousand things. Fine was not one of them.

"Uh huh." she lied, gritting her teeth as she slotted the peg through the cuisse and attempting to fasten the buckle at the back. The thigh plate slipped off the peg before she had the chance, her hands whipping up to brace the upper thigh plate.

Col chuckled softly. She blinked slowly, raising her gaze to his rather amused one. Her cheeks heated, more so at the position of her hands, braced on either side of his thigh.

"You're more than welcome to help." she quipped, one brow raised.

"Where's the fun in that?" he asked, but reached down to hoist the cuisse up again.

She slotted the peg back in with perhaps more force than needed, eyes dashing to his as she buckled it quickly. The muscles at the back of his thigh twitched as she ran her finger over the belt to smooth it down and she swallowed hard.

"Thank you." she said heavily, sitting back again. Col nodded to the top of the cuisse.

"Not done yet, Sparkles. See these holes?" he asked, running a finger over the part of the plate at the very top of his leg. "This is where you will need to tie it to my armour jacket. I hope you're good at knots." he added, head tilted back a little.

Gin's heart now threatened to escape through her mouth as she registered the holes that ran over the top of his thigh. She had absolutely no idea how she was going to tie a knot while her hands trembled like jelly. She could have kicked herself for agreeing to this. But instead of backing out, she took a steady breath, listened to the sound of chatter outside and reminded herself that she was not in Slayton's Hospice. She was free to go if she pleased, and Col would gladly take over from her. But she would not let the fear that crept through her veins take control.

She took the leather ties that hung from the bottom of his jacket, catching his eye as she did so. She was sure he was enjoying this, but the sight of his throat work as her fingers brushed the fabric of his trousers made her question if he was as confident as he made out.

"Do you like bows with your knots, *Master*?" she asked, testing out his logic of humour to deflect from her rising nerves. Their eyes met momentarily.

"Who doesn't?" he said, defiantly.

Gin looked away and smiled softly as her fingers went to work, sure he could feel them shaking.

As she finished fastening the other cuisse, her face so close to his thigh that her breath fogged up the surface of the metal plate, she noticed a large dent in the front, just below a ridge of metal that ran horizontally near the top.

Her brows twitched, and she sat back on her heels slowly, studying it.

"That must have been one hard hit." she said, running her finger over it before letting her arm drop to her lap. Col looked down at the dent, the muscles in his jaw clenching.

"It was. One you feel for a while after, even through the armour. One battle that stays with me the most, in fact." A shiver tiptoed down Gin's spine. He hadn't spoken about the battles he'd fought before and she hadn't the heart to ask.

"The Battle of Towton. March twenty-ninth, 1461. History books tell you that the rivers ran red with blood for days after." he paused, breathing deeply, "A truth that haunts me to this day."

Gin's mouth parted slightly. Her breath hitched in her throat as a feeling of despair crept over her, as if she felt it from him. When he spoke again, his voice sounded weary, as if stretched too far back into harrowed memories.

"We were completely outnumbered. Part of our force hadn't shown up. I was sure that was it... lights out. Part of me was ready for it, too. The part of me that longed to be with Max again." Gin watched his fingers clench by his side and release.

"It wasn't until Lord Fauconberg made the smart move of using the relentless wind that chilled the armour through to our bones, to our advantage. He ordered our archers to the take point. Their arrows found their targets swiftly. But the hours that followed were truly the toughest battle I've ever had the misfortune to be a part of. It felt like days... *days* of endless killing. The hours trickled by, torturously. Hand to hand combat mostly, but for the few of us who were lucky enough to be on horseback, we had the task of taking the brunt of the battle." He brushed his thumb over the deep groove on his armour. "I didn't see the horseman coming straight at me. My lethargy took hold for a second, and that's all it took for his lance to strike. Headed straight for the gap in my armour around the groin. If it weren't for this stop-rib, it would have rendered me among the dead on the ground." His cheeks hollowed, eyes fixed on it.

Gin now shook for a completely different reason. Nausea rippled through her, the feeling of deepest fear and loss grasped at her insides. It was as if she were there, on that bloody battlefield, unarmoured and vulnerable. She didn't speak and wasn't sure the words would leave her mouth even if she tried.

"Instead, I laid among them, very much alive, face to face with my fallen men. Their blood-soaked skin made the whites of their eyes glow like stars on a clear night. The terror... with them until their last breath." His face contorted, and she felt the flash of anger. White hot through her frozen body. How was she feeling the intensity of these emotions as if they were her own? Was it the Crystals? Was their energy linking her feelings with his? Their ability to connect with the Crystals must be more than it seemed.

"In that moment, as I laid there, the Duke of Norfolk's men arrived. It stole the attention of my attacker for long enough that I rose, took up my fallen blade," he clenched his jaw, "and sank it through the same gap in his armour that he'd been aiming for in mine."

Gin closed her eyes and let out a shudder. It drew Col's attention and when she opened them again, he knelt in front of her, searching her face with worry etched into his face.

"Are you ok?" he asked. She rubbed her chest, the wind knocked out of her momentarily. She nodded, despite the shock.

"No, you're not." he grimaced. She met his gaze slowly, trying to let the nausea pass.

"Is it the Crystals? Do they have the ability to make us… *feel* what the other feels sometimes?" she asked, catching her breath. Col frowned, his eyes blazing a trail over her face.

"I'm not sure. It could be. I've met nobody who feels them like you do." he said, searching her eyes. "They've latched onto you, that's for damn sure."

Their gaze lingered, and an entirely new feeling broke the nausea. A tingling in her chest as she skimmed down to the dimples around his mouth. But a squeal from behind her broke the feeling.

"No way!" cried a woman, peering over the low stable door they'd pushed open. "Sir Col! Are you kidding me?" Gin looked around to see a group of visitors being joined by more, eager to get a glimpse of the famous knight. She glanced back at him, surprised to see that he still looked only to her, sighing as he rose.

Gin took a deep breath while he busied himself detaching the breastplate from its stand and stood, knees threatening to give way beneath her. She willed them to steady as she took the breastplate from him. The dimples around his now clean-shaven jaw deepened as he cleared his throat.

"You OK to continue?" he asked, narrowing his eyes.

"Yeah." She didn't have a choice. They had an audience now.

Col scanned the gathering as if reading her thoughts.

"You've joined us as we move to putting on the breastplate. A piece of armour I usually put on myself, through a lot of practice... and a *lot* of swearing. However, my squire is assisting me today." he said, eyes flicking to hers. "Let's see who does the most swearing now." he quirked an eyebrow to laughter from the audience. She cocked her head, ready for the challenge.

Col raised an arm for her to wrap the armour around his chest. He held the bottom that stopped by his ribs and hoisted it up a little.

"The buckles fasten over the shoulder and under the arms." he said to his audience, but she was sure it was more for her sake.

She reached up to the buckles, his arm pressed against her ribs as she stretched. There was no doubt that he could now feel her heart beating against his arm. Their eyes caught and the muscles in his jaw clenched. Was she really capable of making him nervous? Or was it just her projection of feelings he felt because of the crystals? There was so much confusion around her connection to Col.

The placard came next, wrapping around his stomach and fastened down the side. She worked as quickly as she could, all too aware of the eyes that watched her every movement.

The vambrace slipped on to each arm, tying at the point of his shoulder, shielding his arms down to his wrists.

"The pauldrons, they protect the heart from any weapons that might slice in from the side and sit over the shoulder." he said, handing it to her. She pulled the leather straps into a tight knot and moved onto the underside of his biceps, where it buckled. The weight of his armoured arm pressed upon her shoulder as he rested it for her to work. She felt the lightest touch of his fingers against her back. She drew in a sharp breath and straightened as shivers danced over her scars. Col hadn't noticed. His head turned, fetching the other pauldron. She tried to shift so that his fingers moved, but the weight of his arm was too strong now that it was sheathed in armour. Her body flooded with a cold flash as he hauled his arm off and released her, getting the other side done as quickly as possible. She arched her back away from his hand this time, causing her chest to sit flush against him, thankful that his armour sat between them.

"The helmet and gloves will go on last, right before the joust. You'll be wanting to make your way down to the arena if you want to get a good view... which, I'm assuming you do." he said, with a wink to the crowd, who dispersed excitedly. But the girl who had squealed hovered, biting her lip as she swept her golden hair back.

Gin's gaze flitted between her and Col, the girl clearly wanting to approach him. Col, however, was too busy adjusting his armour to notice.

The girl bouncing on the balls of her feet stopped as she looked at Gin. When she first arrived here, Gin would have laughed at this foolishness. But be it the stress of the break-in or hearing about Col's son and Brandon... she found herself putting her guard up. Col did not need this right now. She crossed her arms, matching the glare the girl was shooting her way.

It seemed to have the desired effect. The girl spun on the spot, her long hair whipping around her head, and left.

"First healing, then art, now bodyguard... you're full of hidden talents, Sparkles." said Col, glancing at her. He'd known very well that the girl had lingered. She pursed her lips.

"I merely stopped her from embarrassing herself." she said, picking a piece of straw off her jacket. The corner of Col's mouth twitched.

"Noble," he said. She felt his eyes on her. "Makes me wonder what other talents you're hiding."

Heat flooded her cheeks as she continued to look anywhere but at him. But his footsteps neared, coming to a halt next to her. She dragged her gaze to his, her breathing seeming too loud in the small space between them. Her eyes snagged on the dent over his thigh again, seizing the opportunity to move on from this.

"Why not get the dent hammered out? The other knights are constantly having their squires run back and forth to the blacksmiths. Why keep it when the memories are so painful?"

Col's eyes danced over her face.

"It was part of my life. It shaped me as much as it shaped my armour. I don't want to forget that battle or the man who tried to kill me, only to meet his end instead. Those that fought, both friend and foe, deserve to be remembered. War was not their doing, just their misfortune." His eyes narrowed, lowered, and then met hers again.

Words failed her at that moment. All she could do was nod feebly. He could have faced that part of his life with anger and hatred and have had every right to do so. But he chose to honour those who lived and died through it. She swallowed the lump in her throat. Enough. That was enough of memory lane for today.

"So." she said, stepping back to admire her work. "How did my attempt fare, Master? Would I make the cut for a Medieval Squire?"

Col drew himself up, trying out the movement of his newly donned armour.

"Not bad. But I wouldn't bring you back there for all the whisky in every plane of existence." His eyes roamed over her once and she felt a sudden flash of fire in her belly.

"You don't think I could handle it?" she asked, brows raised as her chin dipped. She survived growing up in literal hell. At this point, the hardships of the Mediaeval times seemed like paradise.

"I don't doubt your backbone, Sparkles. But I would be responsible for your being there, and I'm far too selfish to worry about keeping you safe from the perils of merely stepping outside the castle walls."

She found the tension leave her wound up muscles at his words. No one had ever been *worried* about her wellbeing and it left something warm expanding in her chest as his gaze lingered. She forced the feeling aside and cleared her throat.

"Go easy on Louis out there. I don't want to have to pull another lance out of any part of his body today." she said, patting his cold breastplate, backing away. But Col caught her hand before it left the metal. Gin's mouth parted, staring at his hand on hers. There were those rough hands.

"Don't worry. I'll return your honourable knight to you unscathed." He gave her a lopsided smile, but it didn't reach his eyes. For some reason, the bitterness in his voice twisted her gut. But the way his thumb brushed her fingertips stilled the air in her lungs. She made her feet back up some more, slipping from his grasp, until turning towards the stable door. She lifted her face to the sun as she walked across the courtyard, letting go of a trembling breath. And even as she walked away from Col, she wanted to turn back. As much as the swirling madness he elicited within her spooked and confused her, she found herself seeking those moments. But the reminder of her ties to Louis sat in her stomach like a rock. So did the fact that she had to leave soon. They were on two unique paths. She knew that from the start. Why was that suddenly weighing on her chest differently?

Pushing those maddening thoughts aside, she made her way to the arena, the metal key in her boot rubbing her ankle, reminding her of the looming night ahead. She had absolutely no idea what kind of man she'd meet down there, or if, in fact, he was still a man at all. Perhaps his mind will have taken his humanity completely, leaving some form of beast in his place.

But it would be worth every terror inducing heartbeat to hand Col a Crystal. A chance to give him something in return for his help… before she had to leave him and this place behind her.

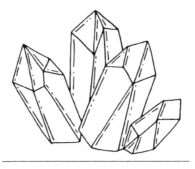

Chapter Twenty-Six

The afternoon brought unseasonal rain and a brisk wind. Visitors huddled under large umbrellas and poured into the cafes and shops, waiting for it to pass. Gin, however, was quite glad of the peace it brought to the stable yard. The knights busied themselves in their individual partitions, their squires at every beck and call. She had tucked herself into the back of Col's bay with his pile of armour, polishing it as she watched the raindrops bounce fiercely in the empty cobbled yard.

Col had taken the job of mucking out the old hay, a job she was grateful he'd shouldered.

There was irony in the weather. Her mood had sullied somewhat as the day went by, her thoughts snagging on the night ahead. The hospice had prepared her well, in a way. The darkness that she used to seek and the patients that she would tend to sometimes lived in a world of their own. But they had never been cold-blooded killers. Goosebumps erupted over her arms and neck.

"You know, armour isn't much use if it has holes in it." Col rested an elbow on the low wall, eyeing his helmet she'd been polishing in the same spot for goodness knows how long. She tore her eyes away from the yard and looked down at the very shiny circular spot under the cloth. Her nose wrinkled into its familiar lines.

"Sorry." she said, starting on a new patch.

"Don't be. I'll be impressed if you can get it all looking as good as that spot."

Gin didn't answer, her mind wandering again. She only looked up when faced with Col, who'd pulled up a low stool, his brows knitted.

"You mulling over something heavy in there?" his eyes roamed up and over her forehead. She shrugged with a shake of her head, staring intently at her work.

"Just thinking about what I want to say in my speech, that's all." She lied, although having thought about that now, she also realised that she needed to think seriously about that too.

Col was quiet for a moment. She almost wondered if he could tell she was not telling him the truth somehow. The full extent of the Crystal's effect on them both was still so undetermined. Who knew what it was capable of?

"Well, if the rain doesn't ease up, there won't be any more shows today. Why don't you take the rest of the afternoon to work on it? I can finish making holes in my helmet." Gin's eyes slid to his. They were lit with a twinkling glow of mischief, one that she found hard not to succumb to the warmth of.

"Are you sure?" she asked.

"Course. We can go over what you come up with this evening."

Gin drew a deep breath and nodded, despite knowing full well that she'd be busy this evening. She'd deal with that issue later.

"Thanks. I appreciate it." she said, wiping her hands on her leggings as she stood.

"Don't mention it. Just tell me, is there a certain direction to rub the cloth to get a nice neat hole, or do I have free rein?" he asked, squinting up at her sideways before jerking backwards as she threw the cloth at him. As she walked out, she heard him call,

"I'll take that as free rein!"

She chuckled to herself as she darted through the yard, holding her hood up against the relentless wind.

Gin had lit no lanterns in her room. The only light came from the fire that sparked gently. And as the clock drew ever closer to midnight, the room became obscured as the fire dwindled, until her surroundings were licked with only the light of the moon.

She peered out of the window, past the silent courtyard and into the shrouded dungeon. If Podraig was there, he had concealed himself well. She clenched her jaw, picked up the key from the table, and marched out into the slumbering castle.

It was a different place at night. The warmth of the fires and buzz of excitement that usually charged the air were replaced by looming shadows of armoured statues and endless hallways. She'd fear the ghosts that dwelled here if they weren't alive and well, slumbering in their beds.

The crisp night air bit through her jumper, raising goosebumps on her arms and neck. The only other sound that met her as she crossed the gravelled courtyard was the distant call of an owl.

She kept to the shadowed edges of the courtyard that hugged the walls, hoping she was still as good at disappearing as she used to be.

The little trees around the dungeon doorway grew nearer and still no sign of Podraig.

Her wide eyes darted around the courtyard and to the castle windows. They were all shuttered except for hers, void of life. She held her breath and dashed across the break in the shadows and behind the curtain of trees. Crouching low, she was faced with the castle wall. Her gaze travelled down, connecting with the top of the dungeon door that peaked out of the stairwell. A ribbon of moonlight illuminated it. She studied the worn wooden door, tracing the grooves with her eyes down to where they disappeared beyond the ridge of the stairs, when suddenly a head popped up, big blue eyes wide in the moon's light.

"Podraig!" exclaimed Gin, slapping a hand to her chest, heart beating wildly.

"*Sorry!*" he winced. "I didn't mean to startle you, just didn't want to risk being seen." He whispered as Gin scampered over to him, crouching at the top of the stairs.

"I haven't been able to settle on anything today. I got here far too early. Can hardly feel my legs." he breathed, blowing into his hands to warm them. Gin gave him a clenched half smile.

"Oh, Podraig. You should've come to find me." he looked away, shuffling on the spot.

"I wouldn't dream of disturbing you in your room." he said, brow furrowed. "That would be improper."

Gin's thoughts wondered to Col and how he had no problem with it. How she'd even woke to find him there. What would Louis have thought if he'd found out? She sighed, pushing those thoughts into the shadows.

"With what I'm asking of you tonight, you're more than welcome to call in on me anytime. Doesn't matter what anyone might think. They have far too much time on their hands if that's what they're concerned about." she glanced behind her, scanning the opening to the secluded area. "I'm going to need you to stay up here to keep watch." she said, meeting his gaping stare. "Someone has to keep watch. And I'm the one that has to go down there." She locked eyes with him, silently daring him to even think about challenging her on this.

"But-"

"Podraig, this isn't up for debate. I have already asked too much of you. You will keep watch." She raised her chin, trying to feel as confident as she sounded.

Podraig's Adam's apple bobbed before he lowered his head and made room for her to join him. She descended the first few steps, the steep decline swallowing her up into the shadow. They stood in front of the small door. The lock looked ridiculously large for such a compact door.

Podraig let out a deep sigh, and she felt his gaze bore into her.

"This door opens up to more stairs. You'll need to go carefully, and take this." He handed her a lantern, lighting it for her with a lighter. Her heart jumped to her throat as he flicked the silver lid open, the click reverberating off the walls of the confined space. It felt as though she'd had the wind knocked from her, hit from nowhere with memories of Slayton, his office, the choking smell of smoke.

She inhaled shakily and let the cold air fill her lungs, reminding herself where she was. No smoke. No Slayton. Not a leather belt raised. And yet her back prickled angrily.

"Once you're at the bottom, the key to the cell door is hung on a hook within an alcove. I've only ever been down there once before when Louis couldn't. But I don't expect it's been moved." She nodded, still staring at the lock as she calmed her mind of anything to do with Slayton. This was the most important task she'd had for a long time, and she would not let *him* mess it up by getting into her head.

Podraig bent down and picked up two stones, weighing them in his palm.

"If anyone comes or I think you need to come back, I'll roll this down the steps. And if you need help, throw this at the wooden door." He paused, eyes wide as she met them, handing her the bigger stone. "Promise me you'll come straight back up if you hear it?" he asked, although it was less of a question, the most authoritative she'd ever heard him.

"I promise." she said, hoping that her promise wouldn't need to be fulfilled and pocketing the stone. He broke her gaze with a grimace as his eyes roamed over the door.

"It terrifies me, the thought of you doing this. I don't even know what he's like. I looked no further than the small serving hatch where I shoved his food. How I wish you'd reconsider." he screwed his eyes shut. Gin opened her mouth to speak. She wished she could say something to reassure him. But it would be a lie. She couldn't even reassure herself about what she was about to come face to face with. It was just something she had to do. She clamped her mouth shut and squeezed his elbow gently instead. It was enough of an answer. His solemn eyes met hers once more before he backed onto the step behind her.

Suddenly, it was time.

All the waiting, the agonising minutes that had dragged by no longer stood in her way. A small part of her wished for them back as she stood alone on that step, key in hand and lock, ready to bear it.

She swallowed hard, but her dry mouth protested.

"If I don't come back within the hour... wake Louis. *Not Col.*" his answering nod was her signal. It was now or never.

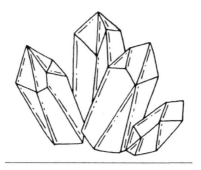

Chapter Twenty-Seven

Cold, damp air hit her as she stood at the top of the staircase. She held the lamp up with a trembling hand, illuminating the first few steps down to Brandon's cell. Shadows consumed the door. Shadows that she would have to bring light to.

She forced her rooted feet to take the steps as she steadied herself with her free hand on the dank wall, slick beneath her palm.

Her breaths came in rippling waves as she descended. The air was growing staler with each step until it turned to a stench of faeces and decay that turned her stomach. She buried her nose into the crook of her arm and winced. It was almost unbearable.

At last, the cell door to her right met the light from her lamp. A small serving hatch, big enough for what she imagined was a tiny portion of food, was cut into it, locked from the outside with a smaller lock.

She slowed as a small barred window came into view. Her free arm dropped to her side as she tried to still the arm that held the lamp. She kept it in her line of vision, eyes wide as her feet met the end of the steps, and flattened herself against the freezing wall opposite. She supposed she should look through the bars first, to see where Brandon was. He must have known by now that someone was here, in the dead of night... the thought alone terrified her, knotting her stomach. She tried to convince herself that perhaps he was asleep too, like any normal person. But she was sure that Brandon was as far as possible from normal.

She blew out a controlled breath and dragged her attention to the wall behind her to locate the key to the cell door. Her search was not long. The alcove was just next to where her head had been; the key hung on a hook at the back. She reached in, her hand brushing against cobwebs, a sign of how little the main door was ever opened.

A wild and unchecked terror crept into every inch of her body with a near paralysing effect. But it was as though she were watching herself from above, all control taken over by some other power, giving her the strength or stupidity to carry on.

She turned back to the door, held her lamp up, only to find an ashen arm, thin enough to fit through the bars, hanging loosely. The other claw-like hand clutched the bars. She almost dropped the lamp as she clamped her hand to her mouth to stifle the scream that threatened to erupt.

Dull grey eyes protruded from sunken sockets over his hand. He winced in the light and the skin of his eyelids drooped like curtains over half his eyes.

Gin feared letting go of her mouth in case the scream still lingered as she panted fiercely through her nose.

Brandon eyed her warily up and down for a moment, only his eyes visible over his bone white knuckles.

"You ain't Max." he said, voice snagging like razor wire on lace. A shiver ran down Gin's spine... Max. Col's Max. She swallowed hard as she moved her hand lower, clasping Col's pendant through the layers of her jumper. She cleared her throat.

"No... I-I'm not." Her voice echoed in the chamber, despite her quietness. "My name is Gin. I'm here for your help. I need to find something that was lost." she said a little louder, hoping to sound unfazed by the murderer that stood before her. "You ain't Max, you can leave." He let go of the bar and turned slowly to the darkness of his cell. She sucked in a breath, desperate to keep him where she could see him.

"Wait! Please! You're the only one who can help me." she pleaded. Brandon turned his head back to the light, his entire face now visible. His thick black beard was a continuation of his matted mass of dark hair that sat atop his head like a knotted and gnarled tree in the middle of winter. His cheek bones cut a sharp angle below his hollow eyes that narrowed angrily in her direction.

"Help? Why should I help you? Why should I help *anyone*?" he sneered, his right eye twitching. Then suddenly his eyes widened and his bony fingers found the bars. Gin pressed herself against the bitingly cold wall again. "Unless you can tell me *where* my Max is? He disappeared a few days ago... shame... he was bloody good company." he added, looking at the floor.

Gin blinked several times as she tried to reason what he'd said, but anger seared through her.

"*Your Max?*" she spat through her teeth, the hatred seeped through the gaps. "You mean the boy you *killed,* along with his mother? He wasn't yours. He had a loving father, who you stole him from." her nose wrinkled in disgust.

Brandon's gaze never left her, but his focus was somewhere else. His distant dead eyed stare lingered in a world of his own. His brows lifted slightly.

"Killed...? I may look it, girl, but I ain't stupid. Anyway, if he was dead, how does he visit me here in my *tomb*?" he released a bone chilling laugh but there was no humour in it. His eye twitched manically again. "Least, he used to." A sour twist crossed his mouth. His lower jaw jutted forward, and he brought a shaky claw to his cheek. "Bloody tooth."

Gin's brows knitted as he rubbed at his sore mouth. He was suffering in every way. Physically, mentally, hallucinating about his victims. Max, coming to visit him in his cell. She swallowed against the dryness in her throat. It was sickening. If Col ever found out about this, it would surely drive him over the edge. Even if it was just a figment of a murderer's delusion. The sting would be just as real.

"Do you not remember what you did to result in your imprisonment?"

Brandon's face seemed to soften like butter. His matted beard shifted, along with the wrinkled leathery corners of his eyes.

"It's one of my favourite things to think about." He was fully focused on her now. His words left her ice cold. His eyes closed slowly.

"But I didn't murder Max." he added as his eyes flashed open. Brandon wheezed out a hacking cough as he laughed.

"What do you mean?" she asked, shaking her head, patience running thin as he amused himself.

"I told you!" he barked as he shot her a look. She would have shrunk back even further if she hadn't already been flat against the wall.

"I ain't *stupid*! I may have been ordered to kill 'em both, but I had my own needs to meet. Made Max watch though, as I strangled the life out of his mother. Mmm... and everything that came after." Gin's eyes widened as her stomach hit the floor. Brandon's smile widened so that she could make out what was left of his rotting, jagged teeth. It was a grin that she'd never forget. He was the very image of a horror filled nightmare.

"But Max? Why would I 'ave killed him when I could make a pretty penny from a lad like that? Strong and handsome, like his father. Lot of folk wanted him... for a lot of different reasons." he whispered, his words cutting through the frigid air like knives. Gin felt them twist in her chest. She squeezed her eyes shut and rubbed at the phantom pain in her chest.

"You *sold him!?*" she seethed. He studied her twisted expression as if it was an achievement, the corner of his mouth twitching up.

"Max has been very forgiving since returning to me. He an' I found our peace. He's like the son I never had... now he's gone again." he stared into nothingness, eye twitching as his dense brows lowered.

Gin's head replayed the words '*sold*', over and over, and the walls seemed to spin.

"Why didn't you tell Col that he wasn't dead?" she breathed.

"You think I'd wanna ease his pain?" he snorted, eyes narrowed to slits. "Was much more fun watching him suffer, knowing that he thought his boy had met the same messy end as his whore of a wife. Did he tell ya she thought she was running off into the sunset with the man of her dreams?" he barked with laughter that made her flinch. "Only to be betrayed by him!" She shook her head, searching the ground as if there were more clarity down there.

"Didn't think so." he added, slowly banging his forehead against the iron bars.

She had so many questions drumming through her mind, she almost forgot why she was here. She had to remind herself of the Crystal. But she also needed to find out who he sold Max to. Col needed to know. Max would be alive when he returned.

She was going to have to play along with his twisted fantasy. If she could convince him she wanted to help him find Max, then he might just give her what she needed. She met his gaze and drew herself away from the wall.

Brandon's cold eyes roamed down her body that she tried to keep from running up the stairs to safety.

"I believe you have something I want. In return, I can help you find Max."

He stopped bashing his forehead, eyes travelling back up to hers.

"Where is he, girl?" His voice was like a low rumble of thunder. "You act like you're innocent. But I ain't a fool. Who took 'im? Who has Max?" he spat through rotting teeth. Gin took a deep breath, both smiling and screaming inwardly. She had him hooked. She just needed to reel him in. It was time to call him out.

"You give me the Crystal you're hiding down here and answer some of my questions, then I'll get your Max back." she said, holding his gaze, her eyes burning.

His eye twitched faster than ever as he roamed his gaze over her. His dry tongue poked out and ran over his lower lip. Queasiness roiled in her stomach as he smacked his lips gently.

"If I'm to trust you, you're gonna have to come in and get it." he said, before slinking into the darkness of his cell.

Gin's mouth fell open, eyes wide as she strained to see where he'd gone. She willed herself not to cry as she gasped for air to fill her tight chest. She was more certain than ever that he did indeed have the Crystal.

She lifted her head to the stone ceiling and bit down hard on her lip, willing the pain to overshadow the fear in her body. Thinking of Hope, what Col was doing to help her get back to her and how she was betraying him at every turn, making plans to leave with Louis. She *had* to do this one thing for him before she left. She had to help him get this Crystal that lay in the one place he'd never enter. And now, she had to find out who bought Max. For there was hope of reuniting Col with his son, as well as justice.

Gin had tasted fear many times, but nothing as potent as this. It was coarse and jagged in the back of her throat. She was about to walk into a psychopathic murderer's cell. Col and Louis would never let her out of sight again if they knew what she was about to do in order to get this Crystal. But they would never have to know. She just needed to keep her wits about her, be smart and get what she needed. With any luck, she'd be long gone by the time Brandon realised she wasn't coming back with Max. That was, if his mind didn't bring him back before she left.

She clenched her fist and glanced up to the sliver of moonlight that seeped through the gap in the door she left ajar at the top of the stairs. The sooner she got this over with, the sooner she could get back to safety.

She faced the cell door and breathed in the rancid air. With shaking hands, she reached for the padlock.

"For Col." she muttered, fiddling with the key until it clicked open the latch.

Her breath hitched in her chest. She listened for any sign of movement from within the depths of the cell, but all she heard was the ferocious beat of her heart drumming in her ears.

As she pushed the door open, it groaned and protested against her, the old hinges so rarely used.

There was no going back.

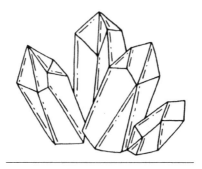

Chapter Twenty-Eight

If Gin thought the air was unwelcome outside the cell, the inside was almost unbearable. She stood in the doorway, half shuttered eyes searching frantically for Brandon as she held her lamp out. She slammed the door shut, keeping her eyes ahead.

"If you do anything stupid your chance of seeing Max again is gone!" she said, trying to sound braver than she was feeling. She just hoped the return of Max was enough to make his sanity come through.

Strange shapes emerged from the darkness as the lamplight drank up the shadows, helped a little by a small barred window, so high in the cavernous walls there was no way of reaching it. If her bearings were right, it opened out to somewhere behind the castle, away from the public.

The moonlight clipped parts of the room, revealing the horrors of his cell; a shallow gutter that ran through the centre, down a tiny shaft to the moat and a bucket that sat in the corner filled with what she did not want to find out.

Then something terrifying glinted above her eye level. Her eyes lifted under thick lashes, to a sight that made her stomach drop. She swallowed hard against the bile that rose and pressed the back of her hand to her mouth. A thick collar hung from the vaulted ceiling by chains. All around the collar were sharp metal spikes, both inside and out.

"One of the kinder devices used for torture." said Brandon, who had turned up at her shoulder. His foul breath caressed her cheek. She couldn't stop the yelp from escaping as she spun around to face him. The lamp shook in her hand as she held it up to his malicious smirk. She backed up and then stopped herself. She had to remain in control. No room for weakness.

"Tightened enough to be absolute torture, but not to do any serious injury. Would keep you in one position, ain't no mistake. The actual punishment came the following days or weeks when you were exhausted and hungry..." She watched him trail off, eyes rolling around in the memory.

"Sir Col's favourite way of trying to break me, when he'd grown tired of doing the dirty work himself." he said. She screwed her eyes up, remembering why Brandon was here. What he did. What Col *thought* he had done to Max. When she opened them again, he was staring at her, head cocked. She pulled her shoulders back.

"Let's not drag this out any longer than we need to."

"Why hurry? Been a lifetime since I've had such pretty company." he shuffled on the spot and turned his head to the other side. His eyes widened slightly, one still twitching. "Shame about those eyes, though. Mars that fair face of yours."

Gin stared at him flatly. He was expecting a reaction; she was sure as the silence followed. She'd learnt to ignore remarks about her abnormality a long time ago. It had always been the least of her worries.

"The Crystal." she said, her voice echoing up through the cavernous room. "You have it, I know you do. It needs to go back to its rightful owner."

Brandon let out a bark of laughter and groaned as he wearily slid down a wall until his frail figure hit the hard ground.

Gin studied him. He was weak. That small amount of time standing had taken strength that his malnourished body was in short supply of.

Brandon's jaw flexed, and he rubbed at his cheek again, the pain from his tooth obviously flaring again.

"The rightful owner... you've some nerve, girl, coming here and pleading his case when he was the one who put me here."

Gin's blood boiled angrily. She clenched her fist. The urge to throw all the things he'd done to actually warrant being cast down here was near impossible to keep a lid on. But that would get her nowhere. She looked down her nose at him as an idea entered her mind...

"You know, Col can heal that raging toothache of yours." she said, with a little sniff. Brandon stopped massaging his cheek and eyed her through the gloom.

"If you were to give me the Crystal and information about who you sold Max to, who you were working for... it would be really easy to make that pain disappear for good." she finished, lips pursed. Brandon shook his head slowly, his coarse matted hair bobbing slightly around his gaunt face.

"He'd never ease my sufferin'. Not when he's hell bent on doing the very opposite." he spat, eyes cast to the ground as he continued massaging the ache again. He was right. Col would never agree to it, but she had no intention of asking him. This was something she'd have to do alone. The idea of easing Brandon's pain after the monstrous things he did was not something that sat well with her. But she'd swallow that bitter pill herself if it meant getting what she needed.

"He wouldn't need to know. I can do it myself." She crouched to his level and set the lamp down between them. The smell of the cold, damp stone filled her nostrils. His eyes narrowed as they flicked from the lamp to her.

He was silent for a moment, and she could see the internal struggle of his mind, battling between giving Col what he wanted and having his throbbing tooth fixed, as well as Max back.

Brandon shuffled towards her, crouched like a frog. In the light, she could see how filthy he was. His sticklike legs and arms were coated in grime that turned to black sludge where he'd been in contact with the damp floor.

She swallowed involuntarily as he studied her.

"What's in it for you, eh?" he asked, his eyes raking over her. She hugged her arms closer. If he didn't look as though he'd snap in a mere breeze, her nerves would have been wrecked already.

"What on earth drove a beauty like you down to my level?" he reached out his claw-like hand to her face but before he could touch her she stood, panting through her flared nostrils. She blinked down at him, his hand still hovering mid air.

"I get the satisfaction of helping a friend."

He cocked his head in a way that seemed almost unnatural, a wicked grin spreading across his face.

"Col don't have friends." he sneered. Gin held back the grimace that tugged at her lips and forced herself to stay on track. She couldn't get dragged into his games. "So what will it be? Do we have a deal or not?" she said flatly, despising every second she was in his presence.

Brandon paused, that sly smirk still plastered on his dirt encrusted face. She held his gaze, her heart pounding. She had no idea what she'd do if he didn't take the offer. But one thing *was* for sure. She wasn't leaving without that Crystal.

After a moment, Brandon raised his frail arm.

"Be a love and help me up? All this excitement... taken it out of me." Her gaze flicked to his hand. The sensation to recoil washed over her like a raging cold wave, caught up in a storm.

With a steel heart, she slapped her hand on to his wrist. His fingers wrapped around her arm, the same fingers that had done unthinkable horrors. The corners of her mouth turned downwards as she yanked him up, his weight surprising despite his stature.

As she went to let go, he grabbed her around the waist and pulled her into an ice cold hold. His hands clawed at her back and she struggled against him, but he'd trapped her arms. His frightening strength, hidden behind smoke and mirrors.

She gritted her teeth and let out a small growl in his face. His eyes were suddenly ablaze with wild abandon, the moonlight making them glow with an ethereal light.

"How I've missed the look of terror in people's eyes." he spat. She held her breath against the rancid odour of his own. "The realisation they ain't immortal and can be snuffed out like a flame... even by an insignificant, lowly being like me." Gin stared in wide-eyed horror as she froze in his iron grip. It seemed impossible for his withered body to harness such strength. "Tell me. Are you feeling your mortality yet, girl?" His eye twitched with manic ferocity and his head trembled of its own accord as he craned his neck forwards, inches from her face.

She writhed in his arms, desperate to free herself. Her breath came in great gasps between holding it while she strained against him. But it only strengthened his grip, his fingers clawing at her scars.

"If you want any chance of getting Max back, you're going about it entirely wrong!" she seethed through gritted teeth, trying to control her panic. He barked with laughter that echoed around the dungeon like a gunshot.

"I 'ave to disagree with you there. *This*" he growled, constricting his arms around her with more force, "is a little reminder, tha' even down here I'm capable of things that would turn Col's wife in her grave... or the parts of her." he sneered. A dreadful flash danced behind his eyes, daring her to try something. She could hardly breathe in the pressure of his grip now, and spots swayed before her eyes in the silvery moonlight. A dizzying array of thoughts clouded her mind. Of what would happen to Hope if she didn't get out of here. Of Col and how if she failed he'd never know the truth about Max. How she was so close to getting this Crystal, she could almost scream.

Gin poured all the strength she had into making this moment count. She locked eyes with him, meeting his unhinged gaze with a piercing one of her own. She honed her breathing into a deep, calming pattern.

"I've met many fools, and you are certainly *not* one of them... but neither am I. You have my word. You can trust me." she said, feeling her nose hitch up as she wielded this lie. Her eyes stung, not daring to look away from him as he continued to study her. She'd not give him any indication of the absolute terror that filled her. She'd hide it, just like she did for Slayton every time he removed his belt, every time she was made to bare her back.

After what felt like an eternity, Brandon's taut features seemed to relax, his nails unhooking slightly from her throbbing back. His eyes flicked over her face as the weakness seemed to return, his body visibly sighing. She pursed her lips, more so to keep the nausea down as she tried to keep her knees from buckling.

Brandon inched backwards, an almost imperceptible nod of his head. Her heart pounded in her chest. This was it. He was going to give her the Crystal. She felt it, almost pulling like a magnet.

But before he had the chance, a force of thunderous rage shot past her. The gust of angry air swirling loose strands of her hair in front of her eyes carried the heartbreaking scent of blackberry and leather. Her red ribbon flapped against her cheek.

A hulking figure stood between her and Brandon, who had been flattened to the ground, arms over his head as he laid there. To her surprise, Brandon was laughing among the coughing, having had the wind knocked from him.

Her wide eyes slid back to the figure before her, his back turned and shoulders rising and falling heavily. If the scent of him hadn't alerted her, she'd have known that silhouette anywhere. Her heart sank to the very depths of her stomach.

"Col…" she breathed, hands cupped over her mouth.

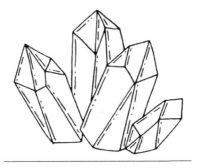

Chapter Twenty-Nine

Gin shook her head, panic scorching through her veins like hot oil. She desperately wanted to explain everything to Col, to let it burst from her lungs. But she had to keep up the premise she'd set for Brandon. Shame sat thickly in her throat at being found down here and unable to say a word in her defence. Not yet.

Col's gaze was fixed firmly on the crumpled heap that Brandon had become. But the laughter that still escaped the prisoner sent a shiver down her spine, as he peeked up at Col's face from behind his rake-like arms. She was thankful for the wall of his heaving back. She didn't think she could stomach the disappointment and anger that would tear from his gaze.

"Sir Col?" wheezed Brandon, lowering his arms fully to get a better look. "As I live and breathe." he said, eye twitching so quickly now that his nose joined in as well. "I thought you vowed never to set eyes on me again. Left me to rot. Hoping you could just forget. What your whore of a wife did to you."

Col's breathing seemed to intensify and Gin felt his surge of anger ripple across her own chest.

"Tell me… how's that working out for you?" A slow burning grin slid across Brandon's face and widened as Col made to deliver his next blow, only to be stopped by Gin, her hands clutched at his tensed arm. It trembled beneath her palms.

"Col, don't! Don't…" she pleaded. Col finally turned to her. The utter torment in his eyes almost shattered her heart. She'd rather face Slayton's belt a thousand times than to have him look at her like this.

Col brought a trembling fist to his lips before lowering it, flexing his fingers. *"Why?"* he growled, his face screwed up in disbelief. A lump formed in her throat and she swallowed painfully against it. She scowled Brandon's way. He was watching them with eager eyes.

"Same reason you lose everyone you care about, I believe. Blasted Crystals of yours." Brandon sneered.

Col's eyes flashed as she looked sheepishly back at him. She pressed her lips together.

"Gin." said Col, his voice broken as he tipped his head back slightly.

"Trust me." she whispered, hoping that would be enough to get them through what had to be done. What she was about to say. The fragile thread had been pulled. Now all she could do was watch it shred him until she could stitch him back together. Her fingers slid down to his trembling hands, trying to keep him grounded to reality, not to lose him to his past. Col's haunted eyes remained on hers, the silence in the confined space almost suffocating as he panted through his nose.

Footsteps descended the steps outside the cell, but neither broke their gaze. Someone came to a shuffled halt in the doorway.

"Oh my god, Gin. Gin!" said Louis, coming to her side. Gin immediately let go of Col's hands, being yanked back into her own reality. Louis grabbed her shoulders, sweeping her hair from her face as he studied her. But she kept her focus on Col, fearing his next move. "What on earth are you doing down here? Are you hurt? Did he… did he hurt you?" he asked, terror electrifying his voice. Still, neither she nor Col gave him their attention, lost in a silent, agonising battle.

"Gin!" Louis shook her gently, finally wrenching her free. She dipped out of Louis's grasp.

"I'm fine." Her focus had to remain on Brandon. She couldn't let him play on Col's anger. It was up to her right now.

"Do we have a deal or not?" she asked Brandon firmly, stepping around Col so that she was between them, snatching her arm away from Col's attempt to pull her back.

"Deal? Oh Christ, Gin, what the hell have you done?" Col rasped from behind her. She ignored him, choosing to concentrate on how she wanted to wipe the smirk from Brandons face for good.

"I'm losing all patience frankly and the longer you drag this out, the less chance you have of *ever* seeing Max again." Her nostrils flared. She could feel Col's look of horror burn her skin without turning to face it.

"*What? What* are you talking about, Gin?" Col's voice cut through the air like a blade. But she held her ground and rose above the look of smug amusement from Brandon. She gritted her teeth against it all until her jaw ached.

"Last chance. *Do we have a deal?*"

Brandon's eyes slid to Col slowly, calculating the power he now held over the man who put him down here. The knowledge that he thought he was going to get the very thing that Col desired. He rolled his head, fragile bones cracking like logs on a fire, before settling his gaze upon her once more. He dragged his body up, knees shaking under him.

Gin pulled her shoulders back as both brothers closed in on either side of her. Both prepared for any sudden moves. But Brandon turned from them and hobbled into a shadowy corner of his cell.

Gin's eyes pushed through the darkness frantically.

"*What the hell, Gin?*" Col's hushed voice rumbled in her ear. It sent goosebumps erupting down her neck. But not as much as the unknown whereabouts of Brandon.

"Never mind *what*, let's just get her *the hell* out of here." Louis seethed by her other ear. She took a few tentative steps forward, away from the heat of their bodies, squinting through the darkness. But they matched her every move.

"Gin, we're leaving. Come on." said Louis, holding her arm. She wrenched it free, not turning as she spoke.

"You are free to go, Louis. But I'm not leaving until I get what I came for." She barely recognised her own voice. It was dark and hollow.

"I am so very close to hauling your ass out of here myself," said Col.

"I'm. Not. Leaving." she gritted out, staring straight ahead. If she took one more look at Col, she would crumble under the weight of shame that sat in her stomach.

The sound of rock hitting rock, somewhere to her left, made her flinch as Col's arm shot in front of her. She didn't move it this time, not missing the muscle in Louis's jaw work as he looked at Col's hand splayed over her stomach.

That's when shuffling feet drew near again.

She swallowed hard, eyes wide, searching for Brandon as her heart pounded in her ears. Visions of rocks hurtling their way and knocking them flat flashed through her mind, quashed only by the reappearance of Brandon, clutching something close to his chest.

Her heart skipped a beat as she stared at his clenched hands, covered in so much grime it was hard to believe skin lay beneath.

Col's breathing had intensified too, his arm lowered. She glanced sideways. He had crumpled before her, his shoulders caved as his chest seemed to grapple for air to fill his lungs.

Brandon stopped, clutching it even closer to his skeletal chest. Her eyes met his furrowed gaze.

"Tooth." he said, jaw jutting out as his gaze flicked between them. She inhaled a shuddering breath. She was going to have to prove herself trustworthy before he handed the Crystal over. But there was no way she was going to subject Col to healing him.

"Col, I need you to do something for me." Her eyes never left Brandon as she spoke. "I need Crystals for healing dental problems. Do you have them?"

Col laughed darkly.

"I'm afraid I'm not in the business of healing murderers." he said, disgust rolling off his tongue with each word.

"Which is why you'll be leaving as soon as you bring them to me." she replied, levelling him with a look now that said she wasn't taking no for an answer. His head fell to the side, painfully slow. She held her trembling shoulders back under his wide-eyed gaze, like he didn't even recognise her.

"Shit, Gin-"

"I will retrieve them myself if I have to. But I would need to look up the correct Crystals and locate them if they're still whole. This will take longer than any of us want it to." she said, cutting him off. Her logic made sense, she knew he couldn't argue. But the incredulous look on his face had her ready for it.

"You honestly think I'm going to set foot outside of this rotting hell hole without you?"

Gin lifted her chin.

"Yes. Because you know I've been dragged through hell myself. And I'm sick of being on my knees. I refuse to be dragged any more. I'm walking through these flames for you now, Col." Her voice was hushed and sharp as she searched his eyes. Her truth surprised her in its aftermath and she glanced sheepishly at Louis, who blinked under a furrowed brow.

Something softened in Col's gaze for a second before turning steely, dipping to Brandon. He ran a hand over his forehead and let it trail down his face.

"I'm here. I'm not going anywhere, Col. Do what she needs, quickly." said Louis, solemnly. Gin couldn't meet Louis's gaze, certain her truth had caused that grimness.

Col sighed heavily through his nose and contemplated the frail man before him. The air seemed to grow colder as Col stepped towards him slowly. Their eyes locked.

"If you so much as *think* about touching her..." he trailed off, his gaze finding the torture collar that loomed above them. "You thought weeks in *that* thing was agonising... try the rest of your goddamn life." he growled.

His threat shivered down Gin's spine and seemed to make the air thicker, harder to inhale, for she knew it was a threat he would follow through with.

Brandon's mouth creeped into a jagged snarling laugh.

"Laugh on." said Col, closing the space between them, his towering frame blocking Brandon from sight. "I sure will, while I take you apart slowly, piece by piece."

"Sounds familiar." was Brandon's reply. Gin's chest tightened at the ruthless remark, aimed to cut deeply.

Louis inched closer to her side. She wasn't sure if it was for her sake or to stop Col if he were to lose it. She closed her eyes, held her breath, each second painfully slow.

"About time I returned the service." said Col, his voice a distant rumble of thunder, waiting for the storm to draw nearer.

With that, he turned on his heel. He stopped in front of Gin, her eyes open once more. A muscle flexed in his jaw. She opened her mouth to speak, but nothing came out. What more could she say while trying to remain neutral to the bastard that destroyed him? Her cheeks heated again against the bitingly cold air. Col licked his lips and looked at the cavernous ceiling. No quick wit or humour was going to spill out of that mouth this time.

She broke through the thickness in her throat and said the only thing she could without losing Brandon's trust.

"I'm sorry." It was a whisper, feeble, but it came from the very bottom of her heart and soul. She felt it leave her with the weight of her sorrow, hoping that it somehow reached a part of him.

But Col didn't reply, his gaze fixed on her as he spoke to Louis.

"Don't so much as blink, brother. Your soulmate appears to have lost her damn mind." he said, lips curled, sliding past her.

Gin inhaled sharply, blinking at the tears that had pooled at the sheer anger she felt from his very core. Before Louis could notice the hurt, she sniffed, straightening against the blow.

"Gin." Louis began, his fingertips bushing hers. The softness in his voice, his touch, irked her. She didn't deserve his kindness. And to be honest, his interference had rattled her even more.

"Don't." She swallowed the sob that wanted to escape and channelled her energy back into Brandon.

"You've got your way. I'll heal you before you hand over the Crystal. But now it's my turn." her voice was low and steady.

"You tell me who you sold Max to and who you worked for, or I'll hit my head against the wall until blood runs down my face. Col won't even ask what happened. You'll be in that collar without a second thought."

"Woah, I think you need to just calm down, alright?" said Louis as Brandon huffed a laugh. But no smile brushed his lips. Instead, she found it slither onto her own. She had him backed into a corner.

"Max won't talk, eh? Don't surprise me, knowing his master... what he would have done to him. After everything I did to his mother it's a wonder how *I've* been his safe place. *Me.*" Brandon glanced at Louis, only laughing more and more. Gin pushed the nauseating sound away.

"You need to stop running your mouth, Brandon. You know not what is real and what isn't!" Louis said, rubbing a hand over his beard. Gin screwed her eyes shut.

"Louis, please!" she said, rounding on him. "Let *me* do the talking." she pleaded. Louis's furrowed gaze darted between her and Brandon.

"Gin, he is not sound of mind. You cannot believe a word of what he says."

"He said he didn't kill Max!" she said incredulously. "I *have* to believe him. If it were Hope, I'd take *every* word out of his mouth as truth until proven otherwise." She whispered, so only Louis could hear. "I didn't ask you to come down here. You don't need to say anything more." His eyes swam over her until finally he gave the smallest of resigned nods.

"I shall give you my silence. But know that you *will* listen when we are done here." She gritted her teeth, no strength left to argue with him now. She turned back to Brandon.

"You must have been a welcome exchange after everything Max went through." she lied. The words felt toxic in her mouth and she thanked the universe that Col had not been here to hear her. "And if you truly care for him, you'll help me bring whoever ordered his death to justice."

Brandon's brows lifted a little. He approached her, his bare feet padding the damp ground. Gin's heart thrummed in her ears and she pulled herself up to full height. He gazed at her, the moonlight washing his grey pallor out almost completely, like a ghost. The twitch in his eye stopped, as if he was trying to reach into her mind and scoop out her true intent. She didn't back away. With an iron will, she forced herself to stand her ground, even as his rancid breath filled her nose. He was testing her resolve, how much she was willing to allow with Col gone for the information she wanted, skirting the boundaries of a forbidden garden.

"I never knew who sent out the orders." He stretched his hand up and stroked the side of her face, sending a wave of ice cold fear through her body but she still held fast, pushing her palm against Louis's chest as he tried to step in, "Weren't told and weren't stupid enough to ask."

Louis sighed behind her. But she pushed on.

"You must have seen someone, though, had a name for whoever gave you the orders." she said, pressing her arms into her sides. Inside her head, she was transported back to Slayton's office, unable to move, just waiting for whatever punishment he chose that day to be over. Only this time, she felt different. She didn't want to just let it happen. Some little fire inside made her want to lash out and break free of Brandon's roaming hands. She almost laughed at the irony of it. "Just instructions, usually from a hooded figure in a dingy corner of the street. Never even saw their face. Could have been a different person each time, for all I know."

She sagged, disappointment dampening her fire. She dipped out of his reach slowly and brushed her cheek where his bitterly cold hand had been.

"Ok, but you must have had dealings with whoever bought Max? You said yourself, *knowing his master...*" She didn't miss the flicker of his gaze as it broke momentarily, meeting Louis's over her shoulder. She narrowed her eyes slightly. Brandon was keeping something from them. "That wasn't just a mysterious hooded figure, was it?"

Brandon looked down at the Crystal he held in his hand and turned it over several times before holding it up to the shaft of moonlight.

Gin's breath hitched in her throat as she saw it properly for the first time. It was unmistakably the Sunstone. The tangerine shade of the Crystal point was flecked with gold that shimmered like frost in the sunrise. She couldn't drag her gaze away. It snared all her senses. Her surroundings seemed to fade even further into darkness, and the sound of her blood rushed through her ears. Even Louis seemed to sag beside her.

Her distraction didn't go unnoticed. Brandon twisted the Sunstone so that she had a better view, moving it to catch the light slowly, watching her transfixed face with curiosity.

"Max loved this Crystal. We'd spend hours just lookin' at it... the way it seems to drink up any light it touches." His voice was near, yet she couldn't for the life of her place him in the room. But the Sunstone seemed to become clearer, bigger... "Like owning a piece of the sun."

The pendant around her neck seemed to vibrate, and she blinked heavily. The world seemed to slow, and she fumbled for the locket through her jumper. It was warm, even through the thick knit and seemed to pulse in time with her heartbeat. She knew Brandon was still talking, but she couldn't recall any of what he'd said. Like trying to hear underwater. Only snippets made their way through, no matter how hard she fought the current of the Crystal, pulling her under. Gin was vaguely aware of Brandon's arm reaching past her head, and barely noticed as he swung the torture device against Louis's skull, knocking him to the ground. The thud of his body collapsing on the stone floor dissolved into the background outside her bubble.

She could not steal her eyes away from the warm glow as it seemingly hovered in front of her, closer... closer... until something told her it was too close. Brandon was too close.

She lifted her limp arms to her eyes, trying to block out the force of the energy, battling with a sensation of pure harmony from the Sunstone and worried for being so vulnerable in Brandon's presence. It was impossible to separate the two. Until she felt an icy tightness around her neck. A cold iron grip as she glimpsed the

Sunstone through her hands, watching it fall impossibly slowly towards the ground.

She blinked heavily as she struggled to gasp, but no air found its way through her constricted throat. That's when the warm glow of the sunstone faded and she crashed back to reality.

The room was dark once more but she could make out Brandon's face, mere inches from her own, a ferralness in his eyes that could easily pass for some wild creature. His pupils, so dilated that his entire eye looked as black as the shadows that ate up most of the room.

She clawed at his hands that had clasped her neck, strength returning to her body at last.

Brandon's gnarled hands were clasped so firmly she could feel every bone in his fingers. As she scratched at his crusty skin, scraping her nails down her own neck in untamed chaos, she could see no way out.

Col would return to find her dead on the floor and she'd never get to explain, never get to tell him his son was not killed. That he would have the chance to find Max.

Her eyes widened, terror rampaging through her body as she stared into his savage face. Her head swirled, time lost all meaning. It felt like an eternity.

Suddenly, she was knocked to the floor, her throat free from the clutches of his hands.

It took a moment for her to refocus, sucking air into her lungs through her burning throat. But as the world came into view, so did the reason she'd slammed into the ground.

Brandon was the one gripped by the neck. Stifled noises spluttered from his mouth as he fought against Col's powerful hands. His thin legs hanging limply as he dangled from the damp wall.

"Was I not *fucking* clear enough for you?" The anger that exploded from Col was palpable throughout the room. His bark bounced around dangerously.

Gin tried calling his name, but her voice caught in her stifled throat. She arched her back, like a dog on all fours, chin dipped to her chest as she tried to muster her voice. But something caught her eye. A blot of colour in the dingy cell. Her elbows quaked as she released a breath, a small smile tracing her lips as she covered the Sunstone with her palm. But the floor felt different beneath her hand, the chill stone of the ground now soft. She blinked away the shadows, focusing upon what the Crystal had landed by. A small notebook, no bigger than her hand, wrinkled with age, the pages crinkled from the damp confines.

She slipped both the sunstone and notebook into her back pocket, heart throbbing in her chest.

Gin clocked Louis's still body to her left. She scrambled to him, palming the air around his chest. She hovered her cheek to his mouth, relief flooding through her at the breath that warmed her cheek. He was alive.

Looking up at Col's surging back, Brandon's beady eyes now bulging as he stared at the man who would gladly finish him.

"Col!" she groaned, before taking a deeper breath through the burning in her throat, "COL!" Brandon's eyes slid to hers and he raised his billowy brows.

She waited, knowing that he heard her desperate cry, and watched as his back stilled, his breath held, not giving up on his prisoner. She sagged, practically seeing the shadows devour Col, dragging him back to the darkness as Brandon's eyes began to flutter.

She panted in the stale air, greedily, preparing to give Col the truth that could either save him... or destroy him.

"He didn't kill Max!" she cried.

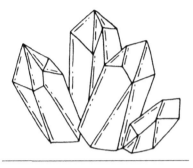

Chapter Thirty

She had done it. She had given him the key to a door that could open a new future for him or send him spiralling into darkness.

Col baulked as he dropped Brandon, letting him slump against the wall. Despite his ordeal, Brandon smirked, half choking, half laughing into nothing.

She winced, hauling herself up from the waterlogged floor. Whether or not Col would forgive her, she had to press on and pray that Brandon would cooperate.

"Who?" she demanded, drawing herself up despite wanting to crumple. "Tell him *who* you sold his son to. Do just *one* good deed in your life."

Col raised his hands to his shaking head.

"He... you..." his broken voice stuttered.

Gin clenched her hands tight to keep from reaching for him, to comfort him. She was most likely the last person he wanted comfort from.

"My son was *alive?"* He rasped, hands clutched at the back of his head. "You're lying... you would have said before. *Why didn't you tell me before?"* he cried, dragging his hands to his mouth, breathing heavily into them.

Brandon's head snapped up, levelling him with crazed amusement, laughing in the face of Col's torment.

Gin watched in horror as Col lost it and pummeled his fist into Brandon's smug face.

"Col!" she called, lurching forwards to grab his arm. His skin was hot and clammy with anger, but he stopped at her touch. Gin's brow raised, half expecting to have been shoved backwards with his rage. But to her relief, he let her take his trembling arm. She daren't let go and break the calm that seemed to seep into him from her touch. She could feel it, like the sun creeping out from behind the clouds, gently warming her skin.

"I had nothing to gain after what I'd done to your wife." He surveyed Col intently, head tilted back as he prepared to fire his next round of poison. "Better to let your mind conjure up his fate."

Gin's lip curled. This monster before her had no remorse, not for anything. In the blink of an eye, Col had ripped himself from her hands and dragged Brandon over to the spiked collar by his arms.

"You are going to tell me who you sold my son to or I swear, you will spend the rest of your pathetic life in this collar! And every time you're close to death, I'll bring you back to do it all over again!" Col's voice had taken on a wildness to match Brandon's appearance. But despite the threat, Brandon continued to survey Col like a cat who had cornered a mouse, his small eyes now wide and hungry. A shiver trickled down Gin's spine as she stared at them, almost black, the whites around them so minimal, it seemed no humanity lived within.

"TELL ME!" he roared. Col was so close to his face now that she could no longer see his expression, only the mechanical laughter that trickled out of Brandon.

"Right under your nose... right... Right under!" he rasped, unable to control himself.

Her shallow breaths were almost turning to sobs. She was at a loss. The panic that had taken over was too strong to be calmed. She watched, frozen to the spot, as Col reached for the collar, his taut biceps straining against his shirt. The clatter of the chains above cut through the room like thunder.

Col threw Brandon to the floor as he fiddled with a lock until it swung open on a hinge. Col sniffed, wiping the back of his hand across his nose and glowered down at him.

"Last damn chance." he said.

Gin clutched her chest, jumper bunched up in her fingers. Bile rose in her throat and tears stung her eyes. She felt nothing but intense hate for the monster on the floor, but more torture? She didn't want Col to live with this shadow over him. She looked away, eyes screwed up tight as she heard him haul Brandon to his feet. His laughter stopped in its tracks.

"Can't say I didn't give you a fair chance."

"Col…" she whispered, too weakly to have stopped him, but the nausea that swirled in her stomach didn't allow for much more.

"Brother!"

Gin twisted, seeing Louis push himself to his feet. Blood trickled down his forehead, mixed with beads of sweat.

Col dragged his gaze away after a moment, nostrils flaring. Then finally, Brandon broke his silence, a laugh skipping around the chamber again. The brothers looked at him, only to be met with more laughter as he looked between them.

Louis plodded past Gin, leaving her staring open-mouthed as he planted a hand on Col's shoulder.

"You're better than this, brother." he said, squeezing his shoulder. "Come, now. Leave it. He is not worth the guilt that would plague you."

Gin noticed the muscles in Col's jaw work before he slowly cocked his head her way. Her insides hollowed. Anger burned in his eyes under his sharp brows. Anger at her for coming down here, anger at himself for not being able to rip into Brandon.

He shoved Brandon to the floor again. "I'm not finished with you. You better wish sanity hasn't completely vanished from my senses when I return."

Brandon's laugh rang around the cell. Whatever was going on in his head had truly taken hold.

"Out." was all Col said to Gin, nodding to the door. She looked at Louis, who nodded gravely.

Her eyes trailed Col as he marched out of the cell, kicked his foot up against the door frame and stared at the bottom step. With one last look towards Brandon, doubled in laughter, she then joined Col, followed by Louis.

The sound of Brandon's laughter dwindled, realisation dawning as the door slammed on him, locking him away once more. Gin watched Louis turn the heavy key in the lock just as hurried shuffling approached the door, hands grasping the bars.

"Wait! Y-y-you ain't held up your end! My tooth won't heal itself! And... and the Sunstone..." Brandon glanced around before disappearing into the dark cell.

Gin felt Col's eyes shift to her, as Brandon scurried about the cell in search of it. She swallowed the dryness in her throat, meeting Col's gaze, and reached into her back pocket to retrieve the Crystal. Though she held the notebook back, curiosity getting the better of her.

This was far from how she envisioned handing over the Crystal. But it was done.

Col gazed down at her hand as Brandon reappeared at the bars, just in time to see Col take it from her. The pain of the evening was written all over Col's wilting frame. She wanted to reach out, to smooth the crease between his brows. Take away his pain. But she was the very reason he was feeling it.

Louis's brow arched as he sucked in a deep breath at the sight of the missing Crystal.

"You owe me my healing!" Brandon barked, spit clinging to his beard.

Gin clenched her teeth. For the first time, she held absolutely no desire to heal the suffering before her.

Col pressed his lips together and squeezed the Crystal in his palm before turning to Brandon. They were mere inches away, the door the only thing that kept them from colliding.

"She owes you *nothing.*" he was quiet, but loud enough to hear in the confines of the stairwell. He didn't look back at her as he swept past and climbed.

"What about Max? You promised! Max for that Crystal! W-when is he coming back?" He was almost pleading now. Col stopped dead in his tracks, fists braced on the damp walls.

Another twist of the knife in her gut. But at least she could tell Brandon the truth now. No more playing his delusion. She stepped towards him, noting Louis closing in next to her.

She raised her chin and fixed him with a stare through the tears that fogged her vision.

"Whenever your twisted mind brings him back." The corner of her mouth twitched up ever so slightly as Brandon's hands trembled on the bars. "Does it hurt? Knowing that *your* Max is just a figment of your sick mind? That you truly are all alone?"

A scream of pure rage emitted from his core. Gin felt Louis's arm around her shoulders, moving her away from his tortured rage. She let him lead her, following Col, wasting no more energy on the monster down here.

As she emerged into the night, the air seemed somewhat milder than it had down in the cell. But the frostiness that Col provided soon made up for it.

She chewed her lip as she clocked him by the bushes, staring out into the courtyard. Podraig gave her a sheepish half smile, which disappeared into guilt at the appearance of Louis. He rounded on the hefty door, closing it on the bellows of Brandon. As the locks were put in place, the sounds disappeared altogether, as though there were some magic spell cast over the door. Gin knew better than to ask at this moment, but didn't put it past the magic of the Crystals she'd witnessed so far.

Louis began walking over to Podraig, the thin line of his lips and puffed up chest signalling that he was not in his best books after helping her. Yet another person she'd let down tonight.

"Louis, wait. It was all my idea. Podraig had nothing to do with it, other than what I asked him to do. This is all on me." she said, sidestepping into his path. Louis stopped to survey her. He took a deep breath before letting it go slowly.

"I know. Still, this fool should have known better than to go along with it." he said, looking pointedly at Podraig. "When I realised my keys were missing tonight, I went straight to Col... who went straight to you... only you weren't there."

Gin looked at her feet as she fiddled with her sleeve.

"I'm sorry. But I had to do what I did." she said, feebly.

"It's not me you need to apologise to." he said, looking over her shoulder. She whirled and noticed that Col had stalked off into the dimly lit courtyard. She gaped and started to go after him.

"Give him some space. He'll come to you when he's ready. Not a moment sooner." said Louis.

Gin's vision blurred again as hot tears stung her eyes. Letting him walk away was hard. She wanted to explain everything, to scream for him to come back. But she knew Louis was right. Col wouldn't be in the headspace for listening to reason right now. She'd betrayed his trust. She dragged her sleeve across her cheek, drying the tears that fell.

"Alright, lad, go get some sleep before I change my mind about going easy on you." Louis told Podraig. She watched him scamper off into the castle and was silent as Louis sidled up to her. Their breath swirled before them for a moment before speaking.

"I never meant for Col to follow me down there. He wasn't supposed to know until I could bring him the Crystal. It was the only place that he'd not searched and I just had a feeling."

Louis sucked the cold air between his teeth.

"Some hunch. I should have thought of it myself. Been down there enough times. Though, never for longer than I have to." A note of annoyance in his voice. She shook her head and huffed.

"I never meant to hurt him. But that's exactly what I have done. I put all of you in danger tonight." She shook her head at the cloudless sky, stars blinking down at her.

"It's not us that Col and I are concerned about." Gin's gaze shifted sidelong to him. "I've been at the receiving end of Brandon's madness before, Gin. He has no boundaries, no sense of right or wrong. Col was scared tonight. And I, Gin, I was terrified." he said weakly. She cocked her head away from him, not wanting to face him. "If anything had happened to you… I would not have been able to forgive myself. It would have destroyed me." he turned to her then, placing his palm on her damp cheek, bringing her gently towards him. Her stomach flipped.

She wasn't sure if she was shaking from cold, shock, or being this close to Louis. His eyes trailed their way down to her lips and her heart threatened to escape her chest as he drew closer. She swallowed, bringing her hand to his, clutching his fingers before dragging them down. She couldn't be trusted with anything in this moment of fraught emotions.

He paused, and they stood hand in hand for a minute longer, their breath swirling in the space between them, before she looked up into his pained eyes. She clamped her lips together, placing his hand on his chest.

"Never let your heart suffer over me, Louis. I am not worthy of that." she said, stepping away from him. He closed his eyes as she turned, treading softly through the stones.

"You are worthy of every ounce of pain that comes with loving you, Gin." came Louis's voice. Gin paused, breath hitched in her chest. She couldn't live with that. She would be no one's source of pain. Not anymore.

"I don't want to be." she breathed.

As she climbed the stairs to her room, she couldn't help but wish that it had been Col who uttered Louis's words. Instead, he couldn't even look at her.

Chapter Thirty-One

August rolled into September, bringing a chill to the warm summer evenings that Gin would spend tucked away in Cora's stable. It had been weeks since that night in the dungeon changed everything. The peace of mind she had found in her path to Hope and certainty in the plan to destroy Slayton had all disappeared.

Along with Col.

She hadn't seen or heard from him since. At first, she understood his absence. She had betrayed his trust, resulting in him having to face his biggest fear head on. His anger was no surprise. But as the days turned into weeks, her acceptance of his actions was wearing thin.

She didn't mind carrying out her duties as squire, taking care of Cora and the stable, polishing the dust that collected on his unused armour and helping Podraig with his duties for Louis when she found herself idle. In the time she had spent with them, she found a bond had formed.

Podraig was the kindest and most genuine person she had ever met. He was selfless in his act of helping her learn and sharing his time without resentment. And though she hated to admit it, Louis had grown on her too. After walking away from their near kiss that night, he hadn't held it against her. Annoyingly, he seemed to respect and care for her even more. As well as his duties, he would help her with those that Col was neglecting, working into lunch and dinner to see that they were done. And when they were finished for the day, he would always make sure they had a meal, often taking what was left from dinner in the kitchens.

It seemed Daphne was happy to have them, relieved that Gin was not brooding over Col's behaviour. She didn't have to ask if Daphne knew the reason for his absence. Daphne knew the ins and outs of everything here… especially where Col was concerned. And certainly wouldn't let him starve.

If the day's work left them with the energy, she and Louis would work on maps for the Hospice, trying out different routes in and out. Her knowledge of the building and the places where they could blend into shadow made the process easier to come to a conclusion.

She had also studied the notebook that she had found in the dungeon, going over it meticulously. It was indeed one of Col's mother's, detailing more Crystals and their purposes. It was all very interesting, but it was little use now that there were so few left.

She had been very amenable when Joseph asked to sit down together and read through the speech he and Slayton had come up with. And though every praising word made her blood boil, she kept a sweet smile in place of her screaming insides. It mattered not in the end. Her words would be her own… if she could just find them.

Even Lady Flora had backed off, somewhat. Now, instead of insults every time their paths crossed, she completely ignored Gin's existence. Which suited her very well.

So why, when everything was plain sailing on the surface, did she feel so unsettled inside? Why did Col's coldness consume her every thought?

It was one such morning, when she had woken before the sun, that Daphne found her in the midst of being lost in her head.

"Oh, good morning, dearie! You're up awfully early." said Daphne, placing a wicker basket of rosy red apples on a barrel. But Gin didn't reply.

Daphne did a double-take, following Gin's gaze to Cora's leather saddle, placed on its stand. Daphne edged closer, hands twisting in front of her chest.

"Uh… everything alright, dearie?" she asked, cautiously.

Gin was silent a moment longer, hands limp by her side. Finally, she spoke, still fixated on the saddle.

"It moves." she said flatly. "I leave the buckles fastened each night and yet every morning they are undone, and it's left slightly lopsided." She finally met Daphne's gaze, which broke from surprise into a forced smile. But she said nothing. Which, for Daphne, told Gin more than words ever could. She was hiding something. Gin angled her body towards her, crossing her arms.

"Daphne?"

Daphne wrung her hands over her large bosom. She tried to keep her smile in place, but under Gin's narrowing eyes it faltered into a grimace.

"Oh, Gin... I didn't know if you'd want to know. I mean, it's just, you seem to have settled into such ease here since..." she trailed off, searching the air for words.

"Since Col stopped speaking to me?" said Gin, finishing for her, a flash of heat striking her chest. Daphne was silent again. "I know you are all thrilled with the way I have bowed to every expectation with a smile, Daphne, but I..." she rubbed her forehead, scrambling for air in the bottled heat of her emotions. "I am not ok!" she finished, eyes burning.

Daphne closed the space between them in an instant, hesitating before helping her sit on the stool beside them.

"Oh Gin." Gin braced her knees, if only to keep her hands from shaking even more.

"You see him, don't you?" Their eyes met and Daphne stilled. "He comes here every night to take Cora out for her ride, doesn't he?" she asked, knowing it needn't be a question. And still, the void of silence stretched out. Daphne's ability to talk for king and country had seemingly dried up. "He hates me." Her head bowed. It was confirmation of the frustrating fear that had built over the past weeks.

Daphne suddenly spurred into action.

"Oh goodness, dearie, no. I don't think he does, not a bit." she crouched down. "Col is perhaps the most complicated, infuriating, intense person I know. But if you're lucky enough to know the part of him he masks... well... you're not someone who he'll just stop caring about. And Gin, believe me when I say he *cares* about you."

Gin's eyes slid to hers, her teeth clenched as she processed her words.

"I very much doubt that now. And I don't need him to care about me." Her voice was dark, distant. Daphne pursed her lips.

"Oh, don't be so quick to refuse people. Especially when the one giving you their fondness gives it so rarely." said Daphne. Gin's cheeks hollowed, refusing to believe that Col cared. Not now. It made her betrayal hurt all the more.

"He wants nothing to do with me, Daphne. He has made that perfectly clear." She stood, picking up an apple from the basket and walking over to Cora's stable.

She clicked her tongue on the roof of her mouth and waited for Cora to make her exceptional appearance, towering over her. Her bond with Cora had also grown. She no longer cowered away from her, accepting her exactly how she was. Daphne tutted loudly.

"He would not come to your room every night, just to check you're still here if that were t-" Daphne halted mid-sentence, mouth open.

Gin's head whipped around, eyes wide. Cora plucked the apple from her palm, startling her.

"What?" she asked, stepping back from Coras's soft probing muzzle.

Daphne seemed to shrink, all too aware she'd put her foot in it.

"Uh, well… now, I promised not to say anything. He thought he went unnoticed! But of course, I'm up all hours of the night sometimes, seeing to the requests of Lady Flora, a-a-and well…" she wiped her hands on her pinafore, "I caught him leaving one night."

Gin's mouth hit the dusty floor. Her heart throbbed, but all she could hear was the ringing in her ears. Daphne's hurried explanations dissolved.

How had she slept through his comings and goings all this time? And why would he even bother when he couldn't even stand to come back to his duties and face her? Only to sedate his need to check on her, but not even care enough to wake her, to *speak* to her. She fumbled over each and every thought until it became too much to even think about.

"Well." She straightened, huffing. "Daphne, I believe you are right about one thing. He really is the most infuriating person. Excuse me." she said, leaving her floundering as she marched away from the yard, out into the open rolling fields that overlooked the arena.

Col's cottage peeked out from behind the wild front garden, no light from within. Just as cold as he had turned out to be.

A few spots of rain landed on her face, simmering the heat of her cheeks. She had been a fool. And what angered her even more was that she had let him under her skin enough to let this bother her so.

Her fingers caressed the necklace he had given her. His promise to never let her down, to always be there…

"Let's see if you really meant it". She said to herself. Through the fog that clouded her mind, one thing stood clear. One thing that Col had taught her himself. She *would* be heard.

The air was sharp as she inhaled through her nose. Her chin rose as she gazed at the arena, its proud walls unnaturally quiet, sleeping with the rest of the castle. The fire that burned her skin in anger now turned to fuel in her belly.

Gin would not wait for Col to decide she was worthy of his breath. She would draw him out the one way she could be sure to get his attention. She would play dirty. And hope that his promise was real.

The rain fell in droves throughout the morning, and visitors crowded into the arena, heading for the shelter of the wooden stalls, ready for their knights.

Gin pushed her way through the hoards of people, fighting her way to the stable yard at the back of the arena, hoping to get a glimpse before they came out. The guard on the door, who she had come to know as Large Larry, spotted her, parting the crowd for her.

"Squire Gin, Sir Col is still not in the joust. Can I assist you?" he asked as she panted her way to him.

"I know. I'm here to help Podraig squire for Sir Louis today." she said, pressing her lips flat. Larry's brows knitted, his enormous shoulders heaving with his breath. She absolutely wasn't here for that reason, but she hoped it was at least believable.

"Right. OK. I think they've arrived already. Didn't mention you were coming, but better hurry if you are to aid them." He nodded to the gate as he opened it for her. Gin grinned, nodding as she slid through the gap and pressed herself against the closed gate.

The yard was mostly empty, the knights all in their stalls, avoiding the pounding rain that dripped heavily from the towering trees. She darted over the puddles and into Louis's stall, averting her eyes as she was met with his shirtless chest, frozen at her appearance.

"Gin. Is everything ok?" he asked, frowning at her bedraggled hair, clinging to her neck. She rubbed idly at her nose as she spoke, trying to avoid looking at his chest.

"Yes, uh… I'm fine." she said, risking a glance. He looked down, noting the cause of her flushed cheeks, and took the padded shirt that Podraig held out, promptly putting it on. Relieved, she settled her wandering gaze.

"I need your help." she said, nostrils flaring. Louis took a step closer to her, head cocked.

"Anything. Always." he said, eyes crinkling around the edges. Gin took a deep breath, not sure he would be so eager to help once he knew what she was asking.

"I need you to step out of the joust."

A bark of laughter leapt from his chest. But his smile slipped as Gin kept a grave eye on him.

"What? why on earth, Gin?" he exclaimed. She considered her next words, afraid to offend him whilst considering the bond they had formed in Col's absence.

"I have tried to ignore Col's silence, Louis. I have tried so hard to just carry on as if everything is fine and I haven't caused an immeasurable amount of suffering for him." Louis's brows twitched momentarily. "But we all know that isn't true." She looked at her hands, twisting a silver ring.

"What does any of that have to do with me stepping out of this joust?" he asked, raising his chin and taking a swig of water from his flask. Gin swallowed.

"I can't carry on being ignored. Being unheard and avoided." She squared her shoulders. "I need to pretend to be Col and take your place today."

Louis choked down his mouthful of water, pressing a fist to his lips. She winced.

"Uh, I'm sorry." he gasped, Podraig coming to stand just behind him, arms crossed, looking thoroughly perplexed. "You want to compete... as Col? Against Sir Tarrick? A knight ten times stronger and heavier than you. Are you absolutely mad, Gin?" he blinked, Podraig shaking his head in agreement. She pursed her lips. She had come prepared for a fight.

"I am quite aware of Sir Tarrick's power and I hope it won't actually come to having to joust." she said, holding her palms out. "I just need Col to hear his name announced over the speaker, so that he will come out of hiding and have to face me!" she pleaded.

"That is completely impulsive and I would be totally irresponsible to let you go ahead with this, Gin." Louis shook his head, face screwed up. "It is far too dangerous. If Col doesn't come, and I've not seen him this morose for a long time so your chances are slim, you will be left on the tilt with Sir Tarrick, who will likely knock you off on the first run!" he said, gasping for breath, hands on his hips.

Gin stilled for a moment.

"You've seen him too." it wasn't a question. She knew the answer. Louis opened his mouth to answer, but she cut him off. It just added more fuel to her already blazing fire.

"It doesn't matter. If he doesn't come and I get hurt, you will take me to Col and make him heal me. Either way, he will stop wallowing and start listening to me." She stepped back with one foot, fixing them both under her gaze.

Louis licked his lips slowly, looking to the rafters. He let a long sigh escape.

"Why do you care so much? You know by now, he is no saint. Why is it so important that you ease his suffering when he has caused a great deal more for others?" he asked. Gin blinked, unsure of how to answer. She didn't know why she cared, only that she did. Perhaps it was because they weren't so different in their quests.

"I understand what it is to love a child." She gave Podraig a fleeting look. His arms unlocked, sagging by his sides. But he remained silent. "What that love could drive you to. I wouldn't wish it on anyone. But if you care for me as much as you say you do, you have to at least understand that the love you hold for a child... that I hold for Hope, is irreplaceable. I only wanted to help Col with some of the challenges he faces, like he's helped me face mine. I know it was stupidly dangerous, but it was worth the risk."

Louis swallowed, clearing his throat as he swept a hand over his beard.

"I should have known my mother would send me a devil-may-care soulmate." he said, looking down his nose at her. She scowled and was ready to argue her case some more, but his face softened.

"If I think it's gone too far, I will tell Joseph and pull the plug," he said. Gin gave him a small smile, nodding. That was better than nothing.

He twisted his head, talking to Podraig but keeping his eyes on Gin.

"Tell Joseph that I have pulled a muscle in my arm... Sir Col will step in."

Podraig chewed his lip, looking between them, clearly not happy with the decision. But he nodded, leaving as instructed.

Gin's heart was beating wildly. She was doing it.

"I had Daphne help me bring Cora down earlier. I just need some help... suiting up." she said, clearing her throat. There was no way she'd be able to do it alone, no matter how uncomfortable she would be.

A muscle worked in Louis's jaw as he frowned, eyes darting around her.

"Come on. Podraig's armour will fit you better. You can use Col's heraldry over the top." he said, motioning to a partitioned wall. "You can dress in the padded undergarments and uh, when you're ready, I'll come and help with the armour." he said, biting his reddening cheeks. She ran a hand through her damp hair, unsticking it from her neck as she scurried past him and into the stall.

As he placed the armour onto different parts of her body a while later, she didn't feel the stifling nerves she had felt when helping Col. Her mind was too preoccupied with what she was about to do. What if he didn't come? What if he didn't even want to heal her afterwards? She was numb to all else except the doubts that crept over her.

Gin barely noticed him finish until she saw him step back to survey her, asking her to try moving. It was ridiculously hard, like trying to move through water. Thankfully, she wouldn't have to walk once mounted.

They dressed Cora, with more difficulty than she'd seen Col do it. She chuffed through it all, fidgeting with more indignation than she'd witnessed before. Gin was sure she could tell something wasn't right, that it wasn't her master underneath the helmet.

"Please tell me you have at least ridden before?" Louis asked, leading Gin on the back of Cora to the stable door. She squeezed her knees to gain her balance.

"Nope." She looked down, focusing on her feet in the stirrups. "Does it show?" Her eyes slid to his. He heaved a sigh, trying to smile, but worry etched his brow.

"Just try to relax. It might feel you need to tense up to stay on, but relaxing makes it a lot easier." He patted Gin's back, causing her to straighten. Even through the armour, her scars protested. "Sit up straight, shoulders back. Hold on tight to the reins and *do not* go into a full canter. Keep it slow, like I showed you."

She nodded, gazing out at the pounding rain bouncing off the ground. She was completely out of her depth, there was no denying it. But it didn't matter to her. All that did was getting through to Col.

The beating of the drums was coming to a crescendo, along with her pulse. It wouldn't be long before Joseph's voice came booming through the arena.

Sir Tarrick made his way slowly through the rain, swaying gently with the movement of his horse. It was time.

Her shoulders heaved upwards as she pushed the visor of her helmet down.

"Thank you, Louis." she said, looking straight ahead. "I really do appreciate your help."

Louis came into view.

"I don't think I could bring myself to not help you, Gin." he said weakly. Gin's heart fluttered in her chest. She knew he meant every word, and that was beginning to create a mix of emotions she wasn't sure she was ready to deal with.

Podraig came running back to the stable, head ducked in the rain. They stood together, looking at her upon the magnificent horse. Louis nodded, squeezing Podraig's shoulder.

"You're Gin's squire today. The weather will not do us any favours, so don't take your eyes away for a second. I will watch from the stalls, ready to step in if needed." He gave her a pointed look. She gave a tight smile, although he couldn't see it.

With that, Podraig led her out, slowly, the rain tapping the metal of her armour like a steel band. She reached a gloved hand out, gliding it over Cora's sinewy neck, and whispered.

"Let's go get our Master back."

Chapter Thirty-Two

"Ladies and gentleman, the moment I know you've been patiently waiting for!
The return of the only knight of his calibre, Sir Col!" Joseph's showman voice
roared through the arena, reaching Gin's ears, muffled by the rain that pounded her
helmet. Her eyes strained through the small gap that allowed her to see. The thick
steam billowed around her, calling her forwards.

She could feel Cora pawing the ground, ready to charge down the tilt. But she had
to keep her steady. She had to take control. Her breath warmed her face in the
confines of her helmet.

"Gin?" came Padraig's strained voice from beside her. She blinked several times,
getting her bearings. She was taking too long.

"Come now, Sir Col! Your people await your glorious return!" The crowd went
into a frenzy at Joseph's words, whipping her into action too.

The gentle squeeze of her legs to get Cora walking turned into a bump... and she
was off.

Gin flew back into the saddle, the force with which Cora galloped out of the gate
knocking the air from her lungs. She held onto the front of the saddle as she tried
to settle into the pounding pace that Cora had slipped into, the motion like
ferocious waves in a storm filled sea. Her surroundings were a blur, even as she
emerged from the smoke. She squeezed her eyes shut, legs gripping Cora's belly
with way too much force than she'd been told. Her heart had never raced so fast as

nausea roiled in her stomach. Trying to calm her breathing, she remembered what Louis had told her.

Relax. Relax.

As Cora approached the podium, Gin tugged on her reins with one hand, slowing her to a steady trot. Although she couldn't make out who was who up there, she knew Joseph and Lady Flora were watching. Her cheeks heated. Surely they would realise in an instant that it was not Col within her armour. She only hoped the pouring rain would cloud their judgement.

With a clenched jaw, she slowly relaxed her legs, releasing the pressure. She pulled her shoulders back and tugged Cora to the right, positioning her at the end of the tilt.

"Ah, it would seem Sir Col is not taking any favours today. He has always been one for strength in his solitude." Joseph quipped.

Crap. Gin realised she had forgotten to take a favour from the audience. She thanked Col's unpredictability, making her mistake not too unusual.

Cora nodded her head feverishly as she waited for what she knew was coming. For what Gin now felt, weighing on her chest. Col had not come.

She would have to joust.

She tightened her fingers around the reins, staring down the tilt at Sir Tarrick, sitting proudly upon his stead. His young squire approached with his lance, which he took with swiftness and grace, making it appear lighter than air.

She looked around for Podraig, clocking him to her right, bringing her own lance. His eyebrows were low as he stopped by her side, squinting up at her through the rain.

"*Gin.*" he whispered. But she could not heed the warning in his voice. She'd come this far. She wouldn't back down now.

She held out a trembling hand, a silent command.

Podraig grimaced, flexing his fingers around the lance before passing it to her.

She nodded once, signalling him to leave as the crowds cheered for their knights to begin.

The weight of the lance pulled her to the right, so much so that she had to pull on the saddle to prop herself up again. She screwed her face up, a groan escaping her, gripping the lance with all the might she had and couched it under her arm. Blowing out a hard breath, she focused upon Sir Tarrick, swallowing the nausea that rocked her.

"Sir Tarrick, Sir Col... as always, may your match be fought in honour, valour and, most of all, respect," said Joseph. Gin was sure there was an edge of uncertainty about his voice. But it only charged the fire within her to make this foolish act count.

Gripping the lance firmly, she trained her sight between Cora's slick ears, steam rising from the heat of her body into the cold, damp air. With a nod of Sir Tarrick's head, she gave one last glance to the gates for Col to have arrived, to save her from what was sure to be an enormous beating. But she was alone. She'd do this the hard way.

"OK, Cora. It's you and me." she whispered before nodding to Sir Tarrick.

The trumpets sounded, and she nudged Cora into action, jarring backwards as she held on tight to the reins, riding the waves that tossed her away from the ground.

She was blind and deaf to all but the pounding of her heart and the rain on her armour. They blazed down the tilt towards an invisible target, gasping for air as she tried not to drown in fear.

On and on.

Bracing for impact at any second.

She pulled her arm into her chest, preparing for the hit...

But it never came.

Cora slowed, falling into the routine of a path taken hundreds of times. Gin blinked hard, trying to see through the pouring rain that battered the ground as she twisted, turning Cora with her.

Sir Tarrick appeared, still in starting position, a brow cocked from his raised visor... and a dark figure stood by his side, legs wide, shoulders heaving.

Gin whipped up her visor, expecting to see Louis, having lost his nerve at the last minute and calling it off. But as Cora plodded over the sodden ground, she was met with the flinty gaze of all too familiar electric sky-blue eyes.

She froze, pulling Cora to a standstill, both panting as raindrops skipped down her cheeks.

Col stared, jaw locked, lip curled as he restrained the anger that simmered below the surface. His usually smooth jaw was shadowed with stubble, his black hair glistening in the rain. The drums continued to pound over the speaker, but the audience was quiet. Watching. Waiting.

Col inclined his head to the side, achingly slow, before marching over to her and grabbing the reins. She swallowed through the dryness of her throat, clutching the saddle as he led them back through the gates, leaving Joseph floundering to save face back in the arena. She was sure he'd find her soon enough. There had been far too many failed jousts since she started for him to overlook this one. His patience would be wearing paper thin.

But her thoughts were good for one thing only, right now. And she had a feeling this was going to make up for the knockout she didn't receive on the tilt.

She kept her eyes trained on Col all the way to the stable, trying to gauge what she was walking into. His silence told her everything she needed to know. He was pissed.

Col stomped around to her left, throwing the wooden dismount block crashing into a puddle. He held out a hand to help her down, eyes cast on the ground before him.

Gin gritted her teeth, riled by his crassness. Pushing herself up in the saddle, with great effort under the weight of armour, she swung her leg over the back of Cora, dismounting without his help. She landed on the block, his sharp gaze finally meeting hers. Heart thumping against her ribs, she waited, willing him to speak first. After a dragged out moment, he stepped out of her way.

"In." he ordered, pushing his stable door open.

Gin curled her fingers. The fact that he was angry did nothing to make her feel guilty this time. She was ready for whatever he had to throw at her. A version of him screaming and shouting was better than the chasm of his absence.

She ripped off her gloves as she marched past him and out of the relentless rain, chucking them onto a bale of hay. Pulling off her helmet, her damp hair stuck to the slick metal of her armour. She watched, breathing hard as Col took Cora's armour off in the stall next to her. She could barely contain her anger as, even now, standing in the very same room, he refused to speak to her.

She pressed her lips together and unbuckled her own armour, with far more aggression than needed. But it felt good. Until she reached the straps at her shoulders, which proved tricky to do alone. She strained, trying to reach them, getting more and more flustered by the second, when a hand landed on hers, moving it away.

She froze, refusing to look at him, her chest heaving as Col took over from behind. His hand brushed her cheek accidentally, filling her senses with that scent of blackberry and leather. She closed her eyes against it, trying to loathe the scent of him. And failing. It felt frustratingly good to smell that familiar scent again.

When he slipped her breastplate off, she spun around. But he had already left her to dress without so much as a second glance.

She wanted to scream. She wanted to run up to him and scream in his face. To make him *feel* something, make him say something, *anything*!

Those thoughts consumed her as she slipped back into her damp squire clothes, wrapping her cold, green jacket around her. She hadn't realised how chilled she had been. Her very bones trembled as she tried to rub some warmth back into her arms.

When she stepped out of the stall, Col was leaning against the door, staring out at the torrential downpour. She halted, lips pursed.

"What in the name of hell, Gin?" he growled, not looking at her.

"So you remember my name then." she said, the corners of her mouth turning downwards. Col's head whipped around.

"Are you absolutely insane? You do realise you could have been seriously injured out there? Beyond the healing capability of what little I have left of the Crystals!" he said, voice rising above the onslaught of the rain, as he closed the space between them.

Heat flushed her neck as he stared her down.

"If you hadn't been so self-absorbed these past few weeks and found the courage to actually talk to me, I wouldn't have *had* to go to extremes to get your attention! But you couldn't see past your own selfishness!" she seethed. Col's eyes danced over her face, leaving a trail of fire.

"Yeah, well, that's me. Don't pretend you didn't know that already." he said, turning to walk into the courtyard.

"That's not good enough, Col! Don't walk away again!" she said, following him out into the pouring rain. "You made a promise!" she held the pendant in her fingers, watching his eyes fall to it as he spun around. His eyes narrowed, jaw set.

"Exactly. I promised I would never let you or Louis down again, which is precisely why I stayed away, Gin." His brows knitted, painfully. "Because you're right. I *am* selfish... but like it or not, you are the one person I *cannot* be selfish with!"

"Then why bother checking up on me every night?" she blurted, unable to bottle it. His lips shrivelled to a thin line as he froze. "Daphne saw you. It was always going to get back to me. Why bother, Col?"

"Because... I..." His stumbling prodded annoyingly at her chest. She didn't want to feel sorry for him in this moment. "I bring out the most reckless version of you, Gin." He wiped the back of his hand across his wet forehead, face screwed up. "You keep putting yourself in situations that I can't protect you from. And for the first time in, I don't even know how long, I seem to care enough for it to scare me!" His eyes were wide with fear as his breathing uneven. "I had to make sure you hadn't run off to Slayton and completely ruined your chances of taking him down. Or worse."

She stared wide eyed, his words softening the edge of her anger. It was the last reason she expected for his absence.

"You can't protect me from myself, Col, and I don't need to be coddled. That version of me has always been there. I've always been reckless. I put myself at risk every time I sneaked around the Hospice at night to help people." She paused. "I don't need anybody's protection."

Col shook his head as he ran a hand through his hair.

"But *you* shouldn't have gone down there, Gin." His voice was strained. "Putting yourself at risk *for me* like that… I lost my damn mind." he panted, raindrops sliding down his face, his black shirt clinging to his skin. "That danger was mine to face. You could have been…" he trailed off. She knew what words were trapped in his throat and a stab of guilt pricked at her chest. "I can't lose you to my demons." His head dropped, eyes to the ground.

Gin's nose wrinkled as she placed her hands on his stubbled cheeks, pulling his eyes back to hers. His words hit her with the weight of a hundred suits of armour.

"I faced it because I couldn't bear the thought of you having to. You trusted me enough to show me the worst part of you, and I couldn't let you revisit that darkness." she said. Deep half-moons of troubles nestled beneath his lashes. They lingered in each other's eyes for a moment too long. She blinked away, pulling herself into reality. The muscles worked in his jaw, her fingers brushing them as she let her hands fall. He shook his head softly.

"You're doing me no favours with my image, Sparkles." he said. "My tough knight reputation seems to be failing ever since you arrived." Gin smirked softly at the return of her nickname on his lips. "I'm getting weaker by the day."

She felt the heat rise in her cheeks and crossed her arms to deflect.

"You are many things, Sir Col, but *weak* is not one of them. To acknowledge the feelings you want to bury is no flaw. It's a strength." For a moment, she nearly lost herself entirely to the intensity of his gaze, the warmth of his breath soft against her face. She blinked through the raindrops, that soul connection to Louis tugging at the back of her mind. She could not continue to allow herself to get so comfortably close with Col. It just seemed to happen so easily.

She swallowed, running a hand through her hair, letting it idle there in the wet tangles. Col's shoulders rose and fell heavily as he weighed her words.

Letting her hand fall, she took a deep breath, bracing herself to tackle the most important thing that had come from her dungeon visit.

"How old would he be?" she asked gently. "When you return." He ran a hand over his forehead, rubbing a phantom pain. His silence unnerved her.

"Col?" she asked.

"Nine... he'd be nine years old. All too aware that his own father didn't come save him." he said bitterly, squinting into the distance.

"But you didn't know!" she breathed, shoulders hitched.

"He didn't know that, though. All he knew was that I left him alone in this world, at just *five* years old, to face god knows what. How could I ever make that right? How could he ever believe that I had no choice?" he said. Gin's nostrils flared as her throat ached and tears pooled. This was all too close to home. And Col realised too late.

"Argh... shit." his chin dipped. She shook her head, trying to shake the pain away with it.

"Gin, this is nothing like you and Hope," he said, stepping closer. "You won't be leaving it for years. We're going to get your baby home before she's old enough to stew on why you left. I promise you that."

Gin pressed her lips together, unable to look at him despite his attempts. Yet another lie that she was imposing on him. She'd be gone before he knew what she and Louis had done. And she didn't know for certain that Hope would even accept her after coming clean, admitting she wasn't her actual mother. Maybe she'd want nothing to do with her. A sickening feeling settled in her stomach at the thought of her actually wanting to stay with Slayton. Who knows what he'd said of her in her absence.

"I know, Col, I know..." she trailed off, searching for a way back to Max, away from her looming fate. "But the love of family is unlike anything. Max won't have given up on you, I just know it." she said, wiping a tear that had settled on her nose. "Just promise me you won't give up on him."

Col was quiet as he surveyed her. He dropped his head and watched his feet shuffle his weight in the puddles.

"There's not a plane of existence where I'd give up on him... I just pray he won't have given up on me."

"You're an impossibly tough person to give up on. Believe me, I've tried." she said, rolling her eyes. He drew up to hers, brows raised, perhaps in realisation of how close he was to losing her. They electrified her core, intoxicating her entire body as they warmed, trailing to her lips. She pressed them together.

"Damn it, Gin..." he paused, lips parted, as if to speak again, when heavy footsteps hurried towards them.

Gin took a step away from the unwise closeness they had found themselves in, to see Louis running over, holding an umbrella over Lady Flora at his heel. She risked a glance at Col, his eyes still burning through her.

"Ah, excellent. You haven't killed each other," he said, catching his breath as he held the brolly over her too. Lady Flora gave her a disapproving look. "I rather think Joseph wants the honour himself." said Louis, wincing at the pair.

Col finally dragged his eyes away, raising a brow at Louis.

"Excellent. It's been too long since I've been a pain in his ass." he said, scuffing his boot through a puddle.

Gin wrapped her arms around herself, the wind biting at her sodden skin.

Lady Flora eyed the pair, no doubt making assumptions in her head about what was going on and why. But she didn't ask, acting as though Gin wasn't even in the equation at all.

"Col, I'm so glad you're out and about again. I've been worried. Come, it's dreadful out here. Let's take tea in my quarters." she said, oblivious to the fact that he wasn't paying her a speck of attention. His gaze was intent upon Gin, unspoken words locked away behind his clenched jaw.

Louis suddenly shoved the brolly into Col's hand, mouth wide as he surveyed Gin's trembling jaw.

"Goodness, look at you. You'll catch your death. Come on, let's get you back up to the castle." he said, removing his jacket and putting it around her shoulders.

She didn't protest the gesture. She was soaked to the bone and freezing from the cold metal armour. But she didn't miss the flash of bitterness on Col's face or the flare of his nostrils as he watched his brother's arms around her. Her chin dipped, trying to hide her reddening cheeks. She couldn't untangle the web of emotions she felt around these two. It was like betrayal whenever her feelings strayed too far for either, from the precarious rope she kept them balanced on.

"You can resume this battle later." said Louis, grabbing the brolly and guiding her away, leaving Lady Flora and Col at the mercy of the rain.

Again, she didn't protest… but she was sure something in her chest did when Col's fingers brushed hers lightly as she was swept away.

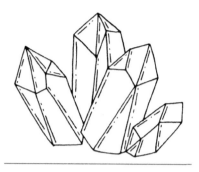

Chapter Thirty-Three

Joseph's resentment hadn't lasted long. Of course, it began with a heavy hand, flat out banning Col from competing for the rest of the season. But Gin was not blind to Col's indifference, even as she watched Joseph turn almost tomato red above his curled moustache, scolding him on everything possible. From bringing shame upon the entire establishment, to putting Gin in harm's way. Outwardly, Col played along with the severity of his punishment. But as soon as they left Joseph's office, he flashed his devil-may-care smirk, sliding his hands into his pockets. As he pointed out, not only would it give them plenty of time to work on her speech and to study the Crystals they had left, but he was quick to add that he didn't have to pretend to like people for the coming weeks.

However, the downtime didn't last long. Three days into his banishment, Joseph interrupted their Crystal study with his tail well and truly between his legs. Apparently, the reception had been flooded with complaints about Sir Col being out of action, and demand for shows had doubled. People actually enjoyed the drama and tension in the arena. It did not surprise Gin that Joseph's concern for anyone's safety had been overshadowed by ticket sales.

Louis had not taken kindly to Joseph's decision. She had no doubt in her mind that he also enjoyed not having to contend with his brother's antics or worry about her safety. Although neither he nor Lady Flora approved of the time they still spent in each other's company while off the field. Sometimes their work had taken them well into the night and she'd fallen asleep, curled up by the fireplace in his cottage. It wasn't lost on her that the fire was still burning in the morning. He always made sure she never woke up cold.

Of course, Daphne had been the first to question her on the nights she had spent there. But there was nothing to tell. Whether either of them felt anything, Col didn't stray from his vow of not letting Louis down and neither had she. The strange pressure of being tied up to Louis on a soul level had meant that she too kept a firm hand on the ever-increasing flutters she felt in her belly around Col that continued to baffle her. She couldn't let it mean anything her mind tried to drown her in. She was not meant for anyone except to be there for Hope. And Louis already complicated that.

This meant that dragging herself away from Col's warm cottage when the hour ticked closer to midnight was crucial. No matter how fast her pulse raced with every goodnight that lingered a few seconds too long.

It was on one morning she'd woken up in the biting cold of her room in the castle, too early for Daphne to have lit her fire, to a voice rolling over her like water on gravel, a voice that didn't belong to the man in her nightmare. A voice she wanted to run to. To get away from the lashings that struck her back and the blinding flashes of white light.

Again.

And again.

And again.

And...

She felt a hand on her arm and immediately lashed out, only to open her eyes to see Col ducking out of her way, crouched down at her bedside. His eyes were wide and intent upon her while her heart hammered in her chest and ears, like it was going to burst out of her ribcage.

"Hey... hey." he whispered. "Nightmare." he winced.

Gin pushed her hair from her face, slick with sweat.

"I'm sorry. It always feels so real." she whispered, looking around, confused as to why he was there before the scurrying of the castle staff had even begun. She peered bleary-eyed at the dark sky beyond the unshuttered window. She liked the stars too much to shut them out. "It can't be morning yet." she said.

Col rubbed his palms together slowly as he inhaled, hedging around his answer.

"Oh god. It is morning… it's today Col." she struggled to get her words out, the air in her lungs seemed too little.

Col swallowed and nodded slowly. He had been sitting here, waiting for her to wake up and register what day it was.

"Happy Halloween." he said, with a gentle lopsided smile, wrapped in concern. She planted her head in her palms, breathing as much of the thin air in as she could. He sighed softly.

"Hey." he said, gently lifting her chin so that her hands fell away. "It's not every Halloween you get to take down a real monster." His eyes narrowed. "You've got this. I know for a fact that you are more than ready to face him."

She shook her head, doubt searing through her chest at the finality of this day. Not only about Slayton, but leaving Col behind tonight. It hurt more than she cared to admit.

"Yes," he said firmly. "*All* the pieces are set. Oldman thinks you're ready to kiss ass tonight with his version of the speech," Gin frowned, remembering the all-praising speech she'd been given. All she had had to do was to add a slight detail here and there. The ribbon that tied up his Ball, ensuring that guests would dig deep in their pockets with those donations.

"But the work you've put in on *your* speech and the times we went over it last night…" She noticed his Adam's apple bob as he searched for words. "It's going to haunt Slayton for the rest of his damn life, and every other snooty-headed person in that room."

Gin forced herself to smile, but it was a grimace that graced her lips. She still hadn't confessed to him about the lashings, afraid of what he might do beforehand if he found out. She had said just enough in her speech that she and Col had worked on making him think she was taking him down with it. But that too was a bluff. Her actual speech was much shorter. Enough to cause irreparable damage once revealing her scars on that stage. They were sure to say more than her words ever could. She'd take him out with fearsome gentleness.

"Thank you... I couldn't have gone into those places of my mind without you." she said, hanging her head.

"It was *you* who went there. Your bravery retrieved those memories. Not mine." he said, taking the pendant that hung around her neck and turning it slowly in his fingers. "You are more powerful than you know." he said, letting go and fixing her with a lopsided gaze. She huffed a small laugh. She wished she could capture the way he looked at her now, eyes soft and glossy, like he truly believed she was everything he built her up to be. No one looked at her the way he did, with total belief. And she was mere hours away from possibly never having that again. She felt her chest deflate as he broke his gaze, pressing his lips together.

These moments of unspoken words that lived only through dragged out gazes were becoming almost unbearable. She was forever at war with herself, longing to know what was on his mind, yet knowing it was safer to remain in the dark.

"It's early yet. Go back to sleep." he said, standing slowly and walking away. A sudden rush of panic tingled through her. She didn't want to go back to sleep, fearing that Slayton would be waiting for her again as soon as she closed her eyes. Her fingers clawed at her shoulders, pulling her knees into her chest.

"Wait." she didn't know what was going to come out of her mouth, but one thing was certain. She didn't want to be left alone. The realisation hit her like a ton of bricks. Alone had always been her security. Alone brought peace. Until this man who didn't even belong in this world erupted into hers. This man who could never be hers. This man whose brother stood like a barrier between them.

Col paused, sinking his hands into his pockets as he looked down at her. She swallowed the dryness in her throat. She was already lost to this maddening effect he had on her. There was no fighting it now. She just had to soak up what she could before tonight and deal with the fallout later.

"Stay. Please... I don't want to wake up alone." Her cheeks heated at the words that left her. But no matter the foolishness, they were true.

Col's brows knitted as he hovered on the edge of whatever battle was going on in his mind. She knew she was asking a lot. Louis would not condone his brother staying in her quarters, even if it was just to sleep. She felt the spike of shame on her cheeks, too. But it wasn't enough to quell her need for Col to stay until the gravity of the day met her.

He walked lazily over to the bed, the mattress giving under his weight as he sat on the edge. She met his weary eyes. Long hours of shows rimmed them with dark circles. She felt a pang of guilt at being another reason to keep him awake at night. Shifting over, she left enough room for him to lie down too. She watched him silently as his eyes slid from the space up to her, assessing her certainty of him laying with her. Despite the rapid beat of her heart, she kept her breathing even. Finally, he stretched out beside her, one hand behind his head, the other on his stomach, focused on the ceiling as she stayed curled up by his chest. Her stomach fluttered uncontrollably as she watched it rise and fall with each breath, his blackberry and leather scent settling on her sheets.

"You're gonna be the death of me, Sparkles." His voice was hoarse, that muscle in his smooth jaw tensing again. Gin's brows rose slightly as she suppressed a smile. She couldn't help but bask in the knowledge that *she* made this fortress of a man cave into the softer side he kept so tightly bound. *She* made him want to check on her in the middle of the night. And there she fell into a peaceful slumber, free from Slayton, with the ghost of a smile on her lips.

The familiar smell of sweet, hot milk filled Gin's senses as she and Col descended the stairs to the kitchen a couple of hours later, before the hubbub of the castle set in.

Daphne stood over a large pot on the fire, stirring the porridge. It was such a familiar sight to Gin now, to see Daphne staring into a pot of bubbling something or other. As she hovered in the doorway, she realised with a pang of sadness that she was going to miss this too. The comfort in knowing that she could always find Daphne if she needed, in the kitchens, preparing food for the hungry mouths of the castle.

She'd have to step up to that role after tonight. She'd not only have to source food for herself, but Hope too… maybe even Louis. Her insides folded.

"Oh! Heavens, you gave me a fright!" she cried, as Col peered over Daphne's shoulder and inhaled deeply. It drew Gin from her thoughts.

"Gotta keep that ticker of yours fine tuned, Daph." he said, putting an arm around her shoulder.

"You'll be the one to stop it one of these days." she said, tutting. Col grinned to Gin, who tried to return it. But she could still feel the lump that had formed in her throat upon seeing Daphne. She cleared her throat.

"Can we do anything to help?" she asked, her voice tight. Daphne glanced over and smiled warmly.

"Bless you, dearie. I'm running behind already! With the castle closed today, Joseph's pulled my staff to help in preparations for tonight, so I'm left to feed an army with my own two hands. Those apples need chopping, if you wouldn't mind, and there should be some ground nutmeg over there on the shelf." She nodded towards row upon row of herbs, spices, pots and pans and wooden ladles. Col retrieved the nutmeg while Gin cut the apples.

They filled their bellies well under strict orders from Daphne, choosing to eat in the kitchen instead. Gin couldn't face what was bound to be a room full of excited people.

As they were scraping the bottom of their bowls, a clatter of footsteps came down the staircase and ended in a flustered-looking Lady Flora and a young maid, who looked just as out of breath.

"Daphne, I must tell you, I really think my dress-" she stopped, noticing the company in the kitchen. Col didn't stop eating on her account, although Gin was sure he had scraped every last drop out of the bowl already.

Lady Flora eyed them both, mouth opening and closing like a fish out of water. Gin stood and took her bowl to wash up, anything to avoid having to be a part of the conversation with her.

"Your dress, my lady?" Daphne prompted, glancing up as she dashed about.

"Uh, yes. It's the neckline. It's not sitting right. We must alter it before this evening."

"Lower, if possible?" came a voice from the stairs. Gin glanced over her shoulder to see Tarrick stroll up behind her, placing a hand on her waist. Lady Flora shifted slightly, eyes darting to Col.

The scraping from Col's bowl ceased and Gin turned to see him wiping his mouth on a napkin, staring at the table.

"Right. I'll come straight to your rooms after breakfast, Lady Flora." said Daphne, as politely as she could, but the undercurrent of annoyance did not go amiss to Gin.

"Thank you." she said, her lips pursed as she fussed with a piece of fluff on her sleeve.

"We'll take breakfast in Lady Flora's rooms too." said Tarrick, his chest thrust out. Lady Flora's eyes flashed and a forced smile plastered onto her lips.

"*Please, Tarrick.*" she berated, "I don't think the whole room needs to hear about where you're having breakfast." Tarrick sighed with a roll of his eyes.

"I beg to differ." he muttered under his breath, gaze sliding to Col.

Gin bit her lip, the whole situation taking a road she didn't want to travel down, drying her hands on a cloth with slow precision. But oddly, she found her gaze drifting to Col as well, curious. She hadn't been aware that he'd stopped seeing Lady Flora.

Col ran his tongue over his lips and threw his napkin onto the table, smirking to himself.

"*What* you eat and *where*, is none of my business, Tarrick." said Col, finally looking up. Lady Flora's cheeks flushed as she tried to find a resting place for her eyes. Gin's cheeks burned too, feeling like she needed to be far from this room right now.

Daphne, however, took control, cleared her throat, running her hands down her apron as she crossed the room to Lady Flora.

"I shall be sure to bring your food to your room, Lady Flora, and we shall see that your dress is absolutely just how you want it." she said with a small scowl flicked towards Tarrick, who looked up from preening his fingernails with a raised brow. "Right. Good." said Lady Flora, trying to gain some composure again. She shook her head slightly, moving her hair from her face, still loose around her shoulders from the night.

Everyone in the room watched them leave, their footsteps light and fast up to the Great Hall. Daphne turned to them finally and raised her eyes skyward.

"As if I needed more added to my list. I thought I'd got her dress fitted properly yesterday and not to mention *both* of you who I've not even got around to doing a final fitting yet!" she said, taking a deep breath and resting a hand on her forehead.

Col's chair scraped backwards, and he made his way over to Daphne, placed his hands on her shoulders and tilted his head.

"Have *you* eaten this morning yet?" he asked. Her bark of laughter was all the answer he needed. He promptly sat her down on a stool, filled a bowl with porridge and sliced apple, setting it before her warmly surprised face, and finished decanting the rest to be taken up to the Great Hall.

Gin smiled as she washed the pots that were strewn around the kitchen. Her chest swelled, watching Col look after Daphne.

"Thank you. *Both* of you." said Daphne, sounding relaxed at last as she ate. "It's been one of those mornings. Well, one of those few weeks." She sighed, taking another mouthful of porridge.

"It'll soon be over and done with." said Col, his gaze meeting Gin's as well. She felt a stab in her chest again.

"Yes! You're all getting your own breakfast tomorrow morning, that's for sure. I plan to sleep! All day!" said Daphne, eyes wide. "Right. You're first Col. After breakfast, you are going to try your suit on." she said, pointing her finger into the air. Col grimaced, but knew better than to argue. "Then I'll get to you, Gin dear. It'll most likely be after lunch though, as I now have to adjust Lady Flora's."

"If that neckline isn't near indecent, she'll never forgive you." said Col, shaking his head. Daphne tutted but failed to suppress a smile before looking at Gin.

"I just can't wait to see you try your dress on. It really is *something else.*" she said, inhaling deeply. Gin swallowed, noting the small glance she sent Col's way. Daphne would be the first person to see her scars before the speech. She would have to bend the truth for a little longer.

"Well, as long as you don't show me up in mine." said Col, studying her from the other side of the kitchen. His eyes had narrowed, catching onto the fear that had settled in her stomach, rendering her unable to speak.

"Mmm, that's if you *actually* turn up. You've failed to attend any and all social events that Joseph has held" Daphne tucked her chin in.

"Oh, I'll be there." His tone was serious.

"We shall see." Daphne quipped. "I'll have Elizabeth make up a nice refreshing bath for you later, then we'll see how this dress fits."

"Oh, you are good to me, Daph." said Col, trying to keep the mood light, but his eyes stayed trained on Gin's anxious eyes.

"I'm not pampering your behind, Col." said Daphne as she made her way over to the serving bowl he had prepared, swiping her napkin at him when she was near enough. He grinned at her, breaking his gaze.

"Thanks Daphne. I'm going to get some air. Thank you for breakfast." Gin said with a tight smile. She needed to clear her head, to focus on all the reasons she was throwing herself to the sharks tonight.

"Always welcome, dearie." she said, busying herself with bowls and spoons.

Col crossed the room to where Gin had been about to leave through the backdoor, touching her elbow lightly. It made her heart beat faster, sure he'd feel it vibrate down her arm.

"I'll come with you." he said, brow furrowed.

"No, I'll be fine. It's just a walk." she said, forcing a smile. "Anyway, I've taken up enough of your time today already." she said, blinking heavily under raised eyebrows. His shoulders lifted with a sigh and opened his mouth to speak, but Daphne cut him off.

"Oh leave her be, Col! Stop fussing and help me get these to the waiting mob upstairs!" moaned Daphne, concentrating on balancing a tower of wooden bowls.

Gin followed his gaze. It was fixed upon his hand that gently held her elbow. Her breath hitched in her chest as he rubbed his thumb in a small circle. He rolled his lips and let go. She nodded towards Daphne.

"Go." she whispered, backing out the back door. He hesitated, eyes dancing on her, before turning slowly.

"Alright. But I am *not* taking food up to Flora and her plaything." she heard him say as she pulled the door closed behind her.

She shivered in the cold air after the warmth of the kitchen. The sun had risen, and it replaced twilight with a golden haze, illuminating the burnt colour palette of Autumn.

Being her last day in the castle, she didn't want to spend it in her room. She had grown to feel safe here. She didn't have to face the wrath of anyone's belt or keep her mouth shut in fear. For the first time ever, she was free… and yet she was not free to stay here. Her chest burned at the cruel irony.

She listened to the gravel crunch beneath her feet as she plodded slowly up the hill, watching as contractors strung lights on the castle walls and people scurry around with their noses buried in clipboards.

She avoided the courtyard and the hubbub, taking the path around the moat instead. The wind whipped her hair about her face and crumpled leaves danced around her ankles. It was her favourite time of year. The garden at Slayton's had been its best when painted with oranges, reds and yellows that outshone the sun. She watched in awe as the castle was slowly transformed before her. By lunch, it was as if she had been transported to some Hollywood film set. White pumpkins wrapped in black lace lined the courtyard pathways, black lanterns with orange candles were placed in between each one.

Every archway was strung with spindly black branches, strung with fairy lights. The steps up to the door of the castle were lined with more pumpkins, some white with black lace, some orange with black lace and some black with white lace.

It took her breath away, even in the daylight when the lanterns weren't glowing and the fairy lights had yet to twinkle. It wasn't as gory or garish as she had imagined, but the most elegantly beautiful Halloween decor possible.

275

As she stepped into the Great Hall, she let out an audible gasp. It was straight out of a fairy tale picture book.

Hung on the wall to her left was a row of black witches' hats, beneath which were black cloaks, each with a unique white broomstick. One broom curled into a spiral at the end, another zigzagged in places along the white wood and the last one comprised lots of branches held together.

Her gaze fell to the staircase, the bannisters hidden under the same black branches and fairy lights as the archways outside, but here they were splashed with small white flowers. From the bottom of the stairs and climbing up halfway were hundreds of small white and orange pumpkins, all varying in size and shape. Pale green foliage sprouted out from beneath them.

It was then that she glimpsed the ceiling, perhaps the most dazzling sight of all. Strung with hundreds, if not thousands, of ornate cobweb shaped fairy lights, each one unique and creeping down onto the walls and windows.

Goosebumps slid across her neck, and it wasn't even completed yet. Dozens of workers scuttled about the hall, carrying yet more decorations and boxes.

"What did I tell you? Tonight is going to be *spectacular!*" said Joseph, appearing at her side pinching his lip as he looked around with pride in his eyes.

Gin looked at him, the passion he had for this place radiating from his core. It truly was his life. A life he had taken for himself, along with all of the people here. She kept silent, not sure she could lie to him right now.

"This is our day, Gin! I know Mr Slayton is so looking forward to seeing you again. You must be thrilled too!" he said, stealing glances to the room between catching her eye.

He walked off without waiting for her reply, directing a man to where he wanted the 'pick your poison' bar to go. She ground her teeth at his obliviousness.

Lunches were sent to their rooms, as the main table was under a cascade of black, white, and orange tulle. She picked at the chicken pie that arrived, between pacing the length of her room, until a knock at the door startled her. She half panicked that it was Slayton, arriving early to see her before the Ball started. But the voice that called out was that of Daphne.

"Gin, dearie. Are you ready for your dress fitting?"

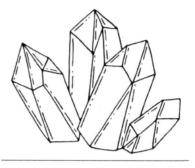

Chapter Thirty-Four

The room filled with the scent of the concoction of oils and herbs that Elizabeth had mixed in Gin's bath. It had done little to ease the nerves that flopped around in her stomach, but she did at least feel fresher than she had in a while, and her skin was softer than it had ever been. She had soaked up the warmth of the water around her shoulders, not knowing when she'd have the luxury of a hot bath again. Everything beyond the Ball was uncertain, even Col's trust, yet again, after going behind his back with Brandon. But one thought drove her forwards. By the end of the night, she'd have Hope in her arms and Slayton would face a life behind bars. Perhaps it would be better if Col hated her for good this time, anyway. He was so close to finding the last Crystal now. Leaving for both of them would be easier if she severed the ties. But the thought still sat sourly in her throat.

She finished towelling off, slipped on a robe and stepped from behind the room divider, where Daphne waited, looking positively fit to burst as she clutched her fists to her chest.

Gin's eyes fell upon what she stood next to. It looked like a river of silver moonlight, the sheer glow of the material enough to take her breath away by itself. Her eyes widened as she stepped closer, taking in every inch of the dress that waited for her. This piece of art had admonished every thought from before. For she'd seen nothing as beautiful. It shimmered as she neared, as if it were alive, flowing with energy. She felt it vibrate in her chest as she ran her fingers over it. It was softer than any material she'd known.

The sheer ivory shawl that draped over the hangers and down the sides glittered with gossamer thread, like dainty cobwebs that glistened in morning dew.

She looked up at Daphne, who was biting her lip behind a wide grin.

"Well?" she squeaked. "What do you think?"

"Daphne... it's beautiful." she breathed. This was more than just a dress to her. It was her truth. It was going to bring freedom. Her heart thumped with the anticipation of it.

"Thank you. *Thank you.*" she said, resting her hand upon Daphne's arm. Daphne stared down at it. Gin could feel her gaze, but she didn't move her hand. It was a rare gesture from her, a touch from one to another that she wanted to share with Daphne. Appreciation, for all that she'd done for her here. Despite making it hard for her to do so sometimes.

"Right! Well, let's not waste time! I'm dying to see you in this! Oh! You have no idea!" Daphne bumbled on as she took the dress from the hanger and waited for Gin to move behind the screen again.

Gin took the dress carefully, afraid the fabric might tear at the slightest touch. It glided over her skin so smoothly, she wasn't sure that she'd even put it on. The fabric floated to the floor and rippled around her feet. She turned to see the train flow out behind her, a small smile growing on her lips. That was until she noticed her scars, tarnishing the beauty of it. But she reminded herself, that was the whole point.

The buttons that needed to be fastened at the back were too far down for her to reach. She took a deep breath and released it slowly. This was it.

She stepped out, facing Daphne, who had a grin that stretched from ear to ear. Daphne drew her hands to her chest and moved closer to her, shaking her head as she went. Gin's eyes shuttered as she began to circle her.

"Oh, Gin, I knew you'd look stunning, but... *really,* there are just no words for how... " She paused mid-sentence and Gin opened her eyes, feeling a shock of electricity through her chest. She'd never felt so naked before, so exposed. Even when Slayton made her strip her top from her body to be lashed, she had never felt as naked and vulnerable as this moment. And for once, Daphne it seemed, was lost for words. It felt like an eternity before she spoke. But Gin kept her chin up, staring right ahead at the wall, patiently, as she let her ugly truth sink in.

"Oh... Gin..." It was a muffled whisper, that she was certain came from behind her hands. "What on earth? How?"

Gin swallowed hard, trying to stop the shaking that racked her chest.

"It's a long story. I'll tell you, I promise. Sooner than you think. Just, not yet." She turned, Daphne's mouth hung open, in shock or disgust Gin wasn't sure. "I need help, though, with the buttons. If you wouldn't mind?" she asked, cheeks aflame, cracking a smile onto her taut face. It felt forced and unnatural, but she hadn't time to break down right now. She had to focus.

It took Daphne a moment to acknowledge what she'd asked.

"Come, turn dearie." she said, her voice breaking slightly as she took her hand and spun her around gently. The train flared out like liquid silver.

"You're a vision!" said Daphne, though her voice was strained. She felt her fasten the buttons, sniffing gently.

A pang of guilt struck Gin at having thrust this upon her in this moment that she'd so looked forward to. She felt like she'd let her down, working so hard on this dress for her, only to be worn by such a hideous body. She looked down, running her palms over the smooth material that hugged her hips.

"I chose this dress for a reason, Daphne, of which I'm sure you now know. I'm sorry I don't live up to expectations for it. But this is more than just a dress to me. I'm not hiding anymore Daphne." she said, her voice trembling.

Daphne's fingers paused on the button she was fastening. She stepped around to face her. She wore an expression she hadn't seen on Daphne. It was not warm, not playful. It was heavy with words that for once stayed on her tongue, careful and selective about which ones to speak.

"You owe me no apology. These scars... I don't know how or why you bear them but... I'm honoured to be the one to help you step out tonight." she trailed off as Gin looked down, lips pressed together. Try as she might, she couldn't stop the sound of Slayton's belt flying through the air play in her mind. She hadn't realised how hard she'd clenched her hands until Daphne took them in hers. She walked her slowly to the full-length mirror. They locked eyes, Gin desperately trying to avoid her own reflection.

"You are radiant, Gin. Look." she said, gently, motioning towards her reflection. Gin blinked, breathing in deeply as her eyes glided hesitantly over the person who stared back. The dress caressed her delicate curves, curves that she didn't know were there, always hidden beneath her layers of protective clothing. She didn't know this girl who looked back at her. But more importantly, she thought she liked her.

"Come, let's get to work on your hair. I've also managed to scrounge some of Lady Flora's make-up. Please say nothing though, I shall never be allowed to forget it."

Gin smiled as Daphne scurried off to bring a basket of bits for her hair and pots of make-up. She was thankful to Daphne for the quiet she worked in.

The time passed calmly as she watched her reflection being transformed. Daphne had plaited her hair softly around her head and to one side, where the ends cascaded in soft curls over her shoulder.

It wasn't long until the sky dissolved into dusk, the lowering sun casting a golden glow through the room. The noise from outside had subdued as everyone headed to their rooms to dress and prepare for the night ahead.

Daphne pressed a rosy shade of powder onto the apples of her cheeks just as a knock at the door broke the silence. Gin's eyes widened as Col's voice called out.

"It's me. Are you decent? I can't stay cooped up in mine for much longer. Not tonight." he said, his muffled voice carrying through the door.

Daphne's hands dropped as she glanced over Gin's shoulder and back with questioning eyes. She was clearly leaving the ball in her court on whether to answer. Gin wasn't sure if she could speak at all until she croaked out a reply.

"Come in." she said, eyes locked on Daphne, who gave a brief nod and stepped back.

This moment had replayed in her mind repeatedly since deciding to do this. She had thought about hiding her back with her shawl until the speech, but she couldn't do that to him. Not when so much was being kept from him already. He deserved this truth to come from her, before the rest of the world knew.

She heard the door unlatch and watched in the mirror as it opened behind her. If he was going to see her scarred back, she would make sure it was done quickly. She barely breathed, frozen to the spot as Col appeared in the doorway.

"Did I ever tell you I can't stand the smell of pumpkin… " His words were lost, swallowing visibly as his eyes fell upon her in the mirror.

Col cleared his throat, trying to speak as he drew nearer, a smile creeping onto his lips before the fall... and there it was. The moment she could never make him unsee.

Her chest caved as his smile slipped away just as quickly as it had appeared, his eyes travelling downwards. She could feel them, as real as if he'd scraped a hot rod down her back. Her skin prickled with goosebumps and she tried to swallow the lump in her throat.

He closed the space between them with a narrowing gaze.

She heard Daphne slip from the room; the door closing quietly behind her. Gin couldn't watch anymore, couldn't bear the look on his face. She closed her eyes against everything.

Col's hand, cold from the brisk walk over here, skimmed gently over her back. A shuddering breath escaped her, her skin set a blaze in his trail, and a tear fell down her powdered cheek. No one had ever touched her back. It was the most alien feeling in the world and stirred an electric current in her chest.

"Gin… tell me this wasn't *Slayton.*" he growled. She blew a shallow breath through her red painted lips, her throat closing up.

"Open your eyes," he uttered after a moment of silence. She gritted her teeth and shook her head. She couldn't do it, couldn't see the look of disgust, not from him.

"Please. Look at me, Gin." His hand ran down her arm and held her hand, with aching gentleness. Before she could find the strength to look at him, he had folded her into his arms. And she crumbled. It was as though all the tears that she'd withheld through every beating were set free in that instant.

"It's alright... It's OK. I've got you. I've got you." he whispered, stroking her hair. They stayed wrapped up like that for what seemed like an eternity, until her sobs became slow, shallow breaths against the gentle rise and fall of his chest.

"I'm gonna rip his fucking throat out." he seethed into her hair. She finally pulled away from the warmth of his body, wiping her cheeks gently, shaking her head.

"We've talked about that." she said, recalling his offer to deal with Slayton himself.

"Hmm." he growled, jaw clenching. He circled to her back again. She hunched her shoulders, hugging her arm at the stroke of his hand down her disfigured back. Electricity erupted once again.

"That was before I knew he did this." he snarled. "Does it hurt?"

"Sometimes. It's tight. Like my ribs are constantly trying to rip through my skin. But I'm used to it. I don't even remember what it felt like before."

Col shook his head solemnly. "They're *so deep*."

She hugged herself tighter, feeling so hideous. Her eyes cast upwards to the ceiling.

"Well, they never had time to heal properly. Every time they got close, he'd..." she paused, swallowing the bile that rose in her throat. Col came back to face her, his brows knitted, waiting with all the patience he could gather. "He'd find a reason to take his belt off again." Col rubbed a hand over his face, his nostrils flaring dangerously. She knew the thoughts of taking this into his own hands were running rampant in his mind, could feel it pulsating from him. His eyes fell to their interlaced fingers and she swallowed involuntarily as he brought them to his chest, squeezing gently as he shook his head. He looked as pained as she'd felt and it seized her chest.

"I could help, I still have the Crystals for this, I could heal them for you." he pleaded, searching her eyes. She smiled a little.

"I know. I know you would." her brow furrowed. "But they're my dents." she said, finally. Col frowned, head tilting. "Like the ones in your armour tell your story. They're a part of your life, a reminder of what you've survived. These are my reminders that I survived Slayton. And that I have to do everything in my power to bring him to justice." She explained, piecing the broken parts of herself together.

Col's shoulders dropped as he stared unblinking at her. He shook his head slowly, pressing his forehead to hers. "You never cease to amaze me." he whispered.

Her breath hitched in her throat as she watched his eyes close. A tug in her gut reminded her that she might not have a moment alone with him again before she would have to leave tonight. This could be it. And she knew they were much too close, and yet she had no desire to pull away. Her mind raced with all the things she wanted to say before she left, all the thank you's and sorry's... all the crazy things that whispered from her heart...

He opened his eyes again, pulled back slightly, and yet all that left her lips was a weak smile. He sighed with the weight of their boundaries.

The sound of the door opening moved them apart, all eyes on Daphne as she stood on the threshold.

"I uh, I think my make-up might need a retouch." said Gin, looking at her interlocked fingers. Daphne held the powder rouge, already prepared, a knowing look upon her face.

In no time, Daphne had her feeling human again, under the watchful eye of Col from the chair in the window, feet upon the table. He picked up the papers that lay on the table. Gin could make out the image of the dress design from the light that the setting sun cast through the window. His brows pinched, and he looked at her, then at the papers again.

"Daph?" he asked. Daphne pursed her lips to hide her smile as she watched him puzzle something out. "Gin's dress." He gaped at it, standing to get a closer look.

"Yes, Col. It is." said Daphne, raising her chin, fixing him with a warm smile.

Gin looked at the pair, both in apparent awe.

"What am I missing?" she asked, slowly. Col's eyes wrinkled around the corners. Daphne sucked in her cheeks and stayed quiet for once, letting Col do the talking.

"Uh... It was my mother's design. One she recreated after time travelling. She kept it hidden because it was so ahead of its time. She always said it would find its place… with someone fit to wear it." He bit his top lip and dragged his eyes over the dress that clung to her delicate curves. "Of course. Who else?"

Gin placed her hands on her stomach, the shock of her choosing this dress, a dress his mother had designed.

"Your mother, Col. Full of surprises. Even now, she's a force of energy the universe keeps alive," said Daphne. Col let out a small laugh, placing his hands in his pockets. Pockets of a suit that Gin had only just realised she'd not fully appreciated yet. A light grey jacket with silver satin lapels gave way to a white shirt underneath, a silver baroque pattern embroidered onto it. His light grey trousers were slim fitting, accentuating his long legs. She averted her lingering stare as her pulse raced. He looked so modern, nothing like the rugged knight she was so used to.

"Thank you, Daphne. For everything." said Gin, truly grateful. "Now, go straight to *your* room and get ready. You have done enough for everyone else. Take some time for yourself, *please*."

Daphne waved a hand in the air.

"Oh, this has been my pleasure, believe me! Louis is going to be stunned at the sight of you!" she said, glancing between the pair. She lingered slightly longer on Col. He looked away from her, brows furrowed, and then Daphne took her leave as ordered.

Gin crossed the room to the window, needing space. They needed to be more careful. Even Daphne seemed to sense the charged energy between them.

The lanterns and fairy lights were coming to life in the low light. Already, guests were arriving in black cars that crunched over the gravel up to the steps, before the doorman let out each exquisitely dressed guest. Their colours reflected the season, burnt amber, reds, golds, blacks and greens.

She sensed Col nearing, pulling her attention away from the courtyard. His warm breath skimmed her bare shoulder as he sighed, making her eyelids flutter. She gripped the window ledge, nerves firing in her belly.

"I hope you realise just how damn beautiful you are." he said.

She dragged her gaze over her shoulder. His face was full of pain as he looked down at her, trailing a hand up her arm. It swept gently over her shoulder and down her scarred back, leaving a blazing trail. Gin pressed her lips together, turning away. Her heart hammered at her ribs as she looked down at the twinkling lights in the courtyard and they blurred in the hot fever that flushed her body. She was suddenly aware of every breath she took.

"If it weren't for the scars-"

"Even your scars. Because they're part of you." He thumbed one softly at the base of her back, his fingers resting softly around her hip. The breath lifted from her lungs, into a dizziness she'd never felt before as her breathing intensified.

"Col." she whispered, unsure what she was even going to say. Her head fell to one side, eyes closed, letting his breath caress her neck. But the warning in her heart told her this had to stop before it went to a place neither of them could come back from.

"We… we shouldn't be... Louis. The prophecy." She swallowed hard as his fingers trailed over her abdomen. She had to remind herself to breathe. This made no sense and yet the barrage of confusing feelings he pulled from her now made perfect sense.

"To hell with the prophecy," he growled. "I'm sick of pretending. Sick of trying not to be selfish with you, for Louis. The guilt consumes me every day, even though I push away every thought of holding you…" His fingers splayed on her stomach before caressing her gently. "Kissing you… " his lips skimmed her neck with a featherlight touch, dragging a breathy sound from her throat, his grip tightening in response. "I've never wanted anyone *so* much. God, all the ways I want to show you how good it can feel to be touched, Gin." he whispered as he pulled her back gently, flush to his chest, causing her stomach to hollow. His words stirred a deep pool of warmth in places she didn't anticipate. "Do you feel what you do to me? How my heart beats wildly for you. Tell me your heart doesn't feel the same. Because I fucking love you, Gin." His voice was hoarse.

Gin's eyes opened. He'd done it. He'd gone there. The room was soft and unfocused in the heat that devoured her, every nerve on fire. The truth was, she could. She felt his heart thumping on her bare skin, his warm sweet scent encompassing her senses. Even his evident arousal that was pressing onto her back, that she was trying desperately to quell the desire to push into. She longed to tell him he wasn't alone, but it terrified her. Not only because of the prophecy, but because she was walking away tonight. Far from the one person who she had ever considered the possibility of wanting in her life with Hope. Walking away with his own brother. So... she had to push him away.

"Col, you just think you love me. It's not real. You love the idea of me because it means one more win over Louis." she said, despite the words feeling like poison.

"That's bullshit and you know it." he said, flatly. She did. But she had to believe this was the right thing to do. "You never would have taken Cora into that arena if you believed that. You *knew* I would come. You knew I loved you then. I love you now and I'll love you with every beat of my misspent heart, through all the ages of this world." he said, voice hushed.

She turned on weak legs, his hand gliding over her hip and resting on the bare small of her back. His Adam's apple bobbed as his eyes travelled to her lips. The very air was charged before them. She could hardly see through the sensation, telling herself this couldn't happen, but paralysed in the moment. She opened her mouth, air catching in her throat as she tried to keep her treacherous heart from spilling out. Never had her mind been so torn. She wanted to give in to him. But Hope... Louis... Max...

There were too many people relying on them. Her nose wrinkled, and she shook her head with heaviness.

"I can't." she breathed. Their chests heaved in the heavy silence for a moment before Col rested his forehead on hers. His hand slipped away from her back to move a loose curl from her cheek and she closed her eyes, nestling into his palm.

"I know. Brother's soulmate, right?" he said, a low, broken rumble. Gin's heart fell off a ledge at his words. He tilted his head the other way, narrowing his eyes. "You're equal parts moonlight and asteroid, you know that?" He gave a pained smile as her eyebrows knitted, "You light up the darkness, without fail. But you honour the path life gives you, no matter the destruction to you. Because you're selfless. Fearless." Tears pooled in her eyes as his words rode through her. "My heart is forever ruined for all others. It will always belong to you, Sparkles." he said, face pinched, trying to keep his wavering smile fixed.

Gin stared, openmouthed as he slid her mother's red ribbon from the table, dipping his head momentarily, catching her scent as it passed before his nose.

"The only thing that's missing." he said, not meeting her eyes as he scooped her ponytail and tied the ribbon around it.

Gin felt utterly hollow inside as she watched him smooth the delicate ribbon into the curls of her hair.

At last, everything clicked. She yielded to what every maddening flutter of her stomach had meant, every time they lingered in each other's presence, just to simply delay parting. And all she could do was watch, as what she finally understood to be the love of her life, slipped through her fingers.

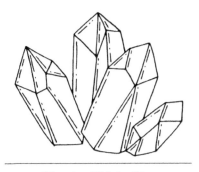

Chapter Thirty-Five

Footsteps erupted on the stairs and, with a bold rap at the door, Louis walked in.

"Ah, sorry. I seem to be late." he said, eyeing his brother. Gin kept her eyes on the spot where Col had been before backing away.

"On the contrary, perfect timing as always, brother." said Col, straightening his jacket sleeves. But Louis had set his gaze firmly upon Gin, who felt another blow to her chest at his words.

"Wow, Gin. You look stunning." he breathed, pushing his shoulders back as he crossed the room.

"Thank you. I uh… I think we should go down now." she said, finally reeling herself in. She swept past him, making sure to not look at Col. The devastation that twisted her gut was raw, and she wasn't sure she'd be able to keep it together if she looked into those sky-blue eyes right now.

She picked up her shawl from the back of a chair and passed it to Louis. He too needed to see her scars before they were thrown into it downstairs.

"Would you mind?" she asked, turning so that he could wrap her shoulders.

"Of course…" he froze. She gritted her teeth, cheeks burning, but the shame that had crippled her with Col seemed to lessen. Perhaps their soul connection had something to do with it. She didn't know or care to think about it anymore.

"Christ, Gin… what happened?" he asked. She didn't need to see his face to see the disgust displayed there. She rolled her shoulders, inhaling a deep, steadying breath.

"Slayton's belt. That's what." she said, staring straight ahead at the door. "Can we please just... go?"

"Wait a minute." said Louis, coming to stand in front of her. Gin's face pinched as she watched him squeeze the bridge of his nose before glancing over her shoulder to his brother.

"You know how I feel about your Crystals." he said to Col, pausing as he dug for words. "But... if there was ever a time to use them. Use them. Now, brother."

Gin lifted her chin, eyeing his fraught face. His repulsion was as she imagined.

"I don't want to heal them, Louis." she said calmly. He gawped at her.

"Gin, you don't have to bear them. Let him heal them." he said, looking to Col for support. "Col?"

Gin could feel Col's eyes burn into her from wherever he stood behind. The silence stood around them like a chasm. Until Col spoke.

"Can't do that, brother."

Gin's chest expanded warmly, silently grateful.

"Why?"

"Because, it's not what she wants." said Col. She watched Louis visibly sag, his eyes flitting between them. The tension between them simmered dangerously.

"And since when do you care so much about what other people want, Col?" spat Louis. Gin froze, pulse racing as she waited out the long pause. If he told Louis how he felt about her, it would put the entire plan into jeopardy.

"Well, I guess having a baby brother who does it so well is finally rubbing off on me." said Col, his voice laced with shade. Louis's lip curled before finally looking at her, his eyes pleading.

"You don't have to live with these wounds, Gin. Please. I can't bear to think of you in pain." His shoulders slumped. She couldn't blame him. He loved her in a deeper way than she could even understand. He only wanted to take care of her. But this wasn't a pain she was willing to part with. She lifted her trembling chin.

"My shawl. Please." she said, her eyes softening as he battled to understand her. Louis's head dropped as he gently bunched the shawl in his fingers before letting out a held breath. Finally, he held it up, brow wrinkled.

290

As she turned, letting him cover her shoulders and back with the light shawl, her eyes finally found Col's. A blaze of heat brushed her skin. He perched on the edge of the table, hands in his pockets. And as she felt Louis caress her shoulders, Col pushed off the table with a flash of bitterness on his face.

"Let's slay this bastard." he said, prowling towards them, his shoes striking the floor. "Shall we?" he said, plastering that feline grin on his lips and wrenching the door open. She hesitated, caught up in the gaze of the only man she'd ever loved, while preparing to face the man she loathed. The mix of conflicting feelings had her body trembling.

"With pleasure." said Louis, holding his arm out for Gin. Col watched her take it, his jaw clenched as her fingers wrapped around the sleeve of his deep blue velvet jacket. If she was to sever the ties between her and Col, she guessed this was a good place to start. And it felt as poisonous as she knew it would.

The music that reached Gin's ears differed from the normal pan flute or beating drum that usually haunted these walls. A raspy voice, hauntingly beautiful, sang amongst drums, piano and guitar. But her own heart in her ears overshadowed the melody as she followed Col down the hallway, still clutching Louis's arm. She was sure her knees would buckle beneath her if she let go.

The bannister was now in view, and she knew that it would lead her to Slayton amongst a room full of strangers.

A shrill ringtone vibrated from Louis's pocket. Her head whipped round as he cursed, taking out the lit up phone.

"Ah, I'm so sorry, Gin. Joseph trusted me to hold the fort while he tended to this evening. I-I have to take this." he winced as he looked up from the screen.

Gin's mouth parted as he slowly stepped back, looking from her to the phone, apologising. She quickly checked herself for being surprised. This was Joseph's golden boy.

"Don't be an idiot, Louis." said Col, coming to Gin's side. "Your priority is not Oldman's precious business tonight." Louis refused to look at his brother, speaking only to Gin.

"I know, and I am all yours after I've taken this call. I promise." he said, tugging her shawl gently into place before answering the phone. Gin watched him disappear back into the depths of the hallway, nausea roiling in her stomach as her eyes flitted to the bannister again.

"He really *is* an idiot." said Col, turning on his heel. But Gin's thoughts were not on Louis.

"It doesn't matter, Col... this is *crazy*. I mean, what if I can't do this? W-what if as soon as I see Slayton, that power he had over me... what if that comes straight back?" She clutched her necklace, staring at the bannister over his shoulder.

"Look at me." he said, turning her chin gently, sending a barrel of butterflies to her stomach. "It might seem impossible to face up here," his finger moved to her head, "but the mind will always try to scare you. That fear, it's all an illusion. I may be a knight, teaching a squire, but *you* taught me that, Gin." she blinked at his words. He laughed softly. "Look at what you've done. From the get go you were fighting. When I stabbed Louis in the shoulder, *you* stepped up. You have worked your ass off as my Squire and to learn about the healing Crystals to heal those in need. You even took my greatest fear and faced it yourself, fully aware of the danger you were walking into. That strength is inside you. It's not something that I or anyone else can teach. You've always had it."

"But you don't know him, Col-"

"But I know *you*," he said, cutting her off, his lips flat. He braced her arms, bringing her out of her mind. "You're *my* goddamn Squire." The corner of his mouth quirked into a smirk. She bit her lip. His words stirred something deep within her. It fizzed in her chest. Perhaps she was more prepared than she thought. She inhaled deeply and let it go, along with all the doubts that fogged her. She nodded slowly. How did he always have a way of talking her down from the edge of losing her mind? Why couldn't Louis do that for her?

Col sighed, chin dropping as he held his arm out for her. Her heart jumped to her throat. She shouldn't have taken it, but prophecy be damned, she did. Her fingers slid over the silk jacket, causing that muscle to tick along his jaw.

Even now, after he handed her his heart, only for her to give it back, he was still unequivocally there for her. Her legs weakened now for an entirely different reason as they began their walk towards the Great Hall.

She gasped at the sea of people, a rainbow of autumnal colours sweeping the floor. The chatter was drowned out by the band on stage. They were dressed in maroon, the lead singer in a velvet bodysuit with diamante detail on the plunging neckline. Metal plates cupped his shoulders like some futuristic knight, his hair a mop of fine curls.

She scanned the room, jaw set, intent upon knowing exactly where Slayton was before going down there. Her heart pounded as her eyes flitted from face to face. She gripped Col's arm tighter. He had to be here, somewhere.

"I don't see him." she breathed, straining her eyes to focus on each unknown face.

"It's OK." he said, his voice calm as he began walking slowly along the balcony.

"I need to know where he is before going down there."

"You don't. *You're* in control, remember? Not him. Not tonight, or any time after." he said, placing his free hand on hers. She glanced up. His eyes, intent upon her, were sad tonight. She couldn't help but feel she was to blame for that. What she'd said moments before. But she couldn't let her mind wander back to that moment in her room with him. His hands on her... his lips almost kissing her neck... the feel of him, hard against her... She swallowed, her mouth so dry it was painful. She continued her search for Slayton instead.

Then, suddenly, a spark of ice spread out from her core. She clocked him. She tensed. Col glanced sidelong at her and followed her gaze to where Slayton stood, drink in one hand, cigarette in the other, talking to Joseph and Alistair.

His hair was slicked back in its usual style, clean shaven and as chiselled as ever. An amassed crowd of admirers eagerly edged their way around him. His men were as obvious as a sore thumb, arms folded in front of their large bodies, scanning the gaggle of people converging upon him.

"That him?" asked Col, his chest swelling beside her as he took a deep breath. She nodded slowly.

A flash of blue caught her eye from his satin jacket as he raised his glass to drink. She couldn't tear her eyes from him, his presence magnetic.

Joseph, who had been engrossed in his attention, clocked their arrival at the top of the stairs. His perfectly groomed handlebar moustache curled upwards as he beamed at her, faltering for a second as he noticed it was Col on her arm and not Louis. But he soon reined in his annoyance.

Then Slayton finally looked her way, double taking as he realised who she was. He lowered his drink and held her gaze for a moment until raising his cigarette to his lips, peering at her through the swirling smoke.

She gripped the railings with her free hand, crushing the foliage that was strung with fairy lights beneath her fingers. Fiery anger burned in her chest, at him being allowed to stand in a room of people with no judgement, no clue about what they allowed to happen behind closed doors.

"I know I said I'd be good, but I'm not gonna lie. I want him dead already." Col growled from beside her. She gritted her teeth. It would be so easy to let him wipe Slayton from the face of this earth. But easy wasn't the right path.

"You cannot end up rotting in a jail cell Col, questioning if you could have gone back and found Max." she stroked her thumb over his arm. He looked sideways at her hand, then met her gaze, his nostrils flaring but resignation in his eyes.

Slayton's narrowed stare was now fully intent upon Col. She gripped his arm tighter, a sudden feeling of needing to protect him flooding her veins. He would not ruin Col's chance at happiness.

"Well just so you know, I'm not leaving your side." he said, both still trained on the man that threatened everything. She felt his words, like a safety blanket, wrapping around her. A feeling she would have to shrug off after tonight.

Hoisting the silken material of her dress, she took the first step down the illuminated staircase, revealing her exquisite ivory shoes, embroidered with silver thread up the length of the heel. She'd never worn heels before. She was very aware of each step she took and the way they made her hips sway in her figure hugging dress.

Slayton's eyes roamed down her body like a predator, moving his cigarette from side to side with his tongue. And then he was stalking towards them, Joseph left gaping after him.

The conversations of those around the hall stopped as all eyes fell upon her and Col. But she barely noticed. Gin held Slayton's gaze, something she had never done before. She reached him at the base of the stairs, stopping on the last step. She would be the one to look down her nose at him, this time.

They were at a standstill, locked in a staring battle of wills. She felt surprisingly under control, the pull of a smile on her lips. To the room, it was a polite greeting. To Gin, it was triumph. And the flicker of confusion behind Slayton's eyes told her he certainly had not expected to see this version of her before him tonight.

His gaze finally flicked to Col, surveying him with another drag on his cigarette. His eyes lingered on their linked arms before he blew a controlled plume of smoke into Gin's face, the familiar snake-like grin slithering onto his lips. Her muscles tensed, not letting it get under her skin. She'd bottle it all until her time to take the stage had come.

Col, however, was teetering already, his body heaving next to her as the wave of anger flowed between them. But this was her moment and he knew that. He held fast, letting her find her strength to overcome him.

It was a standoff, and she was not about to fall at the first hurdle. The room melted into an abyss. It was just her and Slayton. The music seemed to come from another room entirely as he tormented her silently, just like he'd always done so well.

But the moment was broken by the appearance of Joseph by Slayton's side, breathing ragged.

"Ah! Gin! You look absolutely visionary, doesn't she, Mr. Slayton?" he said, beaming at her as her dress shimmered under the sky of fairy lights, dazzling onlookers among a sea of glaring colour.

Slayton's shark-like stare continued as she willed herself not to shrink under it.

"Indeed. A perfect angel, Gin." he said. His thin lips quirked into the slightest smirk.

Angel.

Gin let it slide as she soaked up his icy glare where she would once have drowned in it. She stared so hard that her eyes stung, but it only served to drive her on. Joseph shuffled his feet nervously, rubbing his hands together slowly.

"Ah, Col, what's say we find our guests a round of drinks while Gin and Mr. Slayton catch up? Hm? I'm sure you both have a lot to talk about!" he said merrily, faltering somewhat as he caught sight of their linked arms.

"Yeah, I'm not going anywhere." said Col, slipping his free hand into his pocket with ease. A surge of warmth settled in Gin's chest.

Joseph gave an awkward laugh, glancing around at his guests, whose interest had piqued at the ensuing reunion.

"Don't feel you must stay on my part... Col, was it?" asked Slayton, shooting him a stiff glance and breaking eye contact at last. "I like to keep up with the families and patients who I've cared for when they fly the nest. My sources make sure they're staying safe and I must say, although I have heard a lot about you... I didn't realise you were *quite* so close. I hope Louis doesn't mind." His face remained rigid, unreadable. Gin's eyes narrowed at his admission of having had people watching her. She swallowed the anger that bubbled in her chest. Of course he did.

Col let out a mirthless laugh, scratching his cheek lightly.

"You really can't let her go, can you?" he uttered, so that only Slayton and Gin could hear him over the music. Slayton matched his humourless laugh with his own, revealing what seemed like too many bright white teeth in his mouth, small but perfectly straight. It was a sight that Gin seldom saw, and it raised the hairs on the back of her neck.

"I can assure you it's quite platonic, isn't that right, Sir Col? In fact, he has been training Gin as his Squire here at the castle. Surprised us all with that one!" said Joseph. She'd never seen him so jittery. It seemed Slayton's sway had seeped into the walls here, after all.

"Interesting." Slayton lifted his glass to Gin in a toast. "Well, what a joyous reunion this is to be." He downed the last of his drink, eyes never leaving her, before handing his glass to Joseph. He took it, almost with thanks, and scurried off to find him another, like a puppy trying to please its owner.

"Please, allow me the pleasure of your first dance this evening, Gin." said Slayton, holding out his hand for her to take, his charm on full offence for the occasion.

Gin's mouth parted. She had not expected him to ask this of her.

Col sucked the air between his teeth, wincing.

"Mm, pretty sure that's not gonna happen either." said Col, deathly sweet. Slayton didn't baulk, gaze still set upon his prey.

"Oh, but it is. Isn't that right, Gin?"

Gin stared down at the hand he held out for her. The same hand that had gripped his belt as he sent it soaring down on her back, too many times for her to count, now open for her to hold. The thought was nauseating as she struggled to keep her calm exterior. The glint in his eye told her he was all too aware of it as well. She had no way out. She had to go through with it. For the terrified little girl that he'd beat into silence... she had to.

With a trembling hand, she reached for his. Col cut in, stepping gently in front of her, sliding a hand on her waist and drawing a shudder of breath from her lungs. She looked up at him, a strained smile upon his face, tinged with worry.

"You don't have to do *this*." he whispered, his face inches from hers. She swallowed the ball of nerves.

"I do." she said, letting go of the comfort of Col's arm and slipping it into the clutches of Slayton's hand, forcing the fear that consumed her into the depths of her mind. *It's all in the mind,* she reminded herself. She just needed to tell her heart that, the thudding deafening in her ears.

Slayton sent a smug sneer Cols way as he led her through the throng of people who turned to watch them take the floor.

297

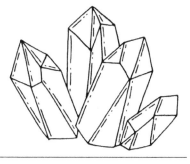

Chapter Thirty-Six

Slayton's grip on her hand was tight, a reminder that he was in control here. But a quiet confidence had kindled in her belly and a smile ghosted her lips... he could have it for now.

They stopped in the middle of the dancefloor, under the watchful eyes of the envious guests. She averted her eyes from their penetrative looks. She would have gladly given her place to any of the fools around her.

Slayton placed his hand over the thin shawl that concealed her back and she froze as he dug his fingers in with a force that said more than words ever could. She gritted her teeth as he pulled her close, a snarl whispering on his lips. If her scars could scream, they'd be bringing the walls down. Her nostrils flared at the ripple of goosebumps that erupted over her tender back. His raised eyebrow told her he knew the discomfort he was causing, daring her to challenge him.

The stage lights of brilliant white panned down, blinding her temporarily as the band played. Slayton moved her around the floor.

"You look remarkably well." he said into her ear. His clammy cheek pressed into hers. The smell of decades of smoke, whisky and aftershave on his clean shaven skin overpowered her senses as the room spun slowly.

"Ironic. These people see the product of me living here for several months and attribute you to that care." she said, pasting on a smile of disbelief that would pass for joy to their audience. "Amazing what being out of your hands can do. Not only to your body," she said, exposing her neck to him as she fixed him with a glare.

"But more importantly, to your mind." His eyes flashed as a deep chuckle escaped him.

"Ah. Would you look at that? The angelic healer becomes the healed." He cocked an eyebrow. "Funny, it didn't take you long to forget about those you left behind, either." He licked his lips slowly, watching as her smile faltered. She swallowed involuntarily, her pulse quickening as he dared to even question her loyalty to Hope. She knew he did it for the rise, to hurt her. After drawing several slow, steady breaths, she managed to find the smile that had slipped away. She would not give him the satisfaction of letting his words find their target. He'd know soon enough just how much she hadn't forgotten about Hope, or anyone that she'd let down at the Hospice. The thought took the edge off her simmering rage and she glanced around the room, leaving him to stew on her silence. Except his answer was to run his hand beneath her shawl, digging his fingers into her bare skin, so that she could feel the sharp bite of his short manicured nails.

She winced, catching sight of Col, who had pushed his way to the front of the gathered crowd. His arms were crossed as he chewed on his lip that he held pinched. A gathering of ladies desperately tried to get his attention and were edging their way closer. He scowled as he watched her and Slayton, oblivious to the crowd he was attracting.

"So, you weren't content enough with healing the sick? You needed knight in training under your *belt* too?" he crooned into her ear, bringing her whirling face to face with him. His beady gaze bore into hers with a deathly smirk upon his face, as if playing with his prey before devouring it. She raised a brow.

"Well, you never know when you're going to need to slay a monster." she said flatly, holding his gaze. Slayton let out a bark of laughter.

"Ah, but the thing about monsters is," he leaned in close to her ear, pressing his hot oily cheek to hers. "You never know who they truly are... until it's too late. They don't need armour, like knights. They're equipped with tough skin and are not afraid to do whatever it takes to destroy anyone that gets in their way." His grip on her back was nearly unbearable now. Playtime was over. Nails scraped over her scars, searing her flesh like an iron rod. She kept her smile in place as the audience continued to admire their *heartwarming* reunion. Inside, her stomach churned with nausea. Her breath pounded through her lungs. She clocked Col again, who must have sensed her shifting mood. He had abandoned the throng of bejewelled ladies and was striding towards her.

The tension left her body as he stayed his course to get her out of Slayton's clutch. But his path was cut short as Louis appeared at their side.

"Ah, you must be the famous Mr Slayton I've heard all about." he said, his eyes smiling above sharp cheekbones. "You wouldn't mind if I stole my dance partner, would you? I'm going to be hard pressed to part with her tonight." he said, eyes trained on her face. Gin blushed under his burning gaze.

Slayton tipped his head back slightly, surveying the man who dared to interrupt. For a moment, she wasn't sure he'd be able to keep a lid on his act. But to her surprise, his fingers slipped from her back and he stepped back graciously.

"Who am I to stand in the way of soulmates?" he said with a simmering smile. Louis wasted no time whisking her into his arms. Her view of Slayton was lost as he moved them. But she knew exactly where he was, for Louis's eyes moved steadily, watching his every movement.

It was then that she saw Col, hands in his pockets, leaned against a column. She wilted at his sunken cheeks, averting his eyes from them.

Guilt riddled her core. She couldn't escape the feeling that she was betraying both of them. Each cared for her and she, too, had grown to care for them. She was tied to Louis in a way that she would be held to forever, in some way. But she was also tied to Col. It may not be the earth shattering epic love that was written in the stars. But she had no idea what that was even supposed to feel like. Only that it hadn't happened yet and it was a form of love she felt for Col. But out of respect for Louis, she couldn't act on her feelings with a clear conscience.

Being in Louis's arms in front of Col, after their moment in her room… it twisted her gut.

"Are you OK?" asked Louis. She looked up at him and swallowed.

"Yes." she lied. Nothing about tonight was OK. He studied her in silence for a moment, clearly trying to read her. She couldn't let that happen. Not with Col ever present on her mind. She cleared her throat.

"I have to apologise. My dancing game is, well... this is my first time dancing at all." She lowered her brows. "I am the worst choice of dance partner in this room." Louis smiled softly, his kind grey eyes watchful.

"In a dress like that, nobody's looking at how you're dancing. Trust me." he said. Gin blushed for the second time under his gaze. She tilted her head away, trying to hide her reddening cheeks.

"I'm sorry," he said, biting his lip. "I'm not usually so crass. You just..." She glanced up at him, holding her breath. "Your beauty is incomparable."
Her brows twitched.

"Even without this shawl?" she asked, recalling his reaction earlier. Louis shook his head.

"You need no shawl, you need not cover up at all, Gin." he said. Gin watched his throat work with narrowed eyes.

"You practically begged me to heal them."

"For your own wellbeing, that is all." he said, slowing their dance. "That is all I care about. You must know that by now?"

She smiled flatly. It didn't matter what he thought. Her reasons were her own. And if he had no desire to love her so fiercely now, she could only thank the gods. It would make her future with Hope far less complicated.

The song ended, and she pulled away.

"Thank you for getting me out of Slayton's hands." she said. Louis licked his lips gently and slowly brought her hand to his lips, watching her intently as he placed a delicate kiss upon it. With a sharp intake of breath, she blushed for a third time. She cursed herself inwardly.

Someone cleared their throat from beside her.

"Mind if I have the next dance?" asked Col, pushing his shoulders back. Gin's stomach flipped as she glanced at Louis, hoping he wouldn't read into this bold move of Col's. He ran his thumb over the spot he'd kissed gently. The satisfied smile resting on his lips axing her worries.

"If you wish to, Gin?" he asked. Gin rubbed at a phantom pain in her chest and nodded with a tight smile. "I'll do some mingling with our guest of honour." said Louis, eyes narrowed as he searched the crowd for his target. Gin swallowed, wondering where Slayton was. She hated not knowing.

"It's OK," said Col, taking her hand and stepping behind her. "I hate parties too." His mouth was next to her ear before raising his arm and twirling her into his body. If she wasn't tethered to his hand, she was sure she'd float away as his sky-blue eyes glimmered under the fairy lights. "Dancing is overrated."
She raised her chin, trying to suppress a smile.

"Dancing certainly isn't my forte. Unless you count Hope standing on my feet while I clumsily plodded around our room." she said, an ache in her chest throbbed at the memory.

"We could try that, if it would make you feel more comfortable?" he suggested, brows raised with a smile that released the tension on her core. She laughed, looking down to where her feet would have been if their bodies weren't so close.

"I can barely hold myself up in these heels, let alone you." she said, just as she noticed the hard stare from Joseph who was frozen at the sight of them, two drinks held in his hand, clearly having lost Slayton. "Mind you, the look on Joseph's face if we did…" She raised an eyebrow. Col laughed softly, following her gaze.

"Almost enough to make crushing your feet appealing, huh?"

"Yep."

They watched him weave into the crowd, his face slightly redder, drinks held up so not to spill them. The two of them smirked at each other. Her old self would cringe at her now, but she was going to miss his sarcasm.

"Poor Joseph." she laughed. She shouldn't, but she did sort of enjoy the fact that they were making his big night difficult. After everything he put Col through, she didn't mind too much.

"Ah, don't worry. He'll add it to his list of reasons to make my life more difficult at some point." he shrugged. Gin didn't laugh, for behind the joke, she knew he was indeed right. She tilted her head to one side, studying the crinkles around his eyes as he gazed down at her. She'd never thought of wrinkles as beautiful before, but she loved those lines. They were symbols of the happy times in his life, lines that signified love and laughter. And she truly wished nothing more for him. Even if it killed her inside that it couldn't be her that gave it to him.

"Listen," he said, chin dipping as they moved in slow circles, "I need to apologise." Her brows bunched, but Col went on. "I shouldn't have put you in that position earlier. It was wrong of me and I promise I won't stand in the way of what you and Louis are meant to find. Whatever that might be. Devil knows, he's a better man than I ever will be." he said with a flash of his lopsided grin before it vanished.

Gin blinked away the sting behind her eyes. Col was giving her the freedom she needed, and yet it sat heavily on her chest. But she was the asteroid. His very words. She had a path to follow and destruction was bound to follow... even if it was her own heart.

She opened her mouth to speak, only to be cut off.

"Good evening, my Lords and Ladies!" Joseph's voice boomed over the speakers, startling them both. She looked over at the stage, eyes wide. Col hung his head as he bit his lip, the warmth of his hand leaving hers as they parted.

"May I just begin with saying how absolutely magnificent you all look? I mean, I thought I had gone over the top with the Halloween decor, but you outshine it all." A round of applause erupted around the hall as everyone congratulated themselves. Gin scowled. The vanity of the room was overpowering, each person dressed to outdo the next. It was written on their faces as they looked over their neighbours with feigned admiration.

"Thank you, all of you, for making the effort to come out tonight, to not only celebrate Halloween, but to support a matter very close to my heart. Indeed, a matter that has become a huge part of our lives here at Lowndes castle." Gin bristled at his words, as if he cared at all about the people at the Hospice. He barely cared about her, the one he adopted into his domain.

"I am sure the man himself needs no introduction." Joseph went on, chest puffed up, the elaborate ruffles on his black shirt splaying like a proud pigeon. "He is the brains and, more importantly, the heart, behind countless charitable ventures, including the fabulous evening before us. So... with no further ado, let's give a very warm welcome on this bitterly cold evening to Mr Slayton himself!" Joseph held his arm out towards the side of the stage and Gin's chest tightened as she watched Slayton make his way on stage, waving to the adoring audience.

In seconds, both Col and Louis had converged on either side of her. She didn't miss the apprehensive look the brothers gave each other over her head. They were ready. It was time to find out if she was.

Slayton's shark toothed smile radiated as he surveyed his audience. He opened the button on his jacket and took his place in front of the microphone. His gaze fell upon Gin, savouring the look of disgust that she couldn't hold in as she witnessed the magnitude of his devoted public. Her toes curled painfully in her delicate shoes. She needed air. She needed to compose herself if she was going to get through her speech. Just a moment by herself.

She weaved through the throng, sliding through the swell of dresses and mixture of a hundred different perfumes and aftershaves, Col and Louis on her heel. But before she could reach the doors to the courtyard, she came face to face with Lady Flora, standing by the wall of witches' cloaks and broomsticks. Sir Tarrick was at her side. He side-stepped to block her way, his flouncy oversized black bowtie flopping with the swift manoeuvre. The doorway was blocked.

Gin gritted her teeth as Lady Flora came to his side like a puppy, her emerald green velvet dress blocking most of the door by itself. Her movement was slowed by the extreme cinched bodice that made it look impossible for her to breathe in, let alone walk.

"Let me pass, please." she said, nostrils flaring. She had no time to waste on fools tonight.

"Not leaving already, are you? I was *so* looking forward to your speech." said Lady Flora, idly playing with her nails. Her bright red lips quivered into a smirk and then slipped at the sight of Col appearing at her shoulder.

"Ah, Col. I was just remarking to Lady Flora how it's such a shame your dear mother couldn't be here tonight. She would have felt right at home among all this freakish decor." said Tarrick. He kicked a broom lazily with his shined shoe.

Gin made to take a step towards him, to do what? She wasn't quite sure, but Col clasped her arm before she could decide.

"Don't waste your energy, Sparkles. You learn to know who is worthy of it with time." he said, lip curled. Lady Flora's eyes flashed at him as she rolled her shoulders. Col released Gin's arm, as Louis made his way through, placing his arm around Gin's waist. She was near boiling point as she slipped out of it. Their competition to protect her was too much. She could hardly breathe.

Thankfully, the cheering and applause had died down enough for them to have to stop their insult match, and was replaced by Slayton's raspy voice. It sent shivers down her spine as she turned to him.

"Thank you. I am always so honoured by the response that I receive at these events. You are all too kind." He placed a hand over his heart. Gin fumed at the faces that ogled him.

"So, you may have heard about my little place up on the hill." He stopped for yet more clapping, chin raised as he lapped it up. "Officially, it's a Hospice. But I like to think of it as a sanctuary. For people who need special care and often have families of their own who have nowhere else to go. Well, Slayton's is *that* place of safety, for the sick and their children to stay together. Because our belief is that the love and support of family is paramount."

Gin's nose wrinkled. He was the last person to know what the love and support of a family was. His father never believed in his ability to take over from him, to be the caregiver that he was. And Slayton had never forgiven him or Gin for being everything he couldn't. Healing in a way he couldn't.

"It's a delicate kind of care that I provide. For not every family leaves together. Some do, but some are parted in this world before they get that chance. So that love and support carries on for the children, until they find a home that will give them just as much love." Gin was practically trembling with the outrage that she tried to conceal. How could he stand up there and lie so easily?

"Which brings me to one very special young lady who is in this room and the very reason that this wonderful event is taking place!" He twisted towards her, speaking to her directly now.

"Gin. You were with me for many years after your beautiful mother left us. You were the angel that we just couldn't find a home special enough for. Until Joseph opened his arms to welcome you into his marvellous castle." He spread his arms. Joseph beamed from the far end of the stage, nodding proudly.

Gin was now seething, wanting nothing more than to rip his throat out herself after all.

"And that little girl that I took into my home and my heart has grown into the most beautiful and inspirational young lady." He tilted his head back, eyes narrowed. "I believe your words tonight will captivate our audience, just as much as your dazzling beauty. Please, join me, Gin." he clapped with his audience.

She ignored the hundreds of pairs of eyes that converged on her, waiting for her to take her place next to Slayton. She willed her feet to move, knowing she must, but they had taken up root. Not only because of the mountain she was about to scale, but when she left Col's side, she didn't know the next time she'd be by it. Or if he'd even look at her again. Louis would whisk her away as soon as she'd finished, slipping away in the pandemonium. Away from his brother's reach.

Then Col leaned in, brushing his hand into hers, whispering gently into her ear.

"This is it." he said. Gin dragged her wide eyes to him. "Finish him, Sparkles." The last small mercy he gave her was that he let go first, leaving her folded speech in her palm.

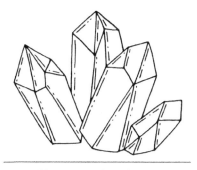

Chapter Thirty-Seven

The sea of people waiting for her to take the stage blurred as her vision honed in on Slayton. *Everything* hung on this moment. Not just the fate of her future with Hope, but the future of everyone in the far pockets of the world who he still held by the tails.

She gathered her silk dress at the thighs as she ascended the steps to the stage, where Slayton beamed at her. She clutched her speech, the paper crinkling between her fingers and the lustrous material of her dress, and took her place, squinting against the glaring lights that hit her. Her elbows jammed into her sides as Slayton clamped his arms around her like a trophy, grinning at his people. She fought the sickness that rolled in her belly and scanned the crowd for Col and Louis. Only the faces nearer the front were illuminated softly. And there, almost directly in front of her was Col, elbowing his way through a couple, their mouths agape at his unexpected rush, Louis close behind.

Col's throat worked before he fixed her with a slow nod. A trace of a smile appeared on his lips as his face softened and her nausea was replaced with a swell of warmth in her chest. He believed in her. And what was more, she finally believed in herself.

She inhaled deeply, anchoring herself before twisting out of Slayton's grasp, her gaze firmly upon him. His head snapped towards her, eyes narrowed for a split second.

He reached for the microphone, but Gin got there first, leaving him looking rather waspish. Her nose wrinkled slightly as she gave him the slowest of smiles. This was *her* moment.

She raised her hand to the crowd, her silver rings glinting in the light as they hushed to listen.

"This man, right here... lurks behind the walls of so many people's lives." She glanced down at her speech, still crumpled in her hand. She knew the words, not like the back of *her* hand but like Col's. All the soft places that rested between the scars and calloused patches. He'd made sure of it, going over it until the words didn't sound like words at all. Of course, she didn't need it. Tonight, she'd speak the truth that she'd kept locked in the darkest part of her.

"More lives than we could possibly know." She licked her lips, taking in the adoring faces that gazed up at them, oblivious to the horror they were soon to witness.

"So, when I was asked to speak tonight about the many years of *special* care I received under his roof, I have to admit, I was terrified. Terrified that I couldn't convey it in the light it deserves." She chewed the inside of her cheek, twisting her head to survey Slayton. His lips were set into a tight smile, eyes darting to Joseph over her shoulder at the side of the stage. She laughed inwardly at the panic they must be feeling at her diversion from the agreed speech and the power she now held in her hands.

"But I soon realised, having spent most of my life with him, I was, in fact, the only one who *could* do him justice. Now, I've listened to many of Joseph's lengthy speeches since coming here to know that short and sweet is the way to go." A chuckle rippled across the audience as they craned their necks to see Joseph, one arm crossed over his chest, the other hand pinching his chin. His smile faltered as he tried to gauge what on earth she was doing. She waved a hand dismissively.

"Thankfully, my words tonight will be just that. And it really is a culmination of the life I lived at Slayton's and the life I've found here that has enabled me to gain my unique perspective." Her eyes slid to Col, a pang in her chest at the space between them that would soon be far greater. "See, I have had the privilege of being Squire to the greatest knight you could ever hope to meet." She swallowed the lump in her throat as Col poked his tongue into his cheek and tucked his hands into his pockets. This was not the speech they'd drummed into her... worry etched his brow.

"Those who enter these gates, day in, day out, are captivated through rose-tinted glasses by the allure of knights in armour. But I have seen what lies behind those glasses." She clenched her jaw, Col's gaze never leaving hers. "The knights you come to see, like some animal in a zoo, have seen things that *no one* should ever have to see. War, blood, evil. Fought on battlefields and made to do things that no one should ever have to even dream of. All because of one person's greed and power hungry ambition." She took a deep breath, watching the exchange of frowns between the audience and Joseph's ashen face as he stood frozen to the spot.

Slayton let out a quick laugh before attempting to take the microphone from Gin, which she sidestepped nimbly. Footwork. Lesson number two, if she remembered col's teachings correctly.

"My speech is not *that* short." she defied, pushing her shoulders back. Slayton pressed his lips together, feigning a laugh at the captive audience, hands clenched into fists beside him. There was nothing he could do. Any move to stop her would only serve against him, and he knew it.

"I have come to realise that there are many different battlefields in life. Some more literal than others, like the ones these knights risked their lives on. However, some are hidden. Behind smoke and mirrors." She watched beads of sweat surface upon Slayton's forehead. "Weapons differ too. Swords, bows and arrows... a belt."

Slayton's skin was now becoming mottled. A blue vein appeared on his temple as his chest rose and fell rapidly. But he smiled all the while, as if he still thought he'd brush this all under the rug. Gin paused for a moment, glanced at Col, who held his chin high, mouth open as he finally realised where this was going.

She turned her body to face Slayton fully, her back against her baffled audience, and gently parted her shawl. Slayton's eyes flashed in warning as they darted to her chest. She watched him, unblinking, as she let the gossamer shawl float like a feather to the ground.

Time slowed. Blood rushed in her ears as his face contorted, lip curling. She couldn't see the look of horror upon the faces in the crowd, but she could hear the gasps that escaped them and the flash of cameras erupting around them. The murmurs that undulated throughout the room grew louder until they were full-blown shrieks between each other. Her secret was no longer weighing her down. She felt lighter than she'd ever felt, even in their repulsion. For in her scars, shining under the stage lights like silver rivers in the moonlight, was the story of her battlefield. And her enemy had just been struck for the first time.

She closed the space between her and Slayton, adrenaline coursing through her body as her heart tried to keep up. A slow and methodical smile crept onto her face, immersing herself in his anguish.

"Let's see how tough your skin really is." she said. His sharp jaw worked the muscles within.

"You don't truly believe you'll get away with this?" he seethed. Gin's eyes swept upwards.

"The sweat on your brow says you may just believe that yourself." she mused. Slayton's eyes darted around the room, blinking rapidly as several men in the audience shouted above the rest. Burly security men bustled up to the front of the stage, battling with Slayton's men.

Joseph came sweeping onto the stage, grappling with his words as he looked between them both, aghast at the carnage she'd dropped them into.

Gin's nostrils flared. Even now, he still struggled to pick a side. Her side. Gin glowered at them.

"If you play with the lives of others, you have to accept that one day they'll have played enough games to beat you." she said, pressing her crumpled speech into Slayton's hands. His lips pursed, almost white, as he straightened his jacket.

She didn't stay long enough for either of them to say anything, before dashing to the right of the stage, towards a shadowy alcove, where she and Louis had planned to meet.

Louis nodded sharply and she paused, hesitating on the steps. She glanced back at the crowd who fought against the security who were keeping them well away from Slayton and Joseph as they conversed furiously. She scanned the faces for Col. But he was nowhere to be seen. Her pitted stomach felt like lead as she dragged herself to Louis.

"Hell's bells, Gin." His brows raised as she approached him. "That'll do it." She took a deep breath, grimacing.

"We can't wait around." she said. He nodded and headed to the kitchens. She whipped her heels off, throwing them into the fireplace as she passed. She paused on the precipice of the stairs, sure she heard a familiar voice call her name, the tug in her chest willing her to turn around. To stay. *Stay.*

Her eyes shuttered as she commanded herself to not look, to take the steps. *To leave.*

Col's voice rang out over the crowd again. There was no mistaking it. Her nails dug into her palm and she slammed her fist into the wall before padding down the cold steps, wrenching the ties to loosen.

Louis was waiting for her in the kitchens, shoulders hunched with his hands on his hips. His uncertain gaze met Gin's before it slid to his left. Gin's heart was in her mouth as she followed to where Daphne stood, no sign of an apron on her deep purple gown, holding both their backpacks in front of the back door. Her heart plummeted at the look of dismay on Daphne's face.

"Daphne... I-I couldn't... I wanted to tell you *everything,* but I couldn't risk it." She stumbled over her words, shrinking under Daphne's watering eyes.

"I'm so sorry. There isn't time to explain this now. I just need you to *trust* me... I *have* to go." she winced, crossing the room to where Daphne stood. The tears in Daphne's eyes threatened to spill, but her face softened and her shoulders dropped. Gin felt a wave of relief as she handed her bag to her. Daphne's lips pressed together briefly.

"I do trust you. I do, I just…" she shook her head, mouth gaping as she searched for the words.

"Worry." said Louis, coming up behind Gin and squeezing her shoulder gently. Daphne looked at him and paused before handing over his bag, lips pursed. "Always." she admitted with a deep sigh. Gin released the tension in her limbs and stepped forward, placing a hand on her arm. Daphne's mouth parted a little, surprised. Gin felt a warmth in her chest and followed a sudden desire to embrace this person, who she was sure she could now call a friend. Her soft skin against her cheek enveloped her in a powdered rose scent. She breathed in deeply, wanting to remember this moment, her deep gratitude overflowing.

"Thank you, Daphne. For everything... I *will* come back. When it's safe, I promise." She pulled back in time to see a tear roll down her cheek as she nodded her head. "Please tell Col... that I'm sorry." she added, as she stepped back to Louis's side. Daphne nodded again, words failing her.

"You make sure you look after her, Sir Louis!" Daphne said, dabbing at her flushed cheeks. "And don't come back without her."

"Promise." he said, shuffling past them and pulling the door open. The cold air hit Gin like a thousand knives, cutting through her thin dress. Her eyes fell on his backpack. He really was leaving the castle behind him for her. She didn't know whether to be relieved or bothered by it. Either way, she'd cross that bridge after she'd got Hope to safety.

Louis handed over her padded black coat and shoes from under a stall by the door. He held her coat up, waiting for her to slip into it. She looked up at him as she pulled it snug around her, unsure of what to say to him. But he gave her a wink and smile, before slipping into the night. She hesitated, watching the darkness swallow him up, before she made to follow. But as she did, Daphne placed a shaky hand on her arm.

"He won't rest." she whispered, out of Louis's earshot. Gin's mouth parted, heart pounding. "Five years Col's searched for those blinkin' Crystals... when he finds out *you've* gone, he'll search the Galaxy for you."

Gin's mood darkened, looking out into the night. She watched her breath swirl before her.

"Tell him he mustn't wait. When he finds that last Crystal, I want him to go." she stammered, keeping her voice steady although she wanted to crumble. "Tell him it's his turn to be the asteroid." She drew herself up, turning away from the warmth of the kitchen and towards the stoic figure of Louis on the path below. She was quiet for a moment, a question playing on her mind.

"Before I go... I never asked. When the time comes, what will your vote be, Daphne? Will you want to stay here or go back?" she asked, finally looking at Daphne. There was a flicker of darkness that danced across her dainty face.

"I always thought I'd go home. Watch over Col. I left many things unfinished. But I'm not so sure now. I have ties to someone here who hasn't the luxury of choice. His life back there was going to end up in his early grave. And that is something that I do not wish to see." she spoke distantly. It sent a wild shiver over Gin's arms. She had no clue who Daphne was talking about, but she did not have the luxury to stay here and ask. Instead, she gave a weighty nod. The heart was something with far greater power than she ever gave it credit for.

"Goodbye, Daphne." she said, letting the darkness leach her from view.

Right now, she had to concentrate on getting Hope to safety, not the scream of her heart as she walked away from the closest thing to home she'd ever felt.

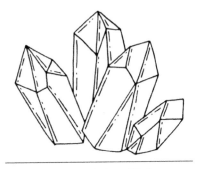

Chapter Thirty-Eight

They travelled on foot, through the fields behind Col's cottage to avoid being seen, sticking close to the hedgerows. She held her dress above her calves, not wanting it to snag and rip on the foliage.

They didn't speak as they traversed their way around, taking paths less travelled under the cover of darkness. Mostly because they didn't want to draw attention to themselves if they could help it. But Gin couldn't help but silently brood over the disruption she'd caused so many good people through this. It sat in the pit of her stomach like a rock. And she still hadn't got Hope out of harm's way. The feeling that this might all be for nothing if she failed the next task simmered in her chest.

They came to the main road that divided the valley, the occasional beam of headlights streaming past, but the town was mostly quiet. Louis unfolded a map of the village that they'd made together.

"The railway track is just over there, up the other side of the valley. It'll take us directly below Slayton's. We'll have to cross the track... dead carefully." he added, keeping his voice low. Gin hugged her arms tighter around herself, brow furrowed.

"It's not as late as I'd hoped. The last train will not have passed yet." she said, shaking her head slowly.

"I know. We will just have to keep our wits about us." he sighed, biting his top lip. Gin inhaled the chilly air, teeth clenched. Louis placed a hand on her elbow.

"I promise I will keep you safe." he said, head inclined. She met his gaze, so different from his brothers. But she knew he spoke the truth. The soul connection was still stronger for him. He would do everything to protect her. She gave him a clenched smile, focusing on the map once more.

"The track runs in a straight line for a stretch there. We should have enough warning if a train comes." she said. Louis nodded, squinting down to where she pointed.

"Right. Onwards." he said, waiting for a moment of quiet in the traffic.

The climb up the other side of the valley soon got her blood pumping and goosebumps were soon a thing of the past. Sweat slicked her back, sticking to her coat.

Lamp posts illuminated the path next to the railway track, the odd one flickering as if about to give up. It was not a path she would have taken alone. Scattered beer cans and broken glass were among the more unsavoury things strewn on the ground.

A cat eyed them from further up the path, its eyes glowing in the light of the lamps. It hissed as they approached and ran under a garden gate.

A few more metres down and her spine stiffened, the scars contorting her skin as she shuddered. There it was. Slayton's Hospice. Looming high above them on the other side of the track, fenced off. It looked smaller than she remembered. It had been her world for most of her life. But her world had grown immeasurably since she last set eyes upon its cold walls.

"Are you ready?" asked Louis, gingerly. Gin couldn't tear her eyes from its hostile walls. Hope was so close and she was more ready than ever to have her in her arms again. But the urge to flee at the sight of this place was strong. She could already smell the polished wood surfaces and could hear the buckle of Slayton's belt. The mere memories were enough to test her resolve. She hoisted her backpack on her shoulders, clutching the straps.

"I don't want Hope in there a second longer than she has to be." she said, still staring upwards. "So I'm as ready as I'll ever be." Louis gave a sharp nod and checked the path for passers-by. Gin's ears strained in the quiet. They were alone. Louis took out a pair of wire cutters from his backpack and smirked at Gin's raised brows.

"I may be ancient but I know how to use a pair of wire cutters." he said as he snipped the thin wires to the train track. She huffed a short laugh while continuing to look up and down the path, knees dancing.

"Argh. There. I'll go first and help you down." he said, pulling the metal open. She watched him, hawk-eyed, as he flattened the area beyond that was thick with weeds.

"Alright, your turn." he said, peeling the fence back further. She pulled her dress up again, stepping onto the grassy verge down to the track.

It was steeper than she thought. Her heart throbbed as she peered down, checking up and down for any sign of an oncoming train. Their eyes met as they listened intently, brows furrowed. When they were both happy, they gave a single nod.

"We'll stop at the bottom and check again." she whispered.

"OK."

They held onto branches of the young trees that grew, finding their footing carefully. She had to let go of her dress with one hand to steady herself, watching as she had no choice but to let it drag through the undergrowth.

By the time she neared the bottom her ankles were covered in scratches. But the adrenaline that coursed through her ceased to reveal her injuries to her.

She clung to the side. The coast still remained clear.

"OK, remember, *don't* touch the third rail on the far side... or game over." she said, recalling the research she'd done to cross here. The third rail was the live one. "You do not want to go playing with electricity." she warned him.

"Alright. Hold my hand and *do not* let go. After three." he said, counting down, both listening with intent for the slightest vibration of the rails. Their feet met the ground, light as a feather, each step considered meticulously.

Gin's breath slowed, her mouth dry as she manoeuvred herself with Louis across the rails. The final rail was just inches away, the first hurdle nearly complete.

She almost collapsed into the verge on the other side, thankful for the sting of the twigs as they jabbed into her palms. She closed her eyes briefly.

"Well done. Let's not linger here." breathed Louis, bracing the hill before them with one hand.

It was steeper this side and tangled with more vegetation. But she was just as eager to get away from the live rail that lay only feet behind them.

It was hard to find good footing; the wet leaves sliding beneath her. Louis put a gap between them, waiting for her to get a good start on her ascent before him. In her haste, she began taking bigger steps, pulling herself up by the matted undergrowth.

The ripping of stems tore through the silence, and she suddenly collided with the ground, powerless to stop herself from sliding down the hill towards the track. She screwed her eyes tight shut as she clawed at the ground until she came to a stop with an almighty thud.

She waited for the jolt of electricity to course through her. The spasms of muscles in shock... but it didn't come.

Instead, upon opening her eyes, she found herself cupped in Louis's arms, against his chest, just as the ground started to vibrate and a rush of air blasted them as a train thundered past.

She tried to calm her heaving chest, arms trembling under her as they hunched down, waiting for the deafening train to pass.

"I got you, Gin, I got you!" he said, panting, his chest rising and falling onto her. And there they stayed until the roar of the engine became a distant rumble.

She tried to catch her breath as he looked down at her, brow pinched. He ran a hand over her cheek, searching her face for any sign of damage.

"Are you ok?" he trembled. Gin nodded, shuffling out from under him, feeling far too crowded.

"Thank you." she rasped. Louis held a hand to his chest in relief and together they scrambled up the hill until she collapsed against the wall at the top, staring down at the tracks.

"We're taking the main road out of here. I'm not risking Hope's safety for a discreet path. I don't care how many of Slayton's men we have to knock out." she said, wide eyed, gripping her stomach. Louis let out a rasp of laughter as he looked at the stone wall they had to scale, hands on his hips.

She turned, placing a hand on the flint wall. The times she'd stood on the other side, wishing to be where she was standing now. That scared girl, too numbed by his power to gather the courage to make it happen.

No more.

She was going to make that little girl proud.

She ran her hand up over the jagged flint, finding one that she could hold on to comfortably, wedged her foot into a suitable foothold and began to climb.

Louis stopped pacing the wall for a weak spot and watched her.

"Well, that's one way." he said, before he followed her lead.

She peered over the top, sweeping the garden for any sign of movement. The place looked almost abandoned. No light came from any of the windows, no guards walked the perimeter. A slight shiver ran down her spine and not because of the crisp October night. But because she had caught sight of the halfmoon window that belonged to Slayton. The room where her scars were born.

"Seems like Slayton took most of his men with him, after all. I can't hear or see any sign of them in their usual spots." she whispered to Louis, who had reached her side.

"He's certainly going to need them with him tonight."

Gin's mind flashed back to the scene they had left, his guards swarming the stage to protect him. In doing so, his lair had been left weakened, as they'd hoped.

She swung herself over the wall and dropped to the ground, crouched in the wall's shadow. Louis landed with a soft thud next to her.

"Och, I'm getting too old for this." he groused, rubbing his back. Gin smiled absently, eyes trained on their surroundings.

"About 700 years too old." she said, ignoring his pointed look, nodding towards the far right of the building. "Look, that's the kitchen sticking out at the end. The fire escape is around the front of the building. It will take us to Slayton's rooms."

"Ok. Stick to the shadows as much as possible, just in case we're not as alone as appearances would have us believe." She gave him a sharp nod and led the way through the garden, taking the cover of bushes and trees until they could slink into the shadow of the building itself.

The kitchen windows were high, which made adhering to the wall easy. They meandered around the bins, the recycling full of supplies that would have been saved for her by Maggie. Her heart sank at the thought of Hope having no purpose to fill her days, no creative outlet to pour herself into. The thought of what he must have been filling her time with crossed her mind, but she squashed it as soon as it entered.

Gin eyed the empty courtyard, before darting across the back entrance to the kitchens, to where the fire escape ladder let out.

She grabbed the railing and placed a foot on the first rung, only to be met with the clang of her shoe against the metal. She winced, glancing down.

"*Shoes off.*" she whispered to Louis, who made quick work of kicking his boots off.

The pain on the soles of her feet as she climbed the thin rungs was a small price to pay for staying undetected. The ladder vibrated as Louis began his ascent behind her.

Upon reaching the top, they faced a heavy duty fire door and a window just to the left of the railings. Louis sidled up behind her as she stared into the window, nose wrinkling.

"This one. It will take us into Slayton's living room. If we can get it open." she said flatly. Gin leaned over the edge of the railing, checking the coast was still clear before trying to open it, only to find Louis had spread his jacket over the railing and was now removing a wool sock. She frowned as he took a rock from his backpack, placed the bunched up sock in a corner of the window and slammed the rock hard into it. He worked quickly, doing the same on all the corners.

"Uh, maybe we should try something…" she trailed off as the centre of the window fragmented. With one last blow to the middle, the glass shattered on the roof of the kitchen. Thankfully, the moss that grew there muffled the landing. She stared incredulously at the shards that sparkled like ice in the moonlight. "I don't even want to ask how you knew to do that." she said as Louis smirked, carving dimples under his high cheekbones.

"Not bad for a 700-year-old," he said, shaking the shards from his jacket, leaving the railing free of broken glass to climb over. Gin pursed her lips as she watched him climb over and into Slayton's office. She gulped as he disappeared, waiting for him to say something. Finally, he popped his head out, holding his hand out to steady her.

"Careful. Step wide when you enter."

She gripped the railing, hoisting her dress up, the snagged and tattered skirt skimming her knees. Louis's eyes lingered on her legs. His cheeks seemed to flush in the moonlight, and she instantly looked away. She couldn't afford any distractions.

The darkened room beyond was a blinding flash of memories. She reminded herself that she had the upper hand now. He was not in there. Just Louis, waiting patiently, arms stretched out to help her over the threshold. And Hope. She was in there, just a few rooms away. Her heart skipped a beat at the thought, and she lurched forwards, grasping the brick as he pulled her in. She landed on the plush carpet, hit with the scent of cigarettes and polished wood. It was *him*. Even though he wasn't here, he was still all around her, seeping into her skin. She swallowed the bile that rose in her throat as she gazed into the dark, unlit room, eyes wide as they adjusted.

Shapes emerged as she exhaled slowly, padding carefully into the sitting room where the silvery moonlight leaked through the halfmoon windows, giving light to objects. His leather sofa stretched the length of the room. The ashtray full of stubbed out butts among a mound of ash. The same ugly ornate clock his late father gave him sat on the mantle with its odd half human, half pig, smoking a pipe painted on the face, the same stupid...

Gin's stomach hardened as she glimpsed something that shouldn't have been there.

"No." she whispered, knees shaking as she made a beeline for the small faded pink hamster teddy that had always sat in the crook of Hope's elbow, now sitting ominously on the mantelpiece. She clutched Penny in her sweaty palms, grinding her teeth.

"What is it?" asked Louis, crossing the room. Her nose twitched with anger at the thought of him taking Hope's one piece of comfort she had left.

"*Hope's...*" was all she could muster through the bubbling rage in her stomach. She pushed past him, heading for the door to the landing.

"Woah, woah!" he hissed as he caught up with her, clutching her arm. She paused on the handle, breathing ragged.

"I need to get to her, now!" she seethed, wrenching free of his grip.

She didn't wait for him to waylay her any further. She was getting her little girl out of here.

The click of the handle echoed softly through the hall beyond. It was lit by several ornate table lamps that ran down the sweeping hallway. Her heart thudded as she stalked across it, eyes feverishly bright in her desperation to reach Hope. The memorised route she used to take to avoid the creaking floorboards flew out of her mind, feet pounding the ground.

Her chest tightened at the sight of her old door as it came into view, where Hope would be sleeping on the other side. She hesitated, staring down at the handle. This moment had replayed over and over in her mind, and it was finally here. She inhaled deeply through her nose, mouth clamped together as she wrapped her fingers around the cold brass and turned it.

She knew she'd remember this moment for the rest of her life. But it wasn't going to be for the relief of finally scooping Hope into her arms like she'd imagined. For she was not asleep in her bed. She was very much awake. Sitting on the edge of her bed, hands bound and mouth gagged.

The click of a lighter turned her blood ice cold, illuminating the monster she thought she'd slain as he lit a cigarette.

Slayton sat next to Hope, leaning against the wall, legs crossed, with a twisted smirk upon his face. A numbingly cold sensation expanded in her core.

"Ah, Angel... what took you so long?"

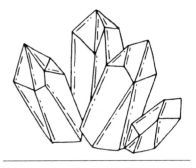

Chapter Thirty-Nine

Penny dropped to Gin's feet. She was sure the blood had drained from her face as a strange sensation filled her head, like being submerged in ice cold water.

Hope's big blue eyes were full of desperation as she tried to cry out from under her gag. Her curly hair was no longer set in pretty ringlets, but matted and unruly. It wrenched Gin's heart from her chest, her lungs refusing to take in the air she needed to breathe.

"I must say, you seem a little lost for words, Gin. Quite the turnaround from earlier with your little speech." he sneered, sitting forward with a long drag of his cigarette.

"It's OK, Hope, I'm here… I won't let anything happen, sweetheart." said Gin, her voice thick through her tight throat. "Untie her or this is going to end very badly for you." said Gin, pulling her eyes away from Hope's quaking frame. "I'm not alone." She looked behind her to Louis as he sauntered in, hand on the hilt of his sword. But the look on his face had her double taking. He was calm, not perturbed at all by the scene that he'd walked into. His emotionless gaze as he eyed her sent a shiver down her spine.

Slayton chuckled darkly.

"Indeed. Yet you may find you are more alone than ever." said Slayton, clicking his lighter shut.

Her shoulders slumped as the crushing realisation settled upon her. Slayton and Louis shared a smug look.

"No…" A bitter smile crept onto her face as she rubbed the cold sweat upon her brow. Not Louis. The one person who she could supposedly count on no matter what. It made no sense. How could he stab her in the back? He was her soulmate.

"Why?" her face screwed up in disgust as he approached with a simper.

"Because it's better this way. You'll see, my love." He tried to caress her cheek, but she immediately hit his arm away as her mind suddenly veered to Col. How angry he'd be. The numbing disappointment outweighed all the anger of his betrayal for her, but for Col… this would cut deep. Louis swallowed visibly, brows lowered.

"See? When will you learn, Gin? I have people *everywhere*." said Slayton, cutting in. "It didn't take long to find a willing candidate at the castle to help me in my crowning moment." With a nod from Slayton, Louis locked her arms behind her in one swift movement, leaving her no time to avoid him. She struggled against his grip, but it was too strong. She just wanted to get to Hope, to hold her and never let her go.

"What are you talking about?" she cried. Slayton jerked his head back and grinned.

"Taking the castle of course! Along with the device. Shame about the healing Crystals. I had big plans for those." He lifted his chin. That's when the penny dropped. Of course.

"You just wanted to outshine your father's legacy. You used me to get to them." she breathed, heart pounding faster with each moment.

Slayton's eye twitched.

"My father. Forever the saviour." His mouth tugged downwards. "And you… how he would have loved you, Gin. Healing the sick, as naturally as breathing." he spat. Louis tugged her arms as she tried to wriggle loose.

"Why else do you think I'd let my angel leave me? You've been part of the plan since the moment you arrived here, all those years ago." She stared at him, aghast, as he paused. He gave a sudden lick of his lips and the grin slipped from his lips. He lodged the cigarette between them.

"Isn't that right, Joseph?" he asked, frowning, eyes flicking to the corner of the room. Gin's head snapped to find Joseph held by one of his men, his handlebar moustache unkempt from its customary pristine shape. There were several cuts to his face, and for the first time ever, he looked utterly deflated. Her stomach roiled with nausea.

"I'm sorry, Gin." he said, chin trembling. She shook her head frantically.

"What have they done to you, Joseph?"

Slayton let out a bark of laughter.

"Is she still calling you that?" he asked, eyes narrowed in amusement. Joseph's chin lowered to his chest as Gin's brow furrowed. "Well, things just got a lot more interesting! I think it's time you reveal your true identity." said Slayton, rubbing his palms together slowly.

"Leave him out of this. You've done enough." said Gin, her chest rising and falling with anger. As much as she didn't care for Joseph, he looked as though he might just disintegrate at the slightest knock right now. His identity was no matter to her, she needed to focus on Hope and Hope alone.

"Let him speak." Gin whipped her head to the familiar voice from the doorway. Her heart skipped several beats at the sight of Col, his face like thunder, leaning against the doorframe. "It says something when a man like Oldman apologises." he said, darky.

"Ah! And the family is all here! Well done, Louis, you've really outdone yourself." said Slayton.

Col ignored the remark, scanning Gin for any injuries before shooting a look that could have sliced through steel at his brother. She couldn't believe he was here. She had prepared for the possibility of never seeing him again, but here he was. Keeping his promise, just like she kept his necklace over her heart at all times.

Louis raised his chin, gripping Gin's arms with more force, causing her to wince as it twisted her sensitive back.

"If there wasn't a child in the room, I'd have some really special words for you, right now, brother." he growled, placing his hands in his pockets slowly. Gin swallowed, looking at Hope, her tiny body shaking as she cowered into the corner of her bed. Gin dug to the depths of her soul to find a smile for her, anything to make her feel less scared.

"Go to hell." said Louis. Col laughed mirthlessly.

"I'd say the same to you, but I really don't wanna see your face there." he said, the pair staring each other out with hate.

"So!" Col spun around to face Joseph. "Talk." he demanded.

Slayton raised a brow as he surveyed Col and waited for Joseph to speak. But Joseph was still slumped over, his breathing ragged.

Gin pleaded with her eyes for Col to just drop this. She wasn't interested in anything other than getting Hope to safety, no matter the cost at this very moment. But Joseph finally spoke, his voice strained with emotion.

"Gin... I-I didn't want you to find out like this," he began. She straightened as much as Louis's hold would allow her. He looked up at her, eyes vacant and glassy. It sent a shiver creeping down her spine. There was no showman within his eyes, no glimmer of the man she saw, day in, day out.

"The reason I took you in. It's... it's because it was me. I left you and your mother here." he said weakly. Gin stared, shock and confusion whirling around her head.

"No... no y-you can't have. That would mean..." she hesitated. Her breath held for a time, unable to collect her words into anything that made sense. But from the way all eyes shifted uneasily to her, they were all thinking the same thing.

"My father left me and my sick mother and *disappeared!*" Even as she spoke, her eyes widened as the pieces of the puzzle slotted together.

"Poof! *Like magic!*" said Slayton, grinning, cigarette between his teeth. Gin's mouth soured.

Col sighed towards the ceiling before stepping towards Gin, placing a hand on her chin.

"Get your damn hands off her." he said to Louis, though his gaze never left her.

"Why not? She's harmless. She wouldn't dare do anything to make her precious *daughter* frown upon her." said Slayton, patting Hope's skinny ankle. Gin whirled out of his grip, snarling at him as she stepped into Col's arms. But she hadn't finished with Joseph. She pushed away from his chest, stalking over the polished wood floor.

Joseph was staring at Hope.

"Daughter?" he asked, sheepishly meeting her gaze. Gin stopped just in front of him, searching his face for any point she could place him in her past. But he was as absent there as he'd been to her at the castle. She huffed a short laugh.

"I'd tell you to say hello to your granddaughter, but you can't even be a father. So what's the point?" she spat. He pressed his lips together as they trembled.

"Gin, I am so sorry. I didn't know your mother would end up so ill. I mean, yes, she struggled from time to time, but not to the extent that she did."

"Well, you left us!" she exploded. "What did you think was going to happen to an already unstable person who is left to care for a child on their own? And how… *how could you leave your own child?*" she held the back of her hand to her mouth, pressing back the tears.

Joseph shrivelled, eyes scanning the ground.

"You were only two. I didn't think you would even remember me, let alone miss me. I had important work to be done, work that couldn't involve distractions!"

"Distractions." laughed Gin, looking to the ceiling.

"The Crystals, the device… it was a world changing discovery!" he pleaded. She pursed her lips, brows raised.

"Yeah. Well, you certainly changed mine and my mother's world." she said, scrunching her nose, before shouldering her jacket down to her elbows, turning so that he could see her scars again. He sighed loudly behind her, flinching from her scars.

"*This* is the world you gave me." her eyes slid to Slayton, who was still revelling in the surrounding devastation.

"Gin, how could I have known?"

"You really never can do wrong, can you?" she asked incredulously.

"Oh, he has a point, though." said Slayton standing, making slow steps towards her. Col strolled right up next to her and Slayton laughed at the gesture, glancing from one to the other, before continuing. "Why would he question me with my reputation? He really did the best thing for you both."

Gin clenched her teeth so hard it sent a searing pain to her jaw.

"Your father told me what he'd found and planned to return when he got back from whatever path the Crystals led him down. And return, he did! With the promise of a bright future for his daughter. Heir to his castle." He stepped closer, stuffing one hand into his pocket and taking his cigarette in the other. She winced as he blew smoke into her face.

"But I had plans of my own. Plans that would end in me securing Lowndes castle and the device with you, my angel, by my side. With me, where you belong. The healing Crystals were the cherry on top." Slayton went to run a hand down her cheek but Col caught his wrist before he touched her.

"Don't even-" Col began, before Slayton landed a blow to his stomach. He doubled over, winded. Gin put her arms around him and stared up at Slayton, her face blanched.

Louis prowled past his brother, straight up to Slayton.

"What do you mean, *by your side?*" he asked in a cautious tone. "I thought we had an understanding. Gin is to marry me."

Every breath Louis took repulsed Gin. He had played her for a complete fool. Slayton bared that toothy grin again, clapping Louis on the back.

"Ah, yes. I almost forgot you were here."

Gin knew that fake pleasantry tone well. She watched them closely as she helped Col to his feet, bunching his jacket beneath her fingers.

"You've been a great asset, Louis. Only, you forgot to mention that minor alteration to Gin's speech this evening." he said, a dangerous smile playing on his lips. Louis held his palms up.

"I knew nothing about that, I swear it!" he said. Gin's eyes widened at the blatant lie. She was ready to call him out, but it appeared Slayton wasn't buying his protest. She waited with bated breath as he brushed an invisible piece of dust from the lapel of his jacket.

"Since this seems to be a night for honesty, you should really follow the trend…
hm?" he prompted with a wink, sucking his lower lip as he surveyed his next
victim. "Firstly, you can admit to destroying the Crystals because of your petty
jealousy of your brother."

Gin watched the colour drain from his face as his gaze flicked to her and Col. She
braced herself for whatever awful truth was about to spill from his lips.

"Slayton," he whispered, closing his eyes. But Slayton just continued to smile, as
if the evening had gone precisely to plan. It chilled her core.

"Secondly, Louis?" he goaded, nostrils flaring above his shark-like smile. Louis's
wide eyes stilled on Slayton, his shoulders shuddering with each breath.

"Come now, brother." said Col, down an intense icy stare, putting himself in front
of Gin. "Can't be any worse than selling out your soulmate."

She bristled at the reminder. The thought of being bound by endless love to this
monster was sickening. But still, Louis remained silent.

"Let's play a little game, shall we, Col? Make this a little more *fun*." said Slayton,
taking a seat next to Hope again. A deep ache settled in Gin's chest. She had
meant to have scooped her into her arms by now. Instead, she sat shaking on the
bed, eyes screwed tight shut to the madness that surrounded her.

"Cast your minds back to the first Joust Gin saw you take part in. I believe our
Angel had already tried to save a life."

"I'm really not in the mood for games, Slayton." said Col, anger rippling from his
core.

"Oh, it's a good one, I promise. Now, tell me… *who* did Gin save that day?"

Gin inhaled deeply, knowing full well they all knew she saved Louis that day.
Slayton cocked a brow impatiently.

"Louis. She tried to save Louis." said Col, grimly. But Slayton clicked his tongue,
raking his gaze over her.

"Wrong answer." he said.

Gin's brows lowered as she caught sight of Louis's fleeting gaze. What was
Slayton trying to do?

"He's right though. I saved Louis that day. But what does this have to do with anything?" she seethed. Slayton smirked.

"To the common observer, yes, that's how it appeared. But think harder, Gin... whose name did you call out that day?" He watched her, eyes alight as she reached into that memory. She swallowed hard.

"Col. I called Col's name." she said flatly. Col's head dipped to the side in front of her as Louis ran a hand over his hair.

"Bingo!" cheered Slayton, throwing a hand into the air.

"What's your damn point?" asked Col, losing patience. Slayton licked his lips slowly.

"Well, was Gin trying to save Louis, or was she trying to save you from making the wrong choice?" he asked, letting his question hang in the air. Gin stilled. She couldn't answer that question and it unsettled her.

"Let's try another." said Slayton, clicking open his lighter, making Gin jump. Col must have sensed it. His fingers brushed hers as he weaved them together. A ripple of goosebumps erupted up her arm and over her shoulders at his touch.

"Whose fear did Gin face, just so that they didn't have to go through the pain themselves?" he asked, brow wrinkling. "Who came to her bedroom *every* night, just to check up on her when they weren't even on speaking terms?"

Col squeezed her hand gently as she shuffled uncomfortably on the spot. But Slayton hadn't finished, even as Louis paced the room, fist clenched to his mouth.

"*Who* came to her rescue when she threw herself into the arena on horseback against Sir Tarrick? *Who* walked her into that ball tonight to face me? *Whose* hand is Gin currently holding?" he cried, incredulous at their pinched brows.

Col's arm heaved against hers.

"*Get to the damn point!*" he shouted, not loosening his hold on her hand. Slayton chuckled darkly.

"Louis was never her soulmate, Col! You are!" he said simply, easing into a relaxed smile. Gin blinked heavily as she looked at Col. His jaw worked as he processed Slayton's words.

"Jealous of his older brother being mummy's golden boy, Louis tried to steal the one thing all men fall to their knees for and yet few really deserve. The love of a woman."

Gin's heart pounded in her ears in the silence that stretched before them. The world around her seemed to slow, as if trudging through water. Did she even hear him right? Did Col even hear the words that were ringing in her ears?

Louis stopped in his tracks, throwing them a shady look and before she knew it, Col's hand that had been laced in hers was pummeling into Louis. Hands soon turned to swords, drawn and clashing dangerously. She brought her palms together in front of her mouth, flinching against every strike. He'd heard alright.

Slayton looked mildly amused before nodding to two of his men, hidden in the shadows, who promptly wrestled the two apart, knocking Col's sword to the floor. Col practically roared as he was dragged away from Louis's bloodied face, both panting as they composed themselves.

"As much as I'd like to see you two fight over the girl who neither of you are going to get, I've more pressing matters to attend to." said Slayton, bringing Hope to her feet. Gin clenched her fingers into an angry fist as she watched her little girl still refuse to look. The terror she must be feeling broke her heart.

"You're forgetting that the entire world will know what kind of person you really are behind these walls by morning." she seethed. Slayton waved a hand dismissively.

"Ah, yes, you put on a hell of a show. See, you had already taken flight before I settled the storm you tried and failed to create." Gin's stomach dropped. "When you left, I set the record straight. Told everyone that I had set this all up. As an example of the sort of patients I help. Clinically insane, in denial of her illness as a result of her father's abuse." His eyes flicked to Joseph. "A man who had been playing the world all this time, sitting comfortably in his castle. Who had hosted them this very evening." he paused, enjoying Gin's ashen face as she feared the worse.

"They won't believe you," she said weakly, grimacing. A tremble erupted in her bones, knowing full well that he had the power to make them believe.

"On the contrary, they applauded my efforts in bringing Joseph's true nature to light. The donations flooded in after that. The rest is history, as they say."

Gin's throat burned with bile as she fought the urge to throw up.

"I told you. I always win." he said, gazing down his nose at her. She heard Joseph sobbing behind her.

"Gentlemen? Col's pockets. You'll find what I need there, I believe." said Slayton. Gin's eyes narrowed as Col laughed mirthlessly. Slayton's men held his arm up, the other reaching into it.

Gin gaped as the man pulled out not one, two, three or four Crystals... but five. The black tourmaline that opened the door to the device, Malachite, Azurite, the Sunstone from the dungeon... and one final Crystal. Dazzling blue. Even in the moonlight's glow through the floor to ceiling windows, it cast rainbows onto the man's hand.

Slayton's eyes gleamed with greed.

"Aqua Aura. The last Crystal." She dragged her eyes to Col, who scraped his teeth over his lower lip, chin dipping. It hit her like a punch to the gut.

"Col... you've had all the Crystals, and you said nothing?" she searched his eyes as he looked up.

"I tried to." His voice was quiet. "At breakfast, before Oldman announced the Ball. Then it seemed so insignificant after that. And I just..." he paused, their eyes locked as their bond filled with an achingly powerful pull. Her breath hitched, and his jaw clenched.

"And there we have it." said Slayton, pulling them out of their hypnotic daze. "The reason we have the pleasure of your company, Col. The folly of the heart. He couldn't bear to leave you." he sneered. Col looked away, nostrils flaring. Gin's cheeks heated. It all fell into place, every maddening feeling, every moment they lingered, every touch that ignited a fire in her belly. She really had called out to save *him* in the joust, not Louis.

He was her soulmate.

"Thanks to your weakness of falling in love with Gin, I have almost everything." Col narrowed his gaze on Slayton.

"So." said Slayton, sucking air between his teeth. "Where is it? Hm?" he asked in feigned delight before the harsh edge returned. "Where is the Galaxy Crystal?"

Gin watched the cogs turn in Col's mind. She had no clue where he kept the one Crystal that gave power to the device. She glanced at Louis, held still by his captor, waiting for Col to speak. Thankfully, it seemed he didn't know either.

"Ok. You win. I'll take you to it." said Col, his voice hoarse. Gin's stomach sank. "But you have to let Gin and Hope go free. Promise right here, right now, that you'll never let your sick mind even *think* of them again." he said, those intense blue eyes staring daggers into Slayton.

"Col, no!" she cried, panic flooding her veins with an ice cold bite. But Col ignored her.

"Nice try, but you are in no position to bargain here. I have Hope tied up, two men on you, one on Joseph... and me." he said, grabbing Gin, her back against his chest, cigarette dangerously close to her cheek. "Who will gladly snap her neck if you don't cooperate."

Hope's muffled scream rang out behind Gin as she hopelessly tried to break free. "It's ok, sweetheart!" she called, "just close your eyes, pretend you're far away... just like we used to do together, remember?" she said, through ragged breaths. Hope's scream subdued a little. Slayton cackled deeply as he looked around.

"*I always win!*" he whispered, all traces of humour gone. Gin flinched as his voice vibrated in her ear, causing the fiery end of his smoke to press against her cheek. It seared her flesh, the stinging sensation so intense it felt bone deep. She bit so hard on the inside of her cheeks, the metallic taste of blood hit her tongue. No scream escaped her, all too used to being on the end of a burning cigarette. Col didn't even notice until his steely gaze caught sight of her screwed-up eyes as the deep red burn ate away at her skin, by which time it was too late.

"*Stop!* You can have it!" he roared, the whites of his eyes shining.

Gin released her pent up breath as Slayton slowly peeled the cigarette away and blew the ash from her wound. The white hot rage from Col matched Gin's burning flesh. It flowed like lava through their unmistakable bond.

"I knew you'd come around," he said calmly.

Col's rage racked his chest, teeth bared as he surveyed her. She shook her head almost imperceptibly, begging with her eyes not to go through with this. But his voice cracked with emotion as he spoke, defeat in every syllable.

"I'll take you to it."

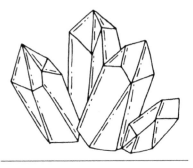

Chapter Forty

Gin stepped carefully into the night, eyes trained straight ahead on the man who held Hope by the arm. She barely registered the pain from the gravel that dug into her bare feet, too preoccupied with the surging anger that fired through her veins. The cruelness of finally being so close to her and not being able to carry her away was torture.

She made to follow her to a black car, but her own captor dragged her to the right. "No! Wait, where are you taking her?" she demanded as she was hauled to Slayton, leaning against the back of another black car. He kicked a foot onto a wheel as he flicked his lighter, smirking as she flinched.

"You don't think I'd let Col take us on a blind road trip without insurance?" he said, brows raised as Col was shoved up against the car. "He knows how much Hope means to you, and I know how much you mean to him, hence... my insurance. Any foul play and it won't just be Gin that gets punished." he said, glancing sideways at a glowering Col. "Hope will be taken to a secure location, along with Louis, until the Galaxy Crystal is in my possession. Not that using him as leverage will do any good now. But I don't have the energy to dispose of his body tonight." he said.

Gin's crestfallen gaze shot to Col, his chance of ever saving Max fading by the minute. His chest caved as his gaze sunk to his feet, fully aware of what he was giving up. And she had no doubt in her mind that he would do it. She could see no way out.

Gin closed her eyes against the horror of this Halloween night, before turning to see Hope trying to call out for her again as she was shoved into the car. Her thin nightgown flapped in the bitter wind.

Gin wept... she couldn't hold it in any longer. She gasped, fighting for air to fill her lungs.

"Take my jacket and give it to Hope, *please!*" she begged Slayton. "Please."

His dead eyes locked on hers, contemplating, as he moved his cigarette between his teeth. Eventually, he nodded to her captor, relief flooding her body. The man pulled her jacket away, the cold metal of her pendant slipping onto her skin. She pressed her arms into her sides against the frigid air. Her exposed back prickled with goosebumps as she watched Slayton take it and walk towards the other car. He stopped halfway, throwing it to the ground, clicking open his lighter and set it ablaze. She stared as the flames danced upwards, her body trembling in anger.

"You bastard!" growled Col, as the flames flickered before them.

Her captor laughed from behind, shoving her towards the car. Slayton followed, opening the door for her, as if he was a perfect gentleman. His smug face crept over her like cobwebs sticking to her skin. Before she could be bundled inside, she took aim and spat. He flinched, mouth turned downwards as he wiped her saliva from his cheekbone. The corners of her mouth tugged upward, adrenaline pumping through her veins.

Slayton cracked his neck from side to side, then brought his palm clear across her face, slapping the side that bore the raw burn. The force knocked her head sideways and if she hadn't been held upright, she would have collided with the gravel.

Col screamed from the other side of the car, the guttural roar wild with anger.

"You need to teach your squire some manners." was Slayton's reply.

"She's doing just fine from where I'm standing." he retorted with a curl of his lip, before he was thrust into the backseat. Gin was plunged into the seat next to him, the doors slamming, leaving them alone for a moment.

"Col, what are you doing? You aren't seriously going to hand the Galaxy Crystal over?" she said, breathless. "Max..." she trailed off, Col's nostrils flaring.

"Let's deal with one problem at a time. Right now, we have more than we can count on one hand." he said, looking sideways at her lap. Gin's throat ached with guilt. "Are you ok?" he asked, grimacing as he brushed loose curls from her burnt cheek.

"Don't worry about me." she said, wincing at the pain. "I'm so sorry." she said, just as Joseph was pushed into the seat next to Col, his crumpled frame in stark contrast to the polished showman. Gin ground her teeth at being reminded of his existence. That he was the reason for all of this.

A sigh pushed out of Col's chest.

"*Sorry* should not be leaving your lips." said Col, staring straight ahead.

Joseph's eyes snagged on hers, deep with sorrow.

"So." said Slayton, sliding into the passenger seat. "Where to?"

They pulled into the courtyard of the castle, the lanterns still lit, the fairy lights still twinkled, everything still just as she left it. Except for the lack of guests.

They were pulled out of the car, her feet raking on the gravel again.

"Where next, Sir Col?" asked Slayton, buttoning his jacket. Col looked up to the top of a turret above Joseph's rooms.

"Up there." he snapped.

Gin's heart jumped to her mouth as Slayton came face to face with him, both staring the other down.

"If you are playing me, one call to my insurance." he said calmly. Too calmly.

"I just want to get as far away as possible from your ego trip. No games." said Col, flatly. Slayton's eyes narrowed before backing up, holding an arm forwards. "Well then. Lead on."

Col didn't look at Gin as he passed. Her captor shunted her forwards, following them with the weight of her guilt upon her shoulders.

The men's shoes clicked on the stone floor across the deserted Great Hall. A stab of longing nestled into her chest at recalling the way Col held her while they danced here. What she would give to go back to that moment, to start again, to do *something* differently. To have turned when Col screamed her name, to have taken him with them. Maybe he would have figured out something was wrong, that Louis was playing them. Her head whirled with regret.

The spiral stone steps to the top of the tower were as uneven and narrow as the rest in the castle and she found it hard to keep her balance with her hands held behind her. They passed Joseph's door, and she wondered if Joseph knew Col had hidden the Galaxy Crystal above his rooms. But Joseph had been kept in the car. What fate awaited him when Slayton had the castle, the device, her and Hope? She swallowed hard. As much anger as she felt towards him, he didn't deserve a fate decided by Slayton.

Col, his captor and Slayton must have reached the top, as she could hear the unlocking of a latch followed by a gust of chilly air. Slayton eyed her as she stepped out onto the high terrace, rubbing his hands to warm them.

"You should have brought a coat, Gin. You'll catch your death up here." he said, sucking the air in between his teeth. She lacked the energy to come back with something witty, letting it wash over her. She just wanted this whole mess to be over with. Her eyes slid to Col, looking out through the crenels in the wall.

Slayton strode towards him casually, taking in their surroundings. She shifted as she realised how high up they were. The town in the valley lit up like a living Christmas card.

"As lovely as it is up here, we haven't come to take in the scenery." said Slayton, clasping his hands behind his back. "The Crystal, Col." His tone matched the temperature as it drifted on the breeze. Col remained stock-still, eyes cast to the sky.

"You could see so much more of the Galaxy 700 years ago."

Slayton laughed, scratching the corner of his mouth.

"Don't waste my time, Col. Or Hope's, for that matter." The threat made Gin's heart race faster, her throat constricting. Col was silent before them as his head lowered slowly.

"Gin has the Crystal." he said, turning to meet her wide eyes. Her body slackened as she fumbled with what he'd just said. He was bluffing. He had to be.

"She'll have to come to me so I can show her. She doesn't know." Col never broke eye contact with her, a calming sensation coming through their bond, like a caress of her cheek. She suddenly realised why she could sometimes feel him like that. The soul connection. It took her breath away for a second, only to be broken by Slayton's bark.

"You heard him, get her over here!"

She found herself flung forwards to face Col, mere inches away. Her breath came in ragged gasps as she looked up at him. He tipped his head back gently, a ghost of a smile upon his lips, for only her to witness.

"You're gonna have to tell these brutes of yours to let go of her for a minute if you want the damn Crystal."

"Yes, fine. Just get the blasted thing, will you? I don't plan on freezing to death up here before morning." said Slayton, blowing into his hands as his patience dwindled.

Gin shook her wrists at their freedom, the blood circulating properly again. She had no idea where Col was going with this. There was no way she really had the Crystal. Col's eyes danced in the way that only his could, before they slipped to the pendant around her neck. Her breath caught in her throat as his hands brushed her skin, scooping the pendant into his fingers. She gaped at him as he placed a finger on each of the inlaid Crystals at the bottom and the same with his other hand on the top. He paused, meeting her gaze, a sad smile upon his lips. She shook her head slowly, in disbelief at what he was doing and what it meant. Her fingers clutched her stomach. She couldn't really have had it all this time…

His eyes slid back to the pendant, and he pressed down on the Crystals gently. She felt the warmth as it heated slightly.

"Col," she breathed, her chest rising and falling against his hand, "please tell me you didn't give me the Galaxy Crystal to protect without knowing."

"Ok… I won't tell you." he said, quietly, before lifting the top half from the base, revealing the most dazzlingly beautiful Crystal she'd ever seen. It glowed from within, as if it really contained the universe. Like she could simply dive in.

"Col, please… don't do this." she whispered.

When she looked up at him, his attention wasn't on the Crystal, but on her. With a sigh that brushed her lips, he said, "I always knew you were special, Sparkles. Didn't need a damn prophecy to tell me that." His brows twitched together for a moment, face pinched. Gin blinked slowly. The guilt stabbed at the back of her throat. All this time he felt the soul connection too… and she never saw it. Never let it penetrate her own armour.

Col moved in one fluid movement towards the Crystal. She grasped the pendant, but it was too late to stop him. He turned to Slayton, his greedy eyes lighting up at the sight of the Crystal in Col's hands. He closed the space between them in seconds and snatched it from his fingers, marvelling at it.

The wind was knocked from Gin's lungs as Slayton now held immeasurable power in his hands. Nausea hit with dizzying force…

He really had won.

But in that split second, Col swung his weight, full force, into his guard behind him, sending him tumbling backwards through the crenel in the wall.

Stunned, she glanced at Slayton, still captivated by the treasure he held.

Col ducked low and rammed himself into the other guard by Gin, knocking him backwards off the tower too. The cry that ripped from the falling guard finally tore Slayton's attention away.

Gin's hands flew to her mouth, frozen to the spot as Slayton let out a roar, clutching the stone and charging towards Col. But something in Slayton's other hand glinted in the moonlight from a white knuckled grip.

A knife.

Numbing horror struck her core as Slayton pelted towards Col, the knife ready to find its mark. Time slowed and yet it was slipping away before her eyes. She needed to act.

Without thinking twice, she threw herself into Col's side. He stumbled, falling to the floor. The next moment, she was crushed beneath Slayton on the ground. Her lungs emptied as her eyes followed the Crystal hurtling into the air. She was paralysed in the fear that clutched her.

The Crystal was on its descent, soaring towards the ground. She watched, unable to do a thing as it exploded into a sea of glittering stars on the stone slabs. Colour expanded from shards, like nebulas escaping from their confines and returning to the sky, along with all hope of ever saving Max and reuniting him with Col. The pain that seared her heart was worse than any injury she'd suffered at Slayton's hands.

After a minute, Slayton raised his head, pushing himself up onto his elbow. His face, like thunder, as he gaped at his empty hand. Both their eyes widened. A sharp wave of pain ignited in her waist, Slayton shocked at having knocked into her instead.

Their eyes travelled down to where his hand still grasped the handle of the knife that was now embedded into her waist.

Gin felt the blood rush from her head as she stared at the dark red patch that had seeped through her silver dress. But as she looked, she began to drift, as if from outside of herself, hovering above.

Slayton let go of the knife as if it were burning his hand and fumbled to stand. His eyes roamed her body, blinking heavily at his slain angel.

Gin's head rolled to her right, where Col fell. Only he was now on his knees by her head, his pain stricken face reeling, as he cupped her cheeks. A tear fell onto her forehead and she realised he was crying. *Screaming.*

But she couldn't hear a thing.

The world was silent as her pain, and that of others, cried out around her. She felt his lips on her forehead before he seemed to fly from her side, straight for Slayton's turned back. She tried to arch her neck to see, but piercing pain cut into her torso, as though it was fire itself.

She lay back, head on the cold floor, and she closed her eyes tightly. Tears rolled down her burning cheeks, searing her skin as reality settled in. She wasn't ready to die. She hadn't even begun to live.

When she opened her eyes, the strangest thing happened in the sky above. The stars danced, and a colour strewn nebula appeared to be descending upon them. But it was the silver eyes, as bright as the moon itself, that held her gaze. She blinked hard and slow, trying to clear the hot mist and fog that clouded her vision. But the eyes remained focused on her. She could hear her own blood rushing through her body… only it came in rhythmic whooshing beats. Like wings.

The pain and fog overpowered her senses, and the world fell into darkness.

Her last thoughts were of Hope…

How she longed to hold her…

Of how very close she'd been…

Of Col… slipping away from him like the tide pulling away from the shore…

And the heat. There was so much heat, wrapping her frozen body in warmth until there was nothing. A space, void of pain in the darkness.

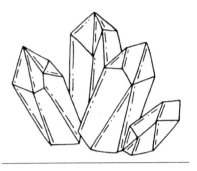

Chapter Forty-One

Gin's reality made itself known long before her eyes discerned it. It started with an ache, deep, squeezing and releasing with the throb of her heart. It consumed her until that strange warmth blanketed her again, soothing the sharpest edge of the pain. She screwed up her eyes, not wanting to wake from the peace she'd found in the darkness. But with a shift of her body, a deep rumble vibrated through her bones and nudged her gently.

One bleary eye opened to take in her surroundings, then the other. The dappled, hazy light streamed through Col's bedroom window. *Col's window.*

She was alive.

The thought sent a buzz of energy through her body as voices from the other room drifted in. One belonged to Col... the other? A little girl. Unmistakably, Hope. She let out a small giggle, and Gin's heart throbbed in her chest at the sound.

Memories of the events that led up to her ending up in this bed came flooding back to her and, blindly, she placed a hand over her waist where the subtle ache resided. She lifted the hem of her top, expecting to feel coarse bandages and tape. But her skin was smooth.

"Alright, alright. But, I *still* don't think this Hangman game is fair, given that you get to use modern day words and I can't use Mediaeval words. You're telling me you don't call breakfast *bellytimber?*" teased Col, much to the amusement of Hope. The sound of her giggle made her chest tighten, the need to hold her nearly too much. She hoisted herself up onto her elbows. But it also stirred something next to her. She froze as warm breath blew her loose hair around her cheeks.

Gin swallowed hard as a purr vibrated the bed that would have sent her running if she'd not been rooted to the spot. Instead, she was met with two bright silver eyes, the same two she swore she'd seen before falling into darkness. They seemed to swirl like molten silver, shimmering as they inspected her serenely.

Gin's voice found her in the form of a scream that pitched through the cottage. The creature cocked its head and leaned back a little. Its black dragon-like body was flecked with what seemed like stars, appearing to swirl as it moved, a cloud like nebula billowing onto its chest in dreamlike colours.

Heavy footsteps came charging in and Col collapsed at her bedside with Hope hovering on the threshold, Penny back in the safety of her arm.

Gin's rapid breathing left her feeling hungry for air that just didn't seem to fill her lungs as she looked from Hope to the creature and back again.

"Hey, hey, hey. Breathe, *breathe,* Gin." said Col, taking her hand in his. He gave the creature an 'I told you so' look before going back to soothing her. "It's OK. You're OK." he searched her eyes before glancing round at Hope. He beckoned her to come.

"You did it, Gin." he said, as Hope padded softly to his side.

Gin didn't know where to begin, a million things running through her mind. But Hope *was* there. Right in front of her. Despite the creature behind her, that seemed to purr at the arrival of the little girl.

"Mummy?" she whispered. Col put his free arm around her and Gin's heart ached with a feeling so full that she almost burst. She pushed herself up, ignoring the ache in her torso. She'd waited long enough for this moment. Wrapping her in her arms, the tension in Hope's frail body melted away.

"I'm *so sorry,* Hope. I'm here. I'll never leave you again. *I promise.*" she said, through the mass of curls that had been washed and detangled since she saw her on Halloween night. The familiar smell of Lavender and Rose filled her nostrils. Daphne's special.

"I missed you!" she squealed, her grip tightening around her to the point of hurting her tender middle. But there was no way she was going to stop her. This moment was too precious.

Gin's eyes found Col's. They were sheathed in a watery haze that pooled behind the red rims of his eyes. She didn't know how long she'd been out for, but Col had definitely not slept a wink throughout it all. Still, the smile that laced his face was the most beautiful thing she'd ever seen.

"I'm so sorry, sweetheart. I'm so sorry." she pulled back, inspecting her little girl. It didn't seem real. She cupped Hope's cheeks, her smile faltering at the plumpness that had disappeared since leaving her. A wave of anger flushed her face. Slayton.

But she wouldn't bring him up in front of her. She refused to subject her to even the mention of his name.

"I knew you'd come back, mummy. You'd always come back." she said. Gin laughed between tears at her beautiful little girl, and the strength she'd had in her absence.

"Always, sweetheart. *Always.*" said Gin. After a moment of letting herself drown in Hope's arms, she spoke again.

"Col. Please tell me I'm imagining what I think I am in this room." she breathed. As if to answer her question, the creature nudged her cheek ever so lightly with its own, the skin warm and as soft as suede. Her eyes fluttered as she tried not to move.

Col tented his fingers in front of his mouth, looking to where the creature sat behind her, and winced as Hope sat up on her knees.

"Isn't she beautiful, Mummy? She made you better!" she beamed, holding a hand up to the creature. Gin finally turned in time to see it nestle its forehead into Hope's small palm, sending her heart rate soaring.

"Uh, I-I'm not sure... maybe you should stay back a... a bit." Gin stumbled over her words as she watched Hope and the creature. She looked helplessly to Col. He wore a thin-lipped smile, but the ghost of a frown lingered.

"Seems my Grandmother wasn't so loopy with her tales of the Crystal's origin after all." he said, eyeing them. "This... dragon, for want of a better word, appeared..." he paused, eyes squinting as he ambled for words, "right after the Galaxy Crystal was destroyed."

Gin's eyes darkened, the memory of the Crystal shattering on the ground flashing before her. Col looked up at her, smiling weakly.

"But she came out of the universe itself, took you, healed you... and hasn't left your side since. This is the nearest I've been allowed for the past three days. Pretty protective of you, that's for damn sure."

Gin's dazed look swept over the dragon. The more she looked at her, the more she realised she was like a living, breathing version of the Galaxy Crystal. Although she wouldn't call it a dragon. Perhaps the upper half, but the lower was more aquatic. Its tail flared out into a fine fin that seemed to ripple like a breeze on the surface of a lake. It was also missing the hind legs entirely, giving the impression that it must use its wings to get around.

Gin's nose wrinkled as she spoke softly to the creature.

"Well... I suppose I owe you my thanks." The creature stopped nuzzling Hope and turned her attention to Gin, head tilting. It blinked slowly and inched forward, holding one leg up as she gently rested her chin on Gin's head. The breath hitched in Gin's throat as she marvelled at the impossible creature. Its scales seemed to undulate with each powerful breath. She huffed a small laugh and gaped as it pulled back to observe her.

"It's impossible. Just like everything else." she marvelled.

Col cleared his throat and Gin didn't miss the pointed look the creature gave him. She pressed her lips together. Their desire to protect her, clearly in competition. They needed to change the subject, and she had burning questions that needed answering.

"Col... what happened up there? After..." her eyes slid to Hope, idly stroking the dragon's soft scales. "I have no memory of anything after passing out." she whispered, all too aware of little ears.

The line between Col's brow creased, and he leaned over to Hope.

"Hey. I'm pretty sure Daphne has a big bowl of honeyed oats for you up in the kitchens. If you ask *really* nicely, she'll sprinkle chocolate on top too, but don't tell her I told you. What say you take our... *guest*," his eyes flicked to the dragon, who's purring stopped, "up there, and get some bellytimber." he winked. Gin smiled as Hope beamed, followed by a roll of her eyes.

"You mean, *breakfast*." she corrected. Col held his hands up in defeat.

"OK, OK. You win! *Breakfast.*" he conceded. Hope looked at Gin, a flash of worry settling upon her. She reached out and pushed Hope's loose curls behind her ear.

"It's alright, sweetheart. I'm not going anywhere. Go fill that belly of yours." she said, before looking at the creature who had already slunk off the bed with grace, but its eyes were on Col.

"And *you*. Don't worry about him." she said. The creature gazed at her. "He may not look it, but he's one of the good guys." she said. Col raised a dark eyebrow.

"I tried telling you." he said to the dragon, shoulders rising. It spread its wings indignantly, and a rush of warm air swept over them. Gin watched in amazement as it shrunk to fit through the doors, then continued to shrink until it was the size of a robin, perched on Hope's shoulder, before she closed the door behind them. They left Gin gaping.

"Did you..."

"Yeah. Should've seen her when she came out of the sky that night. She *was* the sky." he said, gazing up at Gin, elbows on his knees, hands clenched. Words failed her. What baffled her more was the fact that she felt completely at ease sending Hope off with the thing.

Col sighed, drawing her attention away from the door. She felt a wall crumble around him as he rubbed his hands together, lips clamped, no longer having to be strong for Hope. Then he shuddered, head bowed as he took her hands in his, his forehead against their cupped fists. She swallowed, seeing him so depleted, feeling totally overpowered by the feeling of sheer affection for him. Not only had he been there for her, but for Hope, too. Her chest caved, and she leant her head on top of his, soft beneath her cheek. She inhaled his sweet leathery scent, realising that it wasn't just *his* smell. It had become so familiar, so comforting. It was *home*.

"I thought I'd lost you." he said, sitting up, eyes locked on their hands. A trembling breath left her lungs as her stomach twisted.

"I'm so sorry, Col." she grimaced. Col's head whipped up, ready for battle.

"Don't you dare. Don't try to take the blame for *anything.*"

"But I've brought nothing but trouble for you. If you'd never met me, you'd still have your future." She bit her cheek, "You'd still have the Galaxy Crystal, your chance of going back for Max. While I sit here, reunited with Hope... you must hate me." She looked away, cheeks burning. Her heart ached painfully. But Col let go of her hand and pressed his index finger to her chin, lifting her gaze to his face.

"Hate you?" he asked weakly, his eyes narrowing. "Hell, Gin... how could I hate you?" She opened her mouth to tell him exactly, in detail, all the ways in which she had lied to him, betrayed him, caused destruction of all the Crystals he cherished, but he cut in.

"Don't." he said, brows raised. "Any reason you have will be completely inaccurate." He shook his head a little as he dragged his teeth gently over his lower lip. Gin's heart throbbed in her chest, the pain in her throat building. She wanted to believe him, but it seemed so impossible that he would not blame her for ruining everything good in his life.

"Argh." he sighed before running a hand over his mouth. She was caught under his gaze as he studied her. After a moment, he spoke with care.

"My life has been a constant stream of motion, never standing still. I've watched the people I love travel through time, taking my heart with them with every jump. I've seen things no one should ever have to see, over and over again, on a loop of torture. I never felt truly present... until you." He pressed his forehead against hers, dropping his voice to a whisper. Electricity bubbled in her chest. "With you, time stands still. The world keeps going, the clock still ticks... but you and I? We exist on a plane of life that I never knew existed."

Gin's pulse raced in her ears as he raised his head, their faces mere centimetres apart. She swallowed, though her throat was dry as his eyes caressed her lips.

"I love you so damn much, Gin." he said, his hand sweeping up her arm, raising a cascade of goosebumps. She closed her eyes at his touch as his fingers ran slowly over her collarbone. "And I'm no idiot. I know I don't deserve to even contemplate your love. But… I don't think I'm alone in this. So if I am, Gin, tell me, because I am completely at your feet. And I don't get on my fucking knees for anyone."

Gin pulled back to face him. His eyes were dark and hungry for her. She was tired of pushing her feelings aside, tired of pretending that it meant nothing. Because it meant *everything.* They were soulmates.

She grasped his shoulders, bunching his shirt in her fingers.

"I think this whole soulmate thing finally makes sense," she breathed, running a hand down the back of his head, his eyes shutting momentarily at her touch. "I love you, Col." she whispered.

When his eyes opened, she knew the person he was looking at was the one she'd had to hide for so long, laid bare for him. Yet it felt as natural as breathing.

His brows lowered briefly until he slowly leaned in and kissed her softly. The sensation of his lips on hers sent her mind reeling, sure the world was falling away around them. She leaned into his hand as it laced through her hair, her own hands sliding through the opening of his shirt to touch his warm skin. He swallowed the moan that she couldn't keep from surfacing as his fingers grazed the underside of her breast. She arched into his touch, wishing he'd move just a little higher. But with a grunt, he pulled away, coming up for air. Col's eyes roamed her face, his breathing frayed. She was totally ensnared in his entire being.

"Gin, every selfish bone in my body is telling me to climb into that bed with you and take every moan from those pretty lips," he rasped, eliciting another one to escape her. Col closed his eyes against it, and a low growl met her ears. "But you're healing," he warned.

Gin didn't care. She had never felt this urge before, and she wanted to follow it. Her hands slid to the button on his shirt, wanting it gone. But Col caught her wrists in his hands, eyes flashing as she bit her lip.

"Damn it, Sparkles." he gritted out, eyes devouring her mouth.

"I need you, Col. Please… be selfish with me," she begged, wanting to slip further into this feeling. Col's nostrils flared dangerously.

"Sparkles, when you're healed, you're gonna have to beg me to stop. I can promise you that. But I care about you too much to risk hurting you." He kissed her temple, breathing deeply as they both came back to their senses.

Gin knew he was right. Despite wishing he had given in to his selfishness with her this once. He was even more beautiful for it, though. His soul was imperfect and rough around the edges, but his heart was the purest thing she'd ever known. And she would not be careless with it.

"Two broken souls, huh?" she said, gently.

"I think they're well on their way to healing," he said, bringing her hand to his lips. Gin's stomach fluttered with the beat of a hundred wings.

Col's head dropped, brow furrowed as he exhaled, a weight suddenly settling upon his shoulders. She swallowed. It would be easy to let themselves be swept into a world of their own right now, but there were questions that plagued her about what she had missed. And she could feel the heaviness in his heart, too.

"Tell me everything, Col. Don't keep it here." she said, placing her palm over his heart. He was silent before her. But after a moment, his wary eyes met hers, assessing.

"I made you a promise, Gin. That you'd never have to worry about Slayton again." he paused and her tummy knotted. "When he buried that blade in you, the blade that was meant for *me*... I lost it. I saw red. Shit, I thought I was going to lose you and I…" he shook his head slowly, mouth open but words failing. "*I choked the life out of him.*"

Gin covered her open mouth with a shaky palm before reaching out for him, clutching his arms. He'd killed him because of her. He had risked throwing his life away because of *her*. The warmth that had filled her body moments before leached away.

"Oh Col." she breathed. But he shook his head firmly.

"I'd do it again too. I'd live that timeline again and again, over and over, to see the light leave his eyes, before he ever had a chance to hurt you." he said. She felt a tremble rack his body. Or perhaps it was her own. She no longer knew where she ended and he began, their souls stitched together so tightly.

"Col... they will come for you. This won't go unpunished." she choked as fear squeezed in her chest.

"I'll take whatever punishment comes my way to know that *you* and *Hope* never have to look over your shoulder again." His lips twisted downwards as tears ran down her cheek. She was only aware of them as Col gently brushed them away.

"I'm sor-" she began, but he placed a kiss so fragile on her lips, stopping her in her tracks.

"No more apologies." he frowned. She gritted her teeth, wanting to press him about how much danger he had placed himself in, but he went on, trudging through the events of that night.

"Louis turned up not long after Slayton's men hit the ground. He'd broken free of his captor and brought Hope and Oldman back. The scene he arrived on almost had him pissing his pants. Knife in your side, that dragon creature already healing you, lighting up the night sky and me... pushing myself off Slayton's lifeless body." he spoke into the distance. The pain stemmed along the bond and she took it, willing her bond to take it all from him. Louis's betrayal was a wound that went deep.

"I wanted to ask him why. If he was ever sincere... but I also wanted to rip his head off. And I didn't trust myself enough at that moment not to." The muscle in his jaw worked. "So I told him to leave. To never come back. That if I ever see him again, I'll make him pay with his life. Over and over."

That line that Gin had seen so often between his brows and had longed to smooth appeared again. This time, she let herself. She thumbed it softly, watching his face soften as he met her gaze.

"Joseph had a field day with the press, of course." he rolled his eyes. "Told them that Slayton had planned the whole thing, to take the castle and the device. That he tried to put the blame on him for everything he did to you. Even had my back... told the police one of Slayton's men turned on him." Something that looked like shame flashed across his face, but was gone in seconds. "He's back to being king of his castle again. Even been to see you, twice, every day." He cocked his head, surveying her. The fact he had come to see her sat strangely in her stomach. Not in a good or bad way, just an obvious way. She pushed it aside as her mind wandered to a more pressing matter.

"The patients. Where are the patients from the Hospice?" she asked, heart racing. Col pressed his lips together.

"You've been out for days, Gin. The morning after the ball, they were all moved to what I've been assured is the best care home they can offer. They'll be looked after properly, with their medical needs met. They're all safe now."

"But the healing Crystals... did you... did you manage to heal some?" her voice was quiet, as if she already knew the answer. Col's cheeks hollowed before he answered.

"The Crystals I have left were only successful for a few patients. And even then, there were elements of their illnesses that I couldn't heal." He bit his cheek. "I'm so sorry Gin. I know how important it was to you. I did everything I could." he finished, eyes cast down.

Gin quelled the heaviness in her heart of being unable to help them. She pressed her forehead to his.

"Thank you." she whispered.

They sat with it for a minute or two, letting the disappointment ebb and flow.

"You're free, Sparkles. You're totally and utterly free." said Col, finally breaking the silence.

A bolt of electricity coursed through her at those words. She had Hope. She had freedom from Slayton. And yet there was something she could never be free from.

"Not completely." she said. Col raised a brow in question. "I belong to *you*, Col. You have me. Totally and wholeheartedly."

"You belong to you before anyone, remember that. Prophecy or not." he said, worry etched in his brow. She smiled softly, trying to ply it away.

"I know. It's just, I didn't think I needed anyone in my life apart from Hope. I thought letting people in only ever ended up breaking you. But instead, you stitched all my broken parts back together, Col. You've become a part of my soul that I can't and don't want to live without." she said, taking his hands in hers and running her fingers over the scars. "Every perfect imperfection. Every self-doubt. Every hurt. Every smile. The good, the bad. I want *all* of you." she said, smoothing the unshaven bristles on his jaw as his smile lines dimpled. "You taught me to love all the things I used to hide about myself. That kind of love is powerful." Col's brows rose as his gaze swept over her face, and said,

"That prophecy. Knew what it was doing. *Together, our soul's love is more powerful than any Crystal.*"

Gin nodded, recalling the prophecy, but after a moment she stilled. She stared into his eyes, unseeing as a realisation settled upon her.

"Gin?" asked Col, after a moment of silence. She came out of her thoughts at his voice, blinking rapidly. Her hands dropped, and she swivelled to sit on the edge of the bed, feet on the cold stone floor.

"Easy." he said, putting his hands out in case she was about to fall off. "What is it?" he asked, worry etching his words. She couldn't speak, could hardly believe the idea forming in her mind. All she knew was that if this worked, it could be the answer to more than one problem.

"Do you have *any* Hematite Crystals? Any that survived the break in, even fragments?"

Col's forehead wrinkled.

"Uh, I'm not sure. But I can find out." he said as he surveyed her. "What's going on in there?" he asked, eyes sliding to her forehead. She set her jaw, unwilling to say too much.

"I need you to do something for me." she said, holding her breath under his piqued gaze. "Can you get the patients here?"

Col blew out his cheeks and released a breath.

"I don't know. I mean, I could try. Why?" he asked, eyes narrowed. She bit her lip.

"Do you trust me? To have your best interest at heart and those of others?"

"Of course, that's what worries me." he said, eyes dancing about her face. She swallowed the nerves that bubbled in her chest. There was no way he'd go ahead with part of her plan. But he'd gone to hell and back for her. Now it was her turn.

Chapter Forty-Two

Col held Gin close the entire way to the Great Hall, helping with every step. He also protested for most of it, too, but she wasn't going to waste a second. Not when the pockets of those loyal to Slayton in the police service could decide that Slayton's death was not at the hands of one of his own men. Especially if Louis could spill his secret at any moment. She would not see Col go down for it.

He held the door open for her, the hinges groaning as it swung. The few faces that were taking their seats at the breakfast table froze as they watched Gin hobble over the threshold. She stared right back, feeling completely naked despite the long black coat she'd bundled on top of her clothes. She tugged it onto her shoulders, closing the gap.

Lady Flora and Tarrick were already seated and paused when they clocked the two of them. She was fully prepared for an onslaught of insults about her hideous scars. But it didn't come. What surprised her even more was the civil nod that they exchanged with Col with a furtive glance to her before returning to their plates.

"Didn't anyone ever tell you it's rude to stare?" said Col to the rest of them. The faces soon busied themselves again, slightly redder than before.

"What on earth was *that?*" asked Gin, nose wrinkled.

"What was what?" Gin gave him a pointed look.

"That friendly exchange." she said, exasperated. Col inhaled, looking past her briefly as the table resumed their conversations.

"Well, turns out Louis's plan was to plant the seed of me being steered into trouble the night of the Ball, in Flora's mind. When things went south and Louis left with you, Flora had a bad feeling about it. She came and told me to go, but with caution. And that you might be in danger." he said gruffly. Gin's mouth parted.

"Wow." she said, unable to think of anything more profound.

"Yeah." said Col, frowning at his feet. Silence hung in the air before she spoke.

"She does have a heart." she said.

"Hm, disgusting, isn't it?" he said, easing into a twisted smirk.

She huffed a small laugh before hesitating. She needed Col gone if she was going to get her plan underway.

"You should go. I'll meet you back here. Please do everything you can to get them here as quickly as you can." she said, wringing her hands. Col pursed his lips in thought, nodding.

"Are you sure you're up to this now? I mean, they're safe. One more day won't hurt."

"No, no... I'm fine, honestly. I owe it to them." she said, pulling herself up. Col's jaw worked, but he didn't protest further. He parted with a soft kiss, her cheeks warming at the eyes that zoned in on them. But Col's playful smirk soon had her finding her own, heat pooling in her stomach.

"Just don't do anything to prolong your healing, hm?" he practically growled.

"Yes, Master." she replied, enjoying the look of torment on his face as he left.

With no distractions, her mind was free to focus on what she needed to do.

She gritted her teeth as she walked past the long table, feeling the burning eyes of those in the room. Her fingers clutched the Black Tourmaline that Col had found and her body tingled with hope as she made her way to retrieve the device.

Gin had been pacing the length of the hall for what seemed like hours by the time Col returned. She sighed as her body relaxed at the sight of him, holding the door open for the patients who were being brought in. The corners of his lips twitched as they locked eyes. But she positively beamed at him and the faces that she'd not forgotten. Faces that were fascinated with the surrounding splendour.

Gin bit her cheek, edging her way to Col as the Hall gradually filled up with wheelchairs, while others stood, gazing at the place they'd only ever dreamed of seeing.

She wrapped her arms around Col's, the muscles tensing under her touch.

"Thank you." she said, unable to drag her eyes away from the people that had been a part of the driving force that got her here today.

"It's *you* who freed them. Don't need to thank me." he said, placing a kiss upon her hair. Her chest expanded with warmth. But it was soon replaced with a chill as two faces appeared in the doorway before her.

"Kate... Sam." she said, swallowing hard. The last people she'd let down before she left, refusing to help Sam's Alzheimer suffering mum through an episode of schizophrenia. She'd always had a way with her, been able to calm her through the rough storms. But like everyone else, Gin had left Sam to weather that storm alone. Shame bit angrily at her gut. Col's chest swelled against her, the only thing keeping her grounded.

As Kate's eyes bore into hers, she was certain that any moment now, the anger and hatred that she'd left them in would hit her. But Kate flung her arms around her and held her in a hug that melted the jagged ice in her chest.

After being paralysed for a moment, Gin gained control of her stunned arms and folded them around Kate. She blinked fiercely as tears stung the back of her eyes.

"I'm so sorry." she stammered as Sam joined the embrace, too. After a moment, Kate split the hold. She shook her head firmly.

"You did what no one else could. You could have run, let Slayton ruin all of us. But you didn't. You saved us and we will *never* forget that." she said. Gin's mouth slackened as Sam patted her on the arm before they went to join their mothers.

"Proud of you." Col said from beside her. "So much so that it kinda makes me want to throw up," he added. Gin's shoulders sagged as she threw him a pinched look of amusement. He wiggled his brows and let the door swing closed as the last people entered.

"So… you gonna let me in on what's happening yet?" he asked. She raised her chin, looking over the room. It was time to put her theory to the test.

"We're going to heal them." she said, simply, meeting his cautious stare.

"Gin… I already told you, I-"

"I know. The Crystals are gone, but something you said about the prophecy. Well, it got me thinking." She turned her body towards him, lowering her voice. "It said, *together, our soul's love is more powerful than any Crystal…* well, what if *we* can heal them with that power?" she said, willing his frown to subside.

"I don't know if that's how it works, Gin. I mean, the idea is amazing, but…" he trailed off as he scanned the buzzing room. Gin's nose wrinkled, and she rubbed at her pounding chest.

"Look, I know it sounds crazy, but I really feel this could work. I can't explain, other than something inside me just… has to *try.*" she said, clenching her fists to her.

Col's lips thinned as he surveyed her. She knew how mad it sounded, but everything about her life was defined by what should be deemed as impossible and yet, it was real.

Col shoved his hands into his pockets.

"Well, let's find out if you're as crazy as my grandma." he said, his brow quirking up. Gin rubbed her sweaty palms together.

"I really hope so." she bit her lip, looking at the crowded room.

By the time they'd organised everyone, many of the inhabitants had come to see what was going on. Including Joseph.

"Gin! I didn't expect to see you… good grief…" he said, eyes wide as he surveyed the rows of patients in the hall.

Gin tucked a strand of hair behind her ear as she approached her first patient.

"You're just in time, Joseph." she said, glancing up at him, his face as white as a ghost as Col joined her. "This is Sam and his mother, Fiona. We're about to heal her." she said, trying to sound like she had every bit of confidence.

Joseph floundered for words amid the operation she had on her hands.

Col puckered his lips, patting Joseph on the arm.

"Relax. We have absolutely *nothing* under control." said Col, eyes flashing. Gin narrowed hers at him and held out her left hand for him to take.

"OK, Fiona, we're going to hold your hand now… and hope to the powers that be that my hunch is right." she said, slightly under her breath. Fiona sat, rocking in her wheelchair, oblivious to what they were about to do. Part of Gin was thankful. If it didn't work, she wouldn't know she'd let her down again.

She locked onto Col's electrifying eyes as they both took one of Fiona's frail hands. Gin trembled with each deep breath. But as Col brushed his thumb over her hand, she felt the shudders ebb away, replaced with a feeling of utter peace. It tingled her skin, like a thousand stars erupting over her body. Col's shoulders rose and fell with the energy that sparked between them, coursing through their bodies and building with intensity.

Col's grip on her hand tightened as his gaze narrowed. She wasn't sure what was happening, only that it was *something*.

When the tingling turned to a steady buzz, the force subsided and slowly dwindled until it left them breathless and shaking.

Col's brow furrowed.

"Are you alright?" he asked, drawing nearer. She nodded, ignoring the pounding of her heart as she knelt before Fiona.

"Fiona?" she asked, clutching onto the wheelchair arm. She exchanged a nervous glance with Sam, who knelt on the other side.

"Mum?" he asked, finding his unsteady voice. But it was enough.

Fiona blinked, pulling her head towards him, a giant smile breaking to the surface. "Sam?" she asked, her eyes suddenly alight with recognition.

Gin released the breath she'd been holding as they embraced. Her forehead sank to the armrest, as a total weightlessness took hold.

It worked.

The stars had erupted into the night sky by the time the last patient left the castle and Gin was utterly spent. She watched the last van drive away from the courtyard, emotionally and physically drained. It had taken every fibre of her being to keep going, to heal everyone, in order to go ahead with the next part of her plan with a clear conscience.

Col wrapped his arms around her, enveloping her in his warmth as she raised her head to the stars above. She could feel his trembling muscles, just as weakened as hers.

"You know, I don't think crazy ever looked so damn good." he purred in her ear, before leaving a trail of gentle kisses on her cheekbone. She leaned into his cheek, savouring the sweet blackberry and leather scent of his skin.

"You mean the sort of crazy like you, giving me the Galaxy Crystal to protect without telling me?" she asked, swivelling in his grasp to face him.

"Don't blame me, blame my soul. He was being a complete, hopeless romantic." he said. She hid her smirk in his chest, thinking about what was coming next. He was sure to lose it.

"Well, you're going to need to remember how crazy suits me." she said, slipping from his arms and leading him slowly back to the hall. The entire castle was still congregated there, muttering between themselves about what she and Col had done.

Col tipped his head back, hands shoved in his pockets.

"Oh Sparkles, why do I not like the sound of that?"

She ignored his probing and padded over the flagstones to where Hope sat with the dragon, by the fire, subjecting the tiny creature to playing picnics with Penny. They had been inseparable all day. It warmed Gin's heart to see her happy. To see her safe… as insane as that was in present company. But something deep down told her she needn't fear this creature. She had come to trust those intuitive feelings more and more over recent months.

She reached up to a wooden chest in an alcove by the fire. Holding it to her chest, she took a steadying breath and levelled Col with a guarded gaze.

"For the first time, you don't have the luxury of time." she said, heart pounding as his eyes narrowed. "Slayton may have gone, but his allies are still very much alive, woven into society. It's only a matter of time until someone figures out his death was foul play and comes after you. Especially if Louis saw you. He won't think twice about turning you in." she said. Col shifted his weight, running a hand through his hair. He opened his mouth to speak, but she beat him to it.

"And I believe *we* can make the device work. Just like we healed everyone tonight. You can't stay here... which means Hope and I can't stay here either." Col shook his head, but she stepped closer, continuing, "*You're* our home now. We can go back together and search for Max." she said. Col looked away, laughing softly.

"Gin. Even if it did, there is not a world in this universe where I would let you go back to the 1500s, you know that. It's *too* dangerous."
She gritted her teeth, determined not to be talked out of it.

"Look, if I could assure your safety, it would be different. But *I can't*. The safety of these castle walls does not extend to back then. Even if the Galaxy Crystal had survived, I would have stayed with you until I was no longer needed here. That's why I didn't tell you I had the last Crystal. Until you and Hope were..." he trailed off, his gaze flitting over her shoulder, to Hope.

"Dead." she finished for him, well aware of what he was thinking. His chest caved as he released a heavy sigh. He didn't age here. The harsh reality was not lost on her. She and Hope would grow old and he'd still be exactly the same in his physical form. She swallowed the lump in her throat.

"I am mine before anyone else's." she said. Col cursed to the ceiling. "Those were your words, right?"

"Gin-"

"Well, I choose *this*. Because the Galaxy Crystal has been destroyed. But *we* can make the device work. We can save Max. You'd do it for me, I know you would and I'll do it for you." she said, her voice cracking as she opened the chest, revealing the device.

His eyes slid warily from her face to the box, transfixed for a moment before pinching the bridge of his nose.

"Why do you have to be as annoyingly stubborn as me?" he said. She drew herself up, sharpening her resolve. Col sighed.

"You really think this could work?" he asked, eyeing her.

"My daughter's playing picnics with the dragon that saved me. We just healed a room full of sick people with whatever it is our souls have created together." She stared straight ahead. "At this point, anything is possible."

Col glanced sideways and took his hand from his pocket, taking hers in his. He brought it to his lips for a lingering moment...

"I love you." he said onto the back of her hand. "And I would do everything in my power to protect you and Hope. But that's not enough to keep you both safe back there." His brows pinched. Gin smiled somberly. She would always cherish his desire to protect her. But she knew now in her heart that she was strong enough to protect herself and those she loves too.

"I'm an asteroid, remember?" she quipped, tugging a tight-lipped sigh from him. "I follow the path I know to be right. Nothing can change my course."

Col's eyes closed.

"God, I hate it when my own words bite me on the ass." he breathed, before taking her face in his hands, tipping her head up so that when he spoke, there was barely a space between their lips. "You are all the reasons I don't do love, and all the reasons why I can't fucking help but follow my traitorous heart." His words rumbled through her until she couldn't take the space that kept them parted. She kissed him deeply.

She would be an asteroid... for him.

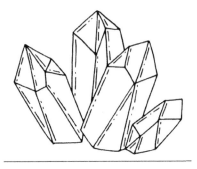

Chapter Forty-Three

Gin placed the device on the table for everyone in the hall to see.

"Gin... what are you..." Joseph stammered. She stood proudly at the head of the table, Hope by her side, where Joseph would have sat, Col leaned over the back of the chair, hands clasped.

"I need you all to listen, and carefully, because this is going to be one of, if not *the* most important decisions of your lives." She looked at Joseph, pointedly. He shrank under her gaze and flitted from face to face around the table.

"I don't have time to explain everything, but I want to give you all the choice. Because as I have come to realise myself, your life is yours and yours alone, before it is anyone else's." She noted the eyes that darted to Joseph and was satisfied that they understood. Col's words had hit their mark with them too, and he visibly shrank under the weight of them.

"You need to decide whether you want to stay here, in this timeline, without the castle, and to make a life for yourself beyond these walls. Or... you can return to your past, where you'll have the chance to live the life you left behind."

The table erupted in whispers and furrowed brows as they processed what she had said. She gave them a minute before continuing. Col tugged on her elbow.

"Gin... you can't. It's all or nothing. There's no going without everyone in the castle going." he reminded her. There were several murmurs of agreement. She spoke louder this time, above the chatter.

"When I found the Sunstone, I also found a notebook. I was going to give it to you, Col, but things got... messy." she said, grimacing. Col tilted his head back. "Go on." he said, gently, no anger in his words. She swallowed.

"From what I can tell, it belonged to your mother. There was a page about a Crystal called Hematite. The most powerful stone for grounding yourself. So powerful that it can make you feel like you're literally being sucked down to the earth. She had worked out that if you're holding onto this, or to someone who is, you won't be shifted in time." she said, studying Col's face. He took a silent deep breath, his brows quirking up as he processed this new information. She scanned the eyes that met hers around the table.

Lady Flora and Tarrick held hands as they took on board the gravity of what she was saying.

"If you remain here, you will not age, be that a blessing or a curse. That's for you to decide." She hesitated, biting her lip. "I am truly sorry for making you choose so quickly. But we need to leave as soon as possible." She turned to face Joseph, who stood with one arm crossed as he chewed the nails of his other hand.

"Joseph. I'm going to give you the opportunity you didn't give these people you call your family." The last word felt sour on her tongue. He had chosen the family he wanted instead of his blood. But she wouldn't make the same mistake as her father. "The choice is whether you stay or come with us. But with that choice comes a second chance." she said, raising her brows as she stepped back to Col's side. He immediately put an arm around her, sensing her weariness.

Joseph stopped biting his nails and clutched both arms, visibly swallowing.

"See, I too have found my family in unconventional ways." She placed a hand on Col's, the other firmly in Hope's. Sweat beaded on Joseph's forehead as he failed to conceal his shame. "I always thought Hope and I were better off on our own. But I was wrong. And if you can find the courage and strength to go back to that period of time that you longed to escape, to come back with us, you might discover the family you didn't think you needed too." She wiped a tear from her cheek, lips pursed, determined not to break down. She didn't need him to choose her. Didn't expect him to do so. He never had before. But for once, she felt the sharpness of that truth.

Col squeezed her shoulder gently, a reminder that he had her, no matter what.

Joseph looked down at his hands before unbuttoning one of his cuffs on his shirt. She watched, brow furrowed, as he rolled up his sleeve to reveal the myriad of faded tattoos. He slid his fingers over a pocket watch design, face pinched.

"One thirty-six am. That was the time you came into this world." he said, reading the time inked on the watch face. The tension in her face relaxed. Had he once cared enough to get a tattoo for her? The thought seemed unfathomable.

"But it seems I need a new tattoo." He glanced at his phone to check the time before chucking it onto the table. "Nine twenty-three pm. The time I really became a father… and Grandfather." he stepped forward, and she inhaled, drawing her arms into her sides as he took her hand with care. He placed his other hand on Hope's head and met Gin's uncertain gaze.

"You two deserve better than me." They both glanced down at Hope's quizzical face. "But I want to make it up to you. I *want* to be a part of your lives. If you'll have me." his voice snagged on the emotion he quelled.

"We'll have you, Mr. Oldman!" said Hope, beaming up at him. Gin's heart could have exploded at her pureness, so willing to accept when she'd every right to distrust and cut people off. Just as she had once done. But time changes people, she was living proof. He deserved the opportunity to change, too.

"If Hope's happy, so am I," said Gin. Joseph nodded, visibly sagging with relief. "Thank you." he whispered, feet shuffling on the ground.

Gin put a hand on his shoulder before facing the table once more. It seems tears had found many of the eyes on her. Decisions had been made. Futures were waiting.

She looked at Daphne, who had been in quiet conversation with Tom in the shadow of an alcove. Daphne met her gaze and her lips trembled. It suddenly hit her with a blazing force. It was Tom. He could not go back. The struggle behind her eyes was clear as day. By staying, she'd be leaving Col, forsaking the promise she made to Josephine. But leaving would mean losing the man she loved.

Gin glanced up at Col, who had also been watching them. She smiled tightly and handed him the Hematite Crystal. She pressed it into his calloused palm and looked at Daphne as she spoke.

"Help her let go of you, so that she can find her happiness." she whispered. Col sniffed, nodding slowly. He padded over to her and held out his hands. Daphne cast a nervous glance between him and then Gin.

"Remember what my mother used to say? *Your heart will not lead you astray, if only your mind gives over the wheel."* he said gently, placing the Hematite in her palm. Daphne closed her eyes briefly before embracing him. "It's time to give up the wheel, Daph." he said, pressing his lips together. Daphne sniffed several times, trying to compose herself.

"I never understood what she meant until we came here. Blimin' foul cars." she said, half laughing, half crying. Col pulled back, squinting through the bittersweet moment.

Tom nodded at Gin, mouthing, *thank you.* She smiled tightly and drew a deep breath. She crossed to Daphne and held her elbow, only to be swept into her warm embrace.

"You're not leaving without a hug, dearie." she said, "You look after them, Col. Or I *will* string you up by the-"

"I promise, Daph. I promise." he said, warmly. "Me and my balls." he said, wincing. She laughed, swatting him on the arm before throwing her arms around him.

Gin crouched, pulling Hope towards her.

"Ok sweetheart. What do you say to an adventure?" she asked, the wide-eyed gleam in her baby girl's eyes already telling her the answer.

"Can we take Skye?" she asked, bouncing on the balls of her feet, pointing to the dragon that watched them with interest. Gin laughed.

"Good name. And yes. I don't think she'd want to stay behind." Hope nodded, her curls bouncing up and down as she hugged Penny in the crook of her arm.

Gin faced the sombre room and walked back to the device, Col in tow. It was time, before those Great Hall doors swung open to the police dragging Col away.

"Ok. If you're staying, place a hand on Daphne. If not…" she paused, releasing a deep breath, "we'll see you on the other side." The room was near enough split, as many staying as going.

Podraig was by her side in a flash, nodding firmly. Gin beamed, glad she didn't have to say goodbye to him.

Lady Flora and Sir Tarrick made their way to Gin and Col's side too. Flora gave a weak smile to Daphne, blowing a delicate kiss, which Daphne pocketed, returning the gesture.

The enormity of Gin's decision tugged painfully at her heart. But so much awaited these people who had been encapsulated in time. The curtain needed to close on this show. Life was waiting.

"God, I hope this works." she whispered. Col cocked his head, that playful smirk dancing behind his beautiful sky-blue eyes that crinkled around his smile.

"It's insane. It's you. It's bound to." he winked before hesitating, chin held high as he studied her. Gin felt sure he was about to change his mind and snatch the device away. But instead, he turned, marched over to the statue of the knight upon his horse and slid the sword from his hand, the sound of metal against metal resounding around the cavernous hall. She watched him warily as he examined it, striding back to her.

"Kneel." he said, eyes sliding down her before dragging back to her very confused ones.

"What? What do you mean, *kneel*?" she asked, shaking her head. Col paused, choosing his next words with care.

"You're nobody's *Squire*, Gin. I'm not having you step a foot back there as anything less than what you truly are." he said, narrowing his eyes. "Kneel." he commanded again. Gin felt the power of his order ripple through her as she lowered her knees to the cold floor, her gaze on his all the way. She had no clue what was happening, but it didn't matter, for the trust her soul had in his was unbreakable.

Satisfied, that feline smirk slid onto his lips ever so slightly. He pulled his broad shoulders back, cutting an impressive stance over her, causing her heart to beat wildly.

"Never have I seen such valour and merit embodied so completely in one person in any of my lifetimes, as I have had the honour to witness in you." he said. Gin's mouth opened as she continued to stare up into his electric eyes.

"There may be no rituals or celebration feast, and you may not be a man. But I've never been one for following rules." he smirked, before gliding his free hand along the flat side of the long gleaming blade. Several gasps of breath erupted around them as they clocked on to what Col was about to do. With a gentle manoeuvre, she watched the blade come down to her shoulder with bated breath.

"Your battlefield has been a lifelong war. You fought with exceptional courage, for everything you believed in, for others as well as yourself... no matter how reckless." He cocked a dark brow. "For this exceptional display, it is with an immense privilege that I dub thee, Dame Knight." he said, bringing the sword up and over her head, onto her other shoulder, as she blinked through clouded vision.

The great hall exploded into applause as she took the sword with trembling hands that Col now offered her. Her chest caved at the sight of it in her hands, the cold metal biting into her palms, letting her know this was real. She was worthy. She had won.

The room was a blur as he braced her arms, raising her gently from the floor, meeting his beaming face.

"Congratulations, Dame Sparkles." he said softly. She blinked the tears away as she laughed.

"Thank you." she breathed, shaking her head slowly, disbelief flooding her.

"I meant every word. You amaze me."

Gin closed her eyes against his lips on her forehead, before glimpsing Daphne's overwhelmed smile as she joined the applause. She had never wanted the glory for anything, only to right the wrongs life had handed her. Never again would she find herself pining for who she could have been. For she knew her path, and it was with those she loved, fighting for them in every moment, never having to seek justice for things she should have changed.

Turning to the device, she blew a sharp breath out, placing the sword on the wooden table, and motioned to Skye to come, not knowing if she'd know what that meant. Thankfully, Skye glided over the flagstone flooring to join her.

"Hope. I need you to hold on to Skye, and *do not* let go. No matter what." her eyes jumped between the pair. Skye responded with a deep purr, shrinking a bit and nuzzling herself under Hope's arm.

"Ok, mummy." She said. Gin stroked her soft cheek and then reached out with a shaking and tentative hand to Skye. Before she could stroke her, Skye had nudged her muzzle into her palm. She smiled, her heart beating wildly at the warm creature that saved her life. With watchful eyes on them, she backed up to Col. In his hands was the device, the four Crystals nestled safely within. A shuddering breath left her as she looked up at him.

"You sure about this?" he asked, eyes narrowing. "I *have* to know you have no doubts about what you're choosing."

She placed a hand on her heart and the other over the device. She licked her lips slowly, nerves sky high.

"I've never been more sure of anything in my life. Let's go find Max." she said.

Col placed his free hand on his heart, exactly as she had, his eyes flashing momentarily as they danced on hers.

"I love you so damn much, Sparkles." he said.

"I love you more." She smiled. Col gave a pinched smile, looking ready to challenge that. And she was ready. Ready for a lifetime of loving him.

The bond vibrated between them as the device grew warm in their hands and began to illuminate. Gin gazed, eyes wide as the room glowed around them in the same dreamlike glow as the night the castle appeared, like a paint drop in water, swirling reality.

They locked eyes as the room grew brighter until finally leaching their surroundings from view.

She felt Col's fingers close around her, and for the first time ever, her scars seemed to soothe at the touch of another as he pulled her into his body, the beat of his heart against her ear. He kissed her head as the world melted away into blinding white light and they were sent soaring towards their future.

Together.

Printed in Great Britain
by Amazon

37760483R10212